THE WORLD'S CLASSICS

CALEB WILLIAMS

WILLIAM GODWIN was born in 1756 in Wisbech, Cambridgeshire. After his education and service for a few years as a Dissenting minister, he went to London and began his career as a writer. His fame was established by the appearance of his two-volume exposition of political anarchism, *Enquiry Concerning Political Justice* (1793), during the time of the French Revolution, and his literary reputation spread the following year with the publication of his best novel, originally titled *Things as They Are, or The Adventures of Caleb Williams*. He was the friend of Hazlitt, Lamb, Coleridge, and Wordsworth. Many considered Godwin the philosophical leader of the English radicals, but when the reaction to the French Revolution set in, he passed from notoriety to obscurity. In 1812, Shelley, then nineteen years old, assumed that Godwin had long been dead, but hearing that he was alive, wrote to, and visited, him, and thus began their important relationship. Godwin wrote many other novels, essays, and histories, but none approached the success of the political treatise or his first full-length novel. His wife, the feminist Mary Wollstonecraft, died giving birth to their child, Mary, who became the wife of Shelley and the author of *Frankenstein*. Godwin died in London in 1836.

DAVID MCCRACKEN is Professor of English at the University of Washington and the author of *Junius and Philip Francis*, and of articles on eighteenth- and nineteenth-century literature.

D0833245

THE WORLD'S CLASSICS

WILLIAM GODWIN
Caleb Williams

Edited with an Introduction by
DAVID McCRACKEN

Oxford   New York
OXFORD UNIVERSITY PRESS

Oxford University Press, Walton Street, Oxford OX2 6DP
Oxford New York
Athens Auckland Bangkok Bombay
Calcutta Cape Town Dar es Salaam Delhi
Florence Hong Kong Istanbul Karachi
Kuala Lumpur Madras Madrid Melbourne
Mexico City Nairobi Paris Singapore
Taipei Tokyo Toronto

and associated companies in
Berlin Ibadan

Oxford is a trade mark of Oxford University Press

Introduction, Notes, Bibliography and Chronology
© Oxford University Press 1970, 1982

First published 1970 by Oxford University Press
First issued, with revisions, as a World's Classics paperback 1982

British Library Cataloguing in Publication Data
Data available

ISBN 0 19-281621 7

7 9 10 8 6

Printed in Great Britain by
BPC Paperbacks Ltd
Aylesbury, Bucks

CONTENTS

CONTENTS

INTRODUCTION

PSYCHOLOGICAL novel, detective, adventure, or pursuit novel, and political novel—these are the labels most often attached to *Caleb Williams*. Critics have called it the first psychological novel because of William Godwin's fascination by the entanglement of human motives, a fascination which leads him to trace and dissect the motives that compel his sometimes insane heroes to action. But this novel has also the momentum, interest, and suspense of a good adventure: at the beginning Caleb is the pursuer of knowledge about past murders, then, becoming his victim's victim, he is himself the pursued outcast. Godwin's success in narrating criminal detection and pursuit led one of his best critics, William Hazlitt, to conceive that 'no one ever began *Caleb Williams* that did not read it through: no one that ever read it could possibly forget it, or speak of it after any length of time but with an impression as if the events and feelings had been personal to himself'.[1] It is, however, as a propaganda or political novel that the work has received the most condemnation and, more recently, the most praise. Especially during the time of the French Revolution, critics in the Establishment found the novel offensively propagandist, but in fact the politics of the novel, if at times merely rhetorical, is usually conceived imaginatively as an integral part of the plot. But whether read as psychological, adventure, or political novel—or as all of these—*Caleb Williams* has a way of appealing to many present-day readers with the immediate and compelling interest that Hazlitt testified it had to readers a century and a half ago.

The name William Godwin, however, was more impressive, or perhaps notorious, in 1794 than it is today. He was among the most famous men of his day, but his fame then had nothing to do with prose fiction. He had formerly been an obscure Calvinist clergyman who quarrelled with his congregation, lost his faith, and became a hack writer in London. His products of this period show little sign of genius: three small novels which disappeared from view almost immediately, some pamphlets, reviews, and editorial

[1] *The Spirit of the Age*, in *Works*, ed. P. P. Howe (1932), xi. 24.

work. But in 1793, during the early period of the French Revolution, Godwin's brilliant, original, and highly subversive *magnum opus* appeared: *Enquiry Concerning Political Justice*. Here, in his calm, objective style, Godwin scrutinized the nature, aims, and institutions of man and presented his revolutionary theses. He found virtually all man's institutions radically corrupt and corrupting—not just the monarchy, aristocracy, legislature, court system, and war, but the entire legal system, blame and punishment, *all* forms of government, customary promises, even disease; all these misshapen growths of history were unnecessarily blocking the way of the Godwinian desiderata, reason and justice. Godwin was the confident spokesman for personal freedom, for the rights and the duties of individual men. He had no trust in groups of men, not even in groups of right-thinking men and especially not in revolutionaries. But he had vast faith in the individual's ability to develop his reason and natural benevolence so that he could live peaceably and usefully with other men, without the restraints of laws or governments. He was aware that history did not always provide obvious support for this optimism and he had profound insight into men's capacity for self-delusion, as *Caleb Williams* demonstrates; but he none the less believed that the English Revolution, the American Revolution, and finally the French Revolution were heralding the advent of a new political society based on man's perfectibility.

Godwin and his friends thought themselves in the enviable position of witnessing a major transition in the history of the human race. Society was inevitably progressing from things as they now are, with men preying on other men, to justice and reason. The change would be radical. Men would not only behave differently but would be spared ill-health and possibly even death. His vision of this new day provided the basis of his political system and it countered the 'other', no less real Godwin who hated contemporary corruptions and vividly perceived what Blake called the 'mind-forg'd manacles'. Godwin's dream for future society sounds like a religious millennium, but for him it was secular, of *this* world, and, he believed, inevitable:

The whole will be a people of men, and not of children. . . . Other improvements may be expected to keep pace with those of health and longevity. There will be no war, no crimes, no administration of justice, as it is called, and no government. Beside this, there will be neither disease, anguish, melancholy, nor resentment. Every man will seek, with ineffable ardour, the good of all. Mind will be active and eager, yet never disappointed. Men will see the progressive advancement of virtue and good. . . .[1]

Just before and during the French Revolution, political philosophers were speculating boldly, and their speculations had great immediacy—greater perhaps than at any time before or since. In France philosophy and politics could not be separated; philosophers became politicians and politicians, philosophers. In England, the Revolution evoked a debate in which nobles and working men alike took part. Alfred Cobban has called it 'perhaps the last real discussion of politics in this country'.[2] For some, like Godwin, the Revolution held promise as a great step forward toward a stateless society based on Truth and Justice; for some, like Thomas Paine, it presaged the general fall of despots and tyrants—his words for kings—and the rise of republicanism; for others, like Edmund Burke, it was a potent threat to the tradition and order embodied in the English Constitution. 'Everything rung and was connected with the Revolution in France,' the Whig lawyer Cockburn said of it; 'Everything, not this thing or that thing, but literally everything, was soaked in this one event.'[3] Thus William Godwin, largely forgotten today and known to many, if at all, only as a parasitic yet influential father-in-law of the poet Shelley, was in 1794 recognized as the intellectual leader of those who believed themselves in the dawn of a new and glorious future. Wordsworth, who for a time felt the excitement and promise of *Political Justice*, wrote in retrospect:

> Bliss was it in that dawn to be alive,
> But to be young was very Heaven![4]

But in a revolutionary age, political bliss and vision to one man is political subversion to another. The Prime Minister, Pitt, is said to have withheld persecution of Godwin, despite Godwin's belief in gradual, non-violent evolution, only because he believed the price of *Political Justice* too high to do much harm. Pitt did not

---

[1] *Enquiry Concerning Political Justice*, ed. F. E. L. Priestley (Toronto, 1946), ii. 528.

[2] *The Debate on the French Revolution*, ed. Alfred Cobban (1950), p. 31.

[3] Henry Thomas Cockburn, *Memorials of His Time* (Edinburgh, 1856), p. 80.

[4] *The Prelude*, xi. 108-9.

anticipate, however, that clubs of working men would buy the book with collective funds and read it aloud.

Godwin no sooner finished the political treatise than he began to think about the novel. In his own words, 'The *Enquiry Concerning Political Justice* was published in February. In this year also I wrote the principal part of the novel of *Caleb Williams*, which may, perhaps, be considered as affording no inadequate image of the fervour of my spirit; it was the offspring of that temper of mind in which the composition of my *Political Justice* left me.'[1] *Political Justice* was completed early in January 1793; Godwin proof-read the entire work by 29 January, and, after one and a half years of writing, saw the two-volume treatise published on 14 February.[2] Ten days later he wrote the first page of *Caleb* and within ten more days he was 'seriously and methodically' writing several pages a day.

According to Godwin's account in the 1832 preface to his third novel, *Fleetwood*, he first conceived the idea of a secret murder, its discovery by a person 'impelled by an unconquerable spirit of curiosity', and his persecution, and then he planned the story from beginning to end. 'I devoted about two or three weeks to the imagining and putting down hints for my story, before I engaged seriously and methodically in its composition. In these hints I began with my third volume, then proceeded to my second, and last of all grappled with the first.' This process of invention began between 12 and 19 February—the week his political treatise was published. The pre-publication fame of *Political Justice* and its immediate reception were, according to Godwin, favourable enough to affect his outlook positively: 'The tone of my mind, both during the period in which I was engaged in the work, and afterwards, acquired a certain elevation, and made me now unwilling to stoop to what was insignificant.' In looking back on the composition of *Caleb Williams* he several times mentioned the unusual inspiration that accompanied it. 'I wrote only when the afflatus was upon me.' And again: 'In *Caleb Williams* and *St. Leon*[3] I was excited to write by a strong idea occurring to my mind, which I conceived, if worked up into a story, with the vein of thinking most congenial to my habits, was capable of a powerful effect. It is

---

[1] C. Kegan Paul, *William Godwin: His Friends and Contemporaries* (1876), i. 78.

[2] Preface to *Fleetwood* (1832 edition). Reprinted in this volume, Appendix II.

[3] Godwin's second major novel, published in 1799.

perhaps but a few times in any man's life that such an idea offers itself to his mind.'[1]

At this time Godwin was more actively engaged in practical politics than at any other period of his life. Largely because of *Political Justice*, he was looked to as the spokesman for the new philosophy, he met with parliamentary leaders and radicals like himself to discuss current political questions, and he actively—and sometimes even effectively—opposed governmental policy. He was torn between the active and contemplative life, but had not yet chosen or been forced by circumstances and his own temperament into the latter. While he was writing his novel, however, the novel was of prime importance, not simply a project for idle moments. Godwin was a slow, methodical writer; he required 'continuous application, and that a continuous number of hours, the flower of every day'[2] in order to write a novel. He usually wrote two or three manuscript pages a day, but in early 1794, when he had reached the early pages of Volume III, he completed only six pages in three months. This was not the result of interruption by more important matters, however; it was simply his constitutional inability to apply himself to his task. The afflatus, he would say, was not upon him. Fortunately, it returned. Volume I was written between 24 February and 28 June 1793; Volume II between 1 July and 25 October; and Volume III between 30 October 1793 and 8 May 1794.[3] He revised as he went along and, as with *Political Justice*, he sent the early pages of the novel to be set in type when he had written only the first half of the book. Thus the writing and type-setting progressed at the same time. The most radical revision in the manuscript occurs at the very end of the book. By the end of April 1794 Godwin had written over one hundred pages of the final volume and was nearing the end. On 30 April he reached what is in the manuscript unmistakably an ending. But he was dissatisfied; after three days, he went back ten pages and began writing a new ending of nine pages. It is this 'new catastrophe'—as he calls it in his diary—which is found in all printed editions. Godwin had spent some fifteen months on *Caleb Williams*; it was published by B. Crosby of London on 28 May 1794.

---

[1] Thomas Constable, *Archibald Constable and His Literary Correspondents* (Edinburgh, 1873), ii. 68. When he wrote this (in 1815) he had also written *Fleetwood*, which is passed by unmentioned, and he never spoke of his later novels in this way.

[2] Constable, ii. 69.   [3] Noted in Godwin's diary (Abinger MSS.).

The preface was written after the novel was completed, and there is some question as to how seriously we should take it. It is without doubt politically inflammatory; and since the State was prosecuting some of Godwin's friends for treason just when *Caleb* was to appear, the publisher thought it prudent to withhold the preface. However, the Treason Trials of 1794[1] ended in acquittal and, after a change of publisher, the preface was printed in the second edition (1796) with a note by Godwin explaining the circumstances of its original withdrawal. But why print the preface at all, when its contents were still inflammatory and it had by no means an obvious connection with the novel itself? It might have been merely an afterthought by Godwin to throw readers off the track or to make the novel appear to be something other (more important, perhaps) than it really was. Or, given the fact that an author's intention is sometimes one thing and the finished product quite another, it might be that the deluded author believed the preface to be a true description of the novel against all evidence to the contrary in the novel itself. This position has considerable support, most notably from Sir Leslie Stephen.[2] Or there remains the possibility, which I am inclined to accept, that the preface was seriously meant by Godwin and that it is an accurate description of what the novel actually achieves, on one level at least. It is, of course, no complete description of the novel; it only indirectly concerns what is of most interest to many modern readers, i.e. the pursuit theme and the exploration of the psychological states of Caleb and Falkland. Furthermore, it has misled many readers into thinking that Godwin was conscious of no essential difference between the rhetorical effect of a treatise and that of a novel. But despite this it is still accurate and indeed explains something about the novel's lasting power as well as its historical context.

Godwin alludes in the preface, though without mentioning names, to the current debate over the French Revolution, a debate not only about the fate of France, but also of England and, more far-reaching, of monarchies and indeed all forms of government. Godwin, of course, declares himself to be on the side of 'reformation and change' and proclaims that the novel unmasks man's un-

---

[1] Several of Godwin's friends, including Horne Tooke and Thomas Holcroft, were charged with high treason by the State. Godwin defended them in a pamphlet entitled *Cursory Strictures*, published in 1794.

[2] Stephen's article on Godwin is listed in the Select Bibliography.

natural inhumanity to man, a sentiment that echoes the original epigraph of the novel: '. . . Man only is the common foe of man.' He does in the novel expose the modes of despotism by which man destroys his own kind—principally through prisons, law, and wealth or property—though these by themselves do not determine the tragic fates of Falkland and Caleb.

The tenant farmer Hawkins, who as an innocent, persecuted, and strong-willed man is closely akin to Caleb, is a victim early in the novel of several types of despotism. He is unjustly expelled from one farm, taken up by the landlord Tyrrel, who on this occasion does the right deed for the wrong reason, and is later ruined by Tyrrel's tyranny of wealth. Through Tyrrel's machinations, Hawkins's son is legally but unjustly imprisoned in the same jail that Caleb suffers in later. Godwin borrowed from John Howard's *State of the Prisons* to torment his hero and to portray the 'unwholesomeness' of prisons, 'their filth, the tyranny of their governors, the misery of their inmates'—to prove, in short, that England *does* have a Bastille.

The system of laws that Godwin mentions in the preface is the object of a much larger and more specific attack in the novel. Hawkins's challenge to Tyrrel—'I have got a lease of my farm. . . . I hope there is some law for poor folk, as well as rich'—produces only scorn from Tyrrel and indeed the events show that the scorn is justifiable. The laws may have been first intended, Caleb as historian[1] charitably acknowledges, as 'safeguards of the poor', but 'wealth and despotism easily know how to engage those laws as the coadjutors of their oppression'. Hawkins is of the opinion that 'law was better adapted for a weapon of tyranny in the hands of the rich, than for a shield to protect the humbler part of the community against usurpations', and he is dramatically proved right, though he underestimates the extent of the truth of his statement. He foolishly resorts to a lawsuit to try to stop Tyrrel's destruction of his property, but Tyrrel retaliates with a legal ruse and has Hawkins's son imprisoned. The 'tyranny of wealth', in the historian's phrase, is thoroughly illustrated and condemned in the

[1] I use Godwin's term 'historian' for the more common term narrator'. Godwin is careful to distinguish between the words of Caleb as 'historian' (the person engaged in writing down the narrative after it has happened) and those of Caleb as 'hero' (the person engaged in the action). See his preface to *Fleetwood*: 'I . . . assumed the first person, making the hero of my tale his own historian.'

passage. Similarly, Tyrrel attempts to excuse his malicious prosecution of his cousin Emily Melvile, which directly leads to her
death, by truthfully commenting: 'I did nothing but what the law
allows.' The specific criticisms of the English laws made in the
novel imply the need for simple reforms and even for drastic
changes. Caleb, who is for a long time jailed without being convicted, has ample occasion to reflect upon his treatment and to
observe with astonishment the effect of the 'boasted laws' of his
country. When he convinces Raymond, an eighteenth-century
Robin Hood, that he is mistaken in thinking his occupation virtuous,
Raymond is unable to change his life because of the laws. His
criticism of them is potent: 'The institutions of countries that
profess to worship . . . God . . . leave no room for amendment, and
seem to have a brutal delight in confounding the demerits of
offenders. It signifies not what is the character of the individual at
the hour of trial. How changed, how spotless, how useful, avails
him nothing.' The law, Caleb learns through his adventures, 'has
neither eyes, nor ears, nor bowels of humanity; and it turns into
marble the hearts of all those that are nursed in its principles'.

The numerous trials in the novel, besides instigating a literary
fad,[1] act cumulatively to condemn the general system of justice.
They are in some cases so obviously corrupt that they stand close
to being the 'faithful delineation', promised in the preface, which
the reader may judge for himself. The first trial scene, however—
the case of the virtuous peasant, which parallels Falkland's history
—hints at protest only through the historian's additional comments. The peasant had obviously acted out of self-defence and
is rather the victim of the man he killed than the reverse. Falkland,
as justice of the peace, discharges the case; thus for the moment,
at least, true justice is done. The main purpose of the scene is not
to sow discontent with the legal system, but dramatically to reveal
Falkland's mind and faults to Caleb. In the second trial scene,
presided over by Forester, Caleb is falsely accused of having stolen
money and valuable property from Falkland, and the evidence,
planted in Caleb's trunk, convinces even Caleb's friends that he is

---

[1] In his diary for 1830 Henry Crabb Robinson mentions an Italian play he saw
in Naples: the play 'is bad enough certainly, but it is worthy remark how this adoption
of *legal* incidents as the source of romantic and dramatic interest, which began with
Godwin, has thus run from one end of Europe to the other . . .'. *Henry Crabb Robinson
on Books and Their Writers*, ed. Edith J. Morley (1938), i. 377.

guilty. Although the historian marvels that 'the principles of equity' could be 'so completely reversed', for the most part he abstains from comment; the reader is allowed to view the despotism and judge accordingly. The injustice is as manifest here as it is later when a magistrate refuses even to listen to Caleb's accusation of Falkland. In that scene, because Caleb had not aided in the crime, was a mere servant, and has no witnesses, he is not given a hearing, even though—as the reader knows—justice is on his side. In both cases, however, even neutral and generally sensible persons are deceived by injustice, and the reader may suspect that he too would act as the magistrates do. But the truth can be seen by the best men; the paragon Brightwel and the virtuous robber Raymond both recognize Caleb's innocence, though lesser men, like magistrates and servants, do not. Godwin presents these trial scenes, and the additional one in which Caleb is accused of a mail robbery, as simple description, without much evaluative comment. They clearly contribute to the protest against law, but while the reader can see and judge the despotism involved, he may not be able to judge immediately how this affects, in the words of the preface, the 'question' regarding 'the existing constitution of society'. Hence Collins's comment: 'Such is the state of mankind, that innocence when involved in circumstances of suspicion can scarcely ever make out a demonstration of its purity, and guilt can often make us feel an insurmountable reluctance to the pronouncing it guilt.' This is the lamentable state of 'Things as They Are', the original title of the novel. Only after Caleb succeeds in his 'hateful mistake' of bringing Falkland to trial at the end does he realize that the system itself abets injustice, even when a 'just' decision is reached.

By the time the reader reaches the end of the novel, he has been led to take a particular view of the debate mentioned in the preface between 'reformation and change' and 'the existing constitution of society'. The novel reader has not only seen the unmitigated corruption of society; he has been led by the author to react in a certain way. The propaganda of the novel is generally negative; it unmasks the despotism that is often not recognized as such, to show that 'things as they are' are corrupt. This is sufficient to argue that reformation and change are necessary. The nature of that change is not of primary importance in the novel, but the reader is assured in several reliable ways that improvement is necessary and possible.

Collins speaks of 'some future period of human improvement' and Brightwel chooses to accept his fate as an innocent prisoner with resignation: 'He talked of the injustice of which we were mutual victims without bitterness, and delighted to believe that the time would come when the possibility of such intolerable oppression would be extirpated.' The wisest character in the novel at the time he is most likely to speak truth—Clare, just before his death—says, 'We should be contemptible indeed, if the prospect of human improvement did not yield us a pure and perfect delight, independently of the question of our existing to partake of it.'

Yet a prevalence of despotic episodes and occasional talk of the delightful prospect of human improvement does not necessarily make a novel propagandist. A fictional character can be thrown into prisons and even pursued by the law without being a propaganda weapon. But in *Caleb Williams* there is an element of intentional protest, always in keeping with the action but consciously didactic and flagrant enough to be termed propaganda. The contemporary novelist Elizabeth Inchbald, fearful for Godwin's well-being at a time when their friends were being tried for treason, suggested that he eliminate it,[1] and he might have done so and still have had a novel to sell. Some propaganda was simply inserted in the manuscript, and might be eliminated as easily. One reviewer thought the novel would be greatly improved by excision: 'The political reflections . . . might in general have been spared; and in a future edition . . . we would recommend to the author to expunge a considerable part of them at least.'[2] The fact that Godwin might have expunged them, however, does not mean the novel would be better if he had done so. Godwin certainly thought otherwise: the 'adventures'—or 'incidents', as he says in his critical writings—are very important, to be sure, but the political message is no less integral a part of the novel. There was sufficient reason for Godwin to refuse to expunge even the overt propaganda concerning the 'modes of despotism'. First, we may be reasonably certain that in composition Godwin's rational analysis of the contemporary modes of despotism and his indignation at them determined his choice of incidents—trials, prisons, wealthy tyrants, etc. More important, most of the propaganda does not simply stand by itself but is dependent on the incidents and characters of the

---

[1] Kegan Paul, i. 139.
[2] *The Critical Review*, xi (July 1794), 290.

novel. Caleb's 'O poverty! thou art indeed omnipotent!' speech
turns out to be the transports of a deluded hero rather than
Godwinian truth. Though it sounds at first like undigested
propaganda, the events following show it to be politically false;
the episode exists to dramatize a new stage in the progression of
Caleb's demonic curiosity.

To pull out one thread of Godwinian precept as the reviewer
suggested would quickly expose another and another until the
novel in its expurgated state would be a tattered thing indeed.
Consider the philosophical and artistic importance of one tenet
crucial to Godwin's thought, expressed in *Political Justice* with
extraordinary dryness and aplomb:

> Sound reasoning and truth, when adequately communicated, must
> always be victorious over error: Sound reasoning and truth are capable
> of being so communicated: Truth is omnipotent: The vices and moral
> weakness of man are not invincible: Man is perfectible, or in other words
> susceptible of perpetual improvement.[1]

To speak of the omnipotence of truth is not, of course, to say that
truth conquers error on every occasion, although those who carica-
ture Godwin as an optimist often fail to make the necessary distinction. Godwin says, 'It is impossible that we should choose any
thing *as* evil',[2] but he does not say it is impossible to choose any-
thing that *is* evil. His belief that man would act appropriately if he
perceived the truth through his understanding was accompanied
by a healthy respect for man's capacity for self-deception. But if
any man could be shorn of his prejudices, most of which are perpetuated by a corrupt government, and be given 'a clear stage',[3]
he would then perceive the truth and would of necessity act upon
it. Godwin's emphasis is always on the individual; that is one
reason why he could be a good novelist as well as a philosopher.
Each man must find truth through his own understanding; then,
chiefly through conversation, the truth could be spread and
ultimately alter the entire society. 'Let truth be incessantly studied,
illustrated and propagated, and the effect is inevitable.'[4] In the
philosophical works Godwin speculates about a future anarchistic

---

[1] *Political Justice*, i. 86. Cf. Blake's aphorism in *The Marriage of Heaven and Hell*:
'Truth can never be told so as to be understood, and not be believed.'

[2] *Political Justice*, i. 276.

[3] Ibid., ii. 225.

[4] Ibid., ii. 227.

society made possible by the spread of truth, but in the novels he deals only with the immediate means to that end—the power of truth in one individual. His fiction illustrates the assertion of his treatise: the man 'who employs the sword and the shield of truth alone . . . calls up his firmness; and knows that a plain story, every word of which is marked with the emphasis of sincerity, will carry conviction to every hearer'.[1] This doctrine, which is fundamental to Godwin's system, is represented in his fiction from the first novel to the last. Each Godwin novel is generally less revolutionary and propagandist than the preceding one, but the representation of this important proposition grows more emphatic and positive. He conceived of it dramatically as the private and determined confrontation of one man possessing truth with another who is in error.

It appears in a negative but important way in the denouement of *Caleb Williams*; the direct and private confrontation of truth with error, testing the power of truth, is what Caleb should have attempted, but did not. That would have been 'the just experiment'. But Caleb resorted to law, a 'hateful mistake'. With remorse he says,

I now see that mistake in all its enormity. I am sure that if I had opened my heart to Mr. Falkland, if I had told to him privately the tale I have now been telling, he could not have resisted my reasonable demand. . . . Mr. Falkland is of a noble nature. Yes; . . . I affirm that he has qualities of the most admirable kind. It is therefore impossible that he could have resisted a frank and fervent expostulation, the frankness and the fervour in which the whole soul is poured out. I despaired while it was yet time to have made the just experiment; but my despair was criminal, was treason against the sovereignty of truth.

This scene, a lament over what might have been, is at once highly dramatic and charged with one of Godwin's most important doctrines. It comes upon the reader with the shock of surprise, for instead of the more likely agony, insanity, and death—as in the original ending[2]—Caleb experiences living remorse and despair for having murdered by his own hateful mistake a man of genius who had earlier been ruined 'in the corrupt wilderness of human society'. Caleb has had sufficient example of the inhumanity and injustice of the law from the fates of the Hawkinses and Emily Melvile, and indeed from his own suffering; but complete recognition does not come until the final courtroom scene, and then it

---

[1] *Political Justice*, ii. 282.   [2] Appendix I.

comes too late. Caleb himself, with his Falkland-like concern for his own reputation, causes his overwhelming remorse as a murderer by ignoring what he should have known about the unjust effect of institutional law, and by failing to test the power of truth through a personal, fervent expostulation with Falkland—the 'just experiment'. Truth does have its power in the final court scene, but that power is tainted by the institution of law. When Caleb is most criminal, the law recognizes no crime in him at all. Truth and justice reside only among individuals in this tale, never in institutions.

The outcome of this unusual confrontation and reversal is made credible by several previous incidents. Caleb, before his persecution, had speculated on the possibilities of the power of truth: 'Virtue . . . defeating by a plain, unvarnished tale all the stratagems of vice . . . was one of the favourite subjects of my youthful reveries.' Before the jurors were moved to belief by Caleb, Brightwel and Raymond had disinterestedly believed his tale, and it is strongly hinted that, if Caleb had insisted, Collins would also have heard and believed him. But between the time of Caleb's learning the secrets in Falkland House and his travelling back, years later, to make his accusation in court, he is no active hero but rather a passive, hunted man. In all their encounters, Falkland (with his power to wilt the animal-like Tyrrel with a torrent of words) is the active agent; Caleb is at first overawed and then forceful in maintaining his own integrity, but he never actively seeks out Falkland to make his 'just experiment', to expostulate privately with fervour and reason for justice. Godwin's belief in the power of truth was not pulled out of his metaphysical filing cabinet at the last moment for a more spectacular ending; that belief is present throughout the novel. But he must have realized after he finished the original ending that he had brought both Caleb and Falkland to where they could credibly undergo a dramatic reversal of fortune through the power of 'a plain story . . . marked with the emphasis of sincerity'.

It is extraordinary that two endings so entirely different can both be credible and effective enough to have critical partisans, as in the case of *Great Expectations*. The original ending not only shows the disastrous end of the hero through a fascinating inside portrayal of a demented mind; it is also more obviously consistent with the preceding action. Caleb and Falkland simply continue their linear movements toward defeat and success. But this is

perhaps why it has less power than the published ending: although
Caleb actively seeks the final trial scene, it cannot be said that he
brings its outcome upon himself; his ultimate punishment is
entirely of a piece with what he experienced from Falkland and
society from the time he left Falkland House. He is at the end a
slaughtered victim. In the published ending, however, Caleb is
more truly an active agent. *He* determines his and Falkland's fates
and recognizes his responsibility in what is now a tragic action.
While the original ending does not embarrass us with any Godwinian
and Blakean notion about the power of truth which we may not be
inclined to accept as an intellectual axiom, to my mind the second
ending, the one which has always appeared as part of the text and
for a long time the only one known, is better Godwin and better
prose fiction. It reveals, through a simultaneous reversal of fortune
and recognition, not only things as they are, but things as they
ought to be. The tragic force comes not from the inexorable course
of events but from Caleb's new understanding of what Falkland's
genius might have been had it not been 'poisoned' by society, and
of what he himself might have done had he not made his 'hateful
mistake'. The final courtroom scene provides an imaginative
glimpse of a power that men like Godwin, Blake, Wordsworth, and
Coleridge, to mention a few from the 1790s, discovered to be a
source of personal nobility and social revolution, but which here is
tragically misused. That power has a way of being rediscovered by
other individuals and other generations; like *Caleb Williams*, it
refuses to be merely a historical mummy.

When Godwin wrote in his prefaces, letters, critiques, and essays
about the effects and techniques of novels, he was concerned with
three topics: the novel as a 'vehicle' for ideas, the novel as a
'delineation of human, consistent character', and the novel as a
unified artistic work. To speak of the novel as a vehicle, as Godwin
does in his 1794 preface, is scarcely unique. In an age when the
novel was expected to have a moral purpose, and especially in the
1790s when there appeared a spate of novels with political purpose,
the term was commonplace. But *Caleb Williams* is successful when
most novels of its kind are not because its ideas—about prisons,
the power of truth, and Falkland's chivalry, for example—are not
independent of its characters and art. One element in Godwin's
political thought that points to his potential as a successful novelist
is his fascination by human motives and his dependence on them

to explain personal and political change. He believed that fiction was a higher form of literature than history because the author could explore with more truth 'the endless intermixture of motive with motive'.[1] He loved, as he confessed, to analyse 'the private and internal operations of the mind, employing my metaphysical dissecting knife in tracing and laying bare the involutions of motive, and recording the gradually accumulating impulses . . .'.[2] And it is precisely this gradual accumulation that gives the novel its artistic unity. For Godwin, a man's motives are manifest in feelings and incidents. If these are progressively developed, with interesting incidents accompanying the new states of mind, the result would be what Godwin called a 'capacious unfolding of a single idea' and 'an entire unity of plot'.[3]

This novel is organized into three parts: the history of Falkland, the intellectual combat between Falkland and Caleb, and the pursuit of Caleb. Throughout, Godwin explores the minds of his two chief characters without sacrificing the coherence that he thought a novel must have. Both Falkland and Caleb are extraordinary men, the first for his benevolence, chivalry, and anguish, the second for his curiosity, ingenuity, and perseverance. But the two heroes of this tale, though quite different in social class, age, and ideas, share the qualities that finally unify rather than divide the novel. In intelligence, in concern with personal reputation, and by the end, even in crime and accompanying remorse, each character mirrors the other. Through expert juggling of the narrative method—at one point having Collins partially take over the narrative from Caleb, and near the end having several breaks in the time of the narrative, as the action overtakes Caleb's writing—Godwin builds interest, suspense, and a tragic climax as he explores the minds of two men who pursue each other in the poisoned atmosphere of 'things as they are'. Thus *Caleb Williams* has established itself as a novel of adventure, psychology, and politics which can stand the test of time. It deals imaginatively and originally with conditions and speculations of the 1790s but refuses to become dated. Obsession and self-love—traits of both Falkland and Caleb—are no less fascinating in the twentieth than in the eighteenth century; the sources, if not the particular forms, of corruption that Godwin attacked have not changed radically; and—though Godwin would

[1] *Cloudesley* (1830), I, ix.   [2] Preface to *Fleetwood*.
[3] Constable, ii. 69; and Preface to *Fleetwood*.

be disappointed in us for this—the tragic miscarriage of justice remains humanly possible and moving because of corruption and unreason more tenacious than he anticipated.

Ironically, if Godwin's vision of gradual progress to a stateless society based on reason and benevolence had proved prophetic, *Caleb Williams* would be dead, a mere historical curiosity. In a letter to his fellow radical novelist Thomas Holcroft, Godwin half-jokingly wrote of 'the fifth monarchy or reign of saints' when the denouement of novels could turn on reasoning rather than incident. Things being what they were, however, a novel of reason could now have only the undesirable effect of impressing upon readers 'an abhorrence of the very name of Political Philosophy'.[1] Godwin believed that the future would offer time enough to write novels for more perfect men. In the meantime, however, he well understood that fiction addresses a different audience and a different faculty from philosophy, and that a fictionalized *Political Justice* had little chance of exciting the imagination. But although there are crucial differences between the two literary forms, it is false to say that Godwin the novelist contradicted, betrayed, or simply ignored Godwin the philosopher. His rational vision of man's perfectibility through the power of truth suffused his imaginative portrayal of things as they are and of the adventures of Caleb Williams. No doubt contrary to his own conviction and desires, Godwin's fiction has proved more durable than his philosophy: *Caleb Williams* still moves readers, as it did one and a half centuries ago, while Godwin's political millennium of reasonable anarchism appears even less imminent.

[1] Godwin's critique of *Anna St. Ives* (Abinger MSS.).

ACKNOWLEDGEMENTS

I wish to express my gratitude to the Victoria and Albert Museum for permission to use Godwin's manuscript as the copy-text for this edition and to print the original ending in an appendix; to the Huntington Library, San Marino, California, for permission to use a copy of their first edition in establishing the text; to the British Museum for permission to print Godwin's account of the composition of this novel from the 1832 edition of *Fleetwood*; and to Lord Abinger, Clees Hall, for permission to quote from his Shelley–Godwin manuscripts in the Introduction. I am especially indebted to Professor Gwin Kolb, who not only located and told me of Godwin's manuscript of the novel, but with characteristic generosity lent me his photographic copy for the preparation of this edition. His advice was generously given and always valuable.

NOTE ON THE TEXT

THE present edition of this novel is based on the extant portion of Godwin's original manuscript of the novel and, for the quarter of the manuscript now lost, on the first published edition of 1794. Incorporated in this text, however, are the numerous substantive corrections and revisions which Godwin made in later editions.

Godwin made no printer's copy from his manuscript; the holograph now located in the Forster Collection of the Victoria and Albert Museum is Godwin's original manuscript from which the printer set type. It has numerous cancellations of words, sentences, and even long sections, with revisions between lines, in the margins, and sometimes on separate scraps of paper with references to the place of insertion. Godwin made these manuscript revisions as he wrote or immediately upon finishing a volume, largely to improve the style but occasionally to make the importance of an incident more explicit or to heighten the suspense of the narrative. Some of them substantially alter Godwin's original ideas. For example, the particulars of the court scene in which Falkland acts as a justice of the peace (II. v) were strikingly altered to provide an analogue to Falkland's character and history. The peasant on trial was originally a boorish peasant who had brutally killed his mother: Caleb says of him, 'I never in my life saw so ferocious a countenance. His features had contracted the most uncouth, discordant and un-human expression. . . . There was the bloatedness of lust, and the iron, harsh and rigid lineaments of cruelty.' On second thought, however, Godwin made the peasant as benevolent as he had been brutal and changed his crime to make him much like Falkland in character and circumstance, though of a different social class. A much more radical revision occurs at the end of the manuscript in the two quite different endings. The first he cancelled and did not send to the printer; it appears here, for the first time in an edition of the novel, in Appendix i. The second ending appears, as it always has, as part of the text.

When Godwin sent the novel to press, he was by no means finished with it; for five editions, from 1794 to 1831, he revised his work, changing style, incidents, and even structure, and the novel was unquestionably improved by his revisions and additions. Between the manuscript and first edition—probably in the proofs—he made over seventy-five substantive revisions, nearly all of them single words. The manuscript variants from the text are all listed in the Textual Notes at the end of this volume. In later editions, however, the revisions are too numerous to record individually in this edition. Those not recorded are summarized by kind in this Note.

The most extensive revisions were made for the second and third editions. Most of the revisions were simple substitutions, additions, or deletions of a word or phrase for stylistic improvement. 'Countenance' is changed to 'face', 'temper' to 'disposition'; 'there was some unknown power' becomes 'there seemed to be some unknown power'; 'very' is often dropped and 'sufficiently satisfied' becomes simply 'satisfied'. He made nearly 400 revisions of this sort in Volume I alone of the second edition—not counting extended revisions of entire episodes. There are about 100 such revisions in Volumes II and III of the second edition and 70-90 per volume in the third edition. Occasionally Godwin can be seen pursuing one particular word; for example, Falkland's mysterious 'chest' becomes a 'trunk' throughout the second edition, and Falkland is changed from Caleb's 'master' to his 'patron' throughout the third. The second also contains several changes of name: 'Doctor Arnold' is altered to 'Doctor Wilson', 'Gines' (Falkland's caretaker) to 'Warnes', 'Jones' (Caleb's pursuer) to 'Gines', 'Barton' to 'Jeckels', and 'Wilson' to 'Larkins'. Some simple grammatical changes are made—verb forms altered, pronouns and antecedents brought into agreement, and necessary pronouns added. It is not unusual to find Godwin striving for clarity by revising the same passage more than once. He originally appended this footnote to a gruesome joke which Caleb witnessed in prison: 'This incident really occurred, and was witnessed by a friend of the author a few years since in Newgate' (II. xi). In the second edition he changed the first part to read, 'An incident exactly similar to this, was witnessed . . .' and in the third edition he changed 'in Newgate' to 'in a visit to the prison of Newgate'. The meaning does not change, but the final version is clearer and perhaps (with 'visit') more prudent.

Many of the revisions, however, were much more extensive. Originally the Hawkins story in Volume I preceded the entire Emily Melvile story, but in the third edition Godwin reorganized the volume by shuffling chapters (see Textual Notes). In his revisions Godwin was especially concerned with making the dialogue more credible. 'Is every body incapable of reason, and making a right estimate of the merits of men?' is an improbable speech for Tyrrel; thus in the second edition it becomes, 'Is every body incapable of saying what kind of stuff a man is made of?' (I. v). The description and character analysis as well as the dialogue of many episodes were rewritten to make them more convincing. In the second edition Godwin substantially revised already existing episodes in I. iii–vii, ix, xi; II. viii–ix; III. iii, x, xiii; and in the third edition in I. v, vii, xi; and II. vii–xi. Also, a number of additions of sentences, paragraphs, and pages were made in the second and third editions, most notably the entire Laura episode in III. xiii. All additions of more than one sentence have been cited in the Textual Notes.

Godwin saw both the fourth edition and the Bentley edition through the press, but he made only a few substantive changes in them. All of these are included in this text.

The punctuation also changed radically during the textual history of the novel. Godwin's punctuation was generally spare: he used commas moderately, and very few quotation marks, preferring instead to let dashes, explanatory comments, or the context indicate a quotation. His printers, however, often changed these accidentals as they pleased; for example, they added in the third edition an unwieldly mass of commas which has been retained in all subsequent editions, and (in the Bentley edition) a great many quotation marks. The additional quotation marks, though closer to modern usage, are, however, not entirely successful, since Caleb as narrator often moves fluently from reflection to quotation and back again without consistent attention to pronoun and tense changes. There are few quotation marks in Godwin's manuscript and in the first through to the fourth editions, but it is always clear who is saying what. It seemed advisable in the present edition to retain the original punctuation, which is equally or more intelligible than subsequent printers' emendations. For Godwin's substantive revisions, the punctuation of the first printed version has been used. The original spelling has been retained, but the manuscript abbreviations have been expanded, the long 's' is discarded, and Godwin's inconsistent spelling of 'knowledge' has been normalized. The brackets and footnotes in the text are Godwin's.

SELECT BIBLIOGRAPHY

GENERAL WORKS ON GODWIN. The most complete bibliography of Godwin's works will be found at the end of Burton R. Pollin, *Education and Enlightenment in the Works of William Godwin* (1962). For critical response to Godwin see Pollin, *Godwin Criticism: A Synoptic Bibliography* (1967). Still the most valuable published source of material about Godwin's life is C. Kegan Paul, *William Godwin, His Friends and Contemporaries*, 2 vols. (1876). Biographies have also been written by Ford K. Brown (1926), George Woodcock (1946), and Don Locke, *A Fantasy of Reason: The Life and Thought of William Godwin* (1980). Other general works are: H. N. Brailsford, *Shelley, Godwin, and their Circle* (1913); John P. Clark, *The Philosophical Anarchism of William Godwin* (1977); David Fleisher, *William Godwin: A Study in Liberalism* (1951); Rosalie Glynn Grylls, *William Godwin and His World* (1953); William Hazlitt, 'William Godwin' in *The Spirit of the Age* (1825; reprinted in *Works*, ed. P. P. Howe (1932), xi. 16–28); David McCracken, 'Godwin's literary Theory', *Philological Quarterly*, xlix (January 1970), 113–33; D. H. Monro, *Godwin's Moral Philosophy* (1953); John Middleton Murry, 'Godwin: The Protestant Dream' in *Heaven—and Earth* (1938), pp. 254–68 (published in the United States of America as *Heroes of Thought*); F. E. L. Priestley, 'Introduction' to Godwin, *Enquiry Concerning Political Justice* (1946), iii. 3–114; Elton E. and Esther G. Smith, *William Godwin* (1965).

EDITIONS OF *CALEB WILLIAMS*. First edition, 1794. Editions revised by Godwin: 2nd, 1796; 3rd, 1797; 4th, 1816; Bentley's 'Standard Novels', No. II', 1831. More than thirty other editions in English (see Bibliography in Pollin, *Education and Enlightenment*, cited above). Translated into French (several times, first in 1794), German (1795, 1797), Russian (1838, 1949), and Polish (1954). Published with introductions by Ernest A. Baker (1903), Van Wyck Brooks (1926), George Sherburn (1960), and Walter Allen (1966).

SPECIAL STUDIES OF *CALEB WILLIAMS*. James T. Boulton, *The Language of Politics* (1963); Marilyn Butler, *Jane Austen and the War of Ideas* (1975); Patrick Cruttwell, 'On *Caleb Williams*', *Hudson Review*, xi (Spring 1958), 87–95; D. Gilbert Dumas, 'Things as They Were:

The Original Ending of *Caleb Williams*', *Studies in English Literature*, vi (July 1966), 575–97; P. N. Furbank, 'Godwin's Novels', *Essays in Criticism*, v (July 1955), 214–28; Gary Kelly, *The English Jacobin Novel 1780–1805* (1976); Robert Kiely, *The Romantic Novel in England* (1972); Ian Ousby, *Bloodhounds of Heaven: The Detective in English Fiction from Godwin to Doyle* (1976); Eric Rothstein, *Systems of Order and Inquiry in Later Eighteenth-Century Fiction* (1975); Leslie Stephen, 'William Godwin's Novels' in *Studies of a Biographer*, 2nd series, iii (1902), 119–54; B. J. Tysdahl, *William Godwin as Novelist* (1981); Angus Wilson, 'The Novels of William Godwin', *World Review*, N.S., xxviii (June 1951), 37–40.

A CHRONOLOGY OF
WILLIAM GODWIN

THINGS AS THEY ARE;

OR, THE

ADVENTURES

OF

CALEB WILLIAMS.

BY WILLIAM GODWIN.

IN THREE VOLUMES.

VOL. I.

Amidst the woods the leopard knows his kind;
The tyger preys not on the tyger brood:
Man only is the common foe of man.

———————

LONDON:
PRINTED FOR B. CROSBY, STATIONERS-COURT,
LUDGATE-STREET.
1794.

Title-page of the first edition, 1794

PREFACE

THE following narrative is intended to answer a purpose more general and important than immediately appears upon the face of it. The question now afloat in the world respecting THINGS AS THEY ARE, is the most interesting that can be presented to the human mind. While one party pleads for reformation and change, the other extols in the warmest terms the existing constitution of society.[1] It seemed as if something would be gained for the decision of this question, if that constitution were faithfully developed in its practical effects. What is now presented to the public is no refined and abstract speculation; it is a study and delineation of things passing in the moral world. It is but of late that the inestimable importance of political principles has been adequately apprehended. It is now known to philosophers that the spirit and character of the government intrudes itself into every rank of society. But this is a truth highly worthy to be communicated to persons whom books of philosophy and science are never likely to reach. Accordingly it was proposed in the invention of the following work, to comprehend, as far as the progressive nature of a single story would allow, a general review of the modes of domestic and unrecorded despotism, by which man becomes the destroyer of man. If the author shall have taught a valuable lesson, without subtracting from the interest and passion by which a performance of this sort ought to be characterised, he will have reason to congratulate himself upon the vehicle he has chosen.

MAY 12, 1794.

This preface was withdrawn in the original edition, in compliance with the alarms of booksellers. Caleb Williams made his first appearance in the world, in the same month in which the sanguinary plot broke out against the liberties of Englishmen,

which was happily terminated by the acquittal of its first intended
victims, in the close of that year. Terror was the order of the day;
and it was feared that even the humble novelist might be shown
to be constructively a traitor.

OCTOBER 29, 1795.

THE ADVENTURES OF
CALEB WILLIAMS

VOLUME I

CHAPTER I

My life has for several years been a theatre of calamity. I have been a mark for the vigilance of tyranny, and I could not escape. My fairest prospects have been blasted. My enemy has shown himself inaccessible to intreaties and untired in persecution. My fame, as well as my happiness, has become his victim. Every one, as far as my story has been known, has refused to assist me in my distress, and has execrated my name. I have not deserved this treatment. My own conscience witnesses in behalf of that innocence my pretensions to which are regarded in the world as incredible. There is now however little hope that I shall escape from the toils that universally beset me. I am incited to the penning of these memoirs, only by a desire to divert my mind from the deplorableness of my situation, and a faint idea that posterity may by their means be induced to render me a justice which my contemporaries refuse. My story will at least appear to have that consistency, which is seldom attendant but upon truth.

I was born of humble parents in a remote county of England. Their occupations were such as usually fall to the lot of peasants, and they had no portion to give me but an education free from the usual sources of depravity, and the inheritance, long since lost by their unfortunate progeny! of an honest fame. I was taught the rudiments of no science, except reading, writing and arithmetic. But I had an inquisitive mind, and neglected no means of information from conversation or books. My improvement was greater than my condition in life afforded room to expect.

There are other circumstances deserving to be mentioned as having influenced the history of my future life. I was somewhat above the middle stature. Without being particularly athletic in appearance or large in my dimensions, I was uncommonly vigorous and active. My joints were supple, and I was formed to excel in youthful sports. The habits of my mind however were to a certain degree at war with the dictates of boyish vanity. I had considerable aversion to the boisterous gaiety of the village gallants, and contrived to satisfy my love of praise with an unfrequent apparition at their amusements. My excellence in these respects however gave a turn to my meditations. I delighted to read of feats of activity, and was particularly interested by tales in which corporeal ingenuity or strength are the means resorted to for supplying resources and conquering difficulties. I inured myself to mechanical pursuits, and devoted much of my time to an endeavour after mechanical invention.

The spring of action which, perhaps more than any other, characterised the whole train of my life, was curiosity. It was this that gave me my mechanical turn; I was desirous of tracing the variety of effects which might be produced from given causes. It was this that made me a sort of natural philosopher; I could not rest till I had acquainted myself with the solutions that had been invented for the phenomena of the universe. In fine, this produced in me an invincible attachment to books of narrative and romance. I panted for the unravelling of an adventure, with an anxiety, perhaps almost equal to that of the man whose future happiness or misery depended on its issue. I read, I devoured compositions of this sort. They took possession of my soul; and the effects they produced, were frequently discernible in my external appearance and my health. My curiosity however was not entirely ignoble: village anecdotes and scandal had no charms for me: my imagination must be excited; and, when that was not done, my curiosity was dormant.

The residence of my parents was within the manor of Ferdinando Falkland, a country squire of considerable opulence. At an early age I attracted the favourable notice of Mr. Collins, this gentleman's steward, who used to call in occasionally at my father's.

He observed the particulars of my progress with approbation, and made a favourable report to his master of my industry and genius.

In the summer of the year   Mr. Falkland visited his estate in our county after an absence of several months. This was a period of misfortune to me. I was then eighteen years of age. My father lay dead in our cottage. I had lost my mother some years before. In this forlorn situation I was surprised with a message from the squire, ordering me to repair to the mansion-house the morning after my father's funeral.

Though I was not a stranger to books, I had no practical acquaintance with men. I had never had occasion to address a person of this elevated rank, and I felt no small uneasiness and awe on the present occasion. I found Mr. Falkland a man of small stature, with an extreme delicacy of form and appearance. In place of the hard-favoured and inflexible visages I had been accustomed to observe, every muscle and petty line of his countenance seemed to be in an inconceivable degree pregnant with meaning. His manner was kind, attentive and humane. His eye was full of animation, but there was a grave and sad solemnity in his air, which for want of experience I imagined was the inheritance of the great, and the instrument by which the distance between them and their inferiors was maintained. His look bespoke the unquietness of his mind, and frequently wandered with an expression of disconsolateness and anxiety.

My reception was as gracious and encouraging as I could possibly desire. Mr. Falkland questioned me respecting my learning, and my conceptions of men and things, and listened to my answers with condescension and approbation. This kindness soon restored to me a considerable part of my self-possession, though I still felt restrained by the graceful, but unaltered dignity of his carriage. When Mr. Falkland had satisfied his curiosity, he proceeded to inform me that he was in want of a secretary, that I appeared to him sufficiently qualified for that office, and that, if in my present change of situation occasioned by the death of my father I approved of the employment, he would take me into his family.

I felt highly flattered by the proposal, and was warm in the expression of my acknowledgements. I set eagerly about the disposal of the little property my father had left, in which I was assisted by Mr. Collins. I had not now a relation in the world, upon whose kindness and interposition I had any direct claim.

But, far from regarding this deserted situation with terror, I formed golden visions of the station I was about to occupy. I little suspected that the gaiety and lightness of heart I had hitherto enjoyed were upon the point of leaving me for ever, and that the rest of my days were devoted to misery and alarm.

My employment was easy and agreeable. It consisted partly in the transcribing and arranging certain papers, and partly in writing from my master's dictation letters of business, as well as sketches of literary composition. Many of these latter consisted of an analytical survey of the plans of different authors, and conjectural speculations upon hints they afforded, tending either to the detection of their errors or the carrying forward their discoveries. All of them bore powerful marks of a profound and elegant mind, well stored with literature, and possessed of an uncommon share of activity and discrimination.

My station was in that part of the house which was appropriated for the reception of books, it being my duty to perform the functions of librarian as well as secretary. Here my hours would have glided in tranquillity and peace, had not my situation included in it circumstances totally different from those which attended me in my father's cottage. In early life my mind had been much engrossed by reading and reflexion. My intercourse with my fellow mortals was occasional and short. But in my new residence I was excited by every motive of interest and novelty to study my master's character, and I found in it an ample field for speculation and conjecture.

His mode of living was in the utmost degree recluse and solitary. He had no inclination to scenes of revelry and mirth. He avoided the busy haunts of men; nor did he seem desirous to compensate for this privation by the confidence of friendship. He appeared a total stranger to every thing which usually bears the appellation of pleasure. His features were scarcely ever relaxed into a smile, nor did that air which bespoke the unhappiness of his mind, at any time forsake them. Yet his manners were by no means such as denoted moroseness and misanthropy. He was compassionate and considerate for others, though the stateliness of his carriage and the reserve of his temper were at no time interrupted. His appearance and general behaviour might have strongly interested all persons in his favour; but the coldness of his address and the impenetrableness of his sentiments seemed to forbid those demonstrations of kindness to which one might otherwise have been prompted.

Such was the general appearance of Mr. Falkland; but his disposition was extremely unequal. The distemper which afflicted him with incessant gloom, had its paroxysms. Sometimes he was hasty, peevish and tyrannical; but this proceeded rather from the torment of his mind than an unfeeling disposition, and, when reflexion recurred, he appeared willing that the weight of his misfortune should fall wholly upon himself. Sometimes he entirely lost his self-possession, and his behaviour was changed into frenzy. He would strike his forehead, his brows became knit, his features distorted, and his teeth ground one against the other. When he felt the approach of these symptoms, he would suddenly rise, and, leaving the occupation whatever it was in which he was engaged, hasten into a solitude upon which no person dared to intrude.

It must not be supposed that the whole of what I am describing was visible to the persons about him; nor indeed was I acquainted with it in the extent here stated, but after a considerable time, and in gradual succession. With respect to the domestics in general, they saw but little of their master. None of them, except myself from the nature of my functions, and Mr. Collins from the antiquity of his service and the respectableness of his character, approached Mr. Falkland, but at stated seasons and for a very short interval. They knew him only by the benevolence of his actions and the principles of inflexible integrity by which he was ordinarily guided; and, though they would sometimes indulge their conjectures respecting his singularities, they regarded him upon the whole with veneration as a being of superior order.

One day when I had been about three months in the service of my patron, I went to a closet or small apartment which was separated from the library by a narrow gallery that was lighted by a small window near the roof. I had conceived that there was no person in the room, and intended only to put any thing in order that I might find out of its place. As I opened the door, I heard at the same instant a deep groan expressive of intolerable anguish. The sound of the door in opening seemed to alarm the person within; I heard the lid of a trunk hastily shut, and the noise as of fastening a lock. I conceived that Mr. Falkland was there, and was going instantly to retire; but at that moment a voice that seemed supernaturally tremendous exclaimed, Who is there? The voice

was Mr. Falkland's. The sound of it thrilled my very vitals. I
endeavoured to answer, but my speech failed, and being incapable
of any other reply, I instinctively advanced within the door into
the room. Mr. Falkland was just risen from the floor upon which
he had been sitting or kneeling. His face betrayed strong symptoms
of confusion. With a violent effort however these symptoms vanished, and instantaneously gave place to a countenance sparkling
with rage. Villain, cried he, what has brought you here? I hesitated
a confused and irresolute answer. Wretch, interrupted Mr. Falkland with uncontrolable impatience, you want to ruin me. You set
yourself as a spy upon my actions. But bitterly shall you repent
your insolence. Do you think you shall watch my privacies with
impunity? I attempted to defend myself. Begone, devil! rejoined
he. Quit the room, or I will trample you into atoms. Saying this,
he advanced towards me. But I was already sufficiently terrified,
and vanished in a moment. I heard the door shut after me with
violence, and thus ended this extraordinary scene.

I saw him again in the evening, and he was then tolerably composed. His behaviour, which was always kind, was now doubly
attentive and soothing. He seemed to have something of which he
wished to disburthen his mind, but to want words in which to
convey it. I looked at him with anxiety and affection. He made
two unsuccessful efforts, shook his head, and then, putting five
guineas into my hand, pressed it in a manner that I could feel
proceeded from a mind pregnant with various emotions, though I
could not interpret them. Having done this, he seemed immediately
to recollect himself, and to take refuge in the usual distance and
solemnity of his manner.

I easily understood that secrecy was one of the things expected
from me, and indeed my mind was too much disposed to meditate
upon what I had heard and seen, to make it a topic of indiscriminate
communication. Mr. Collins however and myself happened to sup
together that evening, which was but seldom the case, his avocations
obliging him to be much abroad. He could not help observing an
uncommon dejection and anxiety in my countenance, and affec-
tionately enquired into the reason. I endeavoured to evade his
questions, but my youth and ignorance of the world gave me little
advantage for that purpose. Beside this, I had been accustomed to
view Mr. Collins with considerable attachment, and I conceived
from the nature of his situation that there could be but small

impropriety in making him my confident in the present instance. I repeated to him minutely every thing that had passed, and concluded with a solemn declaration that, though treated with caprice, I was not anxious for myself: no inconvenience or danger should ever lead me to a pusillanimous behaviour; and I felt only for my patron, who, with every advantage for happiness, and being in the highest degree worthy of it, seemed destined to undergo unmerited distress.

In answer to my communication Mr. Collins informed me that some incidents of a nature similar to that which I related had fallen under his own knowledge, and that from the whole he could not help concluding that our unfortunate patron was at times disordered in his intellects. Alas, continued he, it was not always thus! Ferdinando Falkland was once the gayest of the gay. Not indeed of that frothy sort, who excite contempt instead of admiration, and whose levity argues thoughtlessness rather than felicity. His gaiety was always accompanied with dignity. It was the gaiety of the hero and the scholar. It was chastened with reflexion and sensibility, and never lost sight either of good taste or humanity. Such as it was however, it denoted a genuine hilarity of heart, imparted an inconceivable brilliancy to his company and conversation, and rendered him the perpetual delight of the diversified circles he then willingly frequented. You see nothing of him, my dear Williams, but the ruin of that Falkland, who was courted by sages, and adored by the fair. His youth, distinguished in its outset by the most unusual promise, is tarnished. His sensibility is shrunk up and withered by events the most disgustful to his feelings. His mind was fraught with all the rhapsodies of visionary honour; and in his sense nothing but the grosser part, the mere shell of Falkland, was capable of surviving the wound that his pride has sustained.

These reflexions of my friend Collins strongly tended to inflame my curiosity, and I requested him to enter into a more copious explanation. With this request he readily complied; as conceiving that, whatever delicacy it became him to exercise in ordinary cases, it would be out of place in my situation, and thinking it not improbable that Mr. Falkland, but for the disturbance and inflammation of his mind, would be disposed to a similar communication. I shall interweave with Mr. Collins's story various information which I afterwards received from other quarters, that I may give all possible perspicuity to the series of events. To avoid confusion in my narrative, I shall drop the person of Collins, and assume to be myself the historian of our patron. To the reader it may appear at first sight as if this detail of the preceding life of Mr. Falkland were foreign to my history. Alas, I know from bitter experience that it is otherwise. My heart bleeds at the recollection of his misfortunes as if they were my own. How can it fail to do so? To his story the whole fortune of my life was linked; because he was miserable, my happiness, my name, and my existence have been irretrievably blasted.

CHAPTER II

AMONG the favourite authors of his early years were the heroic poets of Italy. From them he imbibed the love of chivalry and romance. He had too much good sense to regret the times of Charlemagne and Arthur. But, while his imagination was purged by a certain infusion of philosophy, he conceived that there was in the manners depicted by these celebrated poets, something to imitate, as well as something to avoid. He believed that nothing was so well calculated to make men delicate, gallant and humane, as a temper perpetually alive to the sentiments of birth and honour. The opinions he entertained upon these topics were illustrated in his conduct, which was assiduously conformed to the model of heroism that his fancy suggested.

With these sentiments he set out upon his travels at the age at which the grand tour is usually made, and they were rather confirmed than shaken by the adventures that befel him. By inclination he was led to make his longest stay in Italy, and here he fell into company with several young noblemen whose studies and principles were congenial to his own. By them he was assiduously courted and treated with the most distinguished applause. They were delighted to meet with a foreigner who had imbibed all the peculiarities of the most liberal and honourable among themselves. Nor was he less favoured and admired by the softer sex. Though his stature was small, his person had an air of uncommon dignity. His dignity was then heightened by certain additions which were afterwards obliterated, an expression of frankness, ingenuity and unreserve, and a spirit of the most ardent enthusiasm. Perhaps

no Englishman was ever in an equal degree idolised by the inhabitants of Italy.

It was not possible for him to have drunk so deeply of the
fountain of chivalry without being engaged occasionally in affairs
of honour, all of which were terminated in a manner that would
not have disgraced the chevalier Bayard himself.[1] In Italy the
young men of rank divide themselves into two classes, those who
adhere to the pure principles of ancient gallantry, and those who,
being actuated by the same acute sense of injury and insult, accus-
tom themselves to the employment of hired bravoes as their
instruments of vengeance. The whole difference indeed consists in
the precarious application of a generally received distinction. The
most generous Italian conceives that there are certain persons
whom it would be contamination for him to call into the open field.
He nevertheless believes that an indignity cannot be expiated but
with blood, and is persuaded that the life of a man is a trifling consideration in comparison of the indemnification to be made to his
injured honour. There is therefore scarcely any Italian that would
upon some occasions scruple assassination. Men of spirit among
them, notwithstanding the prejudices of their education, cannot
fail to have a secret conviction of its baseness, and will be desirous
of extending as far as possible the cartel of honour. Real or affected
arrogance teaches others to regard almost the whole species as
their inferiors, and of consequence incites them to gratify their
vengeance without danger to their persons. Mr. Falkland met with
some of these. But his undaunted spirit and resolute temper gave
him a decisive advantage even in such perilous rencounters. One
instance among many of his manner of conducting himself among
this proud and high spirited people, it may be proper to relate.
Mr. Falkland is the principal agent in my history; and Mr. Falkland, in the autumn and decay of his vigour such as I found him,
cannot be completely understood without a knowledge of his previous character as it was in all the gloss of youth, yet unassailed by
adversity, and unbroken in upon by anguish or remorse.

At Rome he was received with particular distinction at the house
of marquis Pisani, who had an only daughter, the heir of his immense fortune, and the admiration of all the young nobility of that
metropolis. Lady Lucretia Pisani was tall, of a dignified form and
uncommonly beautiful. She was not deficient in amiable qualities,
but her soul was haughty, and her carriage not unfrequently

contemptuous. Her pride was nourished by the consciousness of
her charms, by her elevated rank and the universal adoration she
was accustomed to receive.

Among her numerous lovers count Malvesi was the individual
most favoured by her father, nor did his addresses seem indifferent
to her. The count was a man of considerable accomplishments, and
of great integrity and benevolence of disposition. But he was too
ardent a lover to be able always to preserve the affability of his
temper. The admirers, whose addresses were a source of gratification to his mistress, were a perpetual uneasiness to him. Placing
his whole happiness in the possession of this imperious beauty,
the most trifling circumstances were capable of alarming him for
the security of his pretensions. But most of all he was jealous of the
English cavalier. Marquis Pisani, who had spent many years in
France, was by no means partial to the suspicious precautions of
Italian fathers, and indulged his daughter in considerable free-
doms. His house and his daughter, within certain judicious restraints, were open to the resort of male visitants. But above all
Mr. Falkland, as a foreigner, and a person little likely to form
pretensions to the hand of Lucretia, was received upon a footing
of great familiarity. The lady herself, conscious of her innocence,
entertained no scruple about trifles, and acted with the confidence
and frankness of one who is superior to suspicion.

Mr. Falkland, after a residence of several weeks at Rome, proceeded to Naples. Mean while certain incidents occurred that
delayed the intended nuptials of the heiress of Pisani. When he
returned to Rome count Malvesi was absent. Lady Lucretia, who
had been considerably amused before with the conversation of Mr.
Falkland, and who had an active and enquiring mind, had conceived in the interval between his first and second residence at
Rome a desire to be acquainted with the English language, inspired
by the lively and ardent encomiums of our best authors that she
had heard from their countryman. She had provided herself with
the usual materials for that purpose, and made some progress
during his absence. But upon his return she was forward to make
use of the opportunity which, if missed, might never occur again
with equal advantage, of reading select passages of our poets in
company with an Englishman of uncommon taste and capacity.

This proposal necessarily led to a more frequent intercourse.
When count Malvesi returned, he found Mr. Falkland established

almost as an inmate of the Pisani palace. His mind could not fail to be struck with the criticalness of the situation. He was perhaps secretly conscious that the qualifications of the Englishman were superior to his own, and he trembled for the progress that each party might have made in the affection of the other, even before they were aware of the danger. He believed that the match was in every respect such as to flatter the ambition of Mr. Falkland, and he was stung even to madness by the idea of being deprived of the object dearest to his heart by this tramontane upstart.

He had however a sufficient share of discretion first to demand an explanation of lady Lucretia. She in the gaiety of her heart trifled with his anxiety. His patience was already exhausted, and he proceeded in his expostulation in language that she was by no means prepared to endure with apathy. Lady Lucretia had always been accustomed to deference and submission; and having got over something like terror that was at first inspired by the imperious manner in which she was now catechised, her next feeling was that of the warmest resentment. She disdained to satisfy so insolent a questioner, and even indulged herself in certain oblique hints calculated to strengthen his suspicions. For some time she described his folly and presumption in terms of the most ludicrous sarcasm, and then suddenly changing her style, bid him never let her see him more except upon a footing of the most distant acquaintance, as she was determined never again to subject herself to so unworthy a treatment. She was happy that he had at length disclosed to her his true character, and would know how to profit of her present experience to avoid a repetition of the same danger. All this passed in the full career of passion on both sides, and lady Lucretia had no time to reflect upon what might be the consequence of thus exasperating her lover.

Count Malvesi left her in all the torments of frenzy. He believed that this was a premeditated scene to find a pretence for breaking off an engagement that was already all but concluded; or rather his mind was racked with a thousand conjectures, he alternately thought that the injustice might be hers or his own, and he quarrelled with lady Lucretia, himself and the whole world. In this temper he hastened to the hotel of the English cavalier. The season of expostulation was now over, and he found himself irresistibly impelled to justify his precipitation with the lady, by taking for granted that the subject of his suspicion was beyond the reach of doubt.

Mr. Falkland was at home. The first words of the count were an abrupt accusation of duplicity in the affair of lady Lucretia, and a challenge. The Englishman had an unaffected esteem for Malvesi, who was in reality a man of considerable merit, and who had been one of Mr. Falkland's earliest Italian acquaintance, they having originally met at Milan. But more than this, the possible consequence of a duel in the present instance burst upon his mind. He had the warmest admiration for lady Lucretia, though his feelings were not those of a lover: and he knew that, however her haughtiness might endeavour to disguise it, she was impressed with a tender regard for count Malvesi. He could not bear to think that any misconduct of his should interrupt the prospects of so deserving a pair. Guided by these sentiments he endeavoured to expostulate with the Italian. But all his attempts were ineffectual. His antagonist was drunk with choler, and would not listen to a word that tended to check the impetuosity of his thoughts. He traversed the room with perturbed steps, and even foamed with anguish and fury. Mr. Falkland, finding that all was to no purpose, told the count that, if he would return tomorrow at the same hour, he would attend him to any scene of action he should think proper to select.

From count Malvesi Mr. Falkland immediately proceeded to the palace of Pisani. Here he found considerable difficulty in appeasing the indignation of lady Lucretia. His ideas of honour would by no means allow him to win her to his purpose by disclosing the cartel he had received; otherwise that disclosure would immediately have operated as the strongest motive that could have been offered to this disdainful beauty. But, though she dreaded such an event, the vague apprehension was not strong enough to induce her instantly to surrender all the stateliness of her resentment. Mr. Falkland however drew so interesting a picture of the disturbance of count Malvesi's mind, and accounted in so flattering a manner for the abruptness of his conduct, that this, together with the arguments he adduced, completed the conquest of lady Lucretia's resentment. Having thus far accomplished his purpose, he proceeded to disclose to her every thing that had passed.

The next day count Malvesi appeared, punctual to his appointment, at Mr. Falkland's hotel. Mr. Falkland came to the door to receive him, but requested him to enter the house for a moment, as he had still an affair of three minutes to dispatch. They proceeded to a parlour. Here Mr. Falkland left him, and presently returned leading in lady Lucretia herself, adorned in all her charms, and those charms heightened upon the present occasion by a consciousness of the spirited and generous condescension she was exerting. Mr. Falkland led her up to the astonished count; and she, gently laying her hand upon the arm of her lover, exclaimed with the most attractive grace, Will you allow me to retract the precipitate haughtiness into which I was betrayed? The enraptured count, scarcely able to believe his senses, threw himself upon his knees before her, and stammered out his reply, signifying that the precipitation had been all his own, that he only had any forgiveness to demand, and, though they might pardon, he could never pardon himself for the sacrilege he had committed against her and this god-like Englishman. As soon as the first tumults of his joy had subsided, Mr. Falkland addressed him thus:

'Count Malvesi, I feel the utmost pleasure in having thus by peaceful means disarmed your resentment, and effected your happiness. But I must confess you put me to a severe trial. My temper is not less impetuous and fiery than your own, and it is not at all times that I should have been thus able to subdue it. But I considered that in reality the original blame was mine. Though your suspicion was groundless, it was not absurd. We have been trifling too much in the face of danger. I ought not, under the present weakness of our nature and forms of society, to have been so assiduous in my attendance upon this enchanting woman. It would have been little wonder, if, having so many opportunities, and playing the preceptor with her as I have done, I had been entangled before I was aware, and harboured a wish which I might not afterwards have had courage to subdue. I owed you an atonement for this imprudence.

'But the laws of honour are in the utmost degree rigid, and there was reason to fear that, however anxious I were to be your friend, I might be obliged to be your murderer. Fortunately the reputation of my courage is sufficiently established, not to expose it to any impeachment by my declining your present defiance. It was lucky however that in our interview of yesterday you found me alone, and that accident by that means threw the management of the affair into my disposal. If the transaction should become known, the conclusion will now become known along with the provocation, and I am satisfied. But, if the challenge had been public, the proofs

I had formerly given of courage would not have excused my present moderation; and, though desirous to have avoided the combat, it would not have been in my power. Let us hence each of us learn to avoid haste and indiscretion, the consequences of which may be inexpiable but with blood; and may heaven bless you in a consort of whom I deem you every way worthy!'

I have already said that this was by no means the only instance in the course of his travels in which Mr. Falkland acquitted himself in the most brilliant manner as a man of gallantry and virtue. He continued abroad during several years, every one of which brought some fresh accession to the estimation in which he was held, as well as to his own impatience of stain or dishonour. At length he thought proper to return to England, with the intention of spending the rest of his days at the residence of his ancestors.

CHAPTER III

FROM the moment he entered upon the execution of this purpose, dictated as it probably was by an unaffected principle of duty, his misfortunes took their commencement. All I have farther to state of his history is the uninterrupted persecution of a malignant destiny, a series of adventures that seemed to take their rise in various accidents, but pointing to one termination. Him they overwhelmed with an anguish he was of all others least qualified to bear; and these waters of bitterness, extending beyond him, poured their deadly venom upon others, I being myself the most unfortunate of their victims.

The person in whom these calamities originated, was Mr. Falkland's nearest neighbour, a man of estate equal to his own, by name, Barnabas Tyrrel. This man one might at first have supposed of all others least qualified from instruction, or inclined by the habits of his life, to disturb the enjoyments of a mind so richly endowed as that of Mr. Falkland. Mr. Tyrrel might have passed for a true model of the English squire. He was early left under the tuition of his mother, a woman of narrow capacity, and who had no other child. The only remaining member of the family it may be necessary to notice, was miss Emily Melvile, the orphan daughter of Mr. Tyrrel's paternal aunt; who now resided in the family mansion, and was wholly dependent on the benevolence of its proprietors. Mrs. Tyrrel appeared to think that there was nothing in the world so precious as her hopeful Barnabas. Every thing must give way to his accommodation and advantage; every one must yield the most servile obedience to his commands. He must not be teased or restricted by any forms of instruction; and of consequence his proficiency even in the arts of writing and reading was extremely slender. From his birth he was muscular and sturdy; and, confined to the *ruelle* of his mother, he made much such a figure as the whelp-lion that a barbarian might have given for a lap-dog to his mistress. But he soon broke loose from these trammels, and formed an acquaintance with the groom and the game-keeper. Under their instruction he proved as ready a scholar as he had been indocile and restive to the pedant who held the office of his tutor. It was now evident that his small proficiency in literature was by no means to be ascribed to want of capacity. He discovered no contemptible sagacity and quick-wittedness in the science of horseflesh, and was eminently expert in the arts of shooting, fishing and hunting. Nor did he confine himself to these, but added the theory and practice of boxing, cudgel-play and quarter-staff. These exercises added tenfold robustness and vigour to his former qualifications. His stature, when grown, was somewhat more than five feet ten inches in height, and his form might have been selected by a painter as a model for that hero of antiquity, whose prowess consisted in felling an ox with his fist, and devouring him at a meal. Conscious of his advantage in this respect, he was insupportably arrogant, tyrannical to his inferiors, and insolent to his equals. The activity of his mind, being diverted from the genuine field of utility and distinction, showed itself in the rude tricks of an over-grown lubber. Here, as in all his other qualifications, he rose above his competitors; and, if it had been possible to overlook the callous and unrelenting disposition which they manifested, one could scarcely have denied his applause to the invention these freaks displayed, and the rough, sarcastic wit with which they were accompanied.

Mr. Tyrrel was by no means inclined to permit these extra-ordinary merits to rust in oblivion. There was a weekly assembly at the nearest market-town, the resort of all the rural gentry. Here he had hitherto figured to the greatest advantage, as grand master of the *cotérie*, no one having an equal share of opulence, and the majority, though still pretending to the rank of gentry, greatly his

inferior in this essential article. The young men in this circle looked
up to this insolent bashaw with timid respect, conscious of the comparative eminence that unquestionably belonged to the powers of
his mind; and he well knew how to maintain his rank with an inflexible hand. Frequently indeed he relaxed his features, and assumed
a temporary appearance of affableness and familiarity; but they
found by experience, that, if any one, encouraged by his condescension, forgot the deference which Mr. Tyrrel considered as
his due, he was soon taught to repent his presumption. It was a
tyger that thought proper to toy with a mouse, the little animal
every moment in danger of being crushed by the fangs of his
ferocious associate. As Mr. Tyrrel had considerable copiousness
of speech and a rich but undisciplined imagination, he was always
sure of an audience. His neighbours crowded round, and joined in
the ready laugh, partly from obsequiousness, and partly from
unfeigned admiration. It frequently happened however that in the
midst of his good humour a characteristic refinement of tyranny
would suggest itself to his mind. When his subjects, encouraged
by his familiarity, had discarded their precaution, the wayward fit
would seize him, a sudden cloud overspread his brow, his voice
transform from the pleasant to the terrible, and a quarrel of a straw
immediately ensue with the first man whose face he did not like.
The pleasure that resulted to others from the exuberant sallies of
his imagination was therefore not unalloyed with sudden qualms
of apprehension and terror. It may be believed that this despotism
did not gain its final ascendancy without being contested in the
outset. But all opposition had been quelled with a high hand by
this rural Antæus.[1] By the ascendancy of his fortune, and his
character among his neighbours, he always reduced his adversary
to the necessity of encountering him at his own weapons, and did
not dismiss him without making him feel his presumption through
every joint in his frame. The tyranny of Mr. Tyrrel would not have
been so patiently endured, had not his colloquial accomplishments
perpetually come in aid of that authority which his rank and
prowess originally obtained.

The situation of our squire with the fair was still more enviable
than that which he maintained among persons of his own sex.
Every mother taught her daughter to consider the hand of Mr.
Tyrrel as the highest object of her ambition. Every daughter
regarded his athletic form and his acknowledged prowess with a

favourable eye. A form eminently athletic is perhaps always well proportioned; and one of the qualifications that women are early taught to look for in the male sex, is that of a protector. As no man was adventurous enough to contest his superiority, so scarcely any woman in this provincial circle would have scrupled to prefer his addresses to those of any other admirer. His boisterous wit had peculiar charms for them; and there was no spectacle more flattering to their vanity than seeing this Hercules exchange his club for a distaff. It was pleasing to them to consider that the fangs of this wild beast, the very idea of which inspired trepidation into the boldest hearts, might be played with by them with the utmost security.

Such was the rival that fortune in her caprice had reserved for the accomplished Falkland. This untamed, though not undiscerning, brute, was found capable of destroying the prospects of a man, the most eminently qualified to enjoy and to communicate happiness. The feud that sprung up between them was nourished by concurring circumstances, till it attained a magnitude difficult to be paralleled; and, because they regarded each other with a deadly hatred, I have become an object of misery and abhorrence.

The arrival of Mr. Falkland gave an alarming shock to the authority of Mr. Tyrrel in the village assembly, and in all scenes of indiscriminate resort. His disposition by no means inclined him to withhold himself from scenes of fashionable amusement; and he and his competitor were like two stars fated never to appear at once above the horizon. The advantages Mr. Falkland possessed in the comparison are palpable; and, had it been otherwise, the subjects of his rural neighbour were sufficiently disposed to revolt against his merciless dominion. They had hitherto submitted from fear not from love; and, if they had not rebelled, it was only for want of a leader. Even the ladies regarded Mr. Falkland with particular complacence. His polished manners were particularly in harmony with feminine delicacy. The sallies of his wit were far beyond those of Mr. Tyrrel in variety and vigour; in addition to which they had the advantage of having their spontaneous exuberance guided and restrained by the sagacity of a cultivated mind. The graces of his person were enhanced by the elegance of his deportment; and the benevolence and liberality of his temper were upon all occasions conspicuous. It was common indeed to Mr. Tyrrel together with Mr. Falkland to be little accessible to

sentiments of awkwardness and confusion. But for this Mr. Tyrrel
was indebted to a self-satisfied effrontery and a boisterous and
overbearing elocution by which he was accustomed to discomfit
his assailants; while Mr. Falkland, with great ingenuity and candour of mind, was enabled, by his extensive knowledge of the world
and acquaintance with his own resources, to perceive almost
instantaneously the proceeding it most became him to adopt.

Mr. Tyrrel contemplated the progress of his rival with uneasiness and aversion. He often commented upon it to his particular
confidents as a thing altogether inconceivable. Mr. Falkland he
described as an animal that was beneath contempt. Diminutive and
dwarfish in his form, he wanted to set up a new standard of human
nature adapted to his miserable condition. He wished to persuade
people that the human species were made to be nailed to a chair,
and to pore over books. He would have them exchange those
robust exercises which made us joyous in the performance and
vigorous in the consequences, for the wise labour of scratching our
heads for a rhyme and counting our fingers for a verse. Monkeys
were as good men as these. A nation of such animals would have
no chance with a single regiment of the old English votaries of
beef and pudding. He never saw any thing come of learning but to
make people foppish and impertinent; and a sensible man would
not wish a worse calamity to the enemies of his nation than to see
them run mad after such pernicious absurdities. It was impossible
that people could seriously feel any liking for such a ridiculous
piece of goods as this outlandish, foreign-made Englishman. But
he knew very well how it was; it was a miserable piece of mummery
that was played only in spite to him. But God for ever blast his
soul, if he were not bitterly revenged upon them all!

If such were the sentiments of Mr. Tyrrel, his patience found
ample exercise in the language which was held by the rest of his
neighbours on the same subject. While he saw nothing in Mr.
Falkland but matter for contempt, they appeared to be never weary
of recounting his praises. Such dignity, such affability, so perpetual an attention to the happiness of others, such delicacy of
sentiment and expression! Learned without ostentation, refined
without foppery, elegant without effeminacy! Perpetually anxious
to prevent his superiority from being painfully felt, it was so much
the more certainly felt to be real; and excited congratulation
instead of envy in the spectator. It is scarcely necessary to remark

that the revolution of sentiment in this rural vicinity, belongs to one of the most obvious features of the human mind. The rudest exhibition of art is at first admired; till a nobler is presented, and we are taught to wonder at the facility with which before we had been satisfied. Mr. Tyrrel thought there would be no end to the commendation; and expected when their common acquaintance would fall down and adore the intruder. The most inadvertent expression of applause inflicted upon him the torment of demons. He writhed with agony, his features became distorted, and his looks inspired terror. Such suffering would probably have soured the kindest temper; what must have been its effect upon Mr. Tyrrel's, always fierce, unrelenting and abrupt?

The advantages of Mr. Falkland seemed by no means to diminish with their novelty. Every new sufferer from Mr. Tyrrel's tyranny immediately went over to the standard of his adversary. The ladies, though treated by their rustic swain with more gentleness than the men, were occasionally exposed to his capriciousness and insolence. They could not help remarking the contrast between these two leaders in the fields of chivalry, the one of whom paid no attention to any one's pleasure but his own, while the other seemed all good humour and benevolence. It was in vain that Mr. Tyrrel endeavoured to restrain the ruggedness of his character. His motive was impatience, his thoughts were gloomy, and his courtship was like the pawings of an elephant. It appeared as if his temper had been more human while he indulged it in its free bent, than now that he sullenly endeavoured to put fetters upon its excesses.

Among the ladies of the village assembly already mentioned there was none that seemed to engage more of the kindness of Mr. Tyrrel than miss Hardingham. She was also one of the few that had not yet gone over to the enemy, either because she really preferred the gentleman who was her oldest acquaintance, or that she conceived from calculation this conduct best adapted to insure her success in a husband. One day however she thought proper, probably only by way of experiment, to show Mr. Tyrrel that she could engage in hostilities, if he should at any time give her sufficient provocation. She so adjusted her manœuvres as to be engaged by Mr. Falkland as his partner for the dance of the evening, though without the smallest intention on the part of that gentleman, who was unpardonably deficient in the sciences of anecdote and match-making, of giving offence to his country neighbour. Though the manners of Mr. Falkland were condescending and attentive, his hours of retirement were principally occupied in contemplations too dignified for scandal, and too large for the altercations of a vestry, or the politics of an election-borough.

A short time before the dances began, Mr. Tyrrel went up to his fair inamorata, and entered into some trifling conversation with her to fill up the time, as intending in a few minutes to lead her forward to the field. He had accustomed himself to neglect the ceremony of soliciting beforehand a promise in his favour, as not supposing it possible that any one should dare dispute his behests; and, had it been otherwise, he would have thought the formality unnecessary in this case, his general preference to miss Hardingham being notorious.

While he was thus engaged, Mr. Falkland came up. Mr. Tyrrel always regarded him with aversion and loathing. Mr. Falkland however slided in a graceful and unaffected manner into the conversation already begun, and the animated ingenuousness of his manner was such, as might for the time have disarmed the devil of his malice. Mr. Tyrrel probably conceived that his accosting miss Hardingham was an accidental piece of general ceremony, and expected every moment when he would withdraw to another part of the room.

The company now began to be in motion for the dance, and Mr. Falkland signified as much to miss Hardingham.—Sir, interrupted Mr. Tyrrel abruptly, that lady is my partner.—I believe not, sir: that lady has been so obliging as to accept my invitation.—I tell you, sir, no. Sir, I have an interest in that lady's affections; and I will suffer no man to intrude upon my claims.—The lady's affections are not the subject of the present question.—Sir, it is to no purpose to parley. Make room, sir!—Mr. Falkland gently repelled his antagonist.—Mr. Tyrrel! returned he with some firmness, let us have no altercation in this business: the master of the ceremonies is the proper person to decide in a difference of this sort, if we cannot adjust it: we can neither of us intend to exhibit our valour before the ladies, and shall therefore chearfully submit to his verdict.—Damn me, sir, if I understand—Softly, Mr. Tyrrel; I intended you no offence. But, sir, no man shall prevent my asserting that to which I have once acquired a claim!

Mr. Falkland uttered these words with the most unruffled

temper in the world. The tone in which he spoke had acquired elevation, but neither roughness nor impatience. There was a fascination in his manner, that made the ferociousness of his antagonist subside into impotence. Miss Hardingham had begun to repent of her experiment, but her alarm was speedily quieted by the dignified composure of her new partner. Mr. Tyrrel walked away without answering a word. He muttered curses as he went, which the laws of honour did not oblige Mr. Falkland to overhear, and which indeed it would have been no easy task to have overheard with accuracy. Mr. Tyrrel would not perhaps have so easily given up his point, had not his own good sense presently taught him that, however eager he might be for revenge, this was not the ground he should desire to occupy. But, though he could not openly resent this rebellion against his authority, he brooded over it in the recesses of a malignant mind; and it was evident enough that he was accumulating materials for a bitter account, to which he trusted his adversary should one day be brought.

CHAPTER IV

This was only one out of innumerable instances that every day seemed to multiply, of petty mortifications which Mr. Tyrrel was destined to endure on the part of Mr. Falkland. In all of them Mr. Falkland conducted himself with such unaffected propriety, as perpetually to add to the stock of his reputation. The more Mr. Tyrrel struggled with his misfortune, the more conspicuous and inveterate it became. A thousand times he cursed his stars, which took, as he apprehended, a malicious pleasure in making Mr. Falkland at every turn the instrument of his humiliation. Smarting under a succession of untoward events, he appeared to feel in the most exquisite manner the distinctions paid to his adversary, even in those points in which he had not the slightest pretensions. An instance of this now occurred.

Mr. Clare, a poet whose works have done immortal honour to the country that produced him, had lately retired, after a life spent in the sublimest efforts of genius, to enjoy the produce of his economy and the reputation he had acquired, in this very neighbourhood. Such an inmate was looked up to by the country gentlemen with a degree of adoration. They felt a conscious pride in recollecting that the boast of England was a native of their vicinity, and they were by no means deficient in gratitude, when they saw him who had left them an adventurer, return into the midst of them in the close of his days crowned with honours and opulence. The reader is acquainted with his works; he has probably dwelt upon them with transport; and I need not remind him of their excellence. But he is perhaps a stranger to his personal qualifications. He does not know that his productions were scarcely more admirable than his conversation. In company he seemed to be the only person ignorant of the greatness of his fame. To the world his writings will long remain a kind of specimen of what the human mind is capable of performing; but no man perceived their defects so acutely as he, or saw so distinctly how much yet remained to be effected. He alone appeared to look upon his works with superiority and indifference. One of the features that most eminently distinguished him was a perpetual suavity of manners, a comprehensiveness of mind, that regarded the errors of others without a particle of resentment, and made it impossible for any one to be his enemy. He pointed out to men their mistakes with frankness and unreserve: his remonstrances produced astonishment and conviction, but without uneasiness in the party to whom they were addressed: they felt the instrument that was employed to correct their irregularities, but it never mangled what it was intended to heal. Such were the moral qualities that distinguished him among his acquaintance. The intellectual accomplishments he exhibited were principally a tranquil and mild enthusiasm, and a richness of conception which dictated spontaneously to his tongue, and flowed with so much ease, that it was only by retrospect you could be made aware of the amazing variety of ideas that had been presented.

Mr. Clare certainly found few men in this remote situation that were capable of participating in his ideas and amusements. It has not seldom been among the weaknesses of great men to fly to solitude, and converse with woods and groves, rather than with a circle of strong and comprehensive minds like their own. From the moment of Mr. Falkland's arrival in the neighbourhood Mr. Clare distinguished him in the most flattering manner. To so penetrating a genius there was no need of long experience and patient observation to discover the merits and defects of any character that presented itself. The materials of his judgment had long since been accumulated, and at the close of so illustrious a life he might almost be said to see through nature at a glance. What wonder that he took some interest in a mind in a certain degree congenial with his own? But to Mr. Tyrrel's diseased imagination every distinction bestowed on his neighbour seemed to be expressly intended as an insult to him. On the other hand Mr. Clare, though gentle and benevolent in his remonstrances to a degree that made the taking offence impossible, was by no means parsimonious of praise, or slow to make use of the deference that was paid him, for the purpose of procuring justice to merit.

It happened at one of those public meetings at which Mr. Falkland and Mr. Tyrrel were present, that the conversation, in one of the most numerous sets into which the company was broken, turned upon the poetical talents of the former. A lady, who was present, and was distinguished for the acuteness of her understanding, said, she had been favoured with the sight of a poem he had just written, entitled, an Ode to the Genius of Chivalry, which appeared to her of exquisite merit. The curiosity of the company was immediately excited, and the lady added, she had a copy in her pocket, which was much at their service, provided its being thus produced would not be disagreeable to the author. The whole circle immediately intreated Mr. Falkland to comply with their wishes, and Mr. Clare, who was one of the company, inforced their petition. Nothing gave this gentleman so much pleasure as to have an opportunity of witnessing and doing justice to the exhibition of intellectual excellence. Mr. Falkland had no false modesty or affectation, and therefore readily yielded his consent.

Mr. Tyrrel accidentally sat at the extremity of this circle. It cannot be supposed that the turn the conversation had taken was by any means agreeable to him. He appeared to wish to withdraw himself, but there seemed to be some unknown power that as it were by enchantment retained him in his place, and made him consent to drink to the dregs the bitter potion which envy had prepared for him.

The poem was read to the rest of the company by Mr. Clare, whose elocution was scarcely inferior to his other accomplishments. Simplicity, discrimination and energy constantly attended him in the act of reading, and it is not easy to conceive a more refined delight than fell to the lot of those who had the good fortune to be his auditors. The beauties of Mr. Falkland's poem were accordingly exhibited with every advantage. The successive passions of the author were communicated to the hearer. What was impetuous and what was solemn were delivered with a responsive feeling, and a flowing and unlaboured tone. The pictures conjured up by the creative fancy of the poet were placed full to view, at one time overwhelming the soul with superstitious awe, and at another transporting it with luxuriant beauty.

The character of the hearers upon this occasion has already been described. They were for the most part plain, unlettered, and of little refinement. Poetry in general they read, when read at all, from the mere force of imitation and with few sensations of pleasure; but this poem had a peculiar vein of glowing inspiration. This very poem would probably have been seen by many of them with little effect; but the accents of Mr. Clare carried it home to the heart. He ended: and, as the countenances of his auditors had before sympathised with the passions of the composition, so now they emulated each other in declaring their approbation. Their sensations were of a sort to which they were little accustomed. One spoke, and another followed by a sort of uncontrolable impulse; and the rude and broken manner of their commendations rendered them the more singular and remarkable. But what was least to be endured was the behaviour of Mr. Clare. He returned the manuscript to the lady from whom he had received it, and then addressing Mr. Falkland said with emphasis and animation: Ha! this is as it should be. It is of the right stamp. I have seen too many hard essays strained from the labour of a pedant, and pastoral ditties distressed in lack of a meaning. They are such as you, sir, that we want. Do not forget however, that the muse was not given to add refinements to idleness, but for the highest and most invaluable purposes. Act up to the magnitude of your destiny.

A moment after, Mr. Clare quitted his seat, and with Mr. Falkland and two or three more withdrew. As soon as they were gone, Mr. Tyrrel edged farther into the circle. He had sat silent so long that he seemed ready to burst with gall and indignation. Mighty pretty verses, said he, half talking to himself, and not addressing any particular person: why, aye, the verses are well enough. Damnation! I should like to know what a ship-load of such stuff is good for.

Why, surely, said the lady who had introduced Mr. Falkland's ode on the present occasion, you must allow that poetry is an agreeable and elegant amusement.

Elegant, quotha!—Why, look at this Falkland! A puny bit of a thing! In the devil's name, madam, do you think he would write poetry if he could do any thing better?

The conversation did not stop here. The lady expostulated. Several other persons, fresh from the sensation they had felt, contributed their share. Mr. Tyrrel grew more violent in his invectives, and found ease in uttering them. The persons who were able in any degree to check his vehemence were withdrawn. One speaker after another shrunk back into silence, too timid to oppose, or too indolent to contend with the fierceness of his passion. He found the appearance of his old ascendancy; but he felt its deceitfulness and uncertainty, and was gloomily dissatisfied.

In his return from this assembly he was accompanied by a young man whom similitude of manners had rendered one of his principal confidents, and whose road home was in part the same as his own. One might have thought that Mr. Tyrrel had sufficiently vented his spleen in the dialogue he had just been holding. But he was unable to dismiss from his recollection the anguish he had endured. Damn Falkland! said he. What a pitiful scoundrel is here to make all this bustle about! But women and fools always will be fools; there is no help for that! Those that set them on have most to answer for; and most of all Mr. Clare. He is a man that ought to know something of the world, and past being duped by gewgaws and tinsel. He seemed too to have some notion of things: I should not have suspected him of hallooing to a cry of mongrels without honesty or reason. But the world is all alike. Those that seem better than their neighbours are only more artful. They mean the same thing, though they take a different road. He deceived me for a while, but it is all out now. They are the makers of the mischief. Fools might blunder, but they would not persist, if people that ought to set them right, did not encourage them to go wrong.

A few days after this adventure Mr. Tyrrel was surprised to receive a visit from Mr. Falkland. Mr. Falkland proceeded without ceremony to explain the motive of his coming.

Mr. Tyrrel, said he, I am come to have an amicable explanation with you.

Explanation! What is my offence?

None in the world, sir; and for that reason I conceive this the fittest time to come to a right understanding.

You are in the devil of a hurry, sir. Are you clear that this haste will not mar, instead of make an understanding?

I think I am, sir. I have great faith in the purity of my intentions, and I will not doubt, when you perceive the view with which I come, that you will willingly cooperate with it.

Mayhap, Mr. Falkland, we may not agree about that. One man thinks one way, and another man thinks another. Mayhap I do not think I have any great reason to be pleased with you already.

It may be so. I cannot however charge myself with having given you reason to be displeased.

Well, sir, you have no right to put me out of humour with myself. If you come to play upon me, and try what sort of a fellow you shall have to deal with, damn me, if you shall have any reason to hug yourself upon the experiment.

Nothing, sir, is more easy for us than to quarrel. If you desire that, there is no fear that you will find opportunities.

Damn me, sir, if I do not believe you are come to bully me.

Mr. Tyrrel! sir—have a care!

Of what, sir?—Do you threaten me? Damn my soul! who are you? what do you come here for?

The fieriness of Mr. Tyrrel brought Mr. Falkland to his recollection.

I am wrong, said he. I confess it. I came for purposes of peace. With that view I have taken the liberty to visit you. Whatever therefore might be my feelings upon another occasion, I am bound to suppress them now.

Ho!—Well, sir: and what have you further to offer?

Mr. Tyrrel, proceeded Mr. Falkland, you will readily imagine that the cause that brought me was not a slight one. I would not have troubled you with a visit but for important reasons. My coming is a pledge how deeply I am myself impressed with what I have to communicate.

We are in a critical situation. We are upon the brink of a whirl-pool which, if once it get hold of us, will render all farther deliberation impotent. An unfortunate jealousy seems to have insinuated itself between us, which I would willingly remove; and I come to ask your assistance. We are both of us nice of temper; we are both apt to kindle, and warm of resentment. Precaution in this stage can be dishonourable to neither; the time may come when we shall wish we had employed it, and find it too late. Why should we be enemies? Our tastes are different; our pursuits need not interfere. We both of us amply possess the means of happiness; we may be respected by all, and spend a long life of tranquillity and enjoyment. Will it be wise in us to exchange this prospect for the fruits of strife? A strife between persons with our peculiarities and our weaknesses, includes consequences that I shudder to think of. I fear, sir, that it is pregnant with death at least to one of us, and with misfortune and remorse to the survivor.

Upon my soul, you are a strange man! Why trouble me with your prophecies and forebodings?

Because it is necessary to your happiness! Because it becomes me to tell you of our danger now, rather than wait till my character will allow this tranquillity no longer!

By quarrelling we shall but imitate the great mass of mankind who could easily quarrel in our place. Let us do better. Let us show that we have the magnanimity to contemn petty misunderstandings. By thus judging we shall do ourselves most substantial honour. By a contrary conduct we shall merely present a comedy for the amusement of our acquaintance.

Do you think so? There may be something in that. Damn me, if I consent to be the jest of any man living.

You are right, Mr. Tyrrel. Let us each act in the manner best calculated to excite respect. We neither of us wish to change roads; let us each suffer the other to pursue his own track unmolested. Be this our compact; and by mutual forbearance let us preserve mutual peace.

Saying this, Mr. Falkland offered his hand to Mr. Tyrrel in token of fellowship. But the gesture was too significant. The wayward rustic, who seemed to have been somewhat impressed by what had preceded, taken as he was by surprise, shrunk back. Mr. Falkland was again ready to take fire upon this new slight, but he checked himself.

All this is very unaccountable, cried Mr. Tyrrel. What the devil can have made you so forward, if you had not some sly purpose to answer by which I am to be overreached?

My purpose, replied Mr. Falkland, is a manly and an honest purpose. Why should you refuse a proposition dictated by reason, and an equal regard to the interest of each? —Mr. Tyrrel had had an opportunity for pause, and fell back into his habitual character.

Well, sir, in all this I must own there is some frankness. Now I will return you like for like. It is no matter how I came by it, my temper is rough, and will not be controled. Mayhap you may think it is a weakness, but I do not desire to see it altered. Till you came, I found myself very well: I liked my neighbours, and my neighbours humoured me. But now the case is entirely altered; and, as long as I cannot stir abroad without meeting with some mortification in which you are directly or remotely concerned, I am determined to hate you. Now, sir, if you will only go out of the county or the kingdom, to the devil if you please, so as I may never hear of you any more, I will promise never to quarrel with you as long as I live. Your rhymes and your rebusses, your quirks and your conundrums may then be every thing that is grand for what I care.

Mr. Tyrrel, be reasonable! Might not I as well desire you to leave the county, as you desire me? I come to you, not as to a master, but an equal. In the society of men we must have something to endure, as well as to enjoy. No man must think that the world was made for him. Let us take things as we find them; and accommodate ourselves as we can to unavoidable circumstances.

True, sir, all this is fine talking. But I return to my text; we are as God made us. I am neither a philosopher nor a poet, to set out upon a wild-goose chase of making myself a different man from what you find me. As for consequences, what must be must be. As we brew, we must bake. And so, do you see, I shall not trouble myself about what is to be, but stand up to it with a stout heart when it comes. Only this I can tell you, that, as long as I find you thrust into my dish every day, I shall hate you as bad as senna and valerian.[1] And damn me, if I do not think I hate you the more for coming to-day in this pragmatical way when nobody sent for you, on purpose to show how much wiser you are than all the world besides.

Mr. Tyrrel, I have done. I foresaw consequences, and came as a friend. I had hoped that by mutual explanation we should have come to a better understanding. I am disappointed; but perhaps when you coolly reflect on what has passed, you will give me credit for my intentions, and think that my proposal was not an unreasonable one.

Having said this, Mr. Falkland departed. Through the interview he, no doubt, conducted himself in a way that did him peculiar credit. Yet the warmth of his temper could not be entirely suppressed: and even when he was most exemplary, there was an apparent loftiness in his manner that was calculated to irritate; and the very grandeur with which he suppressed his passions, operated indirectly as a taunt to his opponent. The interview was prompted by the noblest sentiments; but it unquestionably served to widen the breach it was intended to heal.

For Mr. Tyrrel, he had recourse to his old expedient, and unburthened the tumult of his thoughts to his confidential friend. This, cried he, is a new artifice of the fellow to prove his imagined superiority. We knew well enough that he had the gift of the gab. To be sure, if the world were to be governed by words, he would be in the right box. Oh, yes, he had it all hollow! But what signifies prating? Business must be done in an other-guess way than that. I wonder what possessed me that I did not kick him! But that is all to come. This is only a new debt added to the score which he shall one day richly pay. This Falkland haunts me like a demon. I cannot wake, but I think of him. I cannot sleep, but I see him. He poisons all my pleasures. I should be glad to see him torn with tenter-hooks, and to grind his heart-strings with my teeth. I shall know no joy, till I see him ruined. There may be some things right about him; but he is my perpetual torment. The thought of him hangs like a dead weight upon my heart, and I have a right to shake it off. Does he think I will feel all that I endure for nothing?

In spite of the acerbity of Mr. Tyrrel's feelings, it is probable however he did some justice to his rival. He regarded him indeed with added dislike; but he no longer regarded him as a despicable foe. He avoided his encounter; he forbore to treat him with random hostility; he seemed to lie in wait for his victim, and to collect his venom for a mortal assault.

CHAPTER V

IT was not long after that a malignant contagious distemper broke out in the neighbourhood, which proved fatal to many of the inhabitants, and was of unexampled rapidity in its effects. One of the first persons that was seized with it was Mr. Clare. It may be believed what grief and alarm this incident spread through the vicinity. Mr. Clare was considered by them as something more than mortal. The equanimity of his behaviour, his unassuming carriage, his exuberant benevolence and goodness of heart, joined with his talents, his inoffensive wit and the comprehensiveness of his intelligence made him the idol of all that knew him. In the scene of his rural retreat at least he had no enemy. All mourned the danger that now threatened him. He appeared to have had the prospect of long life, and of going down to his grave full of years and of honour. Perhaps these appearances were deceitful. Perhaps the intellectual efforts he had made, which were occasionally more sudden, violent and unintermitted than a strict regard to health would have dictated, had laid the seed of future disease. But a sanguine observer would infallibly have predicted, that his temperate habits, activity of mind and unabated chearfulness would be able even to keep death at bay for a time, and baffle the attacks of distemper, provided their approach were not uncommonly rapid and violent. The general affliction therefore was doubly pungent upon the present occasion.

But no one was so much affected as Mr. Falkland. Perhaps no man so well understood the value of the life that was now at stake. He immediately hastened to the spot; but he found some difficulty in gaining admission. Mr. Clare, aware of the infectious nature of his disease, had given directions that as few people as possible should approach him. Mr. Falkland sent up his name. He was told that he was included in the general orders. He was not however of a temper to be easily repulsed; he persisted with obstinacy, and at length carried his point, being only reminded in the first instance to employ those precautions which experience has proved most effectual for counteracting infection.

He found Mr. Clare in his bedchamber, but not in bed. He was sitting in his night-gown at a bureau near the window. His appearance was composed and chearful, but death was in his countenance. I had a great inclination, Falkland, said he, not to have suffered you to come in; and yet there is not a person in the world it could give me more pleasure to see. But upon second thoughts I believe there are few people that could run into a danger of this kind with a better prospect of escaping. In your case, at least the garrison will not, I trust, be taken through the treachery of the commander. I cannot tell how it is, that I, who can preach wisdom to you, have myself been caught. But do not be discouraged by my example. I had no notice of my danger, or I would have acquitted myself better.

Mr. Falkland, having once established himself in the apartment of his friend, would upon no terms consent to retire. Mr. Clare considered that there was perhaps less danger in this choice than in the frequent change from the extremes of a pure to a tainted air, and desisted from expostulation. Falkland, said he, when you came in, I had just finished making my will. I was not pleased with what I had formerly drawn up upon that subject, and I did not choose in my present situation to call in an attorney. In fact it would be strange if a man of sense with pure and direct intentions should not be able to perform such a function for himself.

Mr. Clare continued to act in the same easy and disengaged manner as in perfect health. To judge from the chearfulness of his tone and the firmness of his manner, the thought would never once have occurred that he was dying. He walked, he reasoned, he jested, in a way that argued the most perfect self-possession. But his appearance changed perceptibly for the worse every quarter of an hour. Mr. Falkland kept his eye perpetually fixed upon him with mingled sentiments of anxiety and admiration.

Falkland, said he, after having appeared for a short period absorbed in thought, I feel that I am dying. This is a strange distemper of mine. Yesterday I seemed in perfect health, and tomorrow I shall be an insensible corpse. How curious is the line that separates life and death to mortal men! To be at one moment active, gay, penetrating, with stores of knowledge at one's command, capable of delighting, instructing and animating mankind, and the next, lifeless and loathsome, an incumbrance upon the face of the earth. Such is the history of many men, and such will be mine.

I feel as if I had yet much to do in the world; but it will not be. I must be contented with what is past. It is in vain that I muster all my spirits to my heart. The enemy is too mighty and too merciless for me; he will not give me time so much as to breathe. These things are not yet at least in our power. They are parts of a great series that is perpetually flowing. The general welfare, the great business of the universe, will go on, though I bear no farther share in promoting it. That task is reserved for younger strengths, for you, Falkland, and such as you. We should be contemptible indeed, if the prospect of human improvement did not yield us a pure and perfect delight, independently of the question of our existing to partake of it. Mankind would have little to envy to future ages, if they had all enjoyed a serenity as perfect as mine has been for the latter half of my existence.

Mr. Clare sat up through the whole day, indulging himself in easy and chearful exertions, which were perhaps better calculated to refresh and invigorate the frame, than if he had sought repose in its direct form. Now and then he was visited with a sudden pang; but it was no sooner felt, than he seemed to rise above it, and smiled at the impotence of these attacks. They might destroy him, but they could not disturb. Three or four times he was bedewed with profuse sweats, and these again were succeeded by an extreme dryness and burning heat of the skin. He was next covered with small livid spots. Symptoms of shivering followed, but these he drove away with a determined resolution. He then became tranquil and composed, and after some time decided to go to bed, it being already night. Falkland, said he, pressing his hand, the task of dying is not so difficult, as some imagine. When one looks back from the brink of it, one wonders that so total a subversion can take place at so easy a price.

He had now been some time in bed, and, as every thing was still, Mr. Falkland hoped that he slept. But in that he was mistaken. Presently Mr. Clare threw back the curtain, and looked in the countenance of his friend. I cannot sleep, said he. No, if I could sleep, it would be the same thing as to recover; and I am destined to have the worst in this battle.

Falkland, I have been thinking about you. I do not know any one whose future usefulness I contemplate with greater hope. Take care of yourself. Do not let the world be defrauded of your virtues. I am acquainted with your weakness as well as your strength. You have an impetuosity and an impatience of imagined dishonour, that, if once set wrong, may make you as eminently mischievous, as you will otherwise be useful. Think seriously of exterminating this error!

But, if I cannot, in the brief expostulation my present situation will allow, produce this desirable change in you, there is at least one thing I can do. I can put you upon your guard against a mischief I foresee to be imminent. Beware of Mr. Tyrrel. Do not commit the mistake of despising him as an unequal opponent.

Petty causes may produce great mischiefs. Mr. Tyrrel is boisterous, rugged and unfeeling; and you are too passionate, too acutely sensible of injury. It would be truly to be lamented, if a man so inferior, so utterly unworthy to be compared with you, should be capable of changing your whole history into misery and guilt. I have a painful presentiment upon my heart, as if something dreadful would reach you from that quarter. Think of this. I exact no promise from you. I would not shackle you with the fetters of superstition; I would have you governed by reason and justice.

Mr. Falkland was deeply affected with this expostulation. His sense of the generous attention of Mr. Clare at such a moment, was so great as almost to deprive him of utterance. He spoke in short sentences and with visible effort. I will behave better, replied he. Never fear me! Your admonitions shall not be thrown away upon me.

Mr. Clare adverted to another subject. I have made you my executor; you will not refuse me this last office of friendship. It is but a short time that I have had the happiness of knowing you; but in that short time I have examined you well, and seen you thoroughly. Do not disappoint the sanguine hope I have entertained!

I have left some legacies. My former connections, while I lived amidst the busy haunts of men, as many of them as were intimate, are all of them dear to me. I have not had time to summon them about me upon the present occasion, nor did I desire it. The remembrances of me will, I hope, answer a better purpose than such as are usually thought of on similar occasions.

Mr. Clare, having thus unburthened his mind, spoke no more for several hours. Towards morning Mr. Falkland quietly withdrew the curtain, and looked at the dying man. His eyes were open, and were now gently turned towards his young friend. His countenance was sunk, and of a death-like appearance. I hope you are better, said Falkland in a half-whisper, as if afraid of disturbing him. Mr. Clare drew his hand from the bed-clothes, and stretched it forward; Mr. Falkland advanced, and took hold of it. Much better, said Mr. Clare in a voice, inward and hardly articulate; the struggle is now over; I have finished my part; farewel; remember! These were his last words. He lived still a few hours; his lips were sometimes seen to move; he expired without a groan.

Mr. Falkland had witnessed the scene with much anxiety. His

hopes of a favourable crisis, and his fear of disturbing the last moments of his friend, had held him dumb. For the last half hour he had stood up with his eyes intently fixed upon Mr. Clare. He witnessed the last gasp, the last little convulsive motion of the frame. He continued to look; he sometimes imagined that he saw life renewed. At length he could deceive himself no longer, and exclaimed with a distracted accent, And is this all? He would have thrown himself upon the body of his friend; the attendants withheld, and would have forced him into another apartment. But he struggled from them, and hung fondly over the bed. Is this the end of genius, virtue and excellence? Is the luminary of the world thus for ever gone? Oh, yesterday! yesterday! Clare, why could not I have died in your stead? Dreadful moment! Irreparable loss! Lost in the very maturity and vigour of his mind! Cut off from a usefulness ten thousand times greater than any he had already exhibited! Oh, his was a mind to have instructed sages, and guided the moral world! This is all we have left of him! The eloquence of those lips is gone! The incessant activity of that heart is still! The best and wisest of men is gone, and the world is insensible of its loss!

Mr. Tyrrel heard the intelligence of Mr. Clare's death with emotion, but of a different kind. He avowed that he had not forgiven him his partial attachment to Mr. Falkland, and therefore could not recal his remembrance with kindness. But, if he could have overlooked his past injustice, sufficient care, it seems, was taken to keep alive his resentment. Falkland forsooth attended him on his death-bed, as if nobody else were worthy of his confidential communications. But what was worst of all was this executorship. In every thing this pragmatical rascal throws me behind. Contemptible wretch, that has nothing of the man about him! Must he perpetually trample upon his betters! Is every body incapable of saying what kind of stuff a man is made of? caught with mere outside? choosing the flimsy before the substantial? And upon his death-bed too! [Mr. Tyrrel with his uncultivated brutality mixed, as usually happens, certain rude notions of religion.] Sure the sense of his situation might have shamed him. Poor wretch! his soul has a great deal to answer for. He has made my pillow uneasy; and, whatever may be the consequences, it is he we have to thank for them.

The death of Mr. Clare removed the person who could most

effectually have moderated the animosities of the contending parties, and took away the great operative check upon the excesses of Mr. Tyrrel. This rustic tyrant had been held in involuntary restraint by the intellectual ascendancy of his celebrated neighbour; and, notwithstanding the general ferocity of his temper, he did not appear till lately to have entertained a hatred against him. In the short time that had elapsed from the period in which Mr. Clare had fixed his residence in the neighbourhood to that of the arrival of Mr. Falkland from the continent, the conduct of Mr. Tyrrel had even shown tokens of improvement. He would indeed have been better satisfied not to have had even this intruder, into a circle where he had been accustomed to reign. But with Mr. Clare he could have no rivalship; the venerable character of Mr. Clare disposed him to submission; this great man seemed to have survived all the acrimony of contention, and all the jealous subtleties of a mistaken honour.

The effects of Mr. Clare's suavity however, so far as related to Mr. Tyrrel, had been in a certain degree suspended by considerations of rivalship between this gentleman and Mr. Falkland. And, now that the influence of Mr. Clare's presence and virtues was entirely removed, Mr. Tyrrel's temper broke out into more criminal excesses than ever. The added gloom which Mr. Falkland's neighbourhood inspired, overflowed upon all his connections; and the new examples of his sullenness and tyranny which every day afforded, reflected back upon this accumulated and portentous feud.

CHAPTER VI

THE consequences of all this speedily manifested themselves. The very next incident in the story was in some degree decisive of the catastrophe. Hitherto I have spoken only of preliminary matters, seemingly unconnected with each other, though leading to that state of mind in both parties which had such fatal effects. But all that remains is rapid and tremendous. The death dealing mischief advances with an accelerated motion, appearing to defy human wisdom and strength to obstruct its operation.

The vices of Mr. Tyrrel, in their present state of augmentation, were peculiarly exercised upon his domestics and dependents. But the principal sufferer was the young lady mentioned on a former occasion, the orphan daughter of his father's sister. Miss Melvile's mother had married imprudently, or rather unfortunately, against the consent of her relations, all of whom had agreed to withdraw their countenance from her in consequence of that precipitate step. Her husband had turned out to be no better than an adventurer; had spent her fortune, which in consequence of the irreconcilable-ness of her family was less than he expected, and broken her heart. Her infant daughter was left without any resource. In this situation the representations of the people with whom she happened to be placed prevailed upon Mrs. Tyrrel, the mother of the squire, to receive her into her family. In equity perhaps she was entitled to that portion of fortune which her mother had forfeited by her imprudence, and which had gone to swell the property of the male representative. But this idea had never entered into the conceptions of either mother or son. Mrs. Tyrrel conceived that she performed an act of the most exalted benevolence in admitting miss Emily into a sort of equivocal situation, which was neither precisely that of a domestic, nor yet marked with the treatment that might seem due to one of the family.

She had not however at first been sensible of all the mortifica-tions that might have been expected from her condition. Mrs. Tyrrel, though proud and imperious, was not ill natured. The female, who lived in the family in the capacity of housekeeper, was a person who had seen better days, and whose disposition was extremely upright and amiable. She early contracted a friendship for the little Emily, who was indeed for the most part committed to her care. Emily on her side fully repaid the affection of her instructress, and learned with great docility the few accomplish-ments Mrs. Jakeman was able to communicate. But most of all she imbibed her chearful and artless temper, that extracted the agreeable and encouraging from all events, and prompted her to communicate her sentiments, which were never of the cynical cast, without modification or disguise. Beside the advantages Emily derived from Mrs. Jakeman, she was permitted to take lessons from the masters who were employed at Tyrrel Place for the instruction of her cousin; and indeed, as the young gentleman was most frequently indisposed to attend to them, they would com-monly have had nothing to do, had it not been for the fortunate presence of miss Melvile. Mrs. Tyrrel therefore encouraged the studies of Emily on that score; in addition to which she imagined that this living exhibition of instruction might operate as an indirect allurement to her darling Barnabas, the only species of motive she would suffer to be presented. Force she absolutely forbad; and of the intrinsic allurements of literature and knowledge she had no conception.

Emily, as she grew up, displayed an uncommon degree of sensibility, which under her circumstances would have been a source of perpetual dissatisfaction, had it not been qualified with an extreme sweetness and easiness of temper. She was far from being entitled to the appellation of a beauty. Her person was *petite* and trivial; her complexion savoured of the *brunette*; and her face was marked with the small pox, sufficiently to destroy its evenness and polish, though not enough to destroy its expression. But, though her appearance was not beautiful, it did not fail to be in a high degree engaging. Her complexion was at once healthful and delicate; her long dark eye brows adapted themselves with facility to the various conceptions of her mind; and her looks bore the united impression of an active discernment and a good-humoured frankness. The instruction she had received, as it was entirely of a casual nature, exempted her from the evils of untutored ignorance, but not from a sort of native wildness, arguing a mind incapable of guile itself, or of suspecting it in others. She amused, without seeming conscious of the refined sense which her observations contained: or rather, having never been debauched with applause, she set light by her own qualifications; and talked from the pure gaiety of a youthful heart acting upon the stores of a just understanding, and not with any expectation of being distinguished and admired.

The death of her aunt made very little change in her situation. This prudent lady, who would have thought it little less than sacrilege to have considered miss Melvile as a branch of the stock of the Tyrrels, took no more notice of her in her will, than barely putting her down for one hundred pounds in a catalogue of legacies to her servants. She had never been admitted into the intimacy and confidence of Mrs. Tyrrel; and the young squire, now that she was left under his sole protection, seemed inclined to treat her with even more liberality than his mother had done. He had seen her grow up under his eye, and therefore, though there were but six years difference in their ages, he felt a kind of paternal interest in her welfare. Habit had rendered her in a manner necessary to him, and in every recess from the occupations of the field and the pleasures of the table, he found himself solitary and forlorn without the society of miss Melvile. Nearness of kindred and Emily's want of personal beauty prevented him from ever looking on her with the eyes of desire. Her accomplishments were chiefly of the customary and superficial kind, dancing and music. Her skill in the first led him sometimes to indulge her with a vacant corner in his carriage when he went to the neighbouring assembly; and, in whatever light he might himself think proper to regard her, he would have imagined his chambermaid, introduced by him, entitled to an undoubted place in the most splendid circle. Her musical talents were frequently employed for his amusement. She had the honour occasionally of playing him to sleep after the fatigues of the chase; and, as he had some relish for harmonious sounds, she was frequently able to soothe him by their means from the perturbations of which his gloomy disposition was so eminently a slave. Upon the whole she might be considered as in some sort his favourite. She was the mediator to whom his tenants and domestics, when they had incurred his displeasure, were accustomed to apply; the privileged companion that could approach this lion with impunity in the midst of his roarings. She spoke to him without fear; his solicitations were always good natured and disinterested; and, when he repulsed her, he disarmed himself of half his terrors, and was contented to smile at her presumption.

Such had been for some years the situation of miss Melvile. Its precariousness had been beguiled by the uncommon forbearance with which she was treated by her savage protector. But his disposition, always brutal, had acquired a gradual accession of ferocity since the settlement of Mr. Falkland in his neighbourhood. He now frequently forgot the gentleness with which he had been accustomed to treat his good natured cousin. Her little playful arts were not always successful in softening his rage; and he would sometimes turn upon her blandishments with an impatient sternness that made her tremble. The careless ease of her disposition however soon effaced these impressions, and she fell without variation into her old habits.

A circumstance occurred about this time which gave peculiar strength to the acrimony of Mr. Tyrrel, and ultimately brought to its close the felicity, that miss Melvile in spite of the frowns of

fortune had hitherto enjoyed. Emily was exactly seventeen when
Mr. Falkland returned from the continent. At this age she was
peculiarly susceptible of the charms of beauty, grace and moral
excellence, when united in a person of the other sex. She was
imprudent, precisely because her own heart was incapable of guile.
She had never yet felt the sting of the poverty to which she was
condemned, and had not reflected on the insuperable distance that
custom has placed between the opulent and the poorer classes of
the community. She beheld Mr. Falkland, whenever he was thrown
in her way at any of the public meetings, with admiration; and,
without having precisely explained to herself the sentiments she
indulged, her eyes followed him through all the changes of the
scene with eagerness and impatience. She did not see him, as the
rest of the assembly did, born to one of the amplest estates in
the county, and qualified to assert his title to the richest heiress.
She thought only of Falkland, with those advantages which were
most intimately his own, and of which no persecution of adverse
fortune had the ability to deprive him. In a word she was transported when he was present; he was the perpetual subject of her
reveries and her dreams; but his image excited no sentiment in her
mind beyond that of the immediate pleasure she took in his idea.

The notice Mr. Falkland bestowed on her in return appeared
sufficiently encouraging to a mind so full of prepossession as that
of Emily. There was a particular complacency in his looks when
directed towards her. He had said in a company, of which one of
the persons present repeated his remarks to miss Melvile, that she
appeared to him amiable and interesting, that he felt for her unprovided and destitute situation, and that he should have been glad
to be more particular in his notice of her, had he not been apprehensive of doing her a prejudice in the suspicious mind of Mr.
Tyrrel. All this she considered as the ravishing condescension of a
superior nature; for, if she did not recollect with sufficient assiduity
his gifts of fortune, she was on the other hand filled with reverence
for his unrivalled accomplishments. But, while she thus seemingly
disclaimed all comparison between Mr. Falkland and herself, she
probably cherished a confused feeling as if some event that was
yet in the womb of fate might reconcile things apparently the most
incompatible. Fraught with these prepossessions, the civilities,
that had once or twice occurred in the bustle of a public circle, the
restoring her fan which she had dropped, or the disembarrassing

her of an empty tea-cup, made her heart palpitate, and gave birth
to the wildest chimeras in her deluded imagination.

About this time an event happened that helped to give a precise
determination to the fluctuations of miss Melvile's mind. One
evening, a short time after the death of Mr. Clare, Mr. Falkland
had been at the house of his deceased friend in his quality of
executor, and by some accidents of little intrinsic importance had
been detained three or four hours later than he expected. He did
not set out upon his return till two o'clock in the morning. At this
time, in a situation so remote from the metropolis, every thing is
as silent as it would be in a region wholly uninhabited. The moon
shone bright; and the objects around, being marked with strong
variations of light and shade, gave a kind of sacred solemnity to the
scene. Mr. Falkland had taken Collins with him, the business to
be settled at Mr. Clare's being in some respects similar to that to
which this faithful domestic had been accustomed in the routine
of his ordinary service. They had entered into some conversation,
for Mr. Falkland was not then in the habit of obliging the persons
about him by formality and reserve to recollect who he was. The
attractive solemnity of the scene made him break off the talk somewhat abruptly, that he might enjoy it without interruption. They
had not ridden far, before a hollow wind seemed to rise at a distance, and they could hear the hoarse roarings of the sea. Presently
the sky on one side assumed the appearance of a reddish brown,
and a sudden angle in the road placed this phenomenon directly
before them. As they proceeded it became more distinct, and it
was at length sufficiently visible that it was occasioned by a fire.
Mr. Falkland put spurs to his horse; and, as they approached, the
object presented every instant a more alarming appearance. The
flames ascended with fierceness; they embraced a large portion of
the horizon; and, as they carried up with them numerous little
fragments of the materials that fed them, impregnated with fire,
and of an extremely bright and luminous colour, they presented
some feeble image of the tremendous eruption of a volcano.

The flames proceeded from a village directly in their road. There
were eight or ten houses already on fire, and the whole seemed to
be threatened with immediate destruction. The inhabitants were
in the utmost consternation, having had no previous experience of
a similar calamity. They conveyed with haste their moveables and
furniture into the adjoining fields. When any of them had effected

this as far as it could be attempted with safety, they were unable to conceive any farther remedy, but stood wringing their hands and contemplating the ravages of the fire in an agony of powerless despair. The water that could be procured in any mode practised in that place, was but as a drop contending with a whole element in arms. The wind in the mean time was rising, and the flames spread with more and more rapidity.

Mr. Falkland contemplated this scene for a few moments, as if ruminating with himself as to what could be done. He then directed some of the country people about him to pull down a house, next to one that was wholly on fire, but which itself was yet untouched. They seemed astonished at a direction which implied a voluntary destruction of property, and considered the task as too much in the heart of the danger to be undertaken. Observing that they were motionless, he dismounted from his horse, and called upon them in an authoritative voice to follow him. He ascended the house in an instant, and presently appeared upon the top of it as if in the midst of the flames. Having, with the assistance of two or three of the persons that followed him most closely, and who by this time had supplied themselves with whatever tools came next to hand, loosened the support of a stack of chimnies, he pushed them head-long into the midst of the fire. He passed and repassed along the roof; and, having set people to work in all parts, descended in order to see what could be done in any other quarter.

At this moment an elderly woman burst from the midst of a house in flames. The utmost consternation was painted in her looks; and, as soon as she could recollect herself enough to have a proper idea of her situation, the subject of her anxiety seemed in an instant to be totally changed. Where is my child? cried she, and cast an anxious and piercing look among the surrounding crowd. Oh, she is lost! she is in the midst of the flames! Save her! save her! my child! She filled the air with heart-rending shrieks. She turned towards the house. The people that were near endeavoured to prevent her, but she shook them off in a moment. She entered the passage; viewed the hideous ruin; and was then going to plunge into the blazing stair-case. Mr. Falkland saw, pursued, and seized her by the arm; it was Mrs. Jakeman. Stop! he cried, with a voice of grand, yet benevolent, authority. Remain you in the street! I will seek,—and will save her!—Mrs. Jakeman obeyed. He charged the persons who were near to detain her; he enquired which was the apartment of Emily. Mrs. Jakeman was upon a visit to a sister who lived in the village, and had brought Emily along with her. Mr. Falkland ascended a neighbouring house, and entered that in which Emily was, by a window in the roof.

He found her already awaked from her sleep; and, becoming sensible of her danger, she had that instant wrapped a loose gown round her. Such is the almost irresistible result of feminine habits; but, having done this, she examined the surrounding objects with the wildness of despair. Mr. Falkland entered the chamber. She flew into his arms with the rapidity of lightning. She embraced and clung to him, with an impulse that did not wait to consult the dictates of her understanding. Her emotions were indescribable. In a few short moments she had lived an age in love. In two minutes Mr. Falkland was again in the street with his lovely, half-naked burthen in his arms. Having restored her to her affectionate protector, snatched from the immediate grasp of death, from which, if he had not, none would have delivered her, he returned to his former task. By his presence of mind, by his indefatigable humanity and incessant exertions, he saved three-fourths of the village from destruction. The conflagration being at length abated, he sought again Mrs. Jakeman and Emily, who by this time had obtained a substitute for the garments she had lost in the fire. He displayed the tenderest solicitude for the young lady's safety, and directed Collins to go with as much speed as he could, and send his chariot to attend her. More than an hour elapsed in this interval. Miss Melvile had never seen so much of Mr. Falkland upon any former occasion, and the spectacle of such humanity, delicacy, firmness and justice in the form of man, as he crowded into this small space, was altogether new to her, and in the highest degree fascinating. She had a confused feeling as if there had been something indecorous in her behaviour or appearance, when Mr. Falkland had appeared to her relief; and this combined with her other emotions to render the whole critical and intoxicating.

Emily no sooner arrived at the family mansion, than Mr. Tyrrel ran out to receive her. He had just heard of the melancholy accident that had taken place at the village, and was terrified for the safety of his good humoured cousin. He displayed those unpremeditated emotions which are common to almost every individual of the human race. He was greatly shocked at the suspicion that Emily might possibly have become the victim of a catastrophe which had thus broken out in the dead of night. His sensations were of the most pleasing sort, when he folded her in his arms, and fearful apprehension was instantaneously converted into joyous certainty. Emily no sooner entered under the well-known roof, than her spirits were brisk, and her tongue incessant in describing her danger and her deliverance. Mr. Tyrrel had formerly been tortured with the innocent eulogiums she pronounced of Mr. Falkland. But these were tameness itself, compared with the rich and various eloquence that now flowed from her lips. Love had not the same effect upon her, especially at the present moment, which it would have had upon a person instructed to feign a blush, and inured to a consciousness of wrong. She described his activity and his resources, the promptitude with which every thing was conceived, and the cautious, but daring wisdom with which it was executed. All was fairy-land and enchantment in the tenour of her artless tale; you saw a beneficent genius surveying and controling the whole, but could have no notion of any human means by which his purposes were effected.

Mr. Tyrrel listened for a while to these innocent effusions with patience; he could even bear to hear the man applauded by whom he had just obtained so considerable a benefit. But the theme by amplification became nauseous, and he at length with some roughness put an end to the tale. Probably upon recollection it appeared still more insolent and intolerable than while it was passing; the sensation of gratitude wore off, but the hyperbolical praise that had been bestowed still haunted his memory and sounded in his ears: Emily had entered into the confederacy that disturbed his repose. For herself, she was wholly unconscious of offence, and upon every occasion quoted Mr. Falkland as the model of elegant manners and true wisdom. She was a total stranger to dissimulation; and she could not conceive that any one beheld the object of her admiration with less partiality than herself. Her artless love became more fervent than ever. She sometimes flattered herself that nothing less than a reciprocal passion could have prompted Mr. Falkland to the desperate attempt of saving her from the flames; and she trusted that this passion would speedily declare itself, as well as induce the object of her adoration to overlook her comparative unworthiness.

Mr. Tyrrel endeavoured at first with some moderation to check miss Melvile in her applauses, and to convince her by various tokens that the subject was disagreeable to him. He was accustomed to treat her with kindness. Emily on her part was disposed to yield an unreluctant obedience, and therefore it was not difficult to restrain her; but upon the very next occasion her favourite topic would force its way to her lips. Her obedience was the acquiescence of a frank and benevolent heart; but it was the most difficult thing in the world to inspire her with fear. Conscious herself that she would not hurt a worm, she could not conceive that any one would harbour cruelty and rancour against her. Her temper had preserved her from obstinate contention with the persons under whose protection she was placed; and, as her compliance was unhesitating, she had no experience of a severe and rigorous treatment. As Mr. Tyrrel's objection to the very name of Falkland became more palpable and uniform, miss Melvile increased in her precaution: she would stop herself in the half pronounced sentences that were meant to his praise. This circumstance had necessarily an ungracious effect; it was a cutting satire upon the imbecility of her kinsman. Upon these occasions she would sometimes venture upon a good-humoured expostulation: Dear sir! well, I wonder how you can be so ill-natured! I am sure Mr. Falkland would do you any good office in the world: till she was checked by some gesture of impatience and fierceness.

At length she wholly conquered her heedlessness and inattention. But it was too late. Mr. Tyrrel already suspected the existence of that passion which she had thoughtlessly imbibed. His imagination, ingenious in torment, suggested to him all the different openings in conversation in which she would have introduced the praise of Mr. Falkland, had she not been placed under this unnatural restraint. Her present reserve upon the subject was even more insufferable than her former loquacity. All his kindness for this unhappy orphan gradually subsided. Her partiality for the man who was the object of his unbounded abhorrence, appeared to him as the last persecution of a malicious destiny. He figured himself as about to be deserted by every creature in human form, all men under the influence of a fatal enchantment, approving only what was sophisticated and artificial, and holding the rude and genuine offspring of nature in mortal antipathy. Impressed with these gloomy presages, he saw miss Melvile with no sentiments but those of rancorous aversion; and, accustomed as he was to the uncontroled indulgence of his propensities, he determined to wreak upon her a signal revenge.

CHAPTER VII

MR. TYRREL consulted his old confident respecting the plan he should pursue, who, sympathising as he did in the brutality and insolence of his friend, had no idea that an insignificant girl without either wealth or beauty ought to be allowed for a moment to stand in the way of the gratifications of a man of Mr. Tyrrel's importance. The first idea of her now unrelenting kinsman was to thrust her from his doors, and leave her to seek her bread as she could. But he was conscious that this proceeding would involve him in considerable obloquy; and he at length fixed upon a scheme which, at the same time that he believed it would sufficiently shelter his reputation, would much more certainly secure her mortification and punishment.

For this purpose he fixed upon a young man of twenty, the son of one Grimes, who occupied a small farm the property of his confident. This fellow he resolved to impose as a husband on miss Melvile, who he shrewdly suspected, guided by the tender sentiments she had unfortunately conceived for Mr. Falkland, would listen with reluctance to any matrimonial proposal. Grimes he selected as being in all respects the diametrical reverse of Mr. Falkland. He was not precisely a lad of vicious propensities, but in an inconceivable degree boorish and uncouth. His complexion was scarcely human, his features were coarse, and strangely discordant and disjointed from each other. His lips were thick, and the tone of his voice broad and unmodulated. His legs were of equal size from one end to the other, and his feet misshapen and clumsy. He had nothing spiteful or malicious in his disposition, but he was a total stranger to tenderness; he could not feel for those refinements in others, of which he had no experience in himself. He was an expert boxer; his inclination led him to such amusements as were most boisterous; and he delighted in a sort of manual sarcasm, which he could not conceive to be very injurious, as it left no traces behind it. His general manners were noisy and obstreperous; inattentive to others; and obstinate and unyielding, not from any cruelty and ruggedness of temper, but from an incapacity to conceive those finer feelings that make so large a part of the history of persons who are cast in a gentler mould.

Such was the uncouth and half-civilised animal which the

industrious malice of Mr. Tyrrel fixed upon as most happily adapted to his purpose. Emily had hitherto been in an unusual degree exempted from the oppression of despotism. Her happy insignificance had served her as a protection. No one thought it worth his while to fetter her with those numerous petty restrictions, with which the daughters of opulence are commonly tormented. She had the wildness as well as the delicate frame of the bird that warbles unmolested in its native groves.

When therefore she heard from her kinsman the proposal of Mr. Grimes for a husband, she was for a moment silent with astonishment at so unexpected a suggestion. But, as soon as she recovered her speech, she replied: No, sir, I do not want a husband.

You do! Are not you always hankering after the men? It is high time you should be settled.

Mr. Grimes! No, indeed! when I do have a husband, it shall not be such a man as Mr. Grimes neither.

Be silent! How dare you give yourself such unaccountable liberties?

Lord, I wonder what I should do with him. You might as well give me your great rough water-dog, and bid me make him a silk cushion to lie in my dressing room. Besides, sir, Grimes is a common labouring man, and I am sure I have always heard my aunt say that ours is a very great family.

It is a lie. Our family? Have you the impudence to think yourself one of our family?

Why, sir! was not your grandpapa my grandpapa? How then can we be of a different family?

From the strongest reason in the world. You are the daughter of a rascally Scotchman, who spent every shilling of my aunt Lucy's fortune, and left you a beggar. You have got a hundred pounds, and Grimes's father promises to give him as much. How dare you look down upon your equals?

Indeed, sir, I am not proud. But indeed, and indeed, I can never love Mr. Grimes. I am very happy as I am: why should I be married?

Silence your prating. Grimes will be here this afternoon. Look that you behave well to him. If you do not, he will remember and repay, when you least like it.

Now, I am sure, sir—you are not in earnest?

Not in earnest? Damn me but we will see that. I can tell what you would be at. You had rather be Mr. Falkland's miss, than the wife of a plain downright yeoman. But I shall take care of you.— Aye, this comes of indulgence. You must be taken down, miss. You must be taught the difference between high flown notions and realities. Mayhap you may take it a little in dudgeon or so. But never mind that. Pride always wants a little smarting. If you should be brought to shame, it is I that shall bear all the blame of it.

The tone in which Mr. Tyrrel spoke was so different from any thing to which miss Melvile had been accustomed, that she felt herself wholly unable to determine what construction to put upon it. Sometimes she thought he had really formed a plan for imposing upon her a condition, that she could not bear so much as to think of. But presently she rejected this idea as an unworthy imputation upon her kinsman, and concluded that it was only his way, and that all he meant was to try her. To be resolved however she determined to consult her constant adviser, Mrs. Jakeman, and accordingly repeated to her what had passed. Mrs. Jakeman saw the whole in a very different light from that in which Emily had conceived it, and trembled for the future peace of her beloved ward.

Lord bless me, my dear mamma! cried Emily, (this was the appellation she delighted to bestow upon the good housekeeper) you cannot think so. But I do not care. I will never marry Grimes, happen what will.

But how will you help yourself? My master will oblige you.

Nay, now you think you are talking to a child indeed. It is I am to have the man, not Mr. Tyrrel. Do you think I will let any body else chuse a husband for me? I am not such a fool as that neither.

Ah, Emily! you little know the disadvantages of your situation. Your cousin is a violent man, and perhaps will turn you out of doors, if you oppose him.

Oh, mamma, it is very wicked of you to say so. I am sure Mr. Tyrrel is a very good man, though he be a little cross now and then. He knows very well that I am right to have a will of my own in such a thing as this, and nobody is punished for doing what is right.

Nobody ought, my dear child. But there are very wicked and tyrannical men in the world.

Well, well, I will never believe that my cousin is one of these. I hope he is not.

And, if he were, what then? To be sure I should be very sorry to make him angry.

What then? Why then my poor Emily would be a beggar. Do you think I could bear to see that?

No, no. Mr. Tyrrel has just told me that I have a hundred pounds. But, if I had no fortune at all, is not that the case with a thousand other folks? Why should I grieve, for what they bear and are merry? Do not make yourself uneasy, mamma. I am determined that I will do any thing rather than marry Grimes; that is what I will.

Mrs. Jakeman could not bear the uneasy state of suspense in which this conversation left her mind, and went immediately to the squire to have her doubts resolved. The manner in which she proposed the question sufficiently indicated the judgment she had formed of the match.

That is true, said Mr. Tyrrel, I wanted to speak to you about this affair. The girl has got unaccountable notions in her head, that will be the ruin of her. You perhaps can tell where she had them. But, be that as it will, it is high time something should be done. The shortest way is the best, and to keep things well, while they are well. In short I am determined she shall marry this lad: you do not know any harm of him, do you? You have a good deal of influence with her, and I desire, do you see? that you will employ it to lead her to her good: you had best, I can tell you. She is a pert vixen! By and by she would be a whore, and at last no better than a common trull, and rot upon a dunghil, if I were not at all these pains to save her from destruction. I would make her an honest farmer's wife, and my pretty miss cannot bear the thoughts of it!

In the afternoon Grimes came according to appointment, and was left alone with the young lady. Well, miss, said he, it seems the squire has a mind to make us man and wife. For my part, I cannot say I should have thought of it. But, being as how the squire has broke the ice, if so be as you like of the match, why I am your man. Say the word; a nod is as good as a wink to a blind horse.

Emily was already sufficiently mortified at the unexpected proposal of Mr. Tyrrel. She was confounded at the novelty of the situation, and still more at the uncultivated rudeness of her lover, which even exceeded her expectation. This confusion was interpreted by Grimes into diffidence.

Come, come, never be cast down. Put a good face upon it. What though? My first sweetheart was Bet Butterfield, but what of that? What must be must be; grief will never fill the belly. She was a fine strapping wench, that is the truth of it! Five foot ten inches, and as stout as a trooper. Oh, she would do a power of work! Up early and down late; milked ten cows with her own hands; on with her cardinal, rode to market between her panniers, fair weather and foul, hail, blow or snow. It would have done your heart good to have seen her frost-bitten cheeks, as red as a beefen from her own orchard! Ah, she was a maid of mettle; would romp with the harvest men, slap one upon the back, wrestle with another, and had a rogue's trick and a joke for all round. Poor girl! she broke her neck down stairs at a christening. To be sure I shall never meet with her fellow! But never you mind that! I do not doubt that I shall find more in you upon farther acquaintance. As coy and bashful as you seem, I dare say you are rogue enough at bottom. When I have touzled and rumpled you a little, we shall see. I am no chicken, miss, whatever you may think. I know what is what, and can see as far into a milstone as another. Ay, ay; you will come to. The fish will snap at the bait, never doubt it. Yes, yes, we shall rub on main well together.

Emily by this time had in some degree mustered up her spirits, and began, though with hesitation, to thank Mr. Grimes for his good opinion, but to confess that she could never be brought to favour his addresses. She therefore intreated him to desist from all farther application. This remonstrance on her part would have become more intelligible, had it not been for his boisterous manners and extravagant chearfulness, which indisposed him to silence, and made him suppose that at half a word he had a sufficient intimation of another's meaning. Mr. Tyrrel in the mean time was too impatient, not to interrupt the scene before they could have time to proceed far in explanation, and he was studious in the sequel to prevent the young folks from being too intimately acquainted with each other's inclinations. Grimes of consequence attributed the reluctance of miss Melvile to maiden coyness, and the skittish shyness of an unbroken filly. Indeed had it been otherwise, it is not probable that it would have made any effectual impression upon him, as he was always accustomed to consider women as made for the recreation of the men, and to exclaim against the weakness of people who taught them to imagine they were to judge for themselves.

As the suit proceeded and miss Melvile saw more of her new admirer, her antipathy increased. But, though her character was unspoiled by those false wants which frequently make people of family miserable while they have every thing that nature requires within their reach, yet she had been little used to opposition, and was terrified by the growing sternness of her kinsman. Sometimes she thought of flying from a house which was now become her dungeon; but the habits of her youth and her ignorance of the world made her shrink from this project when she contemplated it more nearly. Mrs. Jakeman indeed could not think with patience of young Grimes as a husband for her darling Emily, but her prudence determined her to resist with all her might the idea on the part of the young lady of proceeding to extremities. She could not believe that Mr. Tyrrel would persist in such an unaccountable persecution, and she exhorted miss Melvile to forget for a moment the unaffected independence of her character, and pathetically to deprecate her cousin's obstinacy. She had great confidence in the ingenuous eloquence of her ward. Mrs. Jakeman did not know what was passing in the breast of the tyrant.

Miss Melvile complied with the suggestion of her mamma. One morning immediately after breakfast she went to her harpsichord, and played one after another several of those airs that were most the favourites of Mr. Tyrrel. Mrs. Jakeman had retired; the servants were gone to their respective employments. Mr. Tyrrel would have gone also; his mind was untuned, and he did not take the pleasure he had been accustomed to take in the musical performances of Emily. But her finger was now more tasteful than common. Her mind was probably wrought up to a firmer and bolder tone by the recollection of the cause she was going to plead, at the same time that it was exempt from those incapacitating tremors which would have been felt by one that dared not look poverty in the face. Mr. Tyrrel was unable to leave the apartment. Sometimes he traversed it with impatient steps; then he hung over the poor innocent whose powers were exerted to please him; at length he threw himself in a chair opposite, with his eyes turned towards Emily. It was easy to trace the progress of his emotions. The furrows into which his countenance was contracted were gradually relaxed; his features were brightened into a smile; the kindness with which he had upon former occasions contemplated Emily seemed to revive in his heart.

Emily watched her opportunity. As soon as she had finished one of the pieces, she rose and went to Mr. Tyrrel.

Now have not I done it nicely? And after this will not you give me a reward?

A reward! Ay, come here, and I will give you a kiss.

No, that is not it. And yet you have not kissed me this many a day. Formerly you said you loved me, and called me your Emily. I am sure you did not love me better than I loved you. You have not forgot all the kindness you once had for me? added she anxiously.

Forgot? No, no. How can you ask such a question? You shall be my dear Emily still!

Ah, those were happy times! she replied, a little mournfully. Do you know, cousin, I wish I could wake, and find that the last month,—only about a month,—was a dream?

What do you mean by that? said Mr. Tyrrel with an altered voice. Have a care! Do not put me out of humour. Do not come with your romantic notions now.

No, no. I have no romantic notions in my head. I speak of something upon which the happiness of my life depends.

I see what you would be at. Be silent. You know it is to no purpose to plague me with your stubbornness. You will not let me be in good humour with you for a moment. What my mind is determined on about Grimes, all the world shall not move me to give up.

Dear, dear cousin, why but consider now. Grimes is a rough rustic lout, like Orson in the story-book.[1] He wants a wife like himself. He would be as uneasy and as much at a loss with me, as I with him. Why should we both of us be forced to do what neither of us is inclined to? I cannot think what could ever have put it into your head. But now, for goodness' sake, give it up. Marriage is a serious thing. You should not think of joining two people for a whim, who are neither of them fit for one another in any respect in the world. We should feel mortified and disappointed all our lives. Month would go after month, and year after year, and I could never hope to be my own but by the death of a person I ought to love. I am sure, sir, you cannot mean me all this harm. What have I done, that I should deserve to have you for an enemy?

I am not your enemy. I tell you that it is necessary to put you out of harm's way. But, if I were your enemy, I could not be a worse torment to you than you are to me. Are not you continually singing the praises of Falkland? Are not you in love with Falkland?

That man is a legion of devils to me! I might as well have been a beggar! I might as well have been a dwarf or a monster! Time was when I was thought entitled to respect. But now, debauched by this Frenchified rascal, they call me rude, surly, a tyrant! It is true that I cannot talk in finical phrases, flatter people with hypocritical praise, or suppress the real feelings of my mind! The scoundrel knows his pitiful advantages, and insults me upon them without ceasing. He is my rival and my persecutor. And at last, as if all this were not enough, he has found means to spread the pestilence in my own family. You, whom we took up out of charity, the chance born brat of a stolen marriage! you, must turn upon your bene-factor, and wound me in the point that of all others I could least bear it. If I were your enemy, should I not have reason? Could I ever inflict upon you such injuries as you have made me suffer? And who are you? The lives of fifty such cannot atone for an hour of my uneasiness. If you were to linger for twenty years upon the rack, you would never feel what I have felt. But I am your friend. I see which way you are going, and I am determined to save you from the thief, this hypocritical destroyer of us all. Every moment that the mischief is left to itself it does but make bad worse, and I am determined to save you out of hand.

The angry expostulations of Mr. Tyrrel suggested new ideas to the tender mind of miss Melvile. He had never confessed the emotions of his soul so explicitly before; but the tempest of his thoughts suffered him to be no longer master of himself. She saw with astonishment that he was the irreconcilable foe of Mr. Falk-land, whom she had fondly imagined it was the same thing to know and admire; and that he harboured a deep and rooted resent-ment against herself. She recoiled without well knowing why before the ferocious passions of her kinsman, and was convinced that she had nothing to hope from his implacable temper. But her alarm was the prelude of firmness and not of cowardice.

No, sir, replied she, indeed I will not be driven any way that you happen to like. I have been used to obey you, and in all that is reasonable I will obey you still. But you urge me too far. What do you tell me of Mr. Falkland? Have I ever done any thing to deserve your unkind suspicions? I am innocent, and will continue innocent. Mr. Grimes is well enough, and will no doubt find women that like him. But he is not fit for me, and torture shall not force me to be his wife.

Mr. Tyrrel was not a little astonished at the spirit which Emily displayed upon this occasion. He had calculated too securely upon the general mildness and suavity of her disposition. He now endeavoured to qualify the harshness of his former sentiments.

God damn my soul! And so you can scold, can you? You expect every body to turn out of his way, and fetch and carry, just as you please? I could find in my heart— But you know my mind. I insist upon it that you let Grimes court you, and that you lay aside your sulks, and give him a fair hearing. Will you do that? If then you persist in your wilfulness, why there, I suppose, is an end of the matter. Do not think that any body is going to marry you, whether you will or no. You are no such mighty prize, I assure you. If you knew your own interest, you would be glad to take the young fellow, while he is willing.

Miss Melvile rejoiced in the prospect which the last words of her kinsman afforded her, of a termination at no great distance to her present persecutions. Mrs. Jakeman, to whom she communicated them, congratulated Emily on the returning moderation and good sense of the squire, and herself on her prudence in having urged the young lady to this happy expostulation. But their mutual felicitations lasted not long. Mr. Tyrrel informed Mrs. Jakeman of the necessity in which he found himself of sending her to a distance upon a business which would not fail to detain her several weeks; and, though the errand by no means wore an artificial or ambiguous face, the two friends drew a melancholy presage from this ill-timed separation. Mrs. Jakeman in the mean time exhorted her ward to persevere, reminded her of the compunction which had already been manifested by her kinsman, and encouraged her to hope every thing from her courage and good temper. Emily on her part, though grieved at the absence of her protector and counsellor at so interesting a crisis, was unable to suspect Mr. Tyrrel of such a degree either of malice or duplicity as could afford ground for serious alarm. She congratulated herself upon her delivery from so alarming a persecution, and drew a prognostic of future success from this happy termination of the first serious affair of her life. She exchanged a state of fortitude and alarm for her former pleasing dreams respecting Mr. Falkland. These she bore without impatience. She was even taught by the uncertainty of the event to desire to prolong rather than abridge a situation, which might be delusive, but which was not without its pleasures.

CHAPTER VIII

NOTHING could be farther from Mr. Tyrrel's intention than to suffer his project to be thus terminated. No sooner was he freed from the fear of his housekeeper's interference, than he changed the whole system of his conduct. He ordered miss Melvile to be closely confined to her apartment, and deprived of all the means of communicating her situation to any one out of his own house. He placed over her a female servant in whose discretion he could confide, and who, having formerly been honoured with the amorous notices from the squire, considered the distinctions that were paid to Emily at Tyrrel Place as an usurpation upon her more reasonable claims. The squire himself did every thing in his power to blast the young lady's reputation, and represented to his attendants these precautions as necessary, to prevent her from eloping to his neighbour, and plunging herself in total ruin.

As soon as miss Melvile had been twenty four hours in durance, and there was some reason to suppose that her spirit might be subdued to the emergency of her situation, Mr. Tyrrel thought proper to go to her, to explain the grounds of her present treatment, and acquaint her with the only means by which she could hope for a change. Emily no sooner saw him, than she turned towards him with an air of greater firmness than perhaps she had ever assumed in her life, and accosted him thus:

Well, sir, is it you? I wanted to see you. It seems I am shut up here by your orders. What does this mean? What right have you to make a prisoner of me? What do I owe you? Your mother left me a hundred pounds: have you ever offered to make any addition to my fortune? But, if you had, I do not want it. I do not pretend to be better than the children of other poor parents; I can maintain myself as they do. I prefer liberty to wealth. I see you are surprised at the resolution I exert. But ought I not to turn again, when I am trampled upon? I should have left you before now, if Mrs. Jakeman had not overpersuaded me, and if I had not thought better of you than by your present behaviour I find you deserve. But now, sir, I intend to leave your house this moment, and insist upon it that you do not endeavour to prevent me.

Thus saying, she arose, and went towards the door, while Mr. Tyrrel stood thunderstruck at her magnanimity. Seeing however that she was upon the point of being out of the reach of his power, he recovered himself, and pulled her back.

What is in the wind now? Do you think, strumpet, that you shall get the better of me by sheer impudence? Sit down! rest you satisfied! So you want to know by what right you are here, do you? By the right of possession. This house is mine, and you are in my power. There is no Mrs. Jakeman now to spirit you away; no, nor no Falkland to bully for you. I have countermined you, damn me! and blown up your schemes. Do you think I will be contradicted and opposed for nothing? When did you ever know any body resist my will without being made to repent? And shall I now see myself brow-beaten by a chitty-faced girl? I have not given you a fortune? Damn you, who brought you up? I will make you a bill for clothing and lodging. Do not you know that every creditor has a right to stop his runaway debtor? You may think as you please; but here you are till you marry Grimes. Heaven and earth shall not prevent, but I will get the better of your obstinacy!

Ungenerous, unmerciful man! and so it is enough for you that I have nobody to defend me! But I am not so helpless as you may imagine. You may imprison my body, but you cannot conquer my mind. Marry Mr. Grimes? And is this the way to bring me to your purpose? Every hardship I suffer puts still farther distant the end for which I am thus unjustly treated. You are not used to have your will contradicted! When did I ever contradict it? And in a concern that is so completely my own shall my will go for nothing? Would you lay down this rule for yourself, and suffer no other creature to take the benefit of it? I want nothing of you; how dare you refuse me the privilege of a reasonable being, to live unmolested in poverty and innocence? What sort of a man do you show yourself, you that lay claim to the respect and applause of every one that knows you?

The spirited reproaches of Emily had at first the effect to fill Mr. Tyrrel with astonishment, and make him feel abashed and over-awed in the presence of this unprotected innocent. But his confusion was the result of surprise. When the first emotion wore off, he cursed himself for being moved by her expostulations, and was ten times more exasperated against her, for daring to defy his resentment at a time when she had every thing to fear. His despotic and unforgiving propensities stimulated him to a degree little short of madness. At the same time his habits, which were pensive and gloomy, led him to meditate a variety of schemes to punish her obstinacy. He began to suspect that there was little hope of succeeding by open force, and therefore determined to have recourse to treachery.

He found in Grimes an instrument sufficiently adapted to his purpose. This fellow, without an atom of intentional malice, was fitted by the mere coarseness of his perceptions for the perpetration of the greatest injuries. He regarded both injury and advantage merely as they related to the gratifications of appetite; and considered it an essential in true wisdom to treat with insult the effeminacy of those who suffer themselves to be tormented with ideal misfortunes. He believed that no happier destiny could befal a young woman than to be his wife, and he conceived that that termination would amply compensate for any calamities she might suppose herself to undergo in the interval. He was therefore easily prevailed upon by certain temptations which Mr. Tyrrel knew how to employ, to take a part in the plot into which miss Melvile was meant to be betrayed.

Matters being thus prepared, Mr. Tyrrel proceeded through the means of the jailor, (for the experience he had already had of personal discussion did not incline him to repeat his visits) to play upon the fears of his prisoner. This woman, sometimes under the pretence of friendship, and sometimes with open malice, informed Emily from time to time of the preparations that were making for her marriage. One day 'the squire had rode over to look at a neat little farm which was destined for the habitation of the new-married couple,' and at another 'a quantity of live stock and houshold furniture was procured that every thing might be ready for their reception.' She then told her 'of a licence that was bought, a parson in readiness and a day fixed for the nuptials.' When Emily endeavoured, though with increasing misgivings, to ridicule these proceedings as absolutely nugatory without her consent, her artful gouvernante related several stories of forced marriages, and assured her that neither protestations, nor silence, nor fainting would be of any avail, either to suspend the ceremony, or to set it aside when once performed.

The situation of miss Melvile was in an eminent degree pitiable. She had no intercourse but with her persecutors. She had not a human being with whom to consult, and who might afford her the smallest degree of consolation and encouragement. She had fortitude; but it was neither confirmed nor directed by the dictates of experience. It could not therefore be expected to be so inflexible as with better information it would no doubt have been found. She had a clear and noble spirit; but she had some of her sex's errors. Her mind sunk under the uniform terrors with which she was assailed, and her health became visibly impaired.

Her firmness being thus far undermined, Grimes, in pursuance of his instructions, took care in his next interview to throw out an insinuation, that for his own part he never cared much for the match, and, since she was so averse to it, would be better pleased that it should never take place. Between one and the other however he was got into a scrape, and now he supposed he must marry, will he, nill he. The two squires would infallibly ruin him upon the least appearance of backwardness on his part, as they were accustomed to do every inferior that resisted their will. Emily was rejoiced to find her admirer in so favourable a disposition; and earnestly pressed him to give effect to this humane declaration. Her representations were full of eloquence and energy. Grimes appeared to be moved at the fervency of her manner; but objected the resentment of Mr. Tyrrel and his landlord. At length however he suggested a project in consequence of which he might assist her in her escape, without its ever coming to their knowledge, as indeed there was no likelihood that their suspicions would fix upon him. To be sure, said he, you have refused me in a disdainful sort of a way, as a man may say. Mayhap you thought I was no better 'an a brute. But I bear you no malice, and I will show you that I am more kind-hearted 'an you have been willing to think. It is a strange sort of a vagary you have taken, to stand in your own light, and disoblige all your friends. But, if you are resolute to be off, do you see? I scorn to be the husband of a lass that is not every bit as willing as I; and so I will even help to put you in a condition to follow your own inclinations.

Emily listened to these suggestions at first with eagerness and approbation. But her fervency somewhat abated, when they came to discuss the minute parts of the undertaking. It was necessary, as Grimes informed her, that her escape should be effected in the dead of the night. He would conceal himself for that purpose in the garden, and be provided with false keys by which to deliver her from her prison. These circumstances were by no means adapted to calm her perturbed imagination. To throw herself into the arms of the man, whose intercourse she was employing every method to avoid, and whom under the idea of a partner for life she could least of all men endure, was no doubt an extraordinary proceeding. The attendant circumstances of darkness and solitude aggravated the picture. The situation of Tyrrel Place was uncommonly lonely: it was three miles from the nearest village, and not less than seven from that in which Mrs. Jakeman's sister resided, under whose protection miss Melvile was desirous of placing herself. The ingenuous character of Emily did not allow her once to suspect Grimes of intending to make an ungenerous and brutal advantage of these circumstances; but her mind involuntarily revolted against the idea of committing herself alone to the disposal of a man whom she had lately been accustomed to consider as the instrument of her treacherous relation.

After having for some time revolved these considerations, she thought of the expedient of desiring Grimes to engage Mrs. Jakeman's sister to wait for her at the outside of the garden. But this Grimes peremptorily refused. He even flew into a passion at the proposal. It showed very little gratitude, to desire him to disclose to other people his concern in this dangerous affair. For his part he was determined in consideration of his own safety never to appear in it to any living soul. If miss did not believe him, when he made this proposal out of pure good nature, and would not trust him a single inch, she might even see to the consequences herself. He was resolved to condescend no farther to the whims of a person who in her treatment of him had shown herself as proud as Lucifer himself.

Emily exerted herself to appease his resentment; but all the eloquence of her new confederate could not prevail upon her instantly to give up her objection. She desired till the next day to consider of it. The day after was fixed by Mr. Tyrrel for the marriage ceremony. In the mean time she was pestered with intimations in a thousand different forms of the fate that so nearly awaited her. The preparations were so continued, methodical and regular, as to produce in her the most painful and aching anxiety. If her heart attained a moment's intermission upon the subject, her female attendant was sure by some sly hint or sarcastical remark to put a speedy termination to her tranquillity. She felt herself, as she afterwards remarked, alone, uninstructed, just broken loose as it were from the trammels of infancy, without one single creature to concern himself in her fate. She, who till then had never known an enemy, had now for three weeks not seen the glimpse of a human countenance that she had not good reason to consider as wholly estranged to her at least, if not unrelentingly bent on her destruction. She now for the first time experienced the anguish of never having known her parents, and being cast entirely upon the charity of people with whom she had too little equality to hope to receive from them the offices of friendship.

The succeeding night was filled with the most anxious thoughts. When a momentary oblivion stole upon her senses, her distempered imagination conjured up a thousand images of violence and falshood, she saw herself in the hands of her determined enemies, who did not hesitate by the most daring treachery to complete her ruin. Her waking thoughts were not more consoling. The struggle was too great for her constitution. As morning approached, she resolved at all hazards to put herself into the hands of Grimes. This determination was no sooner made, than she felt her heart sensibly lightened. She could not conceive any evil which could result from this proceeding, that deserved to be put in the balance against those which, under the roof of her kinsman, appeared unavoidable.

When she communicated her determination to Grimes, it was not possible to say whether he received pleasure or pain from the intimation. He smiled indeed, but his smile was accompanied by a certain abrupt ruggedness of countenance, so that it might equally well be the smile of sarcasm or of congratulation. He however renewed his assurances of fidelity to his engagements and punctuality of execution. Meanwhile the day was interspersed with nuptial presents and preparations, all indicating the firmness as well as security of the directors of the scene. Emily had hoped that, as the crisis approached, they might have remitted something of their usual diligence. She was resolved in that case, if a fair opportunity had offered, to give the slip both to her jailors, and to her new and reluctantly chosen confederate. But, though extremely vigilant for that purpose, she found the execution of the idea impracticable.

At length the night so critical to her happiness approached. The mind of Emily could not fail on this occasion to be extremely agitated. She had first exerted all her perspicacity to elude the vigilance of her attendant. This insolent and unfeeling tyrant, instead of any relentings, had only sought to make sport of her anxiety. Accordingly in one instance she hid herself, and, suffering Emily to suppose that the coast was clear, met her at the end of the gallery, near the top of the stair-case. How do you do, my dear?

said she, with an insulting tone. And so the little dear thought itself cunning enough to outwit me, did it? Oh, it was a sly little gipsey! Go, go back, love! troop! Emily felt deeply the trick that was played upon her. She sighed, but disdained to return any answer to this low vulgarity. Being once more in her chamber, she sat down in a chair, and remained buried in reverie for more than two hours. After this she went to her drawers, and turned over in a hurrying, confused way her linen and clothes, having in her mind the provision it would be necessary to make for her elopement. Her jailor officiously followed her from place to place, and observed what she did for the present in silence. It was now the hour of rest. Good night, child, said this saucy girl in the act of retiring. It is time to lock up. For the few next hours the time is your own. Make the best use of it. Do'ee think ee can creep out at the key hole, lovey? At eight o'clock you see me again. And then, and then, added she, clapping her hands, it is all over. The sun is not surer to rise, than you and your honest man to be made one.

There was something in the tone with which this slut uttered her farewel, that suggested the question to Emily, What does she mean? Is it possible she should know what has been planned for the few next hours? This was the first moment that suspicion had offered itself and its continuance was short.—With an aching heart she folded up the few necessaries she intended to take with her. She instinctively listened with an anxiety that would almost have enabled her to hear the stirring of a leaf. From time to time she thought her ear was struck with the sound of feet; but the treading, if treading it were, was so soft, that she could never ascertain whether it were a real sound or the mere creature of the fancy. Then all was still as if the universal motion had been at rest. By and by she conceived she overheard a noise as of buzzing and low muttered speech. Her heart palpitated; for a second time she began to doubt the honesty of Grimes. The suggestion was now more anxious than before; but it was too late. Presently she heard the sound of a key in her chamber door, and the rustic made his appearance. She started, and cried, Are we discovered? did not I hear you speak? Grimes advanced on tiptoe with his finger to his lip. No, no, replied he, all is safe. He took her by the hand, led her in silence out of the house, and then across the garden. Emily examined with her eye the doors and passages as they proceeded, and looked on all sides with fearful suspicion, but every thing was as vacant and still as she

herself could have wished. Grimes opened a back door of the garden
already unlocked, that led into an unfrequented lane. There stood
two horses ready equipped for the journey, and fastened by their
bridles to a post not six yards distant from the garden. Grimes
pushed the door after them. By Gemini, said he, my heart was in
my mouth. As I comed along to you, I saw Mun, coachey, pop along
from the back door to the stables. He was within a hop, step and
jump of me. But he had a lanthorn in his hand, and he did not see
me, being as I was darkling.—Saying this, he assisted miss Melvile
to mount. He troubled her little during the route. On the contrary
he was remarkably silent and contemplative, a circumstance by no
means disagreeable to Emily, to whom his conversation had never
been acceptable.

After having proceeded about two miles, they turned into a wood,
through which the road lay that led to the place of their destination.
The night was extremely dark, at the same time that the air was soft
and mild, it being now the middle of summer. Under pretence of
exploring the way, Grimes contrived, when they had already penetrated into the midst of this gloomy solitude, to get his horse abreast
with that of miss Melvile, and then suddenly reaching out his hand,
seized hold of her bridle. I think we may as well stop here a bit,
said he.

Stop! exclaimed Emily with surprise. Why should we stop? Mr.
Grimes, what do you mean?

Come, come, said he, never trouble yourself to wonder. Did you
think I were such a goose, to take all this trouble merely to gratify
your whim? I' faith, nobody shall find me a pack-horse, to go of
other folks' errands, without knowing a reason why. I cannot say
that I much minded to have you at first; but your ways are enough
to stir the blood of my grandad. Far fetched and dear bought is
always relishing. Your consent was so hard to gain, that squire
thought it was surest asking in the dark. A' said however a' would
have no such doings in his house, and so, do you see, we are come
here.

For God's sake, Mr. Grimes, think what you are about! You
cannot be base enough to ruin a poor creature who has put herself
under your protection!

Ruin! no, no, I will make an honest woman of you, when all is
done. Nay, none of your airs; no tricks upon travellers! I have you
here as safe as a horse in a pound; there is not a house nor a shed

within a mile of us; and, if I miss the opportunity, call me spade. Faith, you are a delicate morsel, and there is no time to be lost.

Miss Melvile had but an instant in which to collect her thoughts. She felt that there was little hope of softening the obstinate and insensible brute in whose power she was placed. But the presence of mind and intrepidity, annexed to her character, did not now desert her. Grimes had scarcely finished his harangue, when with a strong and unexpected jerk she disengaged the bridle from his grasp, and at the same time put her horse upon full speed. She had scarcely advanced twice the length of her horse, when Grimes recovered from his surprise, and pursued her, inexpressibly morti-fied at being so easily overreached. The sound of his horse behind served but to rouse more completely the mettle of that of Emily; whether by accident or sagacity the animal pursued without a fault the narrow and winding way; and the chase continued the whole length of the wood.

At the extremity of this wood there was a gate. The recollection of this softened a little the cutting disappointment of Grimes, as he thought himself secure of putting an end by its assistance to the career of Emily, nor was it very probable that any body would appear to interrupt his designs, in such a place, and in the dead and silence of the night. By the most extraordinary accident however they found a man on horseback in wait at this gate. Help, help! exclaimed the affrighted Emily; thieves! murder! help! The man was Mr. Falkland. Grimes knew his voice, and therefore, though he attempted a sort of sullen resistance, it was feebly made. Two other men, whom by reason of the darkness he had not at first seen, and who were Mr. Falkland's servants, hearing the bustle of the rencounter, and alarmed for the safety of their master, rode up; and then Grimes, disappointed at the loss of his gratification, and admonished by conscious guilt, shrunk from farther parley and rode off in silence.

It may seem strange that Mr. Falkland should thus a second time have been the saviour of miss Melvile, and that under circum-stances the most unexpected and singular. But in this instance it is easily to be accounted for. He had heard of a man who lurked about this wood for robbery or some other bad design, and that it was conjectured this man was Hawkins, another of the victims of Mr. Tyrrel's rural tyranny, whom I shall immediately have occasion to introduce. Mr. Falkland's compassion had already been strongly excited in favour of Hawkins; he had in vain endeavoured to find him, and do him good; and he easily conceived that, if the conjecture which had been made in this instance proved true, he might have it in his power not only to do what he had always intended, but farther to save from a perilous offence against the laws and society a man who appeared to have strongly imbibed the principles of justice and virtue. He took with him two servants, because, going with the express design of encountering robbers, if robbers should be found, he believed he should be inexcusable if he did not go provided against possible accidents. But he had directed them, at the same time that they kept within call, to be out of the reach of being seen; and it was only the eagerness of their zeal that had brought them up thus early in the present encounter.

This new adventure promised something extraordinary. Mr. Falkland did not immediately recognise miss Melvile, and the person of Grimes was that of a total stranger whom he did not recollect to have ever seen. But it was easy to understand the merits of the case, and the propriety of interfering. The resolute manner of Mr. Falkland, combined with the dread which Grimes, oppressed with a sense of wrong, entertained of the opposition of so elevated a personage, speedily put the ravisher to flight. Emily was left alone with her deliverer. He found her much more collected and calm than could reasonably have been expected from a person who had been a moment before in the most alarming situation. She told him of the place to which she desired to be conveyed, and he immediately undertook to escort her. As they went along, she recovered that state of mind which inclined her to make a person to whom she had such repeated obligations, and who was so eminently the object of her admiration, acquainted with the events that had recently befallen her. Mr. Falkland listened with eagerness and surprise. Though he had already known various instances of Mr. Tyrrel's mean jealousy and unfeeling tyranny, this surpassed them all, and he could scarcely credit his ears while he heard the tale. His brutal neighbour seemed to realise all that has been told of the passions of fiends. Miss Melvile was obliged to repeat in the course of her tale her kinsman's rude accusation against her of entertaining a passion for Mr. Falkland; and this she did with the most bewitching simplicity and charming confusion. Though this part of the tale was a source of real pain to her deliverer, yet it is not to be supposed but that the flattering partiality of this unhappy girl increased the interest he felt in her welfare and the indignation he conceived against her infernal kinsman.

They arrived without accident at the house of the good lady under whose protection Emily desired to place herself. Here Mr. Falkland willingly left her as in a place of security. Such conspiracies as that of which she was intended to have been the victim, depend for their success upon the person against whom they are formed being out of the reach of help, and the moment they are detected they are annihilated. Such reasoning will no doubt be generally found sufficiently solid, and it appeared to Mr. Falkland perfectly applicable to the present case. But he was mistaken.

CHAPTER IX

MR. FALKLAND had experienced the nullity of all expostulation with Mr. Tyrrel, and was therefore content in the present case with confining his attention to the intended victim. The indignation with which he thought of his neighbour's character was now grown to such a height, as to fill him with reluctance to the idea of a voluntary interview. There was indeed another affair, which had been contemporary with this, that had once more brought these mortal enemies into a state of contest, and had contributed to raise into a temper little short of madness, the already inflamed and corrosive bitterness of Mr. Tyrrel.

There was a tenant of Mr. Tyrrel, one Hawkins;—I cannot mention his name without recollecting the painful tragedies that are annexed to it! This Hawkins had originally been taken up by Mr. Tyrrel with a view of protecting him from the arbitrary proceedings of a neighbouring squire, though he had now in his turn become an object of persecution to Mr. Tyrrel himself. The first ground of their connection was this. Hawkins, beside a farm which he rented under the abovementioned squire, had a small freehold estate that he inherited from his father. This of course entitled him to a vote in the county elections; and, a warmly contested election having occurred, he was required by his landlord to vote for the candidate in whose favour he had himself engaged. Hawkins refused to obey the mandate, and soon after received notice to quit the farm he at that time rented.

It happened that Mr. Tyrrel had interested himself strongly in behalf of the opposite candidate; and, as Mr. Tyrrel's estate bordered upon the seat of Hawkins's present residence, the ejected countryman could think of no better expedient than that of riding over to this gentleman's mansion, and relating the case to him. Mr. Tyrrel heard him through with attention. Well, friend, said he, it is very true that I wished Mr. Jackman to carry his election; but you know it is usual in these cases for tenants to vote just as their landlords please. I do not think proper to encourage rebellion. —All that is very right, and please you, replied Hawkins; and I would have voted at my landlord's bidding for any other man in the kingdom but squire Marlow. You must know one day his huntsman rode over my fence, and so through my best field of standing corn. It was not above a dozen yards about, if he had kept the cart-road. The fellow had served me the same sauce, an it please your honour, three or four times before. So I only asked him, What he did that for, and whether he had not more conscience than to spoil people's crops o' that fashion? Presently the squire came up. He is but a poor, weazen-face chicken of a gentleman, saving your honour's reverence. And so he flew into a woundy passion, and threatened to horsewhip me. I will do as much in reason to pleasure my landlord as arr a tenant he has; but I will not give my vote to a man that threatens to horsewhip me. And so, your honour, I and my wife and three children are to be turned out of house and home, and what I am to do to maintain them God knows. I have been a hard-working man, and have alway lived very well, and I do think the case is main hard. Squire Underwood turns me out of my farm; and, if your honour do not take me in, I know none of the neighbouring gentry will, for fear as they say of encouraging their own tenants to run rusty too.

This representation was not without its effect upon Mr. Tyrrel. Well, well, man, replied he, we will see what can be done. Order and subordination are very good things; but people should know how much to require. As you tell the story, I cannot see that you are greatly to blame. Marlow is a coxcombical prig, that is the truth on't; and, if a man will expose himself, why, he must even take what follows. I do hate a Frenchified fop with all my soul; and I cannot say that I am much pleased with my neighbour Underwood for taking the part of such a rascal. Hawkins, I think is your name? You may call on Barnes, my steward, tomorrow, and he shall speak to you.

While Mr. Tyrrel was speaking, he recollected that he had a farm vacant of nearly the same value as that which Hawkins at present rented under Mr. Underwood. He immediately consulted his steward, and, finding the thing suitable in every respect, Hawkins was installed out of hand into the catalogue of Mr. Tyrrel's tenants. Mr. Underwood extremely resented this proceeding, which indeed, as being contrary to the understood conventions of the country gentlemen, few people but Mr. Tyrrel would have ventured upon. There was an end, said Mr. Underwood, to all regulation, if tenants were to be encouraged in such disobedience. It was not a question of this or that candidate, seeing that any gentleman, who was a true friend to his country, would rather lose his election, than do a thing which, if once established into a practice, would deprive them for ever of the power of managing any election. The labouring people were sturdy and resolute enough of their own accord; it became every day more difficult to keep them under any subordination; and, if the gentlemen were so ill-advised as to neglect the public good, and encourage them in their insolence, there was no foreseeing where it would end.

Mr. Tyrrel was not of a stamp to be influenced by these remonstrances. Their general spirit was sufficiently conformable to the sentiments he himself entertained; but he was of too vehement a temper to maintain the character of a consistent politician; and, however wrong his conduct might be, he would by no means admit of its being set right by the suggestions of others. The more his patronage of Hawkins was criticised, the more inflexibly he adhered to it; and he was at no loss in clubs and other assemblies to overbear and silence, if not to confute his censurers. Beside which, Hawkins had certain accomplishments which qualified him to be a favourite with Mr. Tyrrel. The bluntness of his manner and the ruggedness of his temper gave him some resemblance to his landlord; and, as these qualities were likely to be more frequently exercised on such persons as had incurred Mr. Tyrrel's displeasure than upon Mr. Tyrrel himself, they were not observed without some degree of complacency. In a word, he every day received new marks of distinction from his patron, and after some time was appointed coadjutor to Mr. Barnes under the denomination of bailiff. It was about the same period that he obtained a lease of the farm of which he was tenant.

Mr. Tyrrel was determined, as occasion offered, to promote

every part of the family of this favoured dependent. Hawkins had a son, a lad of seventeen, of an agreeable person, a ruddy complexion, and of quick and lively parts. This lad was in an uncommon degree the favourite of his father, who seemed to have nothing so much at heart as the future welfare of his son. Mr. Tyrrel had noticed him two or three times with approbation; and the boy, being fond of the sports of the field, had occasionally followed the hounds, and displayed various instances both of agility and sagacity in presence of the squire. One day in particular he exhibited himself with uncommon advantage; and Mr. Tyrrel without farther delay proposed to his father to take him into his family, and make him whipper-in to his hounds, till he could provide him with some more lucrative appointment in his service.

This proposal was received by Hawkins with various marks of mortification. He excused himself with hesitation for not accepting the offered favour; said the lad was in many ways useful to him; and hoped his honour would not insist upon depriving him of his assistance. This apology might perhaps have been sufficient with any other man than Mr. Tyrrel; but it was frequently observed of this gentleman that, when he had once formed a determination however slight in favour of any measure, he was never afterwards known to give it up, and that the only effect of opposition was to make him eager and inflexible in pursuit of that to which he had before been nearly indifferent. At first he seemed to receive the apology of Hawkins with good humour, and to see nothing in it but what was reasonable; but afterwards every time he saw the boy his desire of retaining him in his service was increased, and he more than once repeated to his father the good disposition in which he felt himself towards him. At length he observed that the lad was no more to be seen mingling in his favourite sports, and he began to suspect that this originated in a determination to thwart him in his projects.

Roused by this suspicion, which, to a man of Mr. Tyrrel's character, was not of a nature to brook delay, he sent for Hawkins to confer with him. Hawkins, said he, in a tone of displeasure, I am not satisfied with you. I have spoken to you two or three times about this lad of yours, whom I am desirous of taking into favour. What is the reason, sir, that you seem unthankful and averse to my kindness? You ought to know that I am not to be trifled with. I shall not be contented, when I offer my favours to have them rejected by such fellows as you. I made you what you are; and, if I please, can make you more helpless and miserable than you were when I found you. Have a care!

An it please your honour, said Hawkins, you have been a very good master to me, and I will tell you the whole truth. I hope you will na be angry. This lad is my favourite, my comfort and the stay of my age.

Well, and what then? Is that a reason you should hinder his preferment?

Nay, pray your honour, hear me. I may be very weak for aught I know in this case, but I cannot help it. My father was a clergyman. We have all of us lived in a creditable way; and I cannot bear to think that this poor lad of mine should go to service. For my part, I do not see any good that comes by servants. I do not know, your honour, but, I think, I should not like my Leonard to be such as they. God forgive me, if I wrong them! But this is a very dear case, and I cannot bear to risk my poor boy's welfare, when I can so easily, if you please, keep him out of harm's way. At present he is sober and industrious, and, without being pert or surly, knows what is due to him. I know, your honour, that it is main foolish of me to talk to you thus; but your honour has been a good master to me, and I cannot bear to tell you a lie.

Mr. Tyrrel had heard the whole of this harangue in silence, because he was too much astonished to open his mouth. If a thunderbolt had fallen at his feet, he could not have testified greater surprise. He had thought that Hawkins was so foolishly fond of his son that he could not bear to trust him out of his presence, but had never in the slightest degree suspected what he now found to be the truth.

Oh, ho, you are a gentleman, are you? A pretty gentleman truly! Your father was a clergyman! Your family is too good to enter into my service! Why, you impudent rascal! Was it for this that I took you up, when Mr. Underwood dismissed you for your insolence to him? Have I been nursing a viper in my bosom? Pretty master's manners will be contaminated truly! He will not know what is due to him, but will be accustomed to obey orders! You insufferable villain! Get out of my sight! Depend upon it, I will have no gentlemen on my estate! I will off with them, root and branch, bag and baggage! So, do you hear, sir? come to me tomorrow morning, bring your son, and ask my pardon; or, take my word for it,

I will make you so miserable, you shall wish you had never been born.

This treatment was too much for Hawkins's patience. There is no need, your honour, that I should come to you again about this affair. I have taken up my determination, and no time can make any change in it. I am main sorry to displease your worship, and I know that you can do me a great deal of mischief. But I hope you will not be so hard hearted, as to ruin a father only for being fond of his child, even if so be that his fondness should make him do a foolish thing. But I cannot help it, your honour: you must do as you please. The poorest neger, as a man may say, has some point that he will not part with. I will lose all that I have, and go to day-labour, and my son too, if needs must; but I will not make a gentleman's servant of him.

Very well, friend; very well! replied Tyrrel, foaming with rage. Depend upon it, I will remember you! Your pride shall have a downfal! God damn it! is it come to this? Shall a rascal, that farms his forty acres, pretend to beard the lord of the manor? I will tread you into paste! Let me advise you, scoundrel, to shut up your house and fly as if the devil was behind you! You may think yourself happy, if I be not too quick for you yet, if you escape in a whole skin! I would not suffer such a villain to remain upon my land a day longer, if I could gain the Indies by it!

Not so fast, your honour, answered Hawkins sturdily. I hope you will think better of it, and see that I have not been to blame. But, if you should not, there is some harm that you can do me, and some harm that you cannot. Though I am a plain working man, your honour, do you see? yet I am a man still. No; I have got a lease of my farm, and I shall not quit it o'thaten. I hope there is some law for poor folk, as well as for rich.

Mr. Tyrrel, unused to contradiction, was provoked beyond bearing at the courage and independent spirit of his retainer. There was not a tenant upon his estate, or at least not one of Hawkins's mediocrity of fortune, whom the general policy of land owners, and still more the arbitrary and uncontrolable temper of Mr. Tyrrel, did not effectually restrain from acts of open defiance.

Excellent, upon my soul! God damn my blood! but you are a rare fellow. You have a lease, have you? You will not quit, not you! A pretty pass things are come to, if a lease can protect such fellows as you against the lord of a manor! But you are for a trial of skill?

Oh, very well, friend, very well! With all my soul! Since it is come
to that, we will show you some pretty sport before we have done!
But get out of my sight, you rascal! I have not another word to say
to you! Never darken my doors again!

Hawkins, to borrow the language of the world, was guilty in this
affair of a double imprudence. He talked to his landlord in a more
peremptory manner than the constitution and practices of this
country allow a dependent to assume. But above all, having been
thus hurried away by his resentment, he ought to have foreseen
the consequences. It was mere madness in him to think of contest-
ing with a man of Mr. Tyrrel's eminence and fortune. It was a
fawn contending with a lion. Nothing could have been more easy
to predict, than that it was of no avail for him to have right on his
side, when his adversary had influence and wealth, and therefore
could so victoriously justify any extravagancies that he might think
proper to commit. This maxim was completely illustrated in the
sequel. Wealth and despotism easily know how to engage those
laws as the coadjutors of their oppression which were perhaps at
first intended [witless and miserable precaution!] for the safeguards of the poor.

From this moment Mr. Tyrrel was bent upon Hawkins's destruction; and he left no means unemployed that could either harass
or injure the object of his persecution. He deprived him of his
appointment of bailiff, and directed Barnes and his other dependents to do him ill offices upon all occasions. Mr. Tyrrel by the
tenure of his manor was impropriator of the great tithes,[1] and this
circumstance afforded him frequent opportunities of petty altercation. The land of one part of Hawkins's farm, though covered
with corn, was lower than the rest; and consequently exposed to
occasional inundations from a river by which it was bounded. Mr.
Tyrrel had a dam belonging to this river privately cut about a
fortnight before the season of harvest, and laid the whole under
water. He ordered his servants to pull away the fences of the
higher ground during the night, and to turn in his cattle to the
utter destruction of the crop. These expedients however applied
to only one part of the property of this unfortunate man. But
Mr. Tyrrel did not stop here. A sudden mortality took place
among Hawkins's live stock, attended with very suspicious
circumstances. Hawkins's vigilance was strongly excited by
this event, and he at length succeeded in tracing the matter so

accurately that he conceived he could bring it home to Mr. Tyrrel himself.

Hawkins had hitherto carefully avoided, notwithstanding the injuries he had suffered, the attempting to right himself by legal process, being of opinion that law was better adapted for a weapon of tyranny in the hands of the rich, than for a shield to protect the humbler part of the community against their usurpations. In this last instance however he conceived that the offence was so atrocious as to make it impossible that any rank could protect the culprit against the severity of justice. In the sequel he saw reason to applaud himself for his former inactivity in this respect, and to repent that any motive had been strong enough to persuade him into a contrary system.

This was the very point to which Mr. Tyrrel wanted to bring him, and he could scarcely credit his good fortune, when he was told that Hawkins had entered an action. His congratulation upon this occasion was immoderate, as he now conceived that the ruin of his late favourite was irretrievable. He consulted his attorney, and urged him by every motive he could devise to employ the whole series of his subterfuges in the present affair. The direct repelling of the charge exhibited against him was the least part of his care; the business was, by affidavits, motions, pleas, demurrers, flaws and appeals, to protract the question from term to term and from court to court. It would, as Mr. Tyrrel argued, be the disgrace of a civilized country, if a gentleman, when insolently attacked in law by the scum of the earth, could not convert the cause into a question of the longest purse, and stick in the skirts of his adversary till he had reduced him to beggary.

Mr. Tyrrel however was by no means so far engrossed by his law-suit, as to neglect other methods of proceeding offensively against his tenant. Among the various expedients that suggested themselves there was one, which, though it tended rather to torment than irreparably injure the sufferer, was not rejected. This was derived from the particular situation of Hawkins's house, barns, stacks and out-houses. They were placed at the extremity of a slip of land connecting them with the rest of the farm, and were surrounded on three sides by fields in the occupation of one of Mr. Tyrrel's tenants most devoted to the pleasures of his landlord. The road to the market town ran at the bottom of the largest of these fields, and was directly in view of the front of the house. No inconvenience had yet arisen from that circumstance, as there had always been a broad path, that intersected this field, and led directly from Hawkins's house to the road. This path, or private road, was now by concert of Mr. Tyrrel and his obliging tenant shut up, so as to make Hawkins a sort of prisoner in his own domains, and oblige him to go near a mile about for the purposes of his traffic.

Young Hawkins, the lad who had been the original subject of dispute between his father and the squire, had much of his father's spirit, and felt an uncontrolable indignation against the successive acts of despotism of which he was a witness. His resentment was the greater, because the sufferings to which his parent was exposed, all of them, flowed from affection to him, at the same time that he could not propose removing the ground of dispute, as by so doing he would seem to fly in the face of his father's paternal kindness. Upon the present occasion, without asking any counsel but of his own impatient resentment, he went in the middle of the night and removed all the obstructions that had been placed in the way of the old path, broke the padlocks that had been fixed, and threw open the gates. In these operations he did not proceed unobserved, and the next day a warrant was issued for apprehending him. He was accordingly carried before a meeting of justices, and by them committed to the county jail, to take his trial for the felony at the next assizes. Mr. Tyrrel was determined to prosecute the offence with the greatest severity; and his attorney, having made the proper enquiries for that purpose, undertook to bring it under that clause of the act 9 Geo. I, commonly called The Black Act,[1] which declares that 'any person, armed with a sword or other offensive weapon, and having his face blacked, or being otherwise disguised, appearing in any warren or place where hares or conies have been or shall be usually kept, and being thereof duly convicted, shall be adjudged guilty of felony, and shall suffer death, as in cases of felony, without benefit of clergy.' Young Hawkins, it seemed, had buttoned the cape of his great coat over his face as soon as he perceived himself to be observed; and he was furnished with a wrenching-iron for the purpose of breaking the padlocks. The attorney further undertook to prove, by sufficient witnesses, that the field in question was a warren in which hares were regularly fed. Mr. Tyrrel seized upon these pretences with inexpressible satisfaction. He prevailed upon the justices, by the picture he drew of the obstinacy and insolence of the Hawkinses, fully to commit the lad upon this miserable charge; and it was by no means so certain as paternal affection would have desired, that the same overpowering influence would not cause in the sequel the penal clause to be executed in all its strictness.

This was the finishing stroke to Hawkins's miseries. As he was not deficient in courage, he had stood up against his other persecutions without flinching. He was not unaware of the advantages which our laws and customs give to the rich over the poor in contentions of this kind. But, being once involved, there was a stubbornness in his nature that would not allow him to retract, and he suffered himself to hope rather than expect a favourable issue. But in this last event he was wounded in the point that was nearest his heart. He had feared to have his son contaminated and debased by a servile station, and he now saw him transferred to the seminary of a jail. He was even uncertain as to the issue of his imprisonment, and trembled to think what the tyranny of wealth might effect to blast his hopes for ever.

From this moment his heart died within him. He had trusted to persevering industry and skill to save the wreck of his little property from the vulgar spite of his landlord. But he had now no longer any spirit to exert those efforts which his situation more than ever required. Mr. Tyrrel proceeded without remission in his machinations; Hawkins's affairs every day grew more desperate; and the squire, watching the occasion, took the earliest opportunity of seizing upon his remaining property in the mode of a distress for rent.

It was precisely in this stage of the affair that Mr. Falkland and Mr. Tyrrel accidentally met in a private road near the habitation of the latter. They were on horseback, and Mr. Falkland was going to the house of the unfortunate tenant who seemed upon the point of perishing under his landlord's malice. He had been just made acquainted with the tale of this persecution. It had indeed been an additional aggravation of Hawkins's calamity that Mr. Falkland, whose interference might otherwise have saved him, had been absent from the neighbourhood for a considerable time. He had been three months in London, and from thence had gone to visit his estates in another part of the island. The proud and self-confident spirit of this poor fellow always disposed him to depend as long as possible upon his own exertions. He had avoided applying to Mr. Falkland, or indeed indulging himself in any manner in communicating and bewailing his hard hap, in the beginning of the contention; and, when the extremity grew more urgent, and he would have been willing to recede in some degree from the stubbornness of his measures, he found it no longer in his power. After an absence of considerable duration Mr. Falkland at length returned somewhat unexpectedly; and, having learned among the first articles of country intelligence the distresses of this unfortunate yeoman, he resolved to ride over to his house the next morning, and surprise him with all the relief it was in his power to bestow.

At sight of Mr. Tyrrel in this unexpected rencounter, his face reddened with indignation. His first feeling, as he afterwards said, was to avoid him; but, finding that he must pass him, he conceived that it would be a want of spirit not to acquaint him with his feelings on the present occasion.

Mr. Tyrrel, said he, somewhat abruptly, I am sorry for a piece of news which I have just heard.

And pray, sir, what is your sorrow to me?

A great deal, sir. It is caused by the distresses of a poor tenant of yours, Hawkins. If your steward has proceeded without your authority, I think it right to inform you of what he has done; and, if he has had your authority, I would gladly persuade you to think better of it.

Mr. Falkland, it would be quite as well if you would mind your own business, and leave me to mind mine. I want no monitor, and I will have none.

You mistake, Mr. Tyrrel; I am minding my own business. If I see you fall into a pit, it is my business to draw you out and save your life. If I see you pursuing a wrong mode of conduct, it is my business to set you right and save your honour.

Zounds, sir, do not think to put your conundrums upon me! Is not the man my tenant? Is not my estate my own? What signifies calling it mine, if I am not to have the direction of it? Sir, I pay for what I have; I owe no man a penny; and I will not put my estate to nurse to you, nor the best he that wears a head.

It is very true, said Mr. Falkland, avoiding any direct notice of the last words of Mr. Tyrrel, that there is a distinction of ranks. I believe that distinction is a good thing, and necessary to the peace of mankind. But, however necessary it may be, we must acknowledge that it puts some hardship upon the lower orders of society. It makes one's heart ache to think that one man is born to the inheritance of every superfluity, while the whole share of another, without any demerit of his, is drudgery and starving; and that all this is indispensible. We that are rich, Mr. Tyrrel, must do every thing in our power to lighten the yoke of these unfortunate people. We must not use the advantage that accident has given us, with an unmerciful hand. Poor wretches! they are pressed almost beyond bearing as it is; and, if we unfeelingly give another turn to the machine, they will be crushed into atoms.

This picture was not without its effect even upon the obdurate mind of Mr. Tyrrel.—Well, sir, I am no tyrant. I know very well that tyranny is a bad thing. But you do not infer from thence that these people are to do as they please, and never to meet with their deserts?

Mr. Tyrrel, I see that you are shaken in your animosity. Suffer me to hail the new-born benevolence of your nature. Go with me to Hawkins. Do not let us talk of his deserts! Poor fellow! he has suffered almost all that human nature can endure. Let your forgiveness upon this occasion be the earnest of good neighbourhood and friendship between you and me.

No, sir, I will not go. I own there is something in what you say. I always knew you had the wit to make good your own story, and tell a plausible tale. But I will not be come over thus. It has been my character, when I had once conceived a scheme of vengeance, never to forego it; and I will not change that character. I took up Hawkins when every body forsook him, and made a man of him; and the ungrateful rascal has only insulted me for my pains. Curse me, if ever I forgive him! It would be a good jest indeed, if I were to forgive the insolence of my own creature, at the desire of a man like you that has been my perpetual plague.

For God's sake, Mr. Tyrrel, have some reason in your resentment! Let us suppose that Hawkins has behaved unjustifiably, and insulted you. Is that an offence that can never be expiated? Must the father be ruined, and the son hanged, to glut your resentment?

Damn me, sir, but you may talk your heart out; you shall get nothing of me. I shall never forgive myself for having listened to you for a moment. I will suffer nobody to stop the stream of my resentment; if I ever were to forgive him, it should be at nobody's intreaty but my own. But, sir, I never will. If he and all his family were at my feet, I would order them all to be hanged the next minute, if my power were as good as my will.

And that is your decision, is it? Mr. Tyrrel, I am ashamed of you! Almighty God! to hear you talk gives one a loathing for the institutions and regulations of society, and would induce one to fly the very face of man! But, no! society casts you out; man abominates you. No wealth, no rank can buy out your stain. You will live deserted in the midst of your species; you will go into crowded societies, and no one will deign so much as to salute you. They will fly from your glance, as they would from the gaze of a basilisk. Where do you expect to find the hearts of flint, that shall sympathize with yours? You have the stamp of misery, incessant, undivided, unpitied misery!

Thus saying, Mr. Falkland gave spurs to his horse, rudely pushed beside Mr. Tyrrel, and was presently out of sight. Flaming indignation annihilated even his favourite sense of honour, and he regarded his neighbour as a wretch with whom it was impossible even to enter into contention. For the latter, he remained for the present motionless and petrified. The glowing enthusiasm of Mr. Falkland was such as might well have unnerved the stoutest foe. Mr. Tyrrel, in spite of himself, was blasted with the compunctions of guilt, and unable to string himself for the contest. The picture Mr. Falkland had drawn was prophetic. It described what Mr. Tyrrel chiefly feared; and what in its commencements he thought he already felt. It was responsive to the whispering of his own meditations; it simply gave body and voice to the spectre that haunted him, and to the terrors of which he was an hourly prey.

By and by however he recovered. The more he had been temporarily confounded, the fiercer was his resentment when he came to himself. Such hatred never existed in a human bosom, without marking its progress with violence and death. Mr. Tyrrel however felt no inclination to have recourse to personal defiance. He was the furthest in the world from a coward; but his genius sunk before the genius of Falkland. He left his vengeance to the disposal of circumstances. He was secure that his animosity would neither be forgotten nor diminished by the interposition of any time or events. Vengeance was his nightly dream, and the uppermost of his waking thoughts.

Mr. Falkland had departed from this conference with a confirmed disapprobation of the conduct of his neighbour, and an unalterable resolution to do every thing in his power to relieve the distresses of Hawkins. But he was too late. When he arrived, he found the house already evacuated by its master. The family was removed nobody knew whither; Hawkins was absconded; and, what was still more extraordinary, the boy Hawkins had escaped on the very same day from the county jail. The enquiries Mr. Falkland set on foot after them were fruitless; no traces could be found of the catastrophe of these unhappy people. That catastrophe I shall shortly have occasion to relate; and it will be found pregnant with horror beyond what the blackest misanthropy could readily have suggested.

I go on with my tale. I go on to relate those incidents in which my own fate was so mysteriously involved. I lift the curtain, and bring forward the last act of the tragedy.

CHAPTER X

IT may easily be supposed, that the ill temper cherished by Mr. Tyrrel in his contention with Hawkins, and the increasing animosity between him and Mr. Falkland, added to the impatience with which he thought of the escape of Emily.

Mr. Tyrrel heard with astonishment of the miscarriage of an expedient, of the success of which he had not previously entertained the slightest suspicion. He became frantic with vexation. Grimes had not dared to signify the event of his expedition in person, and the footman whom he desired to announce to his master that miss Melvile was lost, the moment after fled from his presence with the most dreadful apprehensions. Presently he bellowed for Grimes, and the young man at last appeared before him, more dead than alive. Grimes he compelled to repeat the particulars of the tale, which he had no sooner done than he once again slunk away, shocked at the execrations with which Mr. Tyrrel overwhelmed him. Grimes was no coward; but he reverenced the inborn divinity that attends upon rank, as Indians worship the devil. Nor was this all. The rage of Mr. Tyrrel was so ungovernable and fierce, that few hearts could have been found so stout as not to have trembled before it with a sort of unconquerable inferiority.

He no sooner obtained a moment's pause than he began to recal to his tempestuous mind the various circumstances of the case. His complaints were bitter; and in a tranquil observer might have produced the united feeling of pity for his sufferings and horror at his depravity. He recollected all the precautions he had used; he could scarcely find a flaw in the process; and he cursed that blind and malicious power which delighted to cross his most deep laid schemes. Of this malice he was beyond all other human beings the object. He was mocked with the shadow of power; and, when he lifted his hand to smite, it was struck with sudden palsy. [In the bitterness of his anguish, he forgot his recent triumph over Hawkins, or perhaps he regarded it less as a triumph, than an overthrow, because it had failed of coming up to the extent of his malice.] To what purpose had heaven given him a feeling of injury and an instinct to resent, while he could in no case make his resentment felt? It was only necessary for him to be the enemy of any person, to insure that person's being safe against the reach of misfortune. What insults, the most shocking and repeated, had he received from this paltry girl! And by whom was she now torn from his indignation? By that devil that haunted him at every moment, that crossed him at every step, that fixed at pleasure his arrows in his heart, and made mows and mockery at his insufferable tortures.

There was one other reflexion that increased his anguish, and made him careless and desperate as to his future conduct. It was in vain to conceal from himself that his reputation would be cruelly wounded by this event. He had imagined that, while Emily was forced into this odious marriage, she would be obliged by decorum, as soon as the event was decided, to draw a veil over the compulsion she had suffered. But this security was now lost, and Mr. Falkland would take a pride in publishing his dishonour. Though the provocations he had received from miss Melvile would in his own opinion have justified him in any treatment he should have thought proper to inflict, he was sensible the world would see the matter in a different light. This reflexion augmented the violence of his resolutions, and determined him to refuse no means by which he could transfer the anguish that now preyed upon his own mind to that of another.

Meanwhile the composure and magnanimity of Emily had considerably subsided, the moment she believed herself in a place of safety. While danger and injustice assailed her with their menaces, she found in herself a courage that disdained to yield. The succeeding appearance of calm was more fatal to her. There was nothing now powerfully to foster her courage, or excite her energy. She looked back at the trials she had passed, and her soul sickened at the recollection of that which, while it was in act, she had had the fortitude to endure. Till the period at which Mr. Tyrrel had been inspired with this cruel antipathy, she had been in all instances a stranger to anxiety and fear. Uninured to misfortune, she had suddenly and without preparation been made the subject of the most infernal malignity. When a man of robust and vigorous constitution has a fit of sickness, it produces a much more powerful effect than the same indisposition upon a delicate valetudinarian. Such was the case with miss Melvile. She passed the succeeding night sleepless and uneasy, and was found in the morning with a high fever. Her distemper resisted for the present all attempts to assuage it, though there was reason to hope that the goodness of her constitution, assisted by tranquillity and the kindness of those about her, would ultimately surmount it. On the second day she was delirious. On the night of that day she was arrested at the suit of Mr. Tyrrel for a debt contracted for board and necessaries for the last fourteen years.

The idea of this arrest, as the reader will perhaps recollect, first occurred in the conversation between Mr. Tyrrel and miss Melvile soon after he had thought proper to confine her to her chamber. But at that time he had probably no serious conception of ever being induced to carry it into execution. It had merely been mentioned by way of threat, and as the suggestion of a mind whose habits had long been accustomed to contemplate every possible medium of tyranny and revenge. But now that the unlooked-for rescue and escape of his poor kinswoman had wrought up his thoughts to a degree of insanity, and that he revolved in the gloomy recesses of his mind how he might best shake off the load of disappointment which oppressed him, the idea recurred with double force. He was not long in forming his resolution; and, calling for Barnes, his steward, immediately gave him directions in what manner to proceed.

Barnes had been for several years the instrument of Mr. Tyrrel's injustice. His mind was hardened by use, and he could without remorse officiate as the spectator, or even as the author and director of a scene of vulgar distress. But even he was somewhat startled upon the present occasion. The character and conduct of Emily in Mr. Tyrrel's family had been without a blot. She had not a single enemy; and it was impossible to contemplate her youth, her vivacity and her guileless innocence, without emotions of sympathy and compassion.

Your worship?—I do not understand you!—Arrest miss!—miss Emily!

Yes, I tell you! What is the matter with you? Go instantly to Swineard, the lawyer, and bid him finish the business out of hand!

Lord love your honour! Arrest her! Why, she does not owe you a brass farthing; she always lived upon your charity!

Ass! Scoundrel! I tell you she does owe me, owes me—eleven hundred pound.—The law justifies it.—What do you think laws were made for?—I do nothing but right, and right I will have.

Your honour, I never questioned your orders in my life; but I must now. I cannot see you ruin miss Emily, poor girl! nay, and yourself too, for the matter of that, and not say which way you are going. I hope you will bear with me. Why if she owed you ever so much, she cannot be arrested. She is not of age.

Will you have done? Do not tell me of It cannot, and It can. It has been done before, and it shall be done again. Let him dispute it that dares. I will do it now, and stand to it afterwards. Tell Swineard, if he make the least boggling, it is as much as his life is worth; he shall starve by inches.

Pray, your honour, think better of it. Upon my life, the whole country will cry shame of it.

Barnes?——What do you mean? I am not used to be talked to, and I cannot bear it! You have been a good fellow to me upon many occasions. But, if I find you out for making one with them that dispute my authority, damn my soul, if I do not make you sick of your life!

I have done, your honour. I will not say another word, except this. I have heard as how that miss Emily is sick a-bed. You are determined, you say, to put her in jail. You do not mean to kill her, I take it.

Let her die! I will not spare her for an hour. I will not always be insulted. She had no consideration for me, and I have no mercy for her. I am in for it! They have provoked me past all bearing, and they shall feel me! Tell Swineard, in bed or up, day or night, I will not have him hear of an instant's delay.

Such were the directions of Mr. Tyrrel, and in strict conformity to his directions were the proceedings of that respectable limb of the law he employed upon the present occasion. Miss Melvile had been delirious through a considerable part of the day on the evening of which the bailiff and his follower arrived. By the direction of the physician whom Mr. Falkland had ordered to attend her a composing draught was administered; and, exhausted as she was by the wild and distracted images that for several hours had haunted her fancy, she was now sunk into a refreshing slumber. Mrs. Hammond, the sister of Mrs. Jakeman, was sitting by her bed-side, full of compassion for the lovely sufferer and rejoicing in the calm tranquillity that had just taken possession of her, when a little girl, the only child of Mrs. Hammond, opened the street-door to the rap of the bailiff. He said he wanted to speak with miss Melvile, and the child answered that she would go tell her mother. So saying, she advanced to the door of the back-room upon the ground-floor in which Emily lay; but the moment it was opened, instead of waiting for the appearance of the mother, the bailiff entered along with the girl.

Mrs. Hammond looked up. Who are you, said she? Why do you come in here? Hush! be quiet!

I must speak with miss Melvile.

Indeed, but you must not. Tell me your business. The poor child has been light-headed all day. She is just fallen asleep, and must not be disturbed.

That is no business of mine. I must obey orders.

Orders? Whose orders? What is it you mean?

At this moment Emily opened her eyes. What noise is that? Pray let me be quiet.

Miss, I want to speak with you. I have got a writ against you for eleven hundred pound at the suit of squire Tyrrel.

At these words both Mrs. Hammond and Emily were dumb. The latter was scarcely able to annex any meaning to the intelligence; and, though Mrs. Hammond was somewhat better acquainted with the sort of language that was employed, yet in this strange and unexpected connection it was almost as mysterious to her, as to poor Emily herself.

A writ! How can she be in Mr. Tyrrel's debt? A writ against a child!

It is no signification putting your questions to us. We only do as we are directed. There is our authority. Look at it.

Lord Almighty! exclaimed Mrs. Hammond, what does this mean? It is impossible Mr. Tyrrel should have sent you.

Good woman, none of your jabber to us! Cannot you read?

This is all a trick! The paper is forged! It is a vile contrivance to get the poor orphan out of the hands of those with whom only she can be safe. Proceed upon it at your peril!

Rest you content; that is exactly what we mean to do. Take it at my word, we know very well what we are about.

Why, you would not tear her from her bed? I tell you, she is in a high fever; she is light-headed; it would be death to remove her! You are bailiffs, are not you? You are not murderers?

The law says nothing about that. We have orders to take her sick or well. We will do her no harm; except so far as we must perform our office, be it how it will.

Where would you take her? What is it you mean to do?

To the county jail. Bullock, go, order a post-chaise from the Griffin!

Stay, I say! Give no such orders! Wait only three hours; I will send off a messenger express to squire Falkland, and I am sure he will satisfy you as to any harm that can come to you, without its being necessary to take the poor child to jail.

We have particular directions against that. We are not at liberty to lose a minute. Why are not you gone? Order the horses to be put to immediately!

Emily had listened to the course of this conversation, which had sufficiently explained to her whatever was enigmatical at the first appearance of the bailiffs. The painful and incredible reality that was thus presented, effectually dissipated the illusions of frenzy to which she had just been a prey. My dear madam, said she to Mrs. Hammond, do not harass yourself with useless efforts. I am very sorry for all the trouble I have given you. But my misfortune is inevitable. Sir, if you will step into the next room, I will dress myself, and attend you immediately.

Mrs. Hammond began to be equally aware that her struggles were to no purpose; but she could not be equally patient. At one moment she raved upon the brutality of Mr. Tyrrel, whom she affirmed to be a devil incarnate, and not a man. At another she expostulated with bitter invective against the hard-heartedness of the bailiff, and exhorted him to mix some humanity and moderation with the discharge of his function; but he was impenetrable to all she could urge. In the mean while Emily yielded with the sweetest resignation to an inevitable evil. Mrs. Hammond insisted that at least they should permit her to attend her young lady in the chaise; and the bailiff, though the orders he had received were so peremptory that he dared not exercise his discretion as to the execution of the writ, began to have some apprehensions of danger, and was willing to admit of any precaution that was not in direct hostility to his functions. For the rest he understood, that it was in all cases dangerous to allow sickness or apparent unfitness for removal as a sufficient cause to interrupt a direct process, and that accordingly in all doubtful questions and presumptive murders the practice of the law inclined with a laudable partiality to the vindication of its own officers. In addition to these general rules he was influenced by the positive injunctions and assurances of Swineard, and the terror which through a circle of many miles was annexed to the name of Tyrrel. Before they departed Mrs. Hammond dispatched a messenger with a letter of three lines to Mr. Falkland informing him of this extraordinary event. Mr. Falkland was from home when the messenger arrived, and not expected to return till the second day; accident seeming in this instance to favour the vengeance of Mr. Tyrrel, for he had himself been too much under the dominion of an uncontrolable fury to take a circumstance of this sort into his estimate.

The forlorn state of these poor women, who were conducted, the one by compulsion, the other as a volunteer, to a scene so little adapted to their accommodation as that of a common jail, may easily be imagined. Mrs. Hammond however was endowed with a masculine courage and impetuosity of spirit, eminently necessary in the difficulties they had to encounter. She was in some degree fitted by a sanguine temper and an impassioned sense of injustice for the discharge of those very offices which sobriety and calm reflexion might have prescribed. The health of miss Melvile was materially affected by the surprise and removal she had undergone, at the very time that repose was most necessary for her preservation. Her fever became more violent; her delirium was stronger; and the tortures of her imagination were proportioned to the unfavourableness of the state in which the removal had been effected. It was highly improbable she could recover.

In the moments of suspended reason she was perpetually calling on the name of Falkland. Mr. Falkland, she said, was her first and only love, and he should be her husband. A moment after she exclaimed upon him in a disconsolate, yet reproachful tone, for his unworthy deference to the prejudices of the world. It was very cruel of him to show himself so proud, and tell her that he would never consent to marry a beggar. But, if he were proud, she was determined to be proud too. He should see that she would not conduct herself like a slighted maiden, and that, though he could reject her, it was not in his power to break her heart. At another time she imagined she saw Mr. Tyrrel and his engine Grimes, their hands and garments dropping with blood, and the pathetic reproaches she vented against them might have affected a heart of stone. Then the figure of Falkland presented itself to her distracted fancy, deformed with wounds and of a deadly paleness, and she shrieked with agony, while she exclaimed that such was the general hardheartedness, that no one would make the smallest exertion for his rescue. In such vicissitudes of pain, perpetually imagining to herself unkindness, insult, conspiracy and murder, she passed a considerable part of two days.

On the evening of the second Mr. Falkland arrived, accompanied by doctor Wilson, the physician by whom she had previously been attended. The scene he was called upon to witness was such as to be most exquisitely agonizing to a man of his acute sensibility. The news of the arrest had given him an inexpressible shock; he was transported out of himself at the unexampled malignity of its author. But, when he saw the figure of miss Melvile, haggard, and a warrant of death written in her countenance, a victim to the diabolical passions of her kinsman, it seemed too much to be endured. When he entered, she was in the midst of one of her fits of delirium, and immediately mistook her visitors for two assassins. She asked, where they had hid her Falkland, her lord, her life, her husband! and demanded that they should restore to her his mangled corpse, that she might embrace him with her dying arms, breathe her last upon his lips, and be buried in the same grave. She reproached them with the sordidness of their conduct in becoming the tools of her vile cousin, who had deprived her of her reason, and would never be contented till he had murdered her. Mr. Falkland tore himself away from this painful scene, and, leaving doctor Wilson with his patient, desired him when he had given the necessary directions to follow him to his inn.

The perpetual hurry of spirits in which miss Melvile had been kept for several days by the nature of her indisposition was extremely exhausting to her; and in about an hour from the visit of Mr. Falkland her delirium subsided, and left her in so low a state as to render it difficult to perceive any signs of life. Doctor Wilson, who had withdrawn, to soothe, if possible, the disturbed and impatient thoughts of Mr. Falkland, was summoned afresh upon this change of symptoms, and sat by the bed-side during the remainder of the night. The situation of his patient was such as to keep him in momentary apprehension of her decease. While miss Melvile lay in this feeble and exhausted condition, Mrs. Hammond betrayed every token of the tenderest anxiety. Her sensibility was habitually of the acutest sort, and the qualities of Emily were such as powerfully to fix her affection. She loved her like a mother. Upon the present occasion every sound, every motion made her tremble. Doctor Wilson had introduced another nurse in consideration of the incessant fatigue Mrs. Hammond had undergone; and he endeavoured by representations and even by authority to compel her to quit the apartment of the patient. But she was uncontrolable; and he at length found that he should probably do her more injury by the violence that would be necessary to separate her from the suffering innocent, than by allowing her to follow her own inclination. Her eye was a thousand times turned with the most eager curiosity upon the countenance of doctor Wilson, without her daring to breathe a question respecting his opinion, lest he should answer her by a communication of the most fatal tidings. In the mean time she listened with the deepest attention to every thing that dropped either from the physician or the nurse, hoping to collect as it were from some oblique hint the intelligence which she had not courage expressly to require.

Towards morning the state of the patient seemed to take a favourable turn. She dozed for near two hours, and, when she awoke, appeared perfectly calm and sensible. Understanding that Mr. Falkland had brought the physician to attend her, and was himself in her neighbourhood, she requested to see him. Mr. Falkland had gone in the mean time with one of his tenants to bail the debt, and now entered the prison to enquire whether the young lady might be safely removed from her present miserable residence to a more airy and commodious apartment. When he appeared, the sight of him revived in the mind of miss Melvile an imperfect recollection of the wanderings of her delirium. She covered her face with her fingers, and betrayed the most expressive confusion, while she thanked him with her usual unaffected simplicity for the trouble he had taken. She hoped she should not give him much more; she thought she should get better. It was a shame, she said, if a young and lively girl as she was, could not contrive to outlive the trifling misfortunes to which she had been subjected. But, while she said this, she was still extremely weak. She tried to assume a chearful countenance; but it was a faint effort, which the feeble state of her frame did not seem sufficient to support. Mr. Falkland and the doctor joined to request her to keep herself quiet, and to avoid for the present all occasions of exertion.

Encouraged by these appearances, Mrs. Hammond ventured to follow the two gentlemen out of the room in order to learn from the physician what hopes he entertained. Doctor Wilson acknowledged that he found his patient at first in a very unfavourable situation, that the symptoms were changed for the better, and that he was not without some expectation of her recovery. He added however, that he could answer for nothing, that the next twelve hours would be exceedingly critical, but that, if she did not grow worse before morning, he would then undertake to answer for her life. Mrs. Hammond, who had hitherto seen nothing but despair, now became frantic with joy. She burst into tears of transport, blessed the physician in the most emphatic and impassioned terms, and uttered a thousand extravagancies. Doctor Wilson seized this opportunity to press her to give herself a little repose, to which she consented, a bed being first procured for her in the room next to miss Melvile's, she having charged the nurse to give her notice of any alteration in the state of the patient.

Mrs. Hammond enjoyed an interrupted sleep of several hours. It was already night, when she was awaked by an unusual bustle in the next room. She listened for a few moments, and then determined to go and discover the occasion of it. As she opened her door for that purpose, she met the nurse coming to her. The countenance of the messenger told her what it was she had to communicate, without the use of words. She hurried to the bed side, and found miss Melvile expiring. The appearances that had at first been so encouraging were of short duration. The calm of the morning proved to be only a sort of lightning before death. In a few hours the patient grew worse. The bloom of her countenance faded; she drew her breath with difficulty; and her eyes became fixed. Doctor Wilson came in at this period, and immediately perceived that all was over. She was for some time in convulsions; but, these subsiding, she addressed the physician with a composed, though feeble voice. She thanked him for his attention; and expressed the most lively sense of her obligations to Mr. Falkland. She sincerely forgave her cousin, and hoped he might never be visited by too acute a recollection of his barbarity to her. She would have been contented to live; few persons had a sincerer relish of the pleasures of life; but she was well pleased to die rather than have become the wife of Grimes. As Mrs. Hammond entered, she turned her countenance towards her, and with an affectionate expression repeated her name. This was her last word; in less than two hours from that time she breathed her last in the arms of this faithful friend.

CHAPTER XI

SUCH was the fate of miss Emily Melvile. Perhaps tyranny never exhibited a more painful memorial of the detestation in which it deserves to be held. The idea irresistibly excited in every spectator of the scene was that of regarding Mr. Tyrrel as the most diabolical wretch that had ever dishonoured the human form. The very attendants upon this house of oppression, for the scene was acted upon too public a stage not to be generally understood, expressed their astonishment and disgust at his unparalleled cruelty.

If such were the feelings of men bred to the commission of injustice, it is difficult to say what must have been those of Mr. Falkland. He raved, he swore, he beat his head, he rent up his hair. He was unable to continue in one posture, and to remain in one place. He burst away from the spot with a vehemence, as if he sought to leave behind him his recollection and his existence. He seemed to tear up the ground with fierceness and rage. He returned soon again. He approached the sad remains of what had been Emily, and gazed on them with such intentness, that his eyes appeared ready to burst from their sockets. Acute and exquisite as were his notions of virtue and honour, he could not prevent himself from reproaching the system of nature, for having given birth to such a monster as Tyrrel. He was ashamed of himself for wearing the same form. He could not think of the human species with patience. He foamed with indignation against the laws of the universe, that did not permit him to crush such reptiles at a blow, as we would crush so many noxious insects. It was necessary to guard him like a madman.

The whole office of judging what was proper to be done under the present circumstances devolved upon doctor Wilson. The doctor was a man of cool and methodical habits of acting. One of the first ideas that suggested itself to him was, that miss Melvile was a branch of the family of Tyrrel. He did not doubt of the willingness of Mr. Falkland to discharge every expence that might be farther incident to the melancholy remains of this unfortunate victim; but he conceived that the laws of fashion and decorum required that some notification of the event should be made to the head of the family. Perhaps too he had an eye to his interest in his profession, and was reluctant to expose himself to the resentment of a person of Mr. Tyrrel's consideration in the neighbourhood. But, with this weakness, he had nevertheless some feelings in common with the rest of the world, and must have suffered considerable violence before he could have persuaded himself to be the messenger; beside which he did not think it right in the present situation to leave Mr. Falkland.

Doctor Wilson no sooner mentioned these ideas, than they seemed to make a sudden impression on Mrs. Hammond, and she earnestly requested that she might be permitted to carry the intelligence. The proposal was unexpected; but the doctor did not very obstinately refuse his assent. She was determined, she said, to see what sort of impression the catastrophe would make upon the author of it; and she promised to comport herself with moderation and civility. The journey was soon performed.

I am come, sir, said she to Mr. Tyrrel, to inform you that your cousin, miss Melvile, died this afternoon.

Died?

Yes, sir. I saw her die. She died in these arms.

Dead? Who killed her? What do you mean?

Who? Is it for you to ask that question? Your cruelty and malice killed her!

Me?—my?—Poh! she is not dead—It cannot be—It is not a week since she left this house.

Do not you believe me? I say she is dead!

Have a care, woman! This is no matter for jesting. No: though she used me ill, I would not believe her dead for all the world!

Mrs. Hammond shook her head in a manner expressive at once of grief and indignation.

No, no, no, no!—I will never believe that!—No, never!

Will you come with me, and convince your eyes? It is a sight worthy of you, and will be a feast to such a heart as yours!—Saying this, Mrs. Hammond offered her hand, as if to conduct him to the spot.

Mr. Tyrrel shrunk back.

If she be dead, what is that to me? Am I to answer for every thing that goes wrong in the world?—What do you come here for? Why bring your messages to me?

To whom should I bring them, but to her kinsman,—and her murderer?

Murderer?—Did I employ knives or pistols? Did I give her poison? I did nothing but what the law allows. If she be dead, nobody can say that I am to blame!

To blame?—All the world will abhor and curse you. Were you such a fool as to think, because men pay respect to wealth and rank, this would extend to such a deed? They will laugh at so barefaced a cheat. The meanest beggar will spurn and spit at you. Aye, you may well stand confounded at what you have done. I will proclaim you to the whole world, and you will be obliged to fly the very face of a human creature!

Good woman, said Mr. Tyrrel, extremely humbled, talk no more in this strain!—Emmy is not dead! I am sure—I hope—she is not dead!—Tell me that you have only been deceiving me, and I will forgive you every thing.—I will forgive her—I will take her into favour—I will do any thing you please!—I never meant her any harm!

I tell you she is dead! You have murdered the sweetest innocent that lived! Can you bring her back to life, as you have driven her out of it? If you could, I would kneel to you twenty times a day! —What is it you have done? Miserable wretch! did you think you could do and undo, and change the laws this way and that, as you please?

The reproaches of Mrs. Hammond were the first instance in which Mr. Tyrrel was made to drink the full cup of retribution. This was however only a specimen of a long series of contempt, abhorrence and insult that was reserved for him. The words of Mrs. Hammond were prophetic. It evidently appeared that, though wealth and hereditary elevation operate as an apology for many deliquencies, there are some which so irresistibly address themselves to the indignation of mankind, that, like death, they level all distinctions, and reduce their perpetrator to an equality with the most indigent and squalid of his species. Against Mr. Tyrrel, as the tyrannical and unmanly murderer of Emily, those who dared not venture the unreserved avowal of their sentiments, muttered curses, deep, not loud; while the rest joined in an universal cry of abhorrence and execration. He stood astonished at the novelty of his situation. Accustomed as he had been to the obedience and trembling homage of mankind, he had imagined they would be perpetual, and that no excess on his part would ever be potent enough to break the enchantment. Now he looked round and saw sullen detestation in every face, which with difficulty restrained itself, and upon the slightest provocation broke forth with an impetuous tide, and swept away all the mounds of subordination and fear. His large estate could not now purchase civility from the gentry, the peasantry, scarcely from his own servants. In the indignation of all around him he found a ghost that haunted him with every change of place, and a remorse that stung his conscience and exterminated his peace. The neighbourhood appeared more and more every day to be growing too hot for him to endure, and it became evident that he would ultimately be obliged to quit the county. Urged by the flagitiousness of this last example, people learned to recollect every other instance of his excesses, and it was no doubt a fearful catalogue that rose up in judgment against him. It seemed as if the sense of public resentment had long been gathering strength unperceived, and now burst forth into insuppressible violence.

There was scarcely a human being upon whom this sort of retribution could have sat more painfully than upon Mr. Tyrrel. Though he had not a consciousness of innocence prompting him continually to recoil from the detestation of mankind as a thing totally unallied to his character, yet the imperiousness of his temper and the constant experience he had had of the pliability of other men, prepared him to feel the general and undisguised condemnation into which he was sunk with uncommon emotions of anger and impatience. That he, at the beam of whose eye every countenance fell, and to whom in the fierceness of his wrath no one was daring enough to reply, should now be regarded with avowed dislike and treated with unceremonious censure, was a thing he could not endure to recollect or believe. Symptoms of the universal disgust smote him at every instant, and at every blow he writhed with intolerable anguish. His rage was unbounded and raving. He repelled every attack with the fiercest indignation; while the more he struggled, the more desperate his situation appeared to become. At length he determined to collect his strength for a decisive effort, and to meet the whole tide of public opinion in a single scene.

In pursuance of these thoughts he resolved to repair without delay to the rural assembly which I have already mentioned in the course of my story. Miss Melvile had now been dead one month. Mr. Falkland had been absent the last week in a distant part of the country, and was not expected to return for a week longer. Mr. Tyrrel willingly embraced the opportunity, trusting, if he could now effect his re-establishment, that he should easily preserve the ground he had gained even in the face of his most formidable rival. Mr. Tyrrel was not deficient in courage; but he conceived the present to be too important an epoch in his life to allow him to make any unnecessary risk in his chance for future ease and importance.

There was a sort of bustle that took place at his entrance into the assembly, it having been agreed by the gentlemen of the assembly that Mr. Tyrrel was to be refused admittance, as a person with whom they did not choose to associate. This vote had already been notified to him by letter by the master of the ceremonies, but the intelligence was rather calculated with a man of Mr. Tyrrel's disposition to excite defiance than to overawe. At the door of the assembly he was personally met by the master of the ceremonies, who had perceived the arrival of an equipage, and who now endeavoured to repeat his prohibition; but he was thrust aside by Mr. Tyrrel with an air of native authority and ineffable contempt. As he entered, every eye was turned upon him. Presently all the gentlemen in the room assembled round him. Some endeavoured to hustle him, and others began to expostulate. But he found the secret effectually to silence the one set, and to shake off the other. His muscular form, the well-known eminence of his intellectual

powers, the long habits to which every man was formed of acknowledging his ascendancy, were all in his favour. He considered himself as playing a desperate stake, and had roused all the energies he
possessed to enable him to do justice to so interesting a transaction.
Disengaged from the insects that had at first pestered him, he
paced up and down the room with a magisterial stride, and flashed
an angry glance on every side. He then broke silence. 'If any one
had any thing to say to him, he should know where and how to
answer him. He would advise any such person however to consider
well what he was about. If any man imagined he had any thing
personally to complain of, it was very well. But he did expect that
nobody there would be ignorant and raw enough to meddle with
what was no business of theirs, and intrude into the concerns of
any man's private family.'

This being a sort of defiance, one and another gentleman
advanced to answer it. He that was first began to speak; but Mr.
Tyrrel, by the expression of his countenance and a peremptory
tone, by well-timed interruptions and pertinent insinuations,
caused him first to hesitate, and then to be silent. He seemed to be
fast advancing to the triumph he had promised himself. The whole
company were astonished. They felt the same abhorrence and
condemnation of his character; but they could not help admiring
the courage and resources he displayed upon the present occasion.
They could without difficulty have concentred afresh their indignant feelings, but they seemed to want a leader.

At this critical moment Mr. Falkland entered the room. Mere
accident had enabled him to return sooner than he expected.

Both he and Mr. Tyrrel reddened at sight of each other. He
advanced towards Mr. Tyrrel without a moment's pause, and in a
peremptory voice asked him, what he did there?

Here? What do you mean by that? This place is as free to me as
you, and you are the last person to whom I shall deign to give an
account of myself.

Sir, the place is not free to you. Do not you know you have been
voted out? Whatever were your rights, your infamous conduct has
forfeited them.

Mr. what do you call yourself, if you have any thing to say to me,
chuse a proper time and place. Do not think to put on your bullying
airs under shelter of this company! I will not endure it.

You are mistaken, sir. This public scene is the only place where

I can have any thing to say to you. If you would not hear the universal indignation of mankind, you must not come into the society of men. Miss Melvile! Shame upon you, inhuman, unrelenting tyrant! Can you hear her name, and not sink into the earth? Can you retire into solitude, and not see her pale and patient ghost rising to reproach you? Can you recollect her virtues, her innocence, her spotless manners, her unresenting temper, and not run distracted with remorse? Have you not killed her in the first bloom of her youth? Can you bear to think that she now lies mouldering in the grave through your cursed contrivance, that deserved a crown, ten thousand times more than you deserve to live? And do you expect that mankind will ever forget, or forgive such a deed? Go, miserable wretch; think yourself too happy that you are permitted to fly the face of man! Why, what a pitiful figure do you make at this moment! Do you think that any thing could bring so hardened a wretch as you are, to shrink from reproach, if your conscience were not in confederacy with them that reproached you? And were you fool enough to believe that any obstinacy however determined could enable you to despise the keen rebuke of justice? Go, shrink into your miserable self! Begone, and let me never be blasted with your sight again!

And here, incredible as it may appear, Mr. Tyrrel began to obey his imperious censurer. His looks were full of wildness and horror; his limbs trembled; and his tongue refused its office. He felt no power of resisting the impetuous torrent of reproach that was poured upon him. He hesitated; he was ashamed of his own defeat; he seemed to wish to deny it. But his struggles were ineffectual; every attempt perished in the moment it was made. The general voice was eager to abash him. As his confusion became more visible, the outcry increased. It swelled gradually to hootings, tumult, and a deafening noise of indignation. At length he willingly retired from the public scene, unable any longer to endure the sensations it inflicted.

In about an hour and a half he returned. No precaution had been taken against this incident, for nothing could be more unexpected. In the interval he had intoxicated himself with large draughts of brandy. In a moment he was in a part of the room where Mr. Falkland was standing, and with one blow of his muscular arm levelled him with the earth. The blow however was not stunning, and Mr. Falkland rose again immediately. It is obvious to perceive how unequal he must have been to this species of contest. He was scarcely risen, before Mr. Tyrrel repeated his blow. Mr. Falkland was now upon his guard, and did not fall. But the blows of his adversary were redoubled with a rapidity difficult to conceive, and Mr. Falkland was once again brought to the earth. In this situation Mr. Tyrrel kicked his prostrate enemy, and stooped, apparently with the intention of dragging him along the floor. All this passed in a moment, and the gentlemen present had not time to recover their surprise. They now interfered, and Mr. Tyrrel once more quitted the apartment.

It is difficult to conceive of any event more terrible to the individual upon whom it fell, than the treatment which Mr. Falkland in this instance experienced. Every passion of his life was calculated to make him feel it more acutely. He had repeatedly exerted the most uncommon energy and prudence to prevent the misunderstanding between Mr. Tyrrel and himself from proceeding to extremities; but in vain! It was closed with a catastrophe exceeding all that he had feared, or that the most penetrating foresight could have suggested. To Mr. Falkland disgrace was worse than death. The slightest breath of dishonour would have stung him to the very soul. What must it have been with this complication of ignominy, base, humiliating and public? Could Mr. Tyrrel have understood the evil he inflicted, even he under all his circumstances of provocation could hardly have perpetrated it. Mr. Falkland's mind was full of uproar like the war of contending elements, and of such suffering as casts contempt on the refinements of inventive cruelty. He wished for annihilation, to lie down in eternal oblivion, in an insensibility, which compared with what he experienced was scarcely less enviable than beatitude itself. Horror, detestation, revenge, inexpressible longings to shake off the evil, and a persuasion that in this case all effort was powerless, filled his soul even to bursting.

One other event closed the transactions of this memorable evening. Mr. Falkland was baffled of the vengeance that yet remained to him. Mr. Tyrrel was found by some of the company dead in the street, having been murdered at the distance of a few yards from the assembly house.

CHAPTER XII

I SHALL endeavour to state the remainder of this narrative in the words of Mr. Collins. The reader has already had occasion to perceive that Mr. Collins was a man of no vulgar order; and his reflections on this subject were uncommonly judicious.

'This day was the crisis of Mr. Falkland's history. From hence took its beginning that gloomy and unsociable melancholy of which he has since been the victim. No two characters can be in certain respects more strongly contrasted, than the Mr. Falkland of a date prior and subsequent to these events. Hitherto he had been attended by a fortune perpetually prosperous. His mind was sanguine; full of that undoubting confidence in its own powers which prosperity is qualified to produce. Though the habits of his life were those of a serious and sublime visionary, they were nevertheless full of chearfulness and tranquillity. But from this moment his pride and the lofty adventurousness of his spirit were effectually subdued. From an object of envy he was changed into an object of compassion. Life, which hitherto no one had so exquisitely enjoyed, became a burthen to him. No more self-complacency, no more rapture, no more self-approving and heart-transporting benevolence! He, who had lived beyond any man upon the grand and animating reveries of the imagination, seemed now to have no visions but of anguish and despair. His case was peculiarly worthy of sympathy, since no doubt, if rectitude and purity of disposition could give a title to happiness, few men could exhibit a more consistent and powerful claim than Mr. Falkland.

'He was too deeply pervaded with the idle and groundless romances of chivalry ever to forget the situation, humiliating and dishonourable according to his ideas, in which he had been placed upon this occasion. There is a mysterious sort of divinity annexed to the person of a true knight, that makes any species of brute violence committed upon it indelible and immortal. To be knocked down, cuffed, kicked, dragged along the floor! sacred heaven, the memory of such a treatment was not to be endured! No future lustration could ever remove the stain: and, what was perhaps still worse in the present case, the offender having ceased to exist, the lustration which the laws of knight-errantry prescribe was rendered impossible.

'In some future period of human improvement it is probable that that calamity will be in a manner unintelligible, which in the present instance contributed to tarnish and wither the excellence of one of the most elevated and amiable of human minds. If Mr. Falkland had reflected with perfect accuracy upon the case, he would probably have been able to look down with indifference upon a wound which, as it was, pierced to his very vitals. How much more dignity than in the modern duellist do we find in Themistocles, the most gallant of the Greeks; who, when Eurybiades, his commander in chief, in answer to some of his remonstrances, lifted his cane over him with a menacing air, accosted him in that noble apostrophe, Strike, but hear?'

'How would a man of true discernment in such a case reply to his brutal assailant? "I make it my boast that I can endure calamity and pain: shall I not be able to endure the trifling inconvenience that your folly can inflict upon me? Perhaps a human being would be more accomplished, if he understood the science of personal defence; but how few would be the occasions upon which he would be called to exert it? How few human beings would he encounter so unjust and injurious as you, if his own conduct were directed by the principles of reason and benevolence? Beside, how narrow would be the use of this science, when acquired? It will scarcely put the man of delicate make and petty stature upon a level with the athletic pugilist; and, if it did in some measure secure me against the malice of a single adversary, still my person and my life, so far as mere force is concerned, would always be at the mercy of two. Farther than immediate defence against actual violence it could never be of use to me. The man who can deliberately meet his adversary for the purpose of exposing the person of one or both of them to injury, tramples upon every principle of reason and equity. Duelling is the vilest of all egotism, treating the public, which has a claim to all my powers and exertions, as if it were nothing, and myself, or rather an unintelligible chimera I annex to myself, as if it were entitled to my exclusive attention. I am unable to cope with you: what then? Can that circumstance dishonour me? No; I can only be dishonoured by perpetrating an unjust action. My honour is in my own keeping, beyond the reach of all mankind. Strike! I am passive. No injury that you can inflict shall provoke me to expose you or myself to unnecessary evil. I refuse that; but I am not therefore pusillanimous: when I refuse any danger or suffering by which the general good may be promoted, then brand me for a coward!"

'These reasonings, however simple and irresistible they must be found by a dispassionate enquirer, are little reflected on by the world at large, and were most of all uncongenial to the prejudices of Mr. Falkland. But the public disgrace and chastisement that had been imposed upon him, intolerable as they were to be re-collected, were not the whole of the mischief that redounded to our unfortunate patron from the transactions of that day. It was presently whispered that he was no other than the murderer of his antagonist. This rumour was of too much importance to the very continuance of his life, to justify its being concealed from him. He heard it with inexpressible astonishment and horror; it formed a dreadful addition to the load of intellectual anguish that already oppressed him. No man had ever held his reputation more dear than Mr. Falkland; and now in one day he was fallen under the most exquisite calamities, a complicated personal insult, and the imputation of the foulest of crimes. He might have fled; for no one was forward to proceed against a man so adored as Mr. Falk-land, or in revenge of one so universally execrated as Mr. Tyrrel. But flight he disdained. In the mean time the affair was of too serious a magnitude, the rumour unchecked seemed daily to increase in strength. Mr. Falkland appeared sometimes inclined to adopt such steps as might have been best calculated to bring the imputation to a speedy trial. But he probably feared, by too direct an appeal to judicature to render more precise an imputation, the memory of which he deprecated; at the same time that he was sufficiently willing to meet the severest scrutiny, and, if he could not hope to have it forgotten that he had ever been accused, to prove in the most satisfactory manner that the accusation was unjust.

'The neighbouring magistrates at length conceived it necessary to take some steps upon the subject. Without causing Mr. Falkland to be apprehended, they sent to desire he would appear before them at one of their meetings. The proceeding being thus opened, Mr. Falkland expressed his hope that, if the business were likely to stop there, their investigation might at least be rendered as solemn as possible. The meeting was numerous; every person of a respectable class in society, was admitted to be an auditor; the whole town, one of the most considerable in the county, was apprised of the nature of the business. Few trials, invested with all the forms of judgment, have excited so general an interest. A trial, under the present circumstances, was scarcely attainable; and it seemed to be the wish both of principal and umpires, to give to this transaction all the momentary notoriety and decisiveness of a trial.

'The magistrates investigated the particulars of the story. Mr. Falkland, it appeared, had left the rooms immediately after his assailant; and, though he had been attended by one or two of the gentlemen to his inn, it was proved that he had left them upon some slight occasion, as soon as he arrived at it, and that, when they enquired for him of the waiters, he had already mounted his horse and rode home.

'By the nature of the case, no particular facts could be stated in balance against these. As soon as they had been sufficiently detailed, Mr. Falkland therefore proceeded to his defence. Several copies of this defence were made, and Mr. Falkland seemed for a short time to have had the idea of sending it to the press, though for some reason or other he afterwards suppressed it. I have one of the copies in my possession, and I will read it to you.'

Saying this, Mr. Collins rose, and took it from a private drawer in his escritoire. During this action he appeared to recollect himself. He did not, in the strict sense of the word, hesitate; but he was prompted to make some apology for what he was doing.

'You seem never to have heard of this memorable transaction; and indeed that is little to be wondered at, since the good nature of the world is interested in suppressing it, and it is deemed a disgrace to a man to have defended himself from a criminal imputation, though with circumstances the most satisfactory and honourable. It may be supposed that this suppression is particularly acceptable to Mr. Falkland; and I should not have acted in contradiction to his modes of thinking in communicating the story to you, had there not been circumstances of peculiar urgency that seemed to render the communication desirable.' Saying this, he proceeded to read from the paper in his hand.

'Gentlemen,

'I stand here accused of a crime the most black that any human creature is capable of perpetrating. I am innocent. I have no fear that I shall fail to make every person in this company acknowledge my innocence. In the mean time what must be my feelings? Conscious as I am of deserving approbation and not censure, of having passed my life in acts of justice and philanthropy, can any thing be more deplorable than for me to answer a charge of murder? So wretched is my situation, that I cannot accept your gratuitous acquittal, if you should be disposed to bestow it. I must answer to an imputation, the very thought of which is ten thousand times worse to me than death. I must exert the whole energy of my mind to prevent my being ranked with the vilest of men.

'Gentlemen, this is a situation in which a man may be allowed to boast. Accursed situation! No man need envy me the vile and polluted triumph I am now to gain! I have called no witnesses to my character. Great God! what sort of a character is that which must be supported by witnesses? But, if I must speak, look round the company, ask of every one present, enquire of your own hearts! Not one word of reproach was ever whispered against me. I do not hesitate to call upon those who have known me most to afford me the most honourable testimony.

'My life has been spent in the keenest and most unintermitted sensibility to reputation. I am almost indifferent as to what shall be the event of this day. I would not open my mouth upon the occasion, if my life were the only thing that was at stake. It is not in the power of your decision to restore to me my unblemished reputation, to obliterate the disgrace I have suffered, or to prevent it from being remembered that I have been brought to examination upon a charge of murder. Your decision can never have the efficacy to prevent the miserable remains of my existence from being the most intolerable of all burthens.

'I am accused of having committed murder upon the body of Barnabas Tyrrel. I would most joyfully have given every farthing I possess, and devoted myself to perpetual beggary to have preserved his life. His life was precious to me, beyond that of all mankind. In my opinion the greatest injustice committed by his unknown assassin was that of defrauding me of my just revenge. I confess that I would have called him out to the field, and that our encounter should not have been terminated but by the death of one or both of us. This would have been a pitiful and inadequate compensation for his unparalleled insult, but it was all that remained.

'I ask for no pity, but I must openly declare that never was any misfortune so horrible as mine. I would willingly have taken refuge from the recollection of that night in a voluntary death. Life was now stripped of all those recommendations for the sake of which it was dear to me. But even this consolation is denied me. I am compelled to drag for ever the intolerable load of existence, upon penalty, if at any period however remote I shake it off, of having that impatience regarded as confirming a charge of murder. Gentlemen, if by your decision you could take away my life, without that act being connected with my disgrace, I would bless the cord that stopped the breath of my existence for ever.

'You all know how easily I might have fled from this purgation. If I had been guilty, should I not have embraced the opportunity? But, as it was, I could not. Reputation has been the idol, the jewel of my life. I could never have borne to think that a human creature in the remotest part of the globe should believe that I was a criminal. Alas! what a deity it is that I have chosen for my worship! I have entailed upon myself everlasting agony and despair!

'I have but one word to add. Gentlemen, I charge you to do me the imperfect justice that is in your power! My life is a worthless thing. But my honour, the empty remains of honour I have now to boast, is in your judgment, and you will each of you, from this day, have imposed upon yourselves the task of its vindicators. It is little that you can do for me; but it is not less your duty to do that little. May that God who is the fountain of honour and good, prosper and protect you! The man who now stands before you is devoted to perpetual barrenness and blast! He has nothing to hope for beyond the feeble consolation of this day!'

'You will easily imagine that Mr. Falkland was discharged with every circumstance of credit. Nothing is more to be deplored in human institutions than that the ideas of mankind should have annexed a sentiment of disgrace, to a purgation thus satisfactory and decisive. No one entertained the shadow of a doubt upon the subject, and yet a mere concurrence of circumstances made it necessary that the best of men should be publicly put upon his defence, as if really under suspicion of an atrocious crime. It may be granted indeed that Mr. Falkland had his faults, but those very faults placed him at a still farther distance from the criminality in question. He was the fool of honour and fame; a man whom in the pursuit of reputation nothing could divert; who would have purchased the character of a true, gallant and undaunted hero at the expence of worlds, and who thought every calamity nominal but a stain upon his honour. How atrociously absurd to suppose any motive capable of inducing such a man to play the part of a lurking assassin? How unfeeling to oblige him to defend himself from such an imputation? Did any man, and least of all a man of the purest honour, ever pass in a moment from a life unstained by a single act of injury to the consummation of human depravity?

'When the decision of the magistrates was declared, a general murmur of applause and involuntary transport burst forth from every one present. It was at first low, and gradually became louder. As it was the expression of rapturous delight and an emotion disinterested and divine, so there was an indescribable something in the very sound that carried it home to the heart, and convinced every spectator that there was no merely personal pleasure which ever existed that would not be foolish and feeble in the comparison. Every one strove who should most express his esteem of the amiable accused. Mr. Falkland was no sooner withdrawn, than the gentlemen present determined to give a still further sanction to the business by their congratulations. They immediately named a deputation to wait upon him for that purpose. Every one concurred to assist the general sentiment. It was a sort of sympathetic feeling that took hold upon all ranks and degrees. The multitude received him with huzzas, they took his horses from his carriage, dragged him along in triumph, and attended him many miles on his return to his own habitation. It seemed as if a public examination upon a criminal charge, which had hitherto been considered in every event as a brand of disgrace, was converted in the present instance into an occasion of enthusiastic adoration and unexampled honour.

'Nothing could reach the heart of Mr. Falkland. He was not insensible to the general kindness and exertions; but it was too evident that the melancholy that had taken hold of his mind was invincible.

'It was only a few weeks after this memorable scene that the real murderer was discovered. Every part of this story was extraordinary. The real murderer was Hawkins. He was found with his son under a feigned name at a village at about thirty miles distance, in want of all the necessaries of life. He had lived here from the period of his flight in so private a manner, that all the enquiries that had been set on foot by the benevolence of Mr. Falkland or the insatiable malice of Mr. Tyrrel had been insufficient to discover him. The first thing that had led to the detection was a parcel of clothes covered with blood that were found in a ditch, and that, when drawn out, were known by the people of the village to belong to this man. The murder of Mr. Tyrrel was not a circumstance that could be unknown, and suspicion was immediately roused. A diligent search being made, the rusty handle with part of the blade of a knife was found thrown in a corner of his lodging, which being applied to a piece of the point of a knife that had been broken in the wound, appeared exactly to correspond. Upon farther enquiry two rustics, who had been accidentally on the spot, remembered to have seen Hawkins and his son in the town that very evening, and to have called after them, and received no answer, though they were sure of their persons. Upon this accumulated evidence both Hawkins and his son were tried, condemned and afterwards executed. In the interval between the sentence and execution Hawkins confessed his guilt with many marks of compunction; though there are persons by whom this is denied; but I have taken some pains to enquire into the fact, and am persuaded that their disbelief is precipitate and groundless.

'The cruel injustice that this man had suffered from his village tyrant was not forgotten upon the present occasion. It was by a strange fatality that the barbarous proceedings of Mr. Tyrrel seemed never to fall short of their completion; and even his death served eventually to consummate the ruin of a man he hated, a circumstance, which, if it could have come to his knowledge, would perhaps have in some measure consoled him for his untimely end. This poor Hawkins was surely entitled to some pity, since his being finally urged to desperation, and brought, together with his son, to an ignominious fate, was originally owing to the sturdiness of his virtue and independence. But the compassion of the public was in a great measure shut against him, as they thought it a piece of barbarous and unpardonable selfishness, that he had not rather come boldly forward to meet the consequences of his own conduct, than suffer a man of so much public worth as Mr. Falkland, and who had been so desirous of doing him good, to be exposed to the risk of being tried for a murder that he had committed.

'From this time to the present Mr. Falkland has been nearly such as you at present see him. Though it be several years since these transactions, the impression they made is for ever fresh in the mind of our unfortunate patron. From thenceforward his habits became totally different. He had before been fond of public scenes, and acting a part in the midst of the people among whom he immediately resided. He now made himself a rigid recluse. He had no associates, no friends. Inconsolable himself, he yet wished to treat others with kindness. There was a solemn sadness in his manner, attended with the most perfect gentleness and humanity. Every body respects him, for his benevolence is unalterable; but there is a stately coldness and reserve in his behaviour, which makes it difficult for those about him to regard him with the familiarity of affection. These symptoms are uninterrupted, except at certain times when his sufferings become intolerable, and he displays the marks of a furious insanity. At those times his language is fearful and mysterious, and he seems to figure to himself by turns every sort of persecution and alarm which may be supposed to attend upon an accusation of murder. But, sensible of his own weakness, he is anxious at such times to withdraw into solitude; and his domestics in general know nothing of him but the uncommunicative and haughty, but mild dejection that accompanies every thing he does.'

END OF VOLUME I

VOLUME II

CHAPTER I

I HAVE stated the narrative of Mr. Collins, interspersed with such other information as I was able to collect, with all the exactness that my memory, assisted by certain memorandums I made at the time, will afford. I do not pretend to warrant the authenticity of any part of these memoirs except so much as fell under my own knowledge, and that part shall be stated with the same simplicity and accuracy that I would observe towards a court which was to decide in the last resort upon every thing dear to me. The same scrupulous fidelity restrains me from altering the manner of Mr. Collins's narrative to adapt it to the precepts of my own taste; and it will soon be perceived how essential that narrative is to the elucidation of my history:

The intention of my friend in this communication was to give me ease; but he in reality added to my embarrassment. Hitherto I had had no intercourse with the world and its passions; and, though I was not totally unacquainted with them as they appear in books, this proved to be of little service to me when I came to witness them myself. The case seemed entirely altered, when the subject of those passions was continually before my eyes, and the events had happened but the other day as it were, in the very neighbourhood where I lived. There was a connection and progress in this narrative, which made it altogether unlike the little village incidents I had hitherto known. My feelings were successively interested for the different persons that were brought upon the scene. My veneration was excited for Mr. Clare, and my applause for the intrepidity of Mrs. Hammond. I was astonished that any human creature should be so shockingly perverted as Mr. Tyrrel. I paid the tribute of my tears to the memory of the artless miss Melvile. I found a thousand fresh reasons to admire and love Mr. Falkland.

At first I was satisfied with thus considering every incident in its obvious sense. But the story I had heard was for ever in my thoughts, and I was peculiarly interested to comprehend its full import. I turned it a thousand ways, and examined it in every point of view. In the original communication it appeared sufficiently distinct and satisfactory; but, as I brooded over it, it gradually became mysterious. There was something strange in the character of Hawkins. So firm, so sturdily honest and just, as he appeared at first; all at once to become a murderer! His first behaviour under the prosecution, how accurately was it calculated to prepossess one in his favour! To be sure, if he were guilty, it was unpardonable in him to suffer a man of so much dignity and worth as Mr. Falkland to suffer under the imputation of his crime! And yet I could not help bitterly compassionating the honest fellow, brought to the gallows, as he was, strictly speaking, by the machinations of that devil incarnate, Mr. Tyrrel. His son too, that son for whom he voluntarily sacrificed his all, to die with him at the same tree; surely never was a story more affecting!

Was it possible after all that Mr. Falkland should be the murderer? The reader will scarcely believe that the idea suggested itself to my mind that I would ask him. It was but a passing thought; but it serves to mark the simplicity of my character. Then I recollected the virtues of my master, almost too sublime for human nature; I thought of his sufferings so unexampled, so unmerited; and chid myself for the suspicion. The dying confession of Hawkins recurred to my mind; and I felt that there was no longer a possibility of doubting. And yet what was the meaning of all Mr. Falkland's agonies and terrors? In fine, the idea having once occurred to my mind, it was fixed there for ever. My thoughts fluctuated from conjecture to conjecture, but this was the centre about which they revolved. I determined to place myself as a watch upon my patron.

The instant I had chosen this employment for myself, I found a strange sort of pleasure in it. To do what is forbidden always has its charms, because we have an indistinct apprehension of something arbitrary and tyrannical in the prohibition. To be a spy upon Mr. Falkland! That there was danger in the employment served to give an alluring pungency to the choice. I remembered the stern reprimand I had received, and his terrible looks; and the recollection gave a kind of tingling sensation, not altogether unallied to enjoyment. The farther I advanced, the more the sensation was irresistible. I seemed to myself perpetually upon the brink of being countermined, and perpetually roused to guard my designs. The more impenetrable Mr. Falkland was determined to be, the more uncontrolable was my curiosity. Through the whole my alarm and apprehension of personal danger, had a large mixture of frankness and simplicity, conscious of meaning no ill, that made me continually ready to say every thing that was upon my mind, and would not suffer me to believe that, when things were brought to the test, any one could be seriously angry with me.

These reflections led gradually to a new state of my mind. When I had first removed into Mr. Falkland's family, the novelty of the scene rendered me cautious and reserved. The distant and solemn manners of my master seemed to have annihilated my constitutional gaiety. But the novelty by degrees wore off, and my constraint in the same degree diminished. The story I had now heard, and the curiosity it excited, restored to me activity, eagerness and courage. I had always had a propensity to communicate my thoughts; my age was of course inclined to talkativeness; and I ventured occasionally in a sort of hesitating way, as if questioning whether such a conduct might be allowed, to express my sentiments as they arose, in the presence of Mr. Falkland.

The first time I did so, he looked at me with an air of surprise, made me no answer, and presently took occasion to leave me. The experiment was soon after repeated. My master seemed half inclined to encourage me, and yet doubtful whether he might venture. He had been long a stranger to pleasure of every sort, and my artless and untaught remarks appeared to promise him some amusement. Could an amusement of this sort be dangerous? In this uncertainty he could not probably find it in his heart to treat with severity my innocent effusions. I needed but little encouragement; for the perturbation of my mind stood in want of this relief. My simplicity, arising from my being a total stranger to the intercourse of the world, was accompanied with a mind in some degree cultivated with reading, and perhaps not altogether destitute of observation and talent. My remarks were therefore perpetually unexpected, at one time implying extreme ignorance, and at another some portion of acuteness, but at all times having an air of innocence, frankness and courage. There was still an apparent want of design in the manner, even after I was excited accurately to compare my observations and study the inferences to which they led; for the effect of old habit was more visible, than that of a recently conceived purpose which was yet scarcely mature. Mr. Falkland's situation was like that of a fish that plays with the bait employed to entrap him. By my manner he was in a certain degree encouraged to lay aside his usual reserve and relax his stateliness; till some abrupt observation or interrogatory stung him into recollection and brought back his alarm. Still it was evident that he bore about him a secret wound. Whenever the cause of his sorrows was touched, though in a manner the most indirect and remote, his countenance altered, his distemper returned, and it was with difficulty that he could suppress his emotions, sometimes conquering himself with painful effort, and sometimes bursting into a sort of paroxysm of insanity, and hastening to bury himself in solitude. These appearances I too frequently interpreted into grounds of suspicion, though I might with equal probability and more liberality have ascribed them to the cruel mortifications he had encountered in the objects of his darling ambition. Mr. Collins had strongly urged me to secrecy; and Mr. Falkland, whenever my gesture or his consciousness impressed him with the idea of my knowing more than I expressed, looked at me with wistful earnestness, as questioning what was the degree of information I possessed, and how it was obtained. But again at our next interview the simple vivacity of my manner restored his tranquillity, obliterated the emotion of which I had been the cause, and placed things afresh in their former situation. The longer this humble familiarity on my part had continued, the more effort it would require to suppress it; and Mr. Falkland was neither willing to mortify me by a severe prohibition of speech, nor even perhaps to make me of so much consequence as that prohibition might seem to imply. Though I was curious, it must not be supposed that I had the object of my enquiry for ever in my mind, or that my questions and innuendos were perpetually regulated with the cunning of a grey-headed inquisitor. The secret wound of Mr. Falkland's mind was much more uniformly present to his recollection than to mine; and a thousand times he applied the remarks that occurred in conversation, when I had not the remotest idea of such an application till some singularity in his manner brought it back to my thoughts. The consciousness of this morbid sensibility, and the imagination that its influence might perhaps constitute the whole of the case, served probably to spur Mr. Falkland again to the charge, and connect a sentiment of shame with every project that suggested itself for interrupting the freedom of our intercourse.

I will give a specimen of the conversations to which I allude, and as it shall be selected from those which began upon topics the most general and remote, the reader will easily imagine the disturbance that was almost daily endured by a mind so tremblingly alive as that of my patron.

Pray, sir, said I, one day as I was assisting Mr. Falkland in arranging some papers previously to their being transcribed into his collection, how came Alexander of Macedon to be surnamed the Great?

How came it? Did you never read his history?

Yes, sir.

Well, Williams, and could you find no reasons there?

Why, I do not know, sir. I could find reasons why he should be famous; but every man that is talked of, is not admired. Judges differ about the merits of Alexander. Doctor Prideaux says in his Connections[1] that he deserves only to be called the Great Cutthroat, and the author of Tom Jones[2] has written a volume to prove that he and all other conquerors ought to be classed with Jonathan Wild.

Mr. Falkland reddened at these citations.

Accursed blasphemy! Did these authors think that by the coarseness of their ribaldry they could destroy his well-earned fame? Are learning, sensibility and taste no securities to exempt their possessor from this vulgar abuse? Did you ever read, Williams, of a man more gallant, generous and free? Was ever mortal so completely the reverse of every thing engrossing and selfish? He formed to himself a sublime image of excellence, and his only ambition was to realise it in his own story. Remember his giving away every thing when he set out upon his grand expedition, professedly reserving for himself nothing but hope. Recollect his heroic confidence in Philip, the physician, and his entire and unalterable friendship for Ephestion. He treated the captive family of Darius with the most cordial urbanity, and the venerable Sysigambis with all the tenderness and attention of a son to his mother. Never take the judgment, Williams, upon such a subject of a clerical pedant or a Westminster justice.[3] Examine for yourself, and you will find in Alexander a model of honour, generosity and disinterestedness, a man who for the cultivated liberality of his mind and the unparalleled grandeur of his projects must stand alone the spectacle and admiration of all ages of the world.

Ah, sir! it is a fine thing for us to sit here and compose his panegyric. But shall I forget what a vast expence was bestowed in erecting the monument of his fame? Was not he the common disturber of mankind? Did not he overrun nations that would never have heard of him, but for his devastations? How many hundred thousands of lives did he sacrifice in his career? What must I think of his cruelties; a whole tribe massacred for a crime committed by their ancestors one hundred and fifty years before; fifty thousand sold into slavery; two thousand crucified for their gallant defence of their country? Man is surely a strange sort of creature, who never praises any one more heartily than him who has spread destruction and ruin over the face of nations!

The way of thinking you express, Williams, is natural enough, and I cannot blame you for it. But let me hope that you will become more liberal. The death of a hundred thousand men is at first sight very shocking; but what in reality are a hundred thousand such men more than a hundred thousand sheep? It is mind, Williams, the generation of knowledge and virtue that we ought to love. This was the project of Alexander; he set out in a great undertaking to civilise mankind; he delivered the vast continent of Asia from the stupidity and degradation of the Persian monarchy; and, though he was cut off in the midst of his career, we may easily perceive the vast effects of his project. Grecian literature and cultivation, the Seleucidæ, the Antiochuses and the Ptolomies[1] followed, in nations which before had been sunk to the condition of brutes. Alexander was the builder as notoriously as the destroyer of cities.

And yet, sir, I am afraid that the pike and the battle axe are not the right instruments for making men wise. Suppose it were admitted that the lives of men were to be sacrificed without remorse if a paramount good were to result, it seems to me as if murder and massacre were but a very left-handed way of producing civilisation and love. But pray, do not you think this great hero was a sort of a madman? What now will you say to his firing the palace of Persepolis, his weeping for other worlds to conquer, and his marching his whole army over the burning sands of Lybia, merely to visit a temple, and persuade mankind that he was the son of Jupiter Ammon?

Alexander, my boy, has been much misunderstood. Mankind have revenged themselves upon him by misrepresentation, for having so far eclipsed the rest of his species. It was necessary to the realising his project that he should pass for a God. It was the only way by which he could get a firm hold upon the veneration of the stupid and bigoted Persians. It was this, and not a mad vanity, that was the source of his proceeding. And how much had he to struggle with in this respect in the unapprehending obstinacy of some of his Macedonians?

Why then, sir, at last Alexander did but employ means that all politicians profess to use, as well as he. He dragooned men into wisdom, and cheated them into the pursuit of their own happiness. But what is worse, sir, this Alexander in the paroxysm of his head-long rage spared neither friend nor foe. You will not pretend to justify the excesses of his ungovernable passion. It is impossible sure that a word can be said for a man whom a momentary provocation can hurry into the commission of murders——

The instant I had uttered these words, I felt what it was that I had done. There was a magnetical sympathy between me and my patron, so that their effect was not sooner produced upon him, than my own mind reproached me with the inhumanity of the allusion. Our confusion was mutual. The blood forsook at once the transparent complexion of Mr. Falkland, and then rushed back again with rapidity and fierceness. I dared not utter a word, lest I should commit a new error worse than that into which I had just fallen. After a short, but severe, struggle to continue the conversation, Mr. Falkland began with trepidation, but afterwards became calmer:

You are not candid—Alexander—You must learn more clemency—Alexander, I say, does not deserve this rigour. Do you remember his tears, his remorse, his determined abstinence from food, which he could scarcely be persuaded to relinquish? Did not that prove acute feeling and a rooted principle of equity?—Well, well, Alexander was a true and judicious lover of mankind, and his real merits have been little comprehended.

I know not how to make the state of my mind at that moment accurately understood. When one idea has got possession of the soul, it is scarcely possible to keep it from finding its way to the lips. Error, once committed, has a fascinating power, like that ascribed to the eyes of the rattle snake, to draw us into a second error. It deprives us of that proud confidence in our own strength, to which we are indebted for so much of our virtue. Curiosity is a restless propensity, and often does but hurry us forward the more irresistibly, the greater is the danger that attends its indulgence.

Clitus,[1] said I, was a man of very coarse and provoking manners, was he not?

Mr. Falkland felt the full force of this appeal. He gave me a penetrating look as if he would see my very soul. His eyes were then in an instant withdrawn. I could perceive him seized with a convulsive shuddering, which, though strongly counteracted, and therefore scarcely visible, had I know not what of terrible in it. He left his employment, strode about the room in anger, his visage gradually assumed an expression as of supernatural barbarity, he quitted the apartment abruptly, and flung the door with a violence that seemed to shake the house.

Is this, said I, the fruit of conscious guilt, or of the disgust that a man of honour conceives at guilt undeservedly imputed?

CHAPTER II

THE reader will feel how rapidly I was advancing to the brink of the precipice. I had a confused apprehension of what I was doing, but I could not stop myself. Is it possible, said I, that Mr. Falkland, who is thus overwhelmed with a sense of the unmerited dishonour that has been fastened upon him in the face of the world, will long endure the presence of a raw and unfriended youth, who is perpetually bringing back that dishonour to his recollection, and who seems himself the most forward to entertain the accusation?

I felt indeed that Mr. Falkland would not hastily incline to dismiss me, for the same reason that restrained him from many other actions which might seem to favour of a too tender and ambiguous sensibility. But this reflexion was little adapted to comfort me. That he should cherish in his heart a growing hatred against me, and that he should think himself obliged to retain me a continual thorn in his side, was an idea by no means of favourable augury to my future peace.

It was some time after this that in clearing out a case of drawer I found a paper that by some accident had slipped behind one of the drawers, and been overlooked. At another time perhaps my curiosity might have given way to the laws of decorum, and I should have restored it unopened to my master, its owner. But my eagerness for information had been too much stimulated by the preceding incidents to allow me at present to neglect any occasion of obtaining it. The paper proved to be a letter written by the elder Hawkins, and from its contents seemed to have been penned when he had first been upon the point of absconding from the persecutions of Mr. Tyrrel. It was as follows.

Honourable Sir,

I have waited some time in daily hope of your honour's return into these parts. Old Warnes and his dame, who are left to take care of your house, tell me, they cannot say when that will be, nor justly in what part of England you are at present. For my share misfortune comes so thick upon me, that I must determine upon something (that is for certain), and out of hand. Our squire, who I must own at first used me kindly enough, though I am afraid that was partly out of spite to squire Underwood, has since determined to be the ruin of me. Sir, I have been no craven; I fought it up stoutly; for after all, you know, God bless your honour! it is but a man to a man; but he has been too much for me.

Perhaps if I were to ride over to the market town and enquire of Munsle, your lawyer, he could tell me how to direct to you. But having hoped and waited o' this fashion, and all in vain, has put me upon other thoughts. I was in no hurry, sir, to apply to you; for I do not love to be a trouble to any body. I kept that for my last stake. Well, sir, and now that has failed me like, I am ashamed as it were to have thought of it. Have not I, thinks I, arms and legs as well as other people? I am driven out of house and home. Well, and what then? Sure I arn't a cabbage, that if you pull it out of the ground, it must die. I am pennyless. True; and how many hundreds are there that live from hand to mouth all the days of their life? (Begging your honour's pardon) thinks I, if we little folks had but the wit to do for ourselves, the great folks would not be such maggoty changelings as they are. They would begin to look about them.

But there is another thing that has swayed with me more than all the rest. I do not know how to tell you, sir—My poor boy, my Leonard, the pride of my life, has been three weeks in the county jail. It is true indeed, sir. Squire Tyrrel put him there. Now, sir, every time that I lay my head upon my pillow under my own little roof, my heart smites me with the situation of my Leonard. I do not mean so much for the hardship; I do not so much matter that. I do not expect him to go through the world upon velvet; I am not such a fool. But who can tell what may hap in a jail? I have been three times to see him; and there is one man in the same quarter of the prison that looks so wicked! I do not much fancy the looks of the rest. To be sure Leonard is as good a lad as ever lived. I think he will not give his mind to such. But, come what will, I am determined he shall not stay among them twelve hours longer. I am an obstinate old fool perhaps; but I have taken it into my head, and I will do it. Do not ask me what. But, if I were to write to your honour, and wait for your answer, it might take a week or ten days more. I must not think of it!

Squire Tyrrel is very headstrong, and you, your honour, might be a little hottish or so. No, I would not have any body quarrel for me. There has been mischief enough done already; and I will get myself out of the way. So I write this, your honour, merely to unload my mind. I feel myself equally as much bound to respect and love you, as if you had done every thing for me that I believe you would have done if things had chanced differently. It is most likely you will never hear of me any more. If it should be so, set your worthy heart at rest. I know myself too well ever to be tempted to do any thing that is really bad. I have now my fortune to seek in the world. I have been used ill enough, God knows. But I bear no malice; my heart is at peace with all mankind; and I forgive every body. It is like enough that poor Leonard and I may have hardship enough to undergo, among strangers and being obliged to hide ourselves like housebreakers or highwaymen. But I defy all the malice of fortune to make us do an ill thing. That consolation we will always keep against all the crosses of a heart-breaking world.

God bless you!

So prays,

Your honour's humble servant

to command,

Benjamin Hawkins.

I read this letter with considerable attention, and it occasioned me many reflections. To my way of thinking it contained a very interesting picture of a blunt, downright, honest mind. It is a melancholy consideration, said I to myself; but such is man! To have judged from appearances one would have said, This is a fellow, to have taken fortune's buffets and rewards with an incorruptible mind. And yet see where it all ends! This man was capable of afterwards becoming a murderer, and finished his life at the gallows. O poverty! thou art indeed omnipotent! Thou grindest us into desperation; thou confoundest all our boasted and most deep-rooted principles; thou fillest us to the very brim with malice and revenge, and renderest us capable of acts of unknown horror! May I never be visited by thee in the fulness of thy power!

Having satisfied my curiosity with respect to this paper, I took care to dispose of it in such a manner as that it should be found by Mr. Falkland; at the same time that, in obedience to the principle which at present governed me with absolute dominion, I was willing that the way in which it offered itself to his attention, should suggest to him the idea that it had possibly passed through my hands. The next morning I saw him, and I exerted myself to lead the conversation, which by this time I well knew how to introduce, by insensible degrees to the point I desired. After several previous questions, remarks and rejoinders, I continued:

Well, sir, after all, I cannot help feeling very uncomfortably as to my ideas of human nature, when I find that there is no dependence to be placed upon its perseverance, and that, at least among the illiterate, the most promising appearances may end in the foulest disgrace.

You think then that literature and a cultivated mind are the only assurance for the constancy of our principles?

Humh!—why do you suppose, sir, that learning and ingenuity do not often serve people rather to hide their crimes, than to restrain them from committing them? History tells us strange things in that respect.

Williams! said Mr. Falkland, a little disturbed, you are extremely given to censure and severity.

I hope not. I am sure I am most fond of looking on the other side of the picture, and considering how many men have been aspersed, and even at some time or other almost torn to pieces by their fellow creatures, whom, when properly understood, we find worthy of our reverence and love.

Indeed, replied Mr. Falkland with a sigh, when I consider these things, I do not wonder at the dying exclamation of Brutus, O Virtue! I sought thee as a substance, but I find thee an empty name! I am too much inclined to be of his opinion.

Why to be sure, sir, innocence and guilt are too much confounded in human life. I remember an affecting story of a poor man in the reign of queen Elizabeth, who would have infallibly been hanged for murder upon the strength of circumstantial evidence, if the person really concerned had not been himself upon the jury, and prevented it.

In saying this I touched the spring that wakened madness in his mind. He came up to me with a ferocious countenance as if determined to force me into a confession of my thoughts. A sudden pang however seemed to change his design; he drew back with trepidation; and exclaimed, Detested be the universe, and the laws that govern it! Honour, justice, virtue are all the juggle of knaves! If it were in my power, I would instantly crush the whole system into nothing!

I replied; Oh, sir! things are not so bad as you imagine. The world was made for men of sense to do what they will with it. Its affairs cannot be better than in the direction of the genuine heroes; and, as in the end they will be found the truest friends of the whole, so the multitude have nothing to do, but to look on, be fashioned and admire.

Mr. Falkland made a powerful effort to recover his tranquillity. Williams! said he, you instruct me well. You have a right notion of things, and I have great hopes of you. I will be more of a man. I will forget the past, and do better for the time to come. The future, the future is always our own.

I am sorry, sir, that I have given you pain. I am afraid to say all that I think. But it is my opinion that mistakes will ultimately be cleared up, justice done, and the true state of things come to light in spite of the false colours that may for a time obscure it.

The idea I suggested did not give Mr. Falkland the proper degree of delight. He suffered a temporary relapse. Justice!—he muttered. I do not know what is justice. My case is not within the reach of common remedies; perhaps of none. I only know that I am miserable. I began life with the best intentions and the most fervid philanthropy; and here I am—miserable—miserable beyond expression or endurance.

Having said this, he seemed suddenly to recollect himself, and re-assume his accustomed dignity and command. How came this conversation? cried he. Who gave you a right to be my confident? Base, artful wretch that you are! learn to be more respectful! Are my passions to be wound and unwound by an insolent domestic? Do you think I will be an instrument to be played on at your pleasure, till you have extorted all the treasures of my soul? Begone, and fear lest you be made to pay for the temerity you have already committed.

There was an energy and determination in the gestures with which these words were accompanied that did not admit of their being disputed. My mouth was closed; I felt as if deprived of all share of activity, and was only able silently and passively to quit the apartment.

CHAPTER III

Two days subsequent to this conversation Mr. Falkland ordered me to be called to him. [I shall continue to speak in my narrative of the silent, as well as the articulate part of the intercourse between us. His countenance was habitually animated and expressive much beyond that of any other man I have seen. The curiosity, which, as I have said, constituted my ruling passion, stimulated me to make it my perpetual study. It will also most probably happen, while I am thus employed in collecting together the scattered incidents of my history, that I shall upon some occasions annex to appearances an explanation, which I was far from possessing at the time, and was only suggested to me through the medium of subsequent events.]

When I entered the apartment, I remarked in Mr. Falkland's countenance an unwonted composure. This composure however did not seem to result from internal ease, but from an effort which, while he prepared himself for an interesting scene, was exerted to prevent his presence of mind and power of voluntary action from suffering any diminution.

Williams, said he, I am determined, whatever it may cost me, to have an explanation with you. You are a rash and inconsiderate boy, and have given me much disturbance. You ought to have known that, though I allow you to talk with me upon indifferent subjects, it is very improper in you to lead the conversation to any thing that relates to my personal concerns. You have said many things lately in a very mysterious way, and appear to know something more than I am aware of. I am equally at a loss to guess how you came by your knowledge, as of what it consists. But I think I perceive too much inclination on your part to trifle with my peace of mind. That ought not to be, nor have I deserved any such treatment from you. But, be that as it will, the guesses in which you oblige me to employ myself are too painful. It is a sort of sporting with my feeling, which, as a man of resolution, I am determined to bring to an end. I expect you therefore to lay aside all mystery and equivocation, and inform me explicitly what it is upon which your allusions are built. What is it you know? What is it you want? I have been too much exposed already to unparalleled mortification and hardship, and my wounds will not bear this perpetual tampering.

I feel, sir, answered I, how wrong I have been, and am ashamed that such a one as I should have given you all this trouble and displeasure. I felt it at the time; but I have been hurried along I do not know how. I have always tried to stop myself, but the demon that possessed me was too strong for me. I know nothing, sir, but what Mr. Collins told me. He told me the story of Mr. Tyrrel and miss Melvile and Hawkins. I am sure, sir, he said nothing but what was to your honour, and proved you to be more an angel than a man.

Well, sir: I found a letter written by that Hawkins the other day: did not that letter fall into your hands? Did not you read it?

For God's sake, sir, turn me out of your house. Punish me in some way or other, that I may forgive myself. I am a foolish, wicked, despicable wretch. I confess, sir, I did read the letter.

And how dared you read it? It was indeed very wrong of you. But we will talk of that by and by. Well, and what did you say to the letter? You know it seems that Hawkins was hanged.

I say, sir? why it went to my heart to read it. I say, as I said the day before yesterday, that, when I see a man of so much principle, afterwards deliberately proceeding to the very worst of crimes, I can scarcely bear to think of it.

That is what you say? It seems too you know, accursed remembrance! that I was accused of this crime?

I was silent.

Well, sir. You know too perhaps that, from the hour the crime was committed,—yes, sir, that was the date [and, as he said this, there was somewhat frightful, I had almost said diabolical, in his countenance]—I have not had an hour's peace; I became changed from the happiest into the most miserable thing that lives; sleep has fled from my eyes; joy has been a stranger to my thoughts; and annihilation I should prefer a thousand times to the being that I lead. As soon as I was capable of a choice, I chose honour and the esteem of mankind as a good I preferred to all others. You know, it seems, in how many ways my ambition has been disappointed,— I do not thank Collins for having been the historian of my disgrace,—Would to God that night could be blotted from the memory of man!—But the scene of that night, instead of perishing, has been a source of ever new calamity to me, which must flow for ever! Am I then, thus miserable and ruined, a proper subject upon which for you to exercise your ingenuity, and improve your power of tormenting? Was it not enough that I was publicly dishonoured? that I was deprived by the pestilential influence of some demon of the opportunity of avenging my dishonour? No: in addition to this I have been charged with having in this critical moment intercepted my own vengeance by the foulest of crimes. That trial is past. Misery itself has nothing worse in store for me except what you have inflicted: the seeming to doubt of my innocence which after the fullest and most solemn examination has been completely established. You have forced me to this explanation. You have extorted from me a confidence which I had no inclination to make. But it is a part of the misery of my situation, that I am at the mercy of every creature, however little, who feels himself inclined to sport with my distress. Be content. You have brought me low enough.

Oh, sir! I am not content; I cannot be content! I cannot bear to think what I have done. I shall never again be able to look in the face the best of masters and the best of men. I beg of you, sir, to turn me out of your service. Let me go and hide myself where I may never see you more.

Mr. Falkland's countenance had indicated great severity through the whole of this conversation; but now it became more harsh and tempestuous than ever. How now, rascal! cried he. You want to leave me, do you? Who told you that I wished to part with you? But you cannot bear to live with such a miserable wretch as I am! You are not disposed to put up with the caprices of a man so dissatisfied and unjust!

Oh, sir! do not talk to me thus! Do with me any thing you will. Kill me if you please.

Kill you? [Volumes could not describe the emotions with which this echo of my words was given and received.]

Sir, I could die to serve you! I love you more than I can express. I worship you as a being of a superior nature. I am foolish, raw, inexperienced,—worse than any of these;—but never did a thought of disloyalty to your service enter into my heart.

Here our conversation ended; and the impression it made upon my youthful mind it is impossible to describe. I thought with astonishment, even with rapture, of the attention and kindness towards me I discovered in Mr. Falkland through all the roughness of his manner. I could never enough wonder at finding myself, humble as I was by my birth, obscure as I had hitherto been, thus suddenly become of so much importance to the happiness of one of the most enlightened and accomplished men in England. But this consciousness attached me to my patron more eagerly than ever, and made me swear a thousand times as I meditated upon my situation, that I would never prove unworthy of so generous a protector.

CHAPTER IV

Is it not unaccountable that, in the midst of all my increased veneration for my patron, the first tumult of my emotion was scarcely subsided, before the old question that had excited my conjectures recurred to my mind, Was he the murderer? It was a kind of fatal impulse that seemed destined to hurry me to my destruction. I did not wonder at the disturbance that was given to Mr. Falkland by any allusion however distant to this fatal affair. That was as completely accounted for from the consideration of his excessive sensibility in matters of honour, as it would have been upon the supposition of the most atrocious guilt. Knowing as he did, that such a charge had once been connected with his name, he would of course be perpetually uneasy, and suspect some latent insinuation at every possible opportunity. He would doubt and fear, lest every man with whom he conversed harboured the foulest suspicions against him. In my case he found that I was in possession of some information more than he was aware of, without its being possible for him to decide to what it amounted, whether I had heard a just or unjust, a candid or calumniatory tale. He had also reason to suppose that I gave entertainment to thoughts derogatory to his honour, and that I did not form that favourable judgment which the exquisite refinement of his ruling passion made indispensible to his peace. All these considerations would of course maintain in him a state of perpetual uneasiness. But, though I could find nothing that I could consider as justifying me in persisting in the shadow of a doubt, yet, as I have said, the uncertainty and restlessness of my contemplations would by no means depart from me.

The fluctuating state of my mind produced a contention of opposite principles that by turns usurped dominion over my conduct. Sometimes I was influenced by the most complete veneration for my master; I placed an unreserved confidence in his integrity and his virtue, and implicitly surrendered my understanding for him to set it to what point he pleased. At other times the confidence, which had before flowed with the most plenteous tide, began to ebb; I was, as I had already been, watchful, inquisitive, suspicious, full of a thousand conjectures as to the meaning of the most indifferent actions. Mr. Falkland, who was most painfully alive to every thing that related to his honour, saw these variations, and betrayed his consciousness of them now in one manner and now in another, frequently before I was myself aware, sometimes almost before they existed. The situation of both was distressing; we were each of us a plague to the other; and I often wondered that the forbearance and benignity of my master was not at length exhausted, and that he did not determine to thrust from him for ever so incessant an observer. There was indeed one eminent difference between his share in the transaction and mine. I had some consolation in the midst of my restlessness. Curiosity is a principle that carries its pleasures as well as its pains along with it. The mind is urged by a perpetual stimulus; it seems as if it were continually approaching to the end of its race; and, as the insatiable desire of satisfaction is its principle of conduct, so it promises itself in that satisfaction an unknown gratification, which seems as if it were capable of fully compensating any injuries that may be suffered in the career. But to Mr. Falkland there was no consolation. What he endured in the intercourse between us appeared to be gratuitous evil. He had only to wish that there was no such person as myself in the world, and to curse the hour when his humanity led him to rescue me from my obscurity, and place me in his service.

A consequence produced upon me by the extraordinary nature of my situation it is necessary to mention. The constant state of vigilance and suspicion in which my mind was retained worked a very rapid change in my character. It seemed to have all the effect that might have been expected from years of observation and experience. The strictness with which I endeavoured to remark what passed in the mind of one man, and the variety of conjectures into which I was led, appeared as it were to render me a competent adept in the different modes in which the human intellect displays its secret workings. I no longer said to myself, as I had done in the beginning, 'I will ask Mr. Falkland whether he were the murderer.' On the contrary, after having carefully examined the different kinds of evidence of which the subject was susceptible, and recollecting all that had already passed upon the subject, it was not without considerable pain that I felt myself unable to discover any way in which I could be perfectly and unalterably satisfied of my patron's innocence. As to his guilt, I could scarcely bring myself to doubt that in some way or other, sooner or later, I should arrive at the knowledge of that, if it really existed. But I could not endure to think almost for a moment of that side of the alternative as true; and, with all my ungovernable suspicion, arising from the mysteriousness of the circumstances, and all the delight which a young and unfledged mind receives from ideas that give scope to all that imagination can picture of terrible or sublime, I could not yet bring myself to consider Mr. Falkland's guilt as a supposition attended with the remotest probability.

I hope the reader will forgive me for dwelling thus long on preliminary circumstances. I shall come soon enough to the story of my own misery. I have already said that one of the motives which induced me to the penning of this narrative was to console myself in my insupportable distress. I derive a melancholy pleasure from dwelling upon the circumstances which imperceptibly paved the way to my ruin. While I recollect or describe past scenes which occurred in a more favourable period of my life, my attention is called off for a short interval from the hopeless misfortune in which

I am at present involved. The man must indeed possess an uncommon portion of hardness of heart, who can envy me so slight
a relief.—To proceed.

For some time after the explanation which had thus taken place
between me and Mr. Falkland, his melancholy, instead of being in
the slightest degree diminished by the lenient hand of time, went
on perpetually to increase. His fits of insanity, for such I must
denominate them for want of a distinct appellation, though it is
possible they might not fall under the definition that either the
faculty or the court of chancery appropriate to that term, became
stronger and more durable than ever. It was no longer practicable
wholly to conceal them from the family and even from the neighbourhood. He would sometimes without any previous notice
absent himself from his house for two or three days, unaccom-
panied by servant or attendant. This was the more extraordinary,
as it was well known that he paid no visits, nor kept up any sort of
intercourse with the gentlemen of the vicinity. But it was impossible
that a man of Mr. Falkland's distinction and fortune should long
continue in such a practice without its being discovered what was
become of him, though a considerable part of our county was
among the wildest and most desolate districts that are to be found
in South Britain. Mr. Falkland was sometimes seen climbing
among the rocks, reclining motionless for hours together upon the
edge of a precipice, or lulled into a kind of nameless lethargy of
despair by the dashing of the torrents. He would remain for whole
nights together under the naked cope of heaven, inattentive to the
consideration either of place or time, insensible to the variations of
the weather, or rather seeming to be delighted with that uproar of
the elements which partially called off his attention from the dis-
cord and dejection which occupied his own mind.

At first, when we received intelligence at any time of the place
to which Mr. Falkland had withdrawn himself, some person of his
household, Mr. Collins or myself, but most generally myself, as
I was always at home, and always in the received sense of that word
at leisure, went to him to persuade him to return. But after a few
experiments we thought it advisable to desist, and to leave him to
prolong his absence or to terminate it as might happen to suit his
own inclination. Mr. Collins, whose grey hairs and long services
seemed to give him a sort of right to be importunate, sometimes
succeeded; though even in that case there was nothing that could

sit more uneasily upon Mr. Falkland than this insinuation, as if he
wanted a guardian to take care of him, or as if he were in, or in
danger of falling into, a state in which he would be incapable of
deliberately controling his own words and actions. At one time he
would sullenly yield to his humble, venerable friend, murmuring
grievously at the constraint that was put upon him, but without
spirit enough even to complain of it with energy. At another time,
even though complying, he would suddenly burst out in a paroxysm
of resentment. Upon these occasions there was something inconceivably, savagely terrible in his anger, that gave to the person
against whom it was directed the most humiliating and insupportable sensations. Me he always treated at these times with fierceness,
and drove me from him with a vehemence, lofty, emphatical and
sustained beyond any thing of which I should have thought human
nature to be capable. These sallies seemed always to constitute a
sort of crisis in his indisposition; and, whenever he was induced to
such a premature return, he would fall immediately after into a
state of the most melancholy inactivity, in which he usually continued for two or three days. It was by an obstinate fatality that,
whenever I saw Mr. Falkland in these deplorable situations, and
particularly when I lighted upon him after having sought him
among the rocks and precipices, pale, emaciated, solitary and
haggard, the suggestion would continually recur to me, in spite of
inclination, in spite of persuasion and in spite of evidence, Surely
this man is a murderer!

CHAPTER V

It was in one of the lucid intervals, as I may term them, that
occurred during this period, that a peasant was brought before
him, in his character of a justice of peace, upon an accusation of
having murdered his fellow. As Mr. Falkland had by this time
acquired the repute of a melancholy valetudinarian, it is probable
he would not have been called upon to act in his official character
upon the present occasion, had it not been that two or three of the
neighbouring justices were all of them from home at once, so that
he was the only one to be found in a circuit of many miles. The
reader however must not imagine, though I have employed the

word insanity in describing Mr. Falkland's symptoms, that he was by any means reckoned for a madman by the generality of those who had occasion to observe him. It is true that his behaviour at certain times was singular and unaccountable; but then at other times there was in it so much dignity, regularity and economy; he knew so well how to command and make himself respected; his actions and carriage were so condescending, considerate and benevolent; that, far from having forfeited the esteem of the unfortunate or the many, they were loud and earnest in his praises.

I was present at the examination of this peasant. The moment I heard of the errand which had brought this rabble of visitors, a sudden thought struck me. I conceived the possibility of rendering the incident subordinate to the great enquiry which drank up all the currents of my soul. I said, This man is arraigned of murder, and murder is the master key that wakes distemper in the mind of Mr. Falkland. I will watch him without remission. I will trace all the mazes of his thought. Surely at such a time his secret anguish must betray itself. Surely, if it be not my own fault, I shall now be able to discover the state of his plea before the tribunal of unerring justice.

I took my station in a manner most favourable to the object upon which my mind was intent. I could perceive in Mr. Falkland's features as he entered a strong reluctance to the business in which he was engaged; but there was no possibility of retreating. His countenance was embarrassed and anxious; he scarcely saw any body. The examination had not proceeded far before he chanced to turn his eye to the part of the room where I was. It happened in this, as in some preceding instances; we exchanged a silent look by which we told volumes to each other. Mr. Falkland's complexion turned from red to pale, and from pale to red. I perfectly understood his feelings, and would willingly have withdrawn myself. But it was impossible; my passions were too deeply engaged; I was rooted to the spot; though my own life, that of my master, or almost of a whole nation had been at stake, I had no power to change my position.

The first surprise however having subsided, Mr. Falkland assumed a look of determined constancy, and even seemed to increase in self-possession much beyond what could have been expected from his first entrance. This he could probably have maintained, had it not been that the scene, instead of being permanent, was in some sort perpetually changing. The man who was brought before him was vehemently accused by the brother of the deceased as having acted from the most rooted malice. He swore that there had been an old grudge between the parties, and related several instances of it. He affirmed that the murderer had sought the earliest opportunity of wreaking his revenge, had struck the first blow, and, though the contest was in appearance only a common boxing match, had watched the occasion of giving a fatal stroke which was followed by the instant death of his antagonist.

While the accuser was giving in his evidence, the accused discovered every token of the most poignant sensibility. At one time his features were convulsed with anguish, tears unbidden rolled down his manly cheeks; and at another he started with astonishment at the unfavorable turn that was given to the narrative, though without betraying any impatience to interrupt. I never saw a man less ferocious in his appearance. He was tall, well made and comely. His countenance was ingenuous and benevolent, without folly. By his side stood a young woman, his sweetheart, extremely agreeable in her person, and her looks testifying how deeply she interested herself in the fate of her lover. The accidental spectators were divided between indignation against the enormity of the supposed criminal, and compassion for the poor girl that accompanied him. They seemed to take little notice of the favourable appearances visible in the person of the accused, till in the sequel those appearances were more forcibly suggested to their attention. For Mr. Falkland, he was at one moment engrossed by curiosity and earnestness to investigate the tale, while at another he betrayed a sort of revulsion of sentiment which made the investigation too painful for him to support.

When the accused was called upon for his defence, he readily owned the misunderstanding that had existed, and that the deceased was the worst enemy he had in the world. Indeed he was his only enemy, and he could not tell the reason that had made him so. He had employed every possible effort to overcome his animosity, but in vain. The deceased had upon all occasions sought to mortify him, and do him an ill turn; but he had resolved never to be engaged in a broil with him, and till this day he had succeeded. If he had met with a misfortune with any other man, people at least might have thought it accident; but now it would always be believed that he had acted from secret malice and a bad heart.

The fact was that he and his sweetheart had gone to a neighbouring fair, where this man had met them. The man had often
tried to affront him, and his passiveness, interpreted into cowardice,
had perhaps encouraged the other to additional rudeness. Finding
that he had endured trivial insults to himself with an even temper,
the deceased now thought proper to turn his brutality upon the
young woman that accompanied him. He pursued them; he
endeavoured in various manners to harass and vex them; they had
sought in vain to shake him off. The young woman was considerably terrified. The accused expostulated with their persecutor, and
asked him how he could be so barbarous as to persist in frightening
a woman? He replied with an insulting tone, Then the woman
should find some one able to protect her; people that encouraged
and trusted to such a thief as that, deserved no better! The accused
tried every expedient he could invent; at length he could endure it
no longer; he became exasperated, and challenged the assailant.
The challenge was accepted; a ring was formed; he confided the
care of his sweetheart to a bystander; and unfortunately the first
blow he struck proved fatal.

The accused added that he did not care what became of him. He
had been anxious to go through the world in an inoffensive manner,
and now he had the guilt of blood upon him. He did not know but
it would be a kindness in them to hang him out of the way; for his
conscience would reproach him as long as he lived, and the figure
of the deceased, as he had laid senseless and without motion at his
feet, would perpetually haunt him. The thought of this man, at one
moment full of life and vigour, and the next lifted a helpless corpse
from the ground, and all owing to him, was a thought too dreadful
to be endured. He had loved the poor maiden who had been the
innocent occasion of this with all his heart, but from this time he
should never support the sight of her. The sight would bring a
tribe of fiends in its rear. One unlucky minute had poisoned all his
hopes, and made life a burden to him.—Saying this his countenance
fell, the muscles of his face trembled with agony, and he looked the
statue of despair.

This was the story of which Mr. Falkland was called upon to be
the auditor. Though the incidents were for the most part wide of
those which belonged to the adventures of the preceding volume,
and there had been much less policy and skill displayed on either
part in this rustic encounter, yet there were many points which, to

a man who bore the former strongly in his recollection, suggested a sufficient resemblance. In each case it was a human brute persisting in a course of hostility to a man of benevolent character, and suddenly and terribly cut off in the midst of his career. These points perpetually smote upon the heart of Mr. Falkland. He at one time started with astonishment, and at another shifted his posture like a man who is unable longer to endure the sensations that press upon him. Then he new strung his nerves to stubborn patience. I could see, while his muscles preserved an inflexible steadiness, tears of anguish roll down his cheeks. He dared not trust his eyes to glance towards the side of the room where I stood; and this gave an air of embarrassment to his whole figure. But, when the accused came to speak of his own feelings, to describe the depth of his compunction for an involuntary fault, he could endure it no longer. He suddenly rose, and with every mark of horror and despair rushed out of the room.

This circumstance made no material difference in the affair of the accused. The parties were detained about half an hour. Mr. Falkland had already heard the material parts of the evidence in person. At the expiration of that interval, he sent for Mr. Collins out of the room. The story of the culprit was confirmed by many witnesses who had seen the transaction. Word was brought that my master was indisposed, and at the same time the accused was ordered to be discharged. The vengeance of the brother however, as I afterwards found, did not rest here, and he met with a magistrate more scrupulous or more despotic, by whom the culprit was committed for trial.

This affair was no sooner concluded than I hastened into the garden, and plunged into the deepest of its thickets. My mind was full almost to bursting. I no sooner conceived myself sufficiently removed from all observation, than my thoughts forced their way spontaneously to my tongue, and I exclaimed in a fit of uncontrolable enthusiasm: 'This is the murderer! the Hawkinses were innocent! I am sure of it! I will pledge my life for it! It is out! It is discovered! Guilty upon my soul!'

While I thus proceeded with hasty steps along the most secret paths of the garden, and from time to time gave vent to the tumult of my thoughts in involuntary exclamations, I felt as if my animal system had undergone a total revolution. My blood boiled within me. I was conscious to a kind of rapture for which I could not account. I was solemn, yet full of rapid emotion, burning with indignation and energy. In the very tempest and hurricane of the passions, I seemed to enjoy the most soul-ravishing calm. I cannot better express the then state of my mind, than by saying, I was never so perfectly alive as at that moment.

This state of mental elevation continued for several hours, but at length subsided and gave place to more deliberate reflection. One of the first questions that then occurred was, What shall I do with the knowledge I have been so eager to acquire? I had no inclination to turn informer. I felt, what I had had no previous conception of, that it was possible to love a murderer, and, as I then understood it, the worst of murderers. I conceived it to be in the highest degree absurd and iniquitous to cut off a man qualified for the most essential and extensive utility merely out of retrospect to an act which, whatever were its merits, could not be retrieved.

This thought led me to another which had at first passed unnoticed. If I had been disposed to turn informer, what had occurred amounted to no evidence that was admissible in a court of justice. Well then, added I, if it be such as would not be admitted at a criminal tribunal, am I sure it is such as I ought to admit? There were twenty persons beside myself present at the scene from which I pretend to derive such entire conviction. Not one of them saw it in the light that I did. It either appeared to them a casual and unimportant circumstance, or they thought it sufficiently accounted for by Mr. Falkland's infirmity and misfortunes. Did it really contain such an extent of arguments and application, that nobody but I was discerning enough to see?

But all this reasoning produced no alteration in my way of thinking. For this time I could not get it out of my mind for a moment: 'Mr. Falkland is the murderer! He is guilty! I see it! I feel it! I am sure of it!' Thus was I hurried along by an uncontrolable destiny. The state of my passions in their progressive career, the inquisitiveness and impatience of my thoughts, appeared to make this determination unavoidable.

An incident occurred while I was in the garden, that seemed to make no impression upon me at the time, but which I recollected when my thoughts were got into somewhat of a slower motion. In the midst of one of my paroxysms of exclamation, and when I thought myself most alone, the shadow of a man as avoiding me passed transiently by me at a small distance. Though I had scarcely caught a faint glimpse of his person, there was something in the occurrence that persuaded me it was Mr. Falkland. I shuddered at the possibility of his having overheard the words of my soliloquy. But this idea, alarming as it was, had not power immediately to suspend the career of my reflections. Subsequent circumstances however brought back the apprehension to my mind. I had scarcely a doubt of its reality, when dinner time came, and Mr. Falkland was not to be found. Supper and bed-time passed in the same manner. The only conclusion made by his servants upon this circumstance was, that he was gone upon one of his accustomed melancholy rambles.

CHAPTER VI

THE period at which my story is now arrived seemed as if it were the very crisis of the fortune of Mr. Falkland. Incident followed upon incident in a kind of breathless succession. About nine o'clock the next morning an alarm was given that one of the chimnies of the house was on fire. No accident could be apparently more trivial; but presently it blazed with such fury, as to make it clear that some beam of the house, which in the first building had been improperly placed, had been reached by the flames. Some danger was apprehended for the whole edifice. The confusion was the greater in consequence of the absence of the master, as well as of Mr. Collins, the steward. While some of the domestics were employed in endeavouring to extinguish the flames, it was thought proper that others should busy themselves in removing the most valuable moveables to a lawn in the garden. I took some command in the affair, to which indeed my station in the family seemed to entitle me, and for which I was judged qualified by my understanding and mental resources.

Having given some general directions, I conceived that it was not enough to stand by and superintend, but that I should contribute my personal labour in the public concern. I set out for that purpose; and my steps by some mysterious fatality were directed to the private apartment at the end of the library. Here, as I looked round, my eye was suddenly caught by the trunk mentioned in the first pages of my narrative.

My mind was already raised to its utmost pitch. In a window-seat of the room lay a number of chissels and other carpenter's tools. I know not what infatuation instantaneously seized me. The idea was too powerful to be resisted. I forgot the business upon which I came, the employment of the servants and the urgency of general danger. I should have done the same, if the flames that seemed to extend as they proceeded, and already surmounted the house, had reached this very apartment. I snatched a tool suitable for the purpose, threw myself upon the ground, and applied with eagerness to a magazine which inclosed all for which my heart panted. After two or three efforts, in which the energy of uncontrolable passion was added to my bodily strength, the fastenings gave way, the trunk opened, and all that I sought was at once within my reach.

I was in the act of lifting up the lid, when Mr. Falkland entered, wild, breathless, distraction in his looks! He had been brought home from a considerable distance by the sight of the flames. At the moment of his appearance the lid dropt down from my hand. He no sooner saw me, than his eyes emitted sparks of rage. He ran with eagerness to a brace of loaded pistols which hung up in the room, and, seizing one, presented it to my head. I saw his design, and sprang to avoid it; but, with the same rapidity with which he had formed his resolution, he changed it, and instantly went to the window and flung the pistol into the court below. He bade me begone with his usual irresistible energy; and, overcome as I was already by the horror of the detection, I eagerly complied.

A moment after a considerable part of the chimney was tumbled with noise into the court below, and a voice exclaimed that the fire was more violent than ever. These circumstances seemed to produce a mechanical effect upon my patron, who, having first locked the closet, appeared on the outside of the house, ascended the roof, and was in a moment in every place where his presence was required. The flames were at length extinguished.

The reader can with difficulty form a conception of the state to which I was now reduced. My act was in some sort an act of insanity; but how undescribable are the feelings with which I looked back upon it! It was an instantaneous impulse, a short lived and passing alienation of mind; but what must Mr. Falkland think of that alienation? To any man a person, who had once shown himself capable of so wild a flight of the mind, must appear dangerous;

how must he appear to a man under Mr. Falkland's circumstances?
I had just had a pistol held to my head by a man resolved to put a
period to my existence. That indeed was past; but what was it that
fate had yet in reserve for me! The insatiable vengeance of a Falkland, of a man whose hands were to my apprehension red with
blood and his thoughts familiar with cruelty and murder. How
great were the resources of his mind, resources henceforth to be
confederated for my destruction! This was the termination of an
ungoverned curiosity, an impulse that I had represented to myself
as so innocent and so venial!

In the high tide of boiling passion I had overlooked all consequences. It now appeared to me like a dream. Is it in man to leap
from the high-raised precipice, or rush unconcerned into the midst
of flames? Was it possible I could have forgotten for a moment the
awe creating manners of Falkland, and the inexorable fury I should
awake in his soul? No thought of future security had reached my
mind. I had acted upon no plan. I had conceived no means of con-
cealing my deed, after it had once been effected. But it was over
now. One short minute had effected a reverse in my situation, the
suddenness of which the history of man perhaps is unable to
surpass.

I have always been at a loss to account for my having plunged
thus headlong into an act so monstrous. There is something in it
of unexplained and involuntary sympathy. One sentiment flows
by necessity of nature into another sentiment of the same general
character. This was the first instance in which I had witnessed a
danger by fire. All was confusion around me, and all changed into
hurricane within. The general situation to my unpractised apprehension appeared desperate, and I by contagion became alike
desperate. At first I had been in some degree calm and collected,
but that too was a desperate effort, and when it gave way, a kind of
instant insanity became its successor.

I had now every thing to fear. And yet what was my fault? It
proceeded from none of those errors which are justly held up to the
aversion of mankind; my object had been neither wealth, nor the
means of indulgence, nor the usurpation of power. No spark of
malignity had harboured in my soul. I had always reverenced the
sublime mind of Mr. Falkland; I reverenced it still. My offence
had merely been a mistaken thirst of knowledge. Such however it
was as to admit neither of forgiveness nor remission. This epoch

was the crisis of my fate, dividing what may be called the offensive part, from the defensive which was the sole business of my remaining years. Alas, my offence was short, not aggravated by any sinister intention: but the reprisals I was to suffer, are long, and can terminate only with my life!

In the state in which I found myself when the recollection of what I had done flowed back upon my mind, I was incapable of any resolution. All was chaos and uncertainty within me. My thoughts were too full of horror to be susceptible of activity. I felt deserted of my intellectual powers, palsied in mind, and compelled to sit in speechless expectation of the misery to which I was destined. To my own conception I was like a man, who, though blasted with lightning and deprived for ever of the power of motion, should yet retain the consciousness of his situation. Death-dealing despair was the only idea of which I was sensible.

I was still in this situation of mind when Mr. Falkland sent for me. His message roused me from my trance. In recovering I felt those sickening and loathsome sensations, which a man may be supposed at first to endure who should return from the sleep of death. Gradually I recovered the power of arranging my ideas and directing my steps. I understood that the minute the affair of the fire was over Mr. Falkland had retired to his own room. It was evening before he ordered me to be called.

I found in him every token of extreme distress, except that there was an air of solemn and sad composure that crowned the whole. For the present all appearance of gloom, stateliness and austerity was gone. As I entered, he looked up, and, seeing who it was, ordered me to bolt the door. I obeyed. He went round the room, and examined its other avenues. He then returned to where I stood. I trembled in every joint of my frame. I exclaimed within myself, 'What bloody scene of death has Roscius[1] now to act?'

Williams, said he, in a tone that had more in it of sorrow than resentment, I have attempted your life! I am a wretch devoted to the scorn and execration of mankind!—There he stopped.

If there be one being in the whole earth, that feels the scorn and execration due to such a wretch more strongly than another, it is myself. I have been kept in a state of perpetual torture and madness. But I can put an end to it and its consequences; and, so far at least as relates to you, I am determined to do it. I know the price, and——I will make the purchase.

You must swear, said he. You must attest every sacrament, divine and human, never to disclose what I am now to tell you.— He dictated the oath, and I repeated it with an aching heart. I had no power to offer a word of remark.

This confidence, said he, is of your seeking, not of mine. It is odious to me, and is dangerous to you.

Having thus prefaced the disclosure he had to make, he paused. He seemed to collect himself as for an effort of magnitude. He wiped his face with his handkerchief. The moisture that incommoded him appeared not to be tears, but sweat.

Look at me. Observe me. Is it not strange that such a one as I should retain lineaments of a human creature? I am the blackest of villains. I am the murderer of Tyrrel. I am the assassin of the Hawkinses.

I started with terror, and was silent.

What a story is mine! Insulted, disgraced, polluted in the face of hundreds, I was capable of any act of desperation. I watched my opportunity, followed Mr. Tyrrel from the rooms, seized a sharp-pointed knife that fell in my way, came behind him, and stabbed him to the heart. My gigantic oppressor rolled at my feet.

All are but links of one chain. A blow! A murder! My next business was to defend myself, to tell so well digested a lie, as that all mankind should believe it true. Never was a task so harrowing and intolerable!

Well: thus far fortune favoured me. She favoured me beyond my desire. The guilt was removed from me, and cast upon another; but this I was to endure. Whence came the circumstantial evidence against him, the broken knife and the blood, I am unable to tell. I suppose by some miraculous accident Hawkins was passing by, and endeavoured to assist his oppressor in the agonies of death. You have heard his story; you have read one of his letters. But you do not know the thousandth part of the proofs of his simple and unalterable rectitude that I have known. His son suffered with him, that son for the sake of whose happiness and virtue he ruined himself, and would have died a hundred times.——I have had feelings, but I cannot describe them.

This it is to be a gentleman! a man of honour! I was the fool of fame. My virtue, my honesty, my everlasting peace of mind were cheap sacrifices to be made at the shrine of this divinity. But, what is worse, there is nothing that has happened that has in any degree contributed to my cure. I am as much the fool of fame as ever. I cling to it to my last breath. Though I be the blackest of villains, I will leave behind me a spotless and illustrious name. There is no crime so malignant, no scene of blood so horrible, in which that object cannot engage me. It is no matter that I regard these things at a distance with aversion;——I am sure of it; bring me to the test, and I shall yield. I despise myself; but thus I am; things are gone too far to be recalled.

Why is it that I am compelled to this confidence? From the love of fame. I should tremble at the sight of every pistol, or instrument of death that offered itself to my hands; and perhaps my next murder may not be so fortunate as those I have already committed. I had no alternative but to make you my confident or my victim. It was better to trust you with the whole truth under every seal of secrecy, than to live in perpetual fear of your penetration or your rashness.

Do you know what it is you have done? To gratify a foolishly inquisitive humour you have sold yourself. You shall continue in my service, but can never share in my affection. I will benefit you in respect of fortune, but I shall always hate you. If ever an un-guarded word escape from your lips, if ever you excite my jealousy or suspicion, expect to pay for it by your death or worse. It is a dear bargain you have made. But it is too late to look back. I charge and adjure you by every thing that is sacred and that is tremendous, preserve your faith!

My tongue has now for the first time for several years spoken the language of my heart; and the intercourse from this hour shall be shut for ever. I want no pity. I desire no consolation. Surrounded as I am with horrors, I will at least preserve my fortitude to the last. If I had been reserved to a different destiny, I have qualities in that respect worthy of a better cause. I can be mad, miserable and frantic, but even in frenzy I can preserve my presence of mind and discretion.

Such was the story I had been so earnestly desirous to know. Though my mind had brooded upon the subject for months, there was not a syllable of it that did not come to my ear with the most perfect sense of novelty. Mr. Falkland is a murderer! said I, as I retired from the conference. This dreadful appellative 'a murderer,' made my very blood run cold within me. He killed Mr. Tyrrel, for he could not control his resentment and anger: he sacrificed Hawkins the elder and Hawkins the younger, because he could upon no terms endure the public loss of honour: how can I expect that a man thus passionate and unrelenting will not sooner or later make me his victim?

But, notwithstanding this terrible application of the story, an application to which perhaps in some form or other mankind are indebted for nine tenths of their abhorrence against vice, I could not help occasionally recurring to reflections of an opposite nature. Mr. Falkland is a murderer! resumed I. He might yet be a most excellent man, if he did but think so. It is the thinking ourselves vicious then, that principally contributes to make us vicious?

Amidst the shock I received from finding, what I had never suffered myself constantly to believe, that my suspicions were true; I still discovered new cause of admiration for my master. His menaces indeed were terrible. But, when I recollected the offence I had given, so contrary to every received principle of civilized society, so insolent and rude, so intolerable to a man of Mr. Falkland's elevation and in Mr. Falkland's peculiarity of circumstances, I was astonished at his forbearance. There were indeed sufficiently obvious reasons why he might not choose to proceed to extremities with me. But how different from the fearful expectations I had conceived were the calmness of his behaviour and the regulated mildness of his language! In this respect I for a short time imagined that I was emancipated from the mischiefs which had appalled me, and that in having to do with a man of Mr. Falkland's liberality I had nothing rigorous to apprehend.

It is a miserable prospect, said I, that he holds up to me. He imagines that I am restrained by no principles, and deaf to the claims of personal excellence. But he shall find himself mistaken. I will never become an informer. I will never injure my patron; and therefore he will not be my enemy. With all his misfortunes and all his errors, I feel that my soul yearns for his welfare. If he have been criminal, that is owing to circumstances; the same qualities under other circumstances would have been, or rather were sublimely beneficent.

My reasonings were no doubt infinitely more favourable to Mr. Falkland than those which human beings are accustomed to make in the case of such as they style great criminals. This will not be wondered at when it is considered that I had myself just been

trampling on the established boundaries of obligation, and therefore might well have a fellow feeling for other offenders. Add to
which, I had known Mr. Falkland from the first as a beneficent
divinity. I had observed at leisure and with a minuteness which
could not deceive me the excellent qualities of his heart, and I
found him possessed of a mind beyond comparison the most fertile
and accomplished I had ever known.

But, though the terrors which had impressed me were considerably alleviated, my situation was notwithstanding sufficiently
miserable. The ease and light-heartedness of my youth were for
ever gone. The voice of an irresistible necessity had commanded
me to 'sleep no more.' I was tormented with a secret of which I
must never disburthen myself; and this consciousness was at my
age a source of perpetual melancholy. I had made myself a prisoner,
in the most intolerable sense of that term, for years, perhaps for
the rest of my life. Though my prudence and discretion should be
invariable, I must remember that I should have an overseer,
vigilant from conscious guilt, full of resentment at the unjustifiable
means by which I had extorted from him a confession, and whose
lightest caprice might at any time decide upon every thing that was
dear to me. The vigilance even of a public and systematical despotism is poor, compared with a vigilance which is thus goaded by the
most anxious passions of the soul. Against this species of persecution I knew not how to invent a refuge. I dared neither fly from
the observation of Mr. Falkland, nor continue exposed to its
operation. I was at first indeed lulled in a certain degree to security
upon the verge of the precipice. But it was not long before I found
a thousand circumstances perpetually reminding me of my true
situation. Those I am now to relate are among the most memorable.

CHAPTER VII

IN no long time after the disclosure Mr. Falkland had made, Mr.
Forester, his elder brother by the mother's side, came to reside for
a short period in our family. This was a circumstance peculiarly
adverse to my master's habits and inclinations. He had broken off,
as I have already said, all intercourse of visiting his neighbours. He
debarred himself every kind of amusement and relaxation. He

shrunk from the society of his fellows, and thought he could never be sufficiently buried in obscurity and solitude. This principle was in most cases of no difficult execution to a man of firmness. But Mr. Falkland knew not how to avoid the visit of Mr. Forester. This gentleman was just returned from a residence of several years upon the continent, and his demand of an apartment in the house of his half-brother till his own house at the distance of thirty miles should be prepared for his reception, was made with an air of confidence that scarcely admitted of a refusal. Mr. Falkland could only allege that the state of his health and spirits was such, that he feared a residence at his house would be little agreeable to his kinsman; and Mr. Forester conceived that this was a disqualification which would always augment in proportion as it was tolerated, and hoped that his society, by inducing Mr. Falkland to suspend his habits of seclusion, would be the means of essential benefit. Mr. Falkland opposed him no farther. He would have been sorry to be thought unkind to a kinsman for whom he had a particular esteem; and the consciousness of not daring to assign the true reason, made him cautious of adhering to his objection.

The character of Mr. Forester was in many respects the reverse of that of my master. His very appearance indicated the singularity of his disposition. His figure was short and angular. His eyes were sunk far into his head, and were overhung with eye-brows black, thick and bushy. His complexion was swarthy, and his lineaments hard. He had seen much of the world; but, to judge of him from his appearance and manners, one would have thought that he had never moved from his fire-side.

His temper was acid, petulant and harsh. He was easily offended by trifles respecting which, previously to the offence, the persons with whom he had intercourse, could have no suspicion of such a result. When offended, his customary behaviour was exceedingly rugged. He thought only of setting the delinquent right, and humbling him for his error; and, in his eagerness to do this, overlooked the sensibility of the sufferer, and the pains he inflicted. Remonstrance, in such a case, he regarded as the offspring of cowardice, which was to be extirpated with a steady and unshrinking hand, and not soothed with misjudging kindness and indulgence. As is usual in human character, he had formed a system of thinking to suit the current of his feelings. He held that the kindness we entertain for a man, should be veiled and concealed, exerted in substantial benefits, but not disclosed, lest an undue advantage should be taken of it by its object.

With this rugged outside, Mr. Forester had a warm and generous heart. At first sight all men were deterred by his manner, and excited to give him an ill character. But the longer any one knew him, the more they approved him. His harshness was then only considered as habit; and strong sense and active benevolence were uppermost in the recollection of his familiar acquaintance. His conversation, when he condescended to lay aside his snappish, rude and abrupt half-sentences, became flowing in diction, and uncommonly amusing with regard to its substance. He combined with weightiness of expression, a dryness of characteristic humour, that demonstrated at once the vividness of his observation, and the force of his understanding.

The peculiarities of this gentleman's character were not undisplayed in the scene to which he was now introduced. Having much kindness in his disposition, he soon became deeply interested in the unhappiness of his relation. He did every thing in his power to remove it; but his attempts were rude and unskilful. With a mind so accomplished, and a spirit so susceptible as that of Mr. Falkland, Mr. Forester did not venture to let loose his usual violence of manner. But, if he carefully abstained from harshness, he was however wholly incapable of that sweet and liquid eloquence of the soul, which would perhaps have stood the fairest chance, of seducing Mr. Falkland for a moment to forget his anguish. He exhorted his host to rouse up his spirit, and defy the foul fiend; but the tone of his exhortations found no sympathetic chord in the mind of my patron. He had not the skill to carry conviction to an understanding so well fortified in error. In a word, after a thousand efforts of kindness to his entertainer, he drew off his forces, growling and dissatisfied with his own impotence, rather than angry at the obstinacy of Mr. Falkland. He felt no diminution of his affection for him, and was sincerely grieved to find that he was so little capable of serving him. Both parties in this case did justice to the merits of the other; at the same time that the disparity of their humours was such as to prevent the stranger from being in any degree a dangerous companion to the master of the house. They had scarcely one point of contact in their characters; Mr. Forester was incapable of giving Mr. Falkland that degree either of pain or pleasure, which can raise the soul into a tumult and deprive it for a while of tranquillity and self-command.

Our visitor was a man, notwithstanding appearances, of a peculiarly sociable disposition, and, where he was neither interrupted nor contradicted, considerably loquacious. He began to feel himself painfully out of his element upon the present occasion. Mr. Falkland was devoted to contemplation and solitude. He put upon himself some degree of restraint upon the arrival of his kinsman, though even then his darling habits would break out. But when they had seen each other a certain number of times, and it was sufficiently evident that the society of either would be a burthen rather than a pleasure to the other, they consented by a sort of silent compact that each should be at liberty to follow his own inclination. Mr. Falkland was in a sense the greatest gainer by this. He returned to the habits of his choice, and acted as nearly as possible just as he would have done if Mr. Forester had not been in existence. But the latter was wholly at a loss. He had all the disadvantages of retirement, without being able, as he might have done at his house, to bring his own associates or his own amusements about him.

In this situation he cast his eyes upon me. It was his principle to do every thing that his thoughts suggested, without caring for the forms of the world. He saw no reason why a peasant, with certain advantages of education and opportunity, might not be as eligible a companion as a lord; at the same time that he was deeply impressed with the venerableness of old institutions. Reduced as he was to a kind of last resort, he found me better qualified for his purpose than any other of Mr. Falkland's houshold.

The manner in which he began this sort of correspondence was sufficiently characteristical. It was abrupt; but it was strongly stamped with essential benevolence. It was blunt and humorous; but there was attractiveness, especially in a case of unequal intercourse, in that very rusticity by which he levelled himself with the mass of his species. He had to reconcile himself, as well as to invite me; not to reconcile himself to the postponing an aristocratical vanity, for of that he had a very slender portion, but to the trouble of invitation, for he loved his ease. All this produced some irregularity and indecision in his own mind, and gave a very whimsical impression to his behaviour.

On my part I was by no means ungrateful for the distinction

that was paid me. My mind had been relaxed into temporary dejection, but my reserve had no alloy of moroseness or insensibility. It did not long hold out against the condescending attentions of Mr. Forester. I became gradually heedful, encouraged, confiding. I had a most eager thirst for the knowledge of mankind; and, though no person perhaps ever purchased so dearly the instructions he received in that school, the inclination was in no degree diminished. Mr. Forester was the second man I had seen uncommonly worthy of my analysis, and who seemed to my thoughts, arrived as I was at the end of my first essay, almost as much deserving to be studied as Mr. Falkland himself. I was glad to escape from the uneasiness of my reflections; and, while engaged with this new friend, I forgot the criticalness of the evils with which I was hourly menaced.

Stimulated by these feelings I was what Mr. Forester wanted, a diligent and zealous hearer. I was strongly susceptible of impression; and the alternate impressions my mind received, visibly displayed themselves in my countenance and gestures. The observations Mr. Forester had made in his travels, the set of opinions he had formed, all amused and interested me. His manner of telling a story or explaining his thoughts was forcible, perspicuous and original: his style in conversation had an uncommon zest. Every thing he had to relate delighted me; while in return my sympathy, my eager curiosity, and my unsophisticated passions, rendered me to Mr. Forester a most desirable hearer. It is not to be wondered at therefore, that every day rendered our intercourse more intimate and cordial.

Mr. Falkland was destined to be for ever unhappy; and it seemed as if no new incident could occur from which he was not able to extract food for this imperious propensity. He was wearied with a perpetual repetition of similar impressions, and entertained an invincible disgust against all that was new. The visit of Mr. Forester he regarded with antipathy. He was scarcely able to look at him without shuddering; an emotion which his guest perceived, and pitied as the result of habit and disease rather than of judgment. None of his actions passed unremarked; the most indifferent excited uneasiness and apprehension. The first overtures of intimacy between me and Mr. Forester probably gave birth to sentiments of jealousy in the mind of my master. The irregular, variable character of his visitor, tended to heighten them, by producing an appearance of inexplicableness and mystery. At this time he intimated to me that it was not agreeable to him that there should be much intercourse between me and this gentleman.

What could I do? Young as I was, could it be expected that I should play the philosopher, and put a perpetual curb upon my inclinations? Imprudent though I had been, could I voluntarily subject myself to an eternal penance, and estrangement from human society? Could I discourage a frankness so perfectly in consonance with my wishes, and receive in an ungracious way a kindness that stole away my heart?

Besides this I was but ill prepared for the servile submission Mr. Falkland demanded. In early life I had been accustomed to be much my own master. When I first entered into Mr. Falkland's service, my personal habits were checked by the novelty of my situation, and my affections were gained by the high accomplishments of my patron. To novelty and its influence, curiosity had succeeded. Curiosity, so long as it lasted, was a principle stronger in my bosom than even the love of independence. To that I would have sacrificed my liberty or my life; to gratify it, I would have submitted to the condition of a West Indian Negro, or to the tortures inflicted by North American savages. But the turbulence of curiosity had now subsided.

As long as the threats of Mr. Falkland had been confined to generals, I endured it. I was conscious of the unbecoming action I had committed, and this rendered me humble. But, when he went farther, and undertook to prescribe to every article of my conduct, my patience was at an end. My mind, before sufficiently sensible to the unfortunate situation to which my imprudence had reduced me, now took a nearer and a more alarming view of the circumstances of the case. Mr. Falkland was not an old man; he had in him the principles of vigour, however they might seem to be shaken; he might live as long as I should. I was his prisoner: and what a prisoner! All my actions observed; all my gestures marked. I could move neither to the right nor the left, but the eye of my keeper was upon me. He watched me; and his vigilance was a sickness to my heart. For me there was no more of freedom, no more of hilarity, of thoughtlessness, or of youth. Was this the life upon which I had entered with such warm and sanguine expectation? Were my days to be wasted in this chearless gloom; a galley-slave in the hands of the system of nature, whom death only, the death of myself or my inexorable superior, could free?

I had been adventurous in the gratification of an infantine and unreasonable curiosity, and I was resolved not to be less adventurous, if need were, in the defence of every thing that can make life a blessing. I was prepared for an amicable adjustment of interests; I would undertake that Mr. Falkland should never sustain injury through my means; but I expected in return that I should suffer no incroachment, but be left to the direction of my own understanding.

I went on then to seek Mr. Forester's society with eagerness; and it is the nature of an intimacy that does not decline, progressively to increase. Mr. Falkland observed these symptoms with visible perturbation. Whenever I was conscious of their being perceived by him, I betrayed tokens of confusion; this did not tend to allay his uneasiness. One day he spoke to me alone; and, with a look of mysterious, but terrible import, expressed himself thus:

Young man, take warning! Perhaps this is the last time you shall have an opportunity to take it! I will not always be the butt of your simplicity and inexperience, nor suffer your weakness to triumph over my strength! Why do you trifle with me? You little suspect the extent of my power. At this moment you are enclosed with the snares of my vengeance, unseen by you, and at the instant that you flatter yourself you are already beyond their reach, they will close upon you. You might as well think of escaping from the power of the omnipresent God, as from mine! If you could touch so much as my finger, you should expiate it in hours and months and years of a torment of which as yet you have not the remotest idea! Remember! I am not talking at random! I do not utter a word, that, if you provoke me, shall not be executed to the severest letter!

It may be supposed that these menaces were not without their effect. I withdrew in silence. My whole soul revolted against the treatment I endured, and yet I could not utter a word. Why could not I speak the expostulations of my heart, or propose the compromise I meditated? It was inexperience, and not want of strength, that awed me. Every act of Mr. Falkland contained something new, and I was unprepared to meet it. Perhaps it will be found that the greatest hero owes the propriety of his conduct to the habit of encountering difficulties and calling out with promptness the energies of his mind.

I contemplated the proceedings of my patron with the deepest astonishment. Humanity and general kindness were fundamental parts of his character, but in relation to me they were sterile and inactive. His own interest required that he should purchase my kindness; but he preferred to govern me by terror, and watch me with unceasing anxiety. I ruminated with the most mournful sensations upon the nature of my calamity. I believed that no human being was ever placed in a situation so pitiable as mine. Every atom of my frame seemed to have a several existence, and to crawl within me. I had but too much reason to believe that Mr. Falkland's were not empty words. I knew his ability; I felt his ascendancy. If I encountered him, what chance had I of victory? If I were defeated, what was the penalty I had to suffer? Well then, the rest of my life must be devoted to slavish subjection? Miserable sentence! And, if it were, what security had I against the injustice of a man, vigilant, capricious and criminal? I envied the condemned wretch upon the scaffold. I envied the victim of the inquisition in the midst of his torture. They know what they have to suffer. I had only to imagine every thing terrible, and then say, The fate reserved for me is worse than this!

It was well for me that these sensations were transient: human nature could not long support itself under what I then felt. By degrees my mind shook off its burthen. Indignation succeeded to emotions of terror. The hostility of Mr. Falkland excited hostility in me. I determined I would never calumniate him in matters of the most trivial import; much less betray the grand secret upon which every thing dear to him depended. But, totally abjuring the offensive, I resolved to stand firmly upon the defensive. The liberty of acting as I pleased I would preserve, whatever might be the risque. If I were worsted in the contest, I would at least have the consolation of reflecting that I had exerted myself with energy. In proportion as I thus determined, I drew off my forces from petty incursions, and felt the propriety of acting with premeditation and system. I ruminated incessantly upon plans of deliverance, but I was anxious that my choice should not be precipitately made.

It was during this period of my deliberation and uncertainty that Mr. Forester terminated his visit. He observed a strange distance in my behaviour, and in his good-natured, rough way reproached me for it. I could only answer with a gloomy look of mysterious import, and a mournful and expressive silence. He sought me for an explanation, but I was now as ingenious in avoiding, as I had before been ardent to seek him; and he quitted our house, as he afterwards told me, with an impression, that there was some ill destiny that hung over it, which seemed fated to make all its inhabitants miserable, without its being possible for a bystander to penetrate the reason.

CHAPTER VIII

MR. FORESTER had left us about three weeks, when Mr. Falkland sent me upon some business to an estate he possessed in a neighbouring county about fifty miles from his principal residence. The road led in a direction wholly wide of the habitation of our late visitor. I was upon my return from the place to which I had been sent, when I began in fancy to take a survey of the various circumstances of my condition; and by degrees lost in the profoundness of my contemplation all attention to the surrounding objects. The first determination of my mind was to escape from the lynx-eyed jealousy and despotism of Mr. Falkland; the second to provide, by every effort of prudence and deliberation I could devise, against the danger with which I well knew my attempt must be accompanied.

Occupied with these meditations, I rode many miles before I perceived that I had totally deviated from the right path. At length I roused myself, and surveyed the horizon round me; but I could observe nothing with which my organ was previously acquainted. On three sides the heath stretched as far as the eye could reach; on the fourth I discovered at some distance a wood of no ordinary dimension. Before me scarcely a single track could be found to mark that any human being had ever visited the spot. As the best expedient I could devise, I bent my course towards the wood I have mentioned, and then pursued as well as I was able the windings of the inclosure. This led me after some time to the end of the heath, but I was still as much at a loss as ever respecting the road I should pursue. The sun was hid from me by a grey and cloudy atmosphere; I was induced to continue along the skirts of the wood, and surmounted with some difficulty the hedges and other obstacles that from time to time presented themselves. My thoughts were gloomy and disconsolate; the dreariness of the day and the solitude which surrounded me seemed to communicate a sadness to my soul. I had proceeded a considerable way, and was overcome with hunger and fatigue, when I discovered a road and a little inn at no great distance. I made up to them, and upon enquiry found that, instead of pursuing the proper direction, I had taken one that led to Mr. Forester's, rather than to my own habitation. I alighted, and was entering the house, when the appearance of that gentleman struck my eyes.

Mr. Forester accosted me with kindness, invited me into the room where he had been sitting, and enquired what accident had brought me to that place. While he was speaking, I could not help recollecting the extraordinary manner in which we were thus once more brought together, and a train of ideas was by this means suggested to my mind. Some refreshment was by Mr. Forester's order prepared for me; I sat down, and partook of it. Still this thought dwelt upon my recollection:——Mr. Falkland would never be made acquainted with our meeting; I had an opportunity thrown in my way, which if I did not improve, I should deserve all the consequences that may result. I can now converse with a friend, and a powerful friend, without fear of being watched and overlooked. What wonder that I was tempted to disclose, not Mr. Falkland's secret, but my own situation, and receive the advice of a man of worth and experience, which might perhaps be adequately done without entering into any detail injurious to my patron?

Mr. Forester, on his part, expressed a desire to learn why it was I thought myself unhappy, and why I had avoided him during the latter part of his residence under the same roof, as evidently as I had before taken pleasure in his communications. I replied, that I could give him but an imperfect satisfaction upon these points, but what I could I would willingly explain. The fact, I proceeded, was that there were certain reasons which rendered it impossible for me to have a tranquil moment under the roof of Mr. Falkland. I had revolved the matter again and again in my mind, and was finally convinced that I owed it to myself to withdraw from his service. I added, that I was sensible by this half confidence I might rather seem to merit the disapprobation of Mr. Forester than his countenance; but I declared my persuasion that, if he could be acquainted with the whole affair, however strange my behaviour might at present appear, he would applaud my reserve.

He appeared to muse for a moment upon what I had said, and

then asked what reason I could have to complain of Mr. Falkland? I replied, that I entertained the deepest reverence for my patron; I admired his abilities, and considered him as formed for the benefit of his species. I should in my own opinion be the vilest of miscreants, if I uttered a whisper to his disadvantage. But all this did not avail: I was not fit for him; perhaps I was not good enough for him; at all events I must be perpetually miserable so long as I continued to live with him.

I observed Mr. Forester gaze upon me eagerly with curiosity and surprise, but this circumstance I did not think proper to notice. Having recovered himself, he enquired, Why then, that being the case, I did not quit his service? I answered, What he now touched upon was that which most of all contributed to my misfortune. Mr. Falkland was not ignorant of my dislike to my present situation; perhaps he thought it unreasonable, unjust; but I knew that he would never be brought to consent to my giving way to it.

Here Mr. Forester interrupted me; and, smiling, said, I magnified obstacles, and overrated my own importance, adding that he would undertake to remove that difficulty, as well as to provide me with a more agreeable appointment. This suggestion produced in me a serious alarm. I replied, that I must intreat him upon no account to think of applying to Mr. Falkland upon the subject. I added, that perhaps I was only betraying my own imbecility; but in reality, unacquainted as I was with experience and the world, I was afraid, though disgusted with my present residence, to expose myself upon a mere project of my own to the resentment of so considerable a man as Mr. Falkland. If he would favour me with his advice upon the subject, or if he would only give me leave to hope for his protection in case of any unforeseen accident, this was all I presumed to request; and, thus encouraged, I would venture to obey the dictates of my inclination, and fly in pursuit of my lost tranquillity.

Having thus opened myself to this generous friend as far as I could do it with propriety and safety, he sat for some time silent with an air of deep reflection. At length with a countenance of unusual severity, and a characteristic fierceness of manner and voice, he thus addressed me: Young man, perhaps you are ignorant of the nature of the conduct you at present hold. May be, you do not know that, where there is mystery, there is always something at bottom that will not bear the telling. Is this the way to obtain the favour of a man of consequence and respectability? To pretend to make a confidence, and then tell him a disjointed story that has not common sense in it!

I answered, that, whatever were the amount of that prejudice, I must submit. I placed my hope of a candid construction in the present instance, in the rectitude of his nature.

He went on: You do so; do you? I tell you, sir, the rectitude of my nature is an enemy to disguise. Come, boy; you must know that I understand these things better than you. Tell all, or expect nothing from me but censure and contempt.

Sir, replied I, I have spoken from deliberation; I have told you my choice, and whatever be the result I must abide by it. If in this misfortune you refuse me your assistance, here I must end, having gained by the communication only your ill opinion and displeasure.

He looked hard at me, as if he would see me through. At length, he relaxed his features, and softened his manner. You are a foolish, headstrong boy, said he, and I shall have an eye upon you. I shall never place in you the confidence I have done. But——I will not desert you. At present, the balance between approbation and dislike, is in your favour. How long it will last I cannot tell; I engage for nothing. But it is my rule to act as I feel. I will for this time do as you require;——and, pray God, it may answer. I will receive you either now or hereafter under my roof, trusting that I shall not have reason to repent, and that appearances will terminate as favourably as I wish, though I scarcely know how to hope it.

We were engaged in the earnest discussion of subjects thus interesting to my peace, when we were interrupted by an event the most earnestly to have been deprecated. Without the smallest notice, and as if he had dropped upon us from the clouds, Mr. Falkland burst into the room. I found afterwards that Mr. Forester had come thus far upon an appointment to meet Mr. Falkland, and that the place of their intended rendezvous was the next stage. Mr. Forester was detained at the inn where we now were by our accidental rencounter, and in reality had for the moment forgotten his appointment; while Mr. Falkland, not finding him where he expected, proceeded thus far towards the house of his kinsman. To me the meeting was the most unaccountable in the world.

I instantly foresaw the dreadful complication of misfortune that was included in this event. To Mr. Falkland the meeting between me and his relation must appear, not accidental, but on my part at least the result of design. I was totally out of the road I had been travelling by his direction; I was in a road that led directly to the house of Mr. Forester. What must he think of this? How must he suppose I came to that place? The truth, if told, that I came there without design, and purely in consequence of having lost my way, must appear to be the most palpable lie that ever was devised.

Here then I stood detected in the fact of that intercourse which had been so severely forbidden. But in this instance it was infinitely worse, than in those which had already given so much disturbance to Mr. Falkland. It was then frank and unconcealed; and therefore the presumption was that it was for purposes that required no concealment. But the present interview, if concerted, was in the most emphatical degree clandestine. Nor was it less perilous than it was clandestine. It had been forbidden with the most dreadful menaces, and Mr. Falkland was not ignorant how deep an impression those menaces had made upon my imagination. Such a meeting therefore could not have been concerted under such circumstances for a trivial purpose, or for any purpose that his heart did not ache to think of. Such was the amount of my crime; such was the agony my appearance was calculated to inspire; and it was reasonable to suppose that the penalty I had to expect would be proportionable. The threats of Mr. Falkland still sounded in my ears, and I was in a transport of terror.

The conduct of the same man in different circumstances is often so various as to render it very difficult to be accounted for. Mr. Falkland, in this to him terrible crisis, did not seem to be in any degree hurried away by passion. For a moment he was dumb, his eyes glared with astonishment; and the next moment as it were, he had the most perfect calmness and self-command. Had it been otherwise I have no doubt that I should instantly have entered into an explanation of the manner in which I came there, the ingenuousness and consistency of which could not but have been in some degree attended with a favourable event. But as it was, I suffered myself to be overcome; I yielded as in a former instance to the discomfiting influence of surprise. I dared scarcely breathe; I observed the appearances with anxiety and surprise. Mr. Falkland quietly ordered me to return home, and take along with me the groom he had brought with him. I obeyed in silence.

I afterwards understood that he enquired minutely of Mr. Forester the circumstances of our meeting, and that that gentleman, perceiving that the meeting itself was discovered, and guided by habits of frankness, which, when once rooted in a character, it is difficult to counteract, told Mr. Falkland every thing that had passed, together with the remarks it had suggested to his own mind. Mr. Falkland received the communication with an ambiguous and studied silence, which by no means operated to my advantage in the already poisoned mind of Mr. Forester. His silence was partly the direct consequence of a mind watchful, inquisitive and doubting; and partly perhaps was adopted for the sake of the effect it was calculated to produce, Mr. Falkland not being unwilling to encourage prejudices against a character which might one day come in competition with his own.

As to me, I went home indeed, for this was not a moment to resist. Mr. Falkland, with a premeditation to which he had given the appearance of accident, had taken care to send with me a guard to attend upon his prisoner. I seemed as if conducting to one of those fortresses, famed in the history of despotism, from which the wretched victim is never known to come forth alive; and, when I entered my chamber, I felt as if I were entering a dungeon. I reflected that I was at the mercy of a man, exasperated at my disobedience, and who was already formed to cruelty by successive murders. My prospects were now closed; I was cut off for ever from pursuits that I had meditated with ineffable delight; my death might be the event of a few hours. I was a victim at the shrine of conscious guilt that knew neither rest nor satiety; I should be blotted from the catalogue of the living, and my fate remain eternally a secret; the man who added my murder to his former crimes, would show himself the next morning, and be hailed with the admiration and applause of his species.

In the midst of these terrible imaginations one idea presented itself that alleviated my feelings. This was the recollection of the strange and unaccountable tranquillity which Mr. Falkland had manifested when he discovered me in company with Mr. Forester. I was not deceived by this. I knew that the calm was temporary, and would be succeeded by a tumult and whirlwind of the most dreadful sort. But a man under the power of such terrors as now occupied me, catches at every reed. I said to myself, This tranquillity is a period it is incumbent upon me to improve; the shorter its duration may be found, the more speedy am I obliged to be in the use of it. In a word, I took the resolution, because I already stood in fear of the vengeance of Mr. Falkland, to risque the possibility of provoking it in a degree still more inexpiable, and terminate at once my present state of uncertainty. I had now opened my case to Mr. Forester, and he had given me positive assurances of his protection. I determined immediately to address the following letter to Mr. Falkland. The consideration that, if he meditated any thing tragical, such a letter would only tend to confirm him, did not enter into the present feelings of my mind.

Sir,

I have conceived the intention of quitting your service. This is a measure we ought both of us to desire. I shall then be, what it is my duty to be, master of my own actions. You will be delivered from the presence of a person, whom you cannot prevail upon yourself to behold without unpleasing emotions.

Why should you subject me to an eternal penance? Why should you consign my youthful hopes to suffering and despair? Consult the principles of humanity that have marked the general course of your proceedings, and do not let me, I intreat you, be made the subject of a useless severity. My heart is impressed with gratitude for your favours. I sincerely ask your forgiveness for the many errors of my conduct. I consider the treatment I have received under your roof as one almost uninterrupted scene of kindness and generosity. I shall never forget my obligations to you, and will never betray them.

I remain, Sir,
your most grateful, respectful
and dutiful servant,
Caleb Williams.

Such was my employment of the evening of a day, which will be ever memorable in the history of my life. Mr. Falkland not being yet returned, though expected every hour, I was induced to make use of the pretext of fatigue to avoid an interview. I went to bed. It may be imagined that my slumbers were neither deep nor refreshing. The next morning I was informed, that my patron did not come home till late, that he had enquired for me, and, being told that I was in bed, had said nothing farther upon the subject. Satisfied in this respect, I went to the breakfasting parlour, and though full of anxiety and trepidation, endeavoured to busy myself in arranging the books and a few other little occupations, till Mr. Falkland should come down. After a short time I heard his step, which I perfectly well knew how to distinguish, in the passage. Presently, he stopped, and, speaking to some one in a sort of deliberate, but smothered voice, I overheard him repeat my name as enquiring for me. In conformity to the plan I had persuaded myself to adopt I now laid the letter I had written upon the table at which he usually sat, and made my exit at one door as Mr. Falkland entered at the other. This done, I withdrew, with flutterings and palpitation, to a private apartment, a sort of light-closet at the end of the library, where I was accustomed not unfrequently to sit.

I had not been here three minutes when I heard the voice of Mr. Falkland calling me. I went to him in the library. His manner was that of a man labouring with some dreadful thought, and endeavouring to give an air of carelessness and insensibility to his behaviour. Perhaps no carriage of any other sort could have produced a sensation of such inexplicable horror, or have excited in the person who was its object such anxious uncertainty about the event.—That is your letter, said he, throwing it.

My lad, continued he, I believe now you have played all your tricks, and the farce is nearly at an end! With your apishness and absurdity however you have taught me one thing, and, whereas before now I have winced at them with torture, I am now as tough as an elephant. I shall crush you in the end with the same indifference that I would any other little insect that disturbed my serenity.

I am unable to tell what brought about your meeting with Mr. Forester yesterday. It might be design; it might be accident. But, I shall not forget it. You write me here, that you are desirous to quit my service. To that I have a short answer, You never shall quit it with life. If you attempt it, you shall never cease to rue your folly as long as you exist. That is my will; and I will not have it resisted. The very next time you disobey me in that or any other article, there is an end of your vagaries for ever. Perhaps your situation may be a pitiable one; it is for you to look to that. I only know that it is in your power to prevent its growing worse; no time nor chance shall ever make it better.

Do not imagine I am afraid of you! I wear an armour, against which all your weapons are impotent. I have dug a pit for you; and, whichever way you move, backward or forward, to the right or to

the left, it is ready to swallow you. Be still! If once you fall, call as
loud as you will, no man on earth shall hear your cries; prepare a
tale however plausible, or however true, the whole world shall
execrate you for an impostor. Your innocence shall be of no service
to you; I laugh at so feeble a defence. It is I that say it; you may
believe what I tell you. Do you not know, miserable wretch! added
he, suddenly altering his tone, and stamping upon the ground with
fury, that I have sworn to preserve my reputation whatever be the
expence, that I love it more than the whole world and its inhabitants
taken together? And do you think that you shall wound it? Begone,
miscreant! reptile! and cease to contend with unsurmountable
power!

The part of my history which I am now relating is that which I
reflect upon with the least complacency. Why was it that I was
once more totally overcome by the imperious carriage of Mr.
Falkland, and unable to utter a word? The reader will be presented
with many occasions in the sequel in which I wanted neither facility
in the invention of expedients, nor fortitude in entering upon my
justification. Persecution at length gave firmness to my character,
and taught me the better part of manhood. But in the present
instance I was irresolute, overawed and abashed.

The speech I had heard was the dictate of frenzy, and it created
in me a similar frenzy. It determined me to do the very thing against
which I was thus solemnly warned, and fly from my patron's
house. I could not enter into parley with him; I could no longer
endure the vile subjugation he imposed on me. It was in vain that
my reason warned me of the rashness of a measure to be taken
without concert or preparation. I seemed to be in a state in which
reason had no power. I felt as if I could coolly survey the several
arguments of the case, perceive that they had prudence, truth and
common sense on their side; and then answer, I am under the
guidance of a director more energetic than you.

I was not long in executing what I had thus rapidly determined.
I fixed on the evening of that very day as the period of my evasion.
Even in this short interval I had perhaps sufficient time for deliberation. But all opportunity was useless to me; my mind was fixed,
and each succeeding moment only increased the unspeakable
eagerness with which I meditated my escape. The hours usually
observed by our family in this country residence were regular; and
one in the morning was the time I selected for my undertaking.

In searching the apartment where I slept, I had formerly discovered a concealed door, which led to a small apartment of the most secret nature, not uncommon in houses so old as that of Mr. Falkland, and which had perhaps served as a refuge from persecution, or a security from the inveterate hostilities of a barbarous age. I believed no person was acquainted with this hiding place but myself. I felt unaccountably impelled, to remove into it the different articles of my personal property. I could not at present take them away with me. If I were never to recover them, I felt that it would be a gratification to my sentiment, that no trace of my existence should be found after my departure. Having completed their removal, and waited till the hour I had previously chosen, I stole down quietly from my chamber with a lamp in my hand; I went along a passage that led to a small door opening into the garden, and then crossed the garden to a gate that intersected an elm walk and a private horse-path on the outside.

I could scarcely believe my good fortune in having thus far executed my design without interruption. The terrible images Mr. Falkland's menaces had suggested to my mind, made me expect impediment and detection at every step, though the impassioned state of my mind impelled me to advance with desperate resolution. He probably however counted too securely upon the ascendancy of his sentiments, when imperiously pronounced, to think it necessary to take precautions against a sinister event. For myself, I drew a favourable omen as to the final result of my project, from the smoothness of success that attended it in the outset.

CHAPTER IX

THE first plan that had suggested itself to me was, to go to the nearest public road, and take the earliest stage for London. There I believed I should be most safe from discovery, if the vengeance of Mr. Falkland should prompt him to pursue me; and I did not doubt among the multiplied resources of the metropolis to find something which should suggest to me an eligible mode of disposing of my person and industry. I reserved Mr. Forester in my arrangement as a last resource, not to be called forth unless for immediate protection from the hand of persecution and power.

I was destitute of that experience of the world, which can alone render us fertile in resources, or even enable us to institute a just comparison between the resources that offer themselves. I was like the fascinated animal that is seized with the most terrible apprehensions, at the same time that he is incapable of adequately considering for his own safety.

The mode of my proceeding being digested, I traced with a chearful heart the unfrequented path it was now necessary for me to pursue. The night was gloomy, and it drizzled with rain. But these were circumstances I had scarcely the power to perceive; all was sunshine and joy within me. I hardly felt the ground; I repeated to myself a thousand times, I am free. What concern have I with danger and alarm! I feel that I am free; I feel that I will continue so. What power is able to hold in chains a mind ardent and determined? What power can cause that man to die, whose whole soul commands him to continue to live? I looked back with abhorrence to the subjection in which I had been held. I did not hate the author of my misfortunes; truth and justice acquit me of that; I rather pitied the hard destiny to which he seemed condemned. But I thought with unspeakable loathing of those errors, in consequence of which every man is fated to be more or less the tyrant or the slave. I was astonished at the folly of my species, that they did not rise up as one man, and shake off chains so ignominious and misery so insupportable. So far as related to myself, I resolved, and this resolution has never been entirely forgotten by me, to hold myself disengaged from this odious scene, and never fill the part either of the oppressor or the sufferer.

My mind continued in this enthusiastical state, full of confidence, and accessible only to such a portion of fear as served rather to keep up a state of pleasurable emotion, than to generate anguish and distress, during the whole of this nocturnal expedition. After a walk of three hours I arrived without accident at the village from which I hoped to have taken my passage for the metropolis. At this early hour every thing was quiet; no sound of any thing human saluted my ear. It was with difficulty that I gained admittance into the yard of the inn, where I found a single ostler taking care of some horses. From him I received the unwelcome tidings that the coach was not expected till six o'clock in the morning of the day after to-morrow, its route through that town recurring only three times a week.

This intelligence gave the first check to the rapturous inebriation by which my mind had been possessed from the moment I quitted the habitation of Mr. Falkland. The whole of my fortune in ready cash consisted of about eleven guineas. I had about fifty more that had fallen to me from the disposal of my property at the death of my father; but that was so vested as to preclude it from immediate use, and I even doubted whether it would not be found better ultimately to resign it, than by claiming it to risk the furnishing a clue to what I most of all dreaded, the persecution of Mr. Falkland. There was nothing I so ardently desired as the annihilation of all future intercourse between us, that he should not know there was such a person on the earth as myself, and that I should never more hear a name which had been so fatal to my peace.

Thus circumstanced, I conceived frugality to be an object by no means unworthy of my attention, unable as I was to prognosticate what discouragements and delays might present themselves to the accomplishment of my wishes, after my arrival in London. For this and other reasons I determined to adhere to my design of travelling by the stage; it only remaining for me to consider in what manner I should prevent the eventual delay of twenty-four hours from becoming by any untoward event a source of new calamity. It was by no means advisable to remain at the village where I now was, during this interval; nor did I even think it proper to employ it in proceeding on foot along the great road. I therefore decided upon making a circuit, the direction of which should seem at first extremely wide of my intended route, and then suddenly taking a different inclination, should enable me to arrive by the close of day at a market-town twelve miles nearer to the metropolis.

Having fixed the economy of the day, and persuaded myself that it was the best which under the circumstances could be adopted, I dismissed for the most part all farther anxieties from my mind, and eagerly yielded myself up to the different amusements that arose. I rested and went forward at the impulse of the moment. At one time I reclined upon a bank immersed in contemplation, and at another exerted myself to analyse the prospects which succeeded each other. The haziness of the morning was followed by a spirit-stirring and beautiful day. With the ductility so characteristic of a youthful mind, I forgot the anguish which had lately been my continual guest, and occupied myself entirely in dreams of future novelty and felicity. I scarcely ever in the whole course of my existence spent a day of more various or exquisite gratification. It furnished a strong and perhaps not an unsalutary contrast to the terrors which had preceded, and the dreadful scenes that awaited me.

In the evening I arrived at the place of my destination, and enquired for the inn at which the coach was accustomed to call. A circumstance however had previously excited my attention, and reproduced in me a state of alarm.

Though it was already dark before I reached the town, my observation had been attracted by a man, who passed me on horseback in the opposite direction, about half a mile on the other side of the town. There was an inquisitiveness in his gesture that I did not like, and, as far as I could discern his figure, I pronounced him an ill-looking man. He had not passed me more than two minutes before I heard the sound of a horse advancing slowly behind me. These circumstances impressed some degree of uneasy sensation upon my mind. I first mended my pace; and, this not appearing to answer the purpose, I afterwards loitered, that the horseman might pass me. He did so; and, as I glanced him, I thought I saw that it was the same man. He now put his horse into a trot, and entered the town. I followed, and it was not long before I perceived him at the door of an ale-house, drinking a mug of beer. This however the darkness prevented me from discovering, till I was in a manner upon him. I pushed forward, and saw him no more, till, as I entered the yard of the inn where I intended to sleep, the same man suddenly rode up to me, and asked if my name were Williams.

This adventure, while it had been passing, expelled the gaiety of my mind, and filled me with anxiety. The apprehension however that I felt, appeared to me groundless; if I were pursued, I took it for granted it would be by some of Mr. Falkland's people, and not by a stranger. The darkness took from me some of the simplest expedients of precaution. I determined at least to proceed to the inn, and make the necessary enquiries.

I no sooner heard the sound of the horse as I entered the yard, and the question proposed to me by the rider, than the dreadful certainty of what I feared instantly took possession of my mind. Every incident connected with my late abhorred situation was calculated to impress me with the deepest alarm. My first thought was to betake myself to the fields, and trust to the swiftness of my flight for safety. But this was scarcely practicable; I remarked that my enemy was alone; and I believed that, man to man, I might reasonably hope to get the better of him, either by the firmness of my determination, or the subtlety of my invention.

Thus determined, I replied in an impetuous and peremptory tone, that I was the man he took me for; adding, I guess your errand; but it is to no purpose. You come to conduct me back to Falkland House; but no force shall ever drag me to that place alive. I have not taken my resolution without strong reasons; and all the world shall not persuade me to alter it. I am an Englishman; and it is the privilege of an Englishman to be sole judge and master of his own actions.

You are in the devil of a hurry, replied the man, to guess my intentions, and tell your own. But your guess is right, and mayhap you may have reason to be thankful that my errand is not something worse. Sure enough the squire expects you; but I have a letter, and when you have read that, I suppose you will come off a little of your stoutness. If that does not answer, it will then be time to think what is to be done next.

Thus saying, he gave me his letter, which was from Mr. Forester, whom, as he told me, he had left at Mr. Falkland's house. It was as follows:

Williams,

My brother Falkland has sent the bearer in pursuit of you. He expects that, if found, you will return with him. I expect it too. It is of the utmost consequence to your future honour and character. After reading these lines, if you are a villain and a rascal, you will perhaps endeavour to fly. If your conscience tells you, You are innocent, you will out of all doubt come back. Show me then whether I have been your dupe; and, while I was won over by your seeming ingenuousness, have suffered myself to be made the tool of a designing knave. If you come, I pledge myself that, if you clear your reputation, you shall not only be free to go wherever you please, but shall receive every assistance in my power to give. Remember! I engage for nothing farther than that.

Valentine Forester.

What a letter was this? To a mind like mine glowing with the love of virtue, such an address was strong enough to draw the person to whom it was addressed from one end of the earth to the other. My mind was full of confidence and energy. I felt my own innocence, and was determined to assert it. I was willing to be driven out a fugitive; I even rejoiced in my escape, and chearfully went out into the world destitute of every provision, and depending for my future prospects upon my own ingenuity.

Thus much, said I, Falkland! you may do. Dispose of me as you please with respect to the goods of fortune; but you shall neither make prize of my liberty, nor sully the whiteness of my name. I repassed in my thoughts every memorable incident that had happened to me under his roof. I could recollect nothing, except the affair of the mysterious trunk, out of which the shadow of a criminal accusation could be extorted. In that instance my conduct had been highly reprehensible and I had never looked back upon it without remorse and self-condemnation. But I did not believe that it was of the nature of those actions which can be brought under legal censure. I could still less persuade myself that Mr. Falkland, who shuddered at the very possibility of detection, and who considered himself as completely in my power, would dare to bring forward a subject so closely connected with the internal agony in his soul. In a word, the more I reflected on the phrases of Mr. Forester's billet, the less could I imagine the nature of those scenes to which they were to serve as a prelude.

The inscrutableness however of the mystery they contained, did not suffice to overwhelm my courage. My mind seemed to undergo an entire revolution. Timid and embarrassed as I had felt myself, when I regarded Mr. Falkland as my clandestine and domestic foe, I now conceived that the case was entirely altered. Meet me, said I, as an open accuser; if we must contend, let us contend in the face of day; and then, unparalleled as your resources may be, I will not fear you. Innocence and guilt were, in my apprehension, the things in the whole world the most opposite to each other. I would not suffer myself to believe, that the former could be confounded with the latter, unless the innocent man first allowed himself to be sub- dued in mind, before he was defrauded of the good opinion of mankind. Virtue rising superior to every calumny, defeating by a plain, unvarnished tale all the stratagems of vice, and throw- ing back upon her adversary the confusion with which he had hoped to overwhelm her, was one of the favourite subjects of my youthful reveries. I determined never to prove an instrument of destruction to Mr. Falkland; but I was not less resolute to obtain justice to myself.

The issue of all these confident hopes I shall immediately have occasion to relate. It was thus, with the most generous and undoubting spirit, that I rushed upon irretrievable ruin.

Friend, said I to the bearer, after a considerable interval in silence; You are right. This is indeed an extraordinary letter you have brought me; but it answers its purpose. I will certainly go with you now, whatever be the consequence. No person shall ever impute blame to me, so long as I have it in my power to clear myself. I felt, in the circumstances in which I was placed by Mr. Forester's letter, not merely a willingness, but an alacrity and impatience to return. We procured a second horse. We proceeded on our journey in silence. My mind was occupied again in endeavouring to account for Mr. Forester's letter. I knew the inflexibility and sternness of Mr. Falkland's mind in accomplishing the purposes he had at heart; but I also knew that every virtuous and magnanimous principle was congenial to his character.

When we arrived, midnight was already past, and we were obliged to waken one of the servants to give us admittance. I found that Mr. Forester had left a message for me in consideration of the possibility of my arrival during the night, directing me immediately to go to bed, and to take care that I did not come weary and exhausted to the business of the following day. I endeavoured to take his advice; but my slumbers were unrefreshing and disturbed. I suffered however no reduction of courage; the singularity of my situation, my conjectures with respect to the present, my eagerness for the future did not allow me to sink into a languid and inactive state.

Next morning the first person I saw was Mr. Forester. He told me that he did not yet know what Mr. Falkland had to allege against me, for that he had refused to know. He had arrived at the house of his brother by appointment on the preceding day to settle some indispensible business, his intention having been to depart the moment the business was finished, as he knew that conduct on his part would be most agreeable to Mr. Falkland. But he was no sooner come than he found the whole house in confusion, the alarm of my elopement having been given a few hours before. Mr. Falkland had dispatched servants in all directions in pursuit of me; and the servant from the market town arrived at the same moment with Mr. Forester, with intelligence that a person answering to the description he gave had been there very early in the morning enquiring respecting the stage to London.

Mr. Falkland seemed extremely disturbed at this information, and exclaimed upon me with great acrimony as an unthankful and unnatural villain.

Mr. Forester replied: Have more command of yourself, sir! Villain is a very serious appellation, and must not be trifled with. Englishmen are free; and no man is to be charged with villainy because he changes one source of subsistence for another.

Mr. Falkland shook his head, and with a smile expressive of acute sensibility said, Brother, brother, you are the dupe of his art. I always considered him with an eye of suspicion, and was aware of his depravity. But I have just discovered——

Stop, sir! interrupted Mr. Forester. I own I thought that, in a moment of acrimony, you might be employing harsh epithets in a sort of random style. But if you have a serious accusation to state, we must not be told of that, till it is known whether the lad is within reach of a hearing. I am indifferent myself about the good opinion of others. It is what the world bestows and retracts with so little thought, that I can make no account of its decisions. But that does not authorise me lightly to entertain an ill opinion of another. The slenderest allowance I think I can make to such as I consign to be the example and terror of their species, is that of being heard in their own defence. It is a wise principle that requires the judge to come into court, uninformed of the merits of the cause he is to try; and to that principle I am determined to conform as an individual. I shall always think it right to be severe and inflexible in my treatment of offenders; but the severity I exercise in the sequel, must be accompanied with impartiality and caution in what is preliminary.

While Mr. Forester related to me these particulars, he observed me ready to break out into some of the expressions which the narrative suggested, but he would not suffer me to speak. No, said he; I would not hear Mr. Falkland against you; and I cannot hear you in your defence. I come to you at present to speak, and not to hear. I thought it right to warn you of your danger, but I have nothing more to do now. Reserve what you have to say to the proper time. Make the best story you can for yourself; true, if truth, as I hope, will serve your purpose; but, if not, the most plausible and ingenious you can invent. That is what self-defence requires from every man where, as it always happens to a man upon his trial, he has the whole world against him, and has his own battle to fight against the world. Farewell, and God send you a good deliverance! If Mr. Falkland's accusation, whatever it be, shall appear premature, depend upon having me more zealously your friend than ever. If not, this is the last act of friendship you will ever receive from me!

It may be believed that this address, so singular, so solemn, so big with conditional menace, did not greatly tend to encourage me. I was totally ignorant of the charge to be advanced against me; and not a little astonished, when it was in my power to be in the most formidable degree the accuser of Mr. Falkland, to find the principles of equity so completely reversed, as for the innocent, but instructed individual to be the party accused and suffering, instead of having, as was natural, the real criminal at his mercy. I was still more astonished at the super-human power Mr. Falkland seemed to possess of bringing back the object of his persecution within the sphere of his authority; a reflection attended with some check to that eagerness and boldness of spirit which now constituted the ruling passion of my mind.

But this was no time for meditation. To the sufferer the course of events is taken out of his direction, and he is hurried along with an irresistible force, without finding it within the compass of his efforts to check their rapidity. I was allowed only a short time to recollect myself when my trial commenced. I was conducted to the library where I had passed so many happy and so many contemplative hours, and found there Mr. Forester and three or four of the servants already assembled in expectation of me and my accuser. Every thing was calculated to suggest to me that I must trust only in the justice of the parties concerned, and had nothing to hope from their indulgence. Mr. Falkland entered at one door, almost as soon as I entered at the other.

HE began: It has been the principle of my life never to inflict a wilful injury upon any thing that lives; I need not express my regret when I find myself obliged to be the promulgator of a criminal charge. How gladly would I pass unnoticed the evil I have sustained; but I owe it to society to detect an offender, and prevent other men from being imposed upon, as I have been, by an appearance of integrity.

It would be better, interrupted Mr. Forester, to speak directly to the point. We ought not, though unwarily, by apologising for ourselves, to create at such a time a prejudice against an individual, against whom a criminal accusation will always be prejudice enough.

I strongly suspect, continued Mr. Falkland, this young man, who has been peculiarly the object of my kindness, of having robbed me to a considerable amount.

What, replied Mr. Forester, are the grounds of your suspicion?

The first of them is the actual loss I have sustained in notes, jewels and plate. I have missed bank notes to the amount of nine hundred pounds, three gold repeaters[1] of considerable value, a complete set of diamonds the property of my late mother, and several other articles.

And why, continued my arbitrator, astonishment, grief, and a desire to retain his self-possession strongly contending in his countenance and voice, do you fix on this young man as the instrument of the depredation?

I found him, on my coming home upon the day when every thing was in disorder from the alarm of fire, in the very act of quitting the private apartment where these things were deposited. He was confounded at seeing me, and hastened to withdraw as soon as he possibly could.

Did you say nothing to him, take no notice of the confusion your sudden appearance produced?

I asked what was his errand in that place. He was at first so terrified and overcome that he could not answer me. Afterwards with a good deal of faltering he said that, when all the servants were engaged in endeavouring to save the most valuable part of my property, he had come hither with the same view; but that he had as yet removed nothing.

Did you immediately examine to see that every thing was safe?

No. I was accustomed to confide in his honesty, and I was suddenly called away in the present instance to attend to the increasing progress of the flames. I therefore only took out the key from the door of the apartment, having first locked it; and, putting it in my pocket, hastened to go where my presence seemed indispensibly necessary.

How long was it before you missed your property?

The same evening. The hurry of the scene had driven the circumstance entirely out of my mind, till going by accident near the apartment, the whole affair, together with the singular and equivocal behaviour of Williams, rushed at once upon my recollection. I immediately entered, examined the trunk in which these things were contained, and to my astonishment found the locks broken, and the property gone.

What steps did you take upon this discovery?

I sent for Williams, and talked to him very seriously upon the subject. But he had now perfectly recovered his self command, and calmly and stoutly denied all knowledge of the matter. I urged him with the enormousness of the offence, but I made no impression. He did not discover either the surprise and indignation one would have expected from a person entirely innocent, or the uneasiness that generally attends upon guilt. He was rather silent and reserved. I then informed him, that I should proceed in a manner different from what he might perhaps expect. I would not, as is too frequent in such cases, make a general search, for I had rather lose my property for ever without redress, than expose a multitude of innocent persons to anxiety and injustice. My suspicion for the present unavoidably fixed upon him. But in a matter of so great consequence I was determined not to act upon suspicion. I would neither incur the possibility of ruining him being innocent, nor be the instrument of exposing others to his depredations, if guilty. I should therefore merely insist upon his continuing in my service. He might depend upon it he should be well watched, and I trusted the whole truth would eventually appear. Since he avoided confession now, I advised him to consider how far it was likely he would come off with impunity at last. This I was determined on, that the moment he attempted an escape, I would consider that as an indication of guilt and proceed accordingly.

What circumstances have occurred from that time to the present?

None upon which I can infer a certainty of guilt. Several that agree to favour a suspicion. From that time Williams was perpetually uneasy in his situation, always desirous, as it now appears, to escape, but afraid to adopt such a measure without certain precautions. It was not long after, that you, Mr. Forester, became my visitor. I observed with dissatisfaction the growing intercourse between you, reflecting on the equivocalness of his character, and the attempt he would probably make to render you the dupe of his hypocrisy. I accordingly threatened him severely, and I believe you observed the change that presently after took place in his behaviour with relation to you.

I did, and it appeared at that time mysterious and extraordinary.

Some time after, as you well know, a rencounter took place between you, whether accidental or intentional on his part I am not able to say, when he confessed to you the uneasiness of his mind without discovering the cause, and openly proposed to you to assist him in his flight, and stand in case of necessity between him and my resentment. You offered, it seems, to take him into your service, but nothing, as he acknowledged, would answer his purpose, that did not place his retreat wholly out of my power to discover.

Did it not appear extraordinary to you that he should hope for any effectual protection from me, while it remained perpetually in your power to satisfy me of his unworthiness?

Perhaps he had hopes that I should not proceed to that step, at least so long as the place of his retreat should be unknown to me, and of consequence the event of my proceeding dubious. Perhaps he confided in his own powers, which are far from contemptible, to construct a plausible tale, especially as he had taken care to have the first impression in his favour. After all, this protection on your part was merely reserved in case all other expedients failed. He does not appear to have had any other sentiment upon the subject, than that, if he were defeated in his projects for placing himself beyond the reach of justice, it was better to have bespoken a place in your patronage than to be destitute of every resource.

Mr. Falkland having thus finished his evidence, called upon Robert, the valet, to confirm that part of it which related to the day of the fire.

Robert stated, that he happened to be coming through the library that day a few minutes after Mr. Falkland's being brought home by the sight of the fire, that he had found me standing there with every mark of perturbation and fright, that he was so struck with my appearance that he could not help stopping to notice it, that he had spoken to me two or three times before he could obtain an answer, and that all he could get from me at last was that I was the most miserable creature alive.

He farther said, that in the evening of the same day Mr. Falkland called him into the private apartment adjoining to the library, and bid him bring a hammer and some nails. He then showed him a trunk standing in the apartment with its locks and fastenings broken, and ordered him to observe and remember what he saw, but not to mention it to any one. Robert did not at that time know what Mr. Falkland intended by these directions, which were given in a manner uncommonly solemn and significant; but he entertained no doubt that the fastenings were broken and wrenched by the application of a chissel or such like instrument with the intention of forcibly opening the trunk.

Mr. Forester observed upon this evidence, that as much of it as related to the day of the fire seemed indeed to afford powerful reasons for suspicion, and that the circumstances that had occurred since strangely concurred to fortify that suspicion. Meantime, that nothing proper to be done might be omitted, he asked whether in my flight I had removed my property, and proposed searching my boxes, to see whether, by that means, any trace could be discovered to confirm the imputation. Mr. Falkland treated this suggestion slightly, saying that, if I were the thief, I had no doubt taken the precaution to obviate so palpable a means of detection. To this Mr. Forester only replied, that conjecture, however skilfully formed, was not always realised in the actions and behaviour of mankind; and ordered that my boxes and trunks, if found, should be brought into the library. I listened to this suggestion with pleasure; and, uneasy and confounded as I was at the appearances combined against me, I trusted in this appeal to give a new face to my cause. I was eager to declare the place where my property was deposited; and the servants, guided by my direction, presently produced what was enquired for.

The two boxes that were first opened contained nothing to confirm the accusation against me; in the third were found a watch and several jewels that were immediately known to be the property of Mr. Falkland. The production of this seemingly decisive evidence excited emotions of astonishment and concern; but no person's astonishment appeared to be greater, than that of Mr. Falkland. That I should have left the stolen goods behind me, would of itself have appeared incredible; but, when it was considered what a secure place of concealment I had found for them, the wonder diminished; and Mr. Forester observed, that it was by no means impossible I might conceive it easier to obtain possession of them afterwards, than to remove them at the period of my precipitate flight.

Here, however, I thought it necessary to interfere. I fervently urged my right to a fair and impartial construction. I asked Mr. Forester, whether it were probable, if I had stolen these things, that I should not have contrived, at least to remove them along with me? And again, whether, if I had been conscious they would be found among my property, I should myself have indicated the place where I had concealed it?

The insinuation I conveyed against Mr. Forester's impartiality, overspread his whole countenance for an instant with the flush of anger.

Impartiality, young man! yes, be sure, from me you shall experience an impartial treatment! God send that may answer your purpose! Presently you shall be heard at full in your own defence.

You expect us to believe you innocent, because you did not remove these things along with you. The money is removed. Where, sir, is that? We cannot answer for the inconsistencies and oversights of any human mind, and least of all, if that mind should appear to be disturbed with the consciousness of guilt.

You observe that it was by your own direction these boxes and trunks have been found. That is indeed extraordinary. It appears little less than infatuation. But to what purpose appeal to probabilities and conjecture, in the face of incontestible facts? There, sir, are the boxes. You alone knew where they were to be found. You alone had the keys. Tell us then how this watch and these jewels came to be contained in them?

I was silent.

To the rest of the persons present I seemed to be merely the subject of detection; but in reality I was of all the spectators that individual who was most at a loss to conceive through every stage of the scene what would come next, and who listened to every word that was uttered with the most uncontrolable amazement. Amazement however alternately yielded to indignation and horror. At first I could not refrain from repeatedly attempting to interrupt; but I was checked in these attempts by Mr. Forester, and I presently felt how necessary it was to my future peace that I should collect the whole energy of my mind to repel the charge, and assert my innocence.

Every thing being now produced that could be produced against me, Mr. Forester turned to me with a look of concern and pity, and told me that now was the time if I chose to allege any thing in my defence. In reply to this invitation I spoke nearly as follows:

I am innocent. It is in vain that circumstances are accumulated against me: there is not a person upon earth less capable than I of the things of which I am accused. I appeal to my heart; I appeal to my looks; I appeal to every sentiment my tongue ever uttered.

I could perceive that the fervour with which I spoke made some impression upon every one that heard me. But in a moment their eyes were turned upon the property that lay before them, and their countenances changed. I proceeded:

One thing more I must aver; Mr. Falkland is not deceived: he perfectly knows that I am innocent.

I had no sooner uttered these words than an involuntary cry of indignation burst from every person in the room. Mr. Forester turned to me with a look of extreme severity, and said:

Young man, consider well what you are doing! It is the privilege of the party accused to say whatever he thinks proper; and I will take care that you shall enjoy that privilege in its utmost extent. But do you think it will conduce in any respect to your benefit to throw out such insolent and intolerable insinuations?

I thank you most sincerely, replied I, for your caution; but I well know what it is I am doing. I make this declaration not merely because it is solemnly true, but because it is inseparably connected with my vindication. I am the party accused, and I shall be told that I am not to be believed in my own defence. I can produce no other witnesses of my innocence; I therefore call upon Mr. Falkland to be my evidence. I ask him,

Did you never boast to me in private of your power to ruin me? Did you never say that, if once I brought on myself the weight of your displeasure, my fall should be irreparable? Did you not tell me that, though I should prepare in that case a tale how ever

plausible or how ever true, you would take care that the whole
world should execrate me as an impostor? Were not those your
very words? Did you not add that my innocence should be of no
service to me, and that you laughed at so feeble a defence? I ask
you farther, Did you not receive a letter from me the morning of
the day on which I departed, requesting your consent to my
departure? Should I have done that, if my flight had been that of a
thief? I challenge any man to reconcile the expressions of that
letter with this accusation. Should I have begun with stating that I
had conceived a desire to quit your service, if my desire and the
reasons for it had been of the nature that is now alleged? Should
I have dared to ask for what reason I was thus subjected to an
eternal penance?

Saying this, I took out a copy of my letter and laid it open upon
the table.

Mr. Falkland returned no immediate answer to my interrogations. Mr. Forester turned to him, and said, Well, sir, what is your
reply to this challenge of your servant?

Mr. Falkland answered: Such a mode of defence hardly stands
in need of a reply. But I answer, I held no such conversation; I
never used such words; I received no such letter. Surely it is no
sufficient refutation of a criminal charge, that the criminal repels
what is alleged against him with volubility of speech and intrepidity
of manner?

Mr. Forester then turned to me. If, said he, you trust your
vindication to the plausibility of your tale, you must take care to
render it consistent and complete. You have not told us what was
the cause of the confusion and anxiety in which Robert professes
to have found you, why you were so impatient to quit the service of
Mr. Falkland, or how you account for certain articles of his property being found in your possession?

All that, sir, answered I, is true. There are certain parts of my
story that I have not told. If they were told, they would not conduce
to my disadvantage, and they would make the present accusation
appear still more astonishing. But I cannot, as yet at least, prevail
upon myself to tell them. Is it necessary to give any particular and
precise reasons why I should wish to change the place of my
residence? You all of you know the unfortunate state of Mr.
Falkland's mind. You know the sternness, reservedness and distance of his manners. If I had no other reasons, surely it would

afford small presumption of criminality that I should wish to change his service for another.

The question of how these articles of Mr. Falkland's property came to be found in my possession is more material. It is a question I am wholly unable to answer. Their being found there was at least as unexpected to me as to any one of the persons now present. I only know that, as I have the most perfect assurance of Mr. Falkland's being conscious of my innocence, for, observe! I do not shrink from that assertion, I reiterate it with new confidence; I therefore firmly and from my soul believe that their being there is of Mr. Falkland's contrivance.

I no sooner said this, than I was again interrupted by an involuntary exclamation from every one present. They looked at me with furious glances, as if they could have torn me to pieces. I proceeded:

I have now answered every thing that is alleged against me.

Mr. Forester, you are a lover of justice; I conjure you not to violate it in my person. You are a man of penetration; look at me, do you see any of the marks of guilt? Recollect all that has ever passed under your observation; is it compatible with a mind capable of what is now alleged against me? Could a real criminal have shown himself so unabashed, composed and firm as I have now done?

Fellow servants! Mr. Falkland is a man of rank and fortune; he is your master. I am a poor country lad without a friend in the world. That is a ground of real difference to a certain extent; but it is not a sufficient ground for the subversion of justice. Remember, that I am in a situation that is not to be trifled with, that a decision given against me now, in a case in which I solemnly assure you I am innocent, will for ever deprive me of reputation and peace of mind, combine the whole world in a league against me, and determine perhaps upon my liberty and my life. If you believe, if you see, if you know that I am innocent, speak for me. Do not suffer a pusillanimous timidity to prevent you from saving a fellow creature from destruction, who does not deserve to have a human being for his enemy. Why have we the power of speech, but to communicate our thoughts? I will never believe that a man conscious of innocence, cannot make other men perceive that he has that thought. Do not you feel that my whole heart tells me, I am not guilty of what is imputed to me?

To you, Mr. Falkland, I have nothing to say. I know you, and know that you are impenetrable. At the very moment that you are urging such odious charges against me, you admire my resolution and forbearance. But I have nothing to hope from you. You can look upon my ruin without pity or remorse. I am most unfortunate indeed in having to do with such an adversary. You oblige me to say ill things of you; but I appeal to your own heart whether my language is that of exaggeration or revenge.

Every thing that could be alleged on either side being now concluded, Mr. Forester undertook to make some remarks upon the whole. Williams, said he, the charge against you is heavy; the direct evidence strong; the corroborating circumstances numerous and striking. I grant that you have shown considerable dexterity in your answers; but you will learn, young man, to your cost, that dexterity, however powerful it may be in certain cases, will avail little against the stubbornness of truth. It is fortunate for mankind that the empire of talents has its limitations, and that it is not in the power of ingenuity to subvert the distinctions of right and wrong. Take my word for it that the true merits of the case against you will be too strong for sophistry to overturn, that justice will prevail, and impotent malice be defeated.

To you, Mr. Falkland, society is obliged for having placed this black affair in its true light. Do not suffer the malignant aspersions of the criminal to give you any uneasiness. Depend upon it that they will be found of no weight. I have no doubt that your character in the judgment of every person that has heard them stands higher than ever. We feel for your misfortune in being obliged to hear such calumnies from a person who has injured you so grossly. But you must be considered in that respect as a martyr in the public cause. The purity of your motives and dispositions is beyond the reach of malice; and truth and equity will not fail to award to your calumniator infamy, and to you the love and approbation of mankind.

I have now told you, Williams, what I think of your case. But I have no right to assume to be your ultimate judge. Desperate as it appears to me, I will give you one piece of advice as if I were retained as a counsel to assist you. Leave out of it whatever tends to the disadvantage of Mr. Falkland. Defend yourself as well as you can, but do not attack your master. It is your business to create in those that hear you a prepossession in your favour. But the recrimination you have been now practising will always create indignation. Dishonesty will admit of some palliation. The deliberate malice you have now been showing is a thousand times more atrocious. It proves you to have the mind of a demon rather than a felon. Wherever you shall repeat it, those who hear you will pronounce you guilty upon that, even if the proper evidence against you were glaringly defective. If therefore you would consult your interest, which seems to be your only consideration, it is incumbent upon you by all means immediately to retract that. If you desire to be believed honest, you must in the first place show that you have a due sense of merit in others. You cannot better serve your cause than by begging pardon of your master, and doing homage to rectitude and worth even when they are employed in vengeance against you.

It is easy to conceive that my mind sustained an extreme shock from the decision of Mr. Forester; but his call upon me to retract and humble myself before my accuser penetrated my whole soul with indignation. I answered:

I have already told you I am innocent. I believe that I could not endure the effort of inventing a plausible defence, if it were otherwise. You have just affirmed that it is not in the power of ingenuity to subvert the distinctions of right and wrong, and in that very instant I find them subverted. This is indeed to me a very awful moment. New to the world, I know nothing of its affairs but what has reached me by rumour, or is recorded in books. I have come into it with all the ardour and confidence inseparable from my years. In every fellow being I expected to find a friend. I am unpractised in its wiles, and have even no acquaintance with its injustice. I have done nothing to deserve the animosity of mankind, but, if I may judge from the present scene, I am from henceforth to be deprived of the benefits of integrity and honour. I am to forfeit the friendship of every one I have hitherto known, and to be precluded from the power of acquiring that of others. I must therefore be reduced to derive my satisfaction from myself. Depend upon it I will not begin that career by dishonourable concessions. If I am to despair of the good will of other men, I will at least maintain the independence of my own mind. Mr. Falkland is my implacable enemy. Whatever may be his merits in other respects, he is acting towards me without humanity, without remorse and without principle. Do you think I will ever make any submissions to a man by whom I am thus treated, that I will fall down at the feet of one who is to me a devil, or kiss the hand that is red with my blood?

In that respect, answered Mr. Forester, do as you shall think proper. I must confess that your firmness and consistency astonish me. They add something to what I had conceived of human powers. Perhaps you have chosen the part which all things considered may serve your purpose best, though I think more moderation would be more conciliating. The exterior of innocence will, I grant, stagger the persons who may have the direction of your fate, but it will never be able to prevail against plain and incontrovertible facts. But I have done with you. I see in you a new instance of that abuse which is so generally made of talents the admiration of an undiscerning public. I regard you with horror. All that remains is that I should discharge my duty in consigning you as a monster of depravity to the justice of your country.

No, rejoined Mr. Falkland, to that I can never consent. I have put a restraint upon myself thus far, because it was right that evidence and enquiry should take their course. I have suppressed all my habits and sentiments, because it seemed due to the public that hypocrisy should be unmasked. But I can suffer this violence no longer. I have through my whole life interfered to protect, not overbear the sufferer; and I must do so now. I feel not the smallest resentment of his impotent attacks upon my character; I smile at their malice; and they make no diminution in my benevolence to their author. Let him say what he pleases; he cannot hurt me. It was proper that he should be brought to public shame, that other people might not be deceived by him as we have been. But there is no necessity for proceeding farther; and I must insist upon it that he be permitted to depart wherever he pleases. I am sorry that public interest affords so gloomy a prospect for his future happiness.

Mr. Falkland, answered Mr. Forester, these sentiments do honour to your humanity; but I must not give way to them. They only serve to set in a stronger light the venom of this serpent, this monster of ingratitude, who first robs his benefactor, and then reviles him. Wretch that you are, will nothing move you? Are you inaccessible to remorse? Are you not struck to the heart with the unmerited goodness of your master? Vile calumniator! you are the abhorrence of nature, the opprobrium of the human species, and the earth can only be freed from an insupportable burthen by your being exterminated! Recollect, sir, that this monster, at the very moment that you are exercising such unexampled forbearance in his behalf, has the presumption to charge you with prosecuting a crime of which you know him to be innocent, nay, with having conveyed the pretended stolen goods among his property for the express purpose of ruining him. By this unexampled villainy he makes it your duty to free the world from such a pest, and your interest to admit no relaxing in your pursuit of him, lest the world should be persuaded by your clemency to credit his vile insinuations.

I care not for consequences, replied Mr. Falkland, I will obey the dictates of my own mind. I will never lend my assistance to the reforming mankind by axes and gibbets; I am sure things will never be as they ought, till honour and not law be the dictator of mankind, till vice is taught to shrink before the resistless might of inborn dignity, and not before the cold formality of statutes. If my calumniator were worthy of my resentment I would chastise him with my own sword, and not that of the magistrate; but in the present case I smile at his malice, and resolve to spare him, as the generous lord of the forest spares the insect that would disturb his repose.

The language you now hold, said Mr. Forester, is that of romance, and not of reason. Yet I cannot but be struck with the contrast exhibited before me of the magnanimity of virtue and the obstinate, impenetrable injustice of guilt. While your mind overflows with goodness, nothing can touch the heart of this thrice bred villain. I shall never forgive myself for having once been entrapped by his detestable arts. This is no time for us to settle the question between chivalry and law. I shall therefore simply insist as a magistrate, having taken the evidence in this felony, upon my right and duty of following the course of justice, and committing the accused to the county jail.

After some farther contest Mr. Falkland, finding Mr. Forester obstinate and impracticable, withdrew his opposition. Accordingly a proper officer was summoned from the neighbouring village, a mittimus made out, and one of Mr. Falkland's carriages prepared to conduct me to the place of custody. It will easily be imagined that this sudden reverse was very painfully felt by me. I looked round on the servants who had been the spectators of my examination, but not one of them either by word or gesture expressed any compassion for my calamity. The robbery of which I was accused appeared to them atrocious from its magnitude, and whatever sparks of compassion might otherwise have sprung up in their ingenuous and undisciplined minds, were totally obliterated by indignation at my supposed profligacy in recriminating upon their worthy and excellent master. My fate being already determined, and one of the servants dispatched for the officer, Mr. Forester and Mr. Falkland withdrew, and left me in the custody of two others.

One of these was the son of a farmer at no great distance, who had been in habits of long established intimacy with my late father. I was willing accurately to discover the state of mind of those who had been witnesses of this scene and who had had some previous opportunity of observing my character and manners. I therefore endeavoured to open a conversation with him. Well, my good Thomas, said I, in a querulous tone and with a hesitating manner, am I not a most miserable creature?

Do not speak to me, master Williams! You have given me a shock that I shall not get the better of for one while. You were hatched by a hen, as the saying is, but you came of the spawn of a cockatrice. I am glad to my heart, that honest farmer Williams is dead, your villainy would else have made him curse the day that ever he was born.

Thomas, I am innocent! I swear by the great God that shall judge me another day, I am innocent!

Pray, do not swear! for goodness sake, do not swear! Your poor soul is damned enough without that. For your sake, lad, I will never take any body's word, nor trust to appearances, thof it should be an angel. Lord bless us! how smoothly you palavered it over, for all the world as if you had been as fair as a new-born babe. But it will not do; you will never be able to persuade people that black is white. For my own part I have done with you. I loved you yesterday, all one as if you had been my own brother. To-day I love you so well, that I would go ten miles with all the pleasure in life to see you hanged.

Good God! Thomas, have you the heart? What a change! I call God to witness I have done nothing to deserve it! What a world do we live in!

Hold your tongue, boy! It makes my very heart sick to hear you! I would not lie a night under the same roof with you for all the world! I should expect the house to fall and crush such wickedness! I admire that the earth does not open and swallow you alive! It is poison so much as to look at you! If you go on at this hardened rate, I believe from my soul that the people you talk to will tear you to pieces, and you will never live to come to the gallows. Oh, yes, you do well to pity yourself: poor, tender thing! that spit venom all round you like a toad, and leave the very ground upon which you crawl infected with your slime.

Finding the person with whom I talked thus impenetrable to all I could say, and considering that the advantage to be gained was but small even if I could overcome his prepossession, I took his advice and was silent. It was not much longer before every thing was prepared for my departure, and I was conducted to the same prison which had so lately inclosed the wretched and innocent Hawkinses. They too had been the victims of Mr. Falkland. He exhibited, upon a contracted scale indeed, but in which the truth of delineation was faithfully sustained, a copy of what monarchs are, who reckon among the instruments of their power prisons of state.

CHAPTER XI

FOR my own part I had never seen a prison, and like the majority of my brethren had given myself little concern to enquire what was the condition of those who committed offence against, or became obnoxious to suspicion from the community. Oh, how enviable is the most tottering shed under which the labourer retires to rest, compared with the residence of these walls!

To me every thing was new, the massy doors, the resounding locks, the gloomy passages, the grated windows, and the characteristic looks of the keepers, accustomed to reject every petition, and to steel their hearts against feeling and pity. Curiosity and a sense of my situation induced me to fix my eyes on the faces of these men, but in a few minutes I drew them away with unconquerable loathing. It is impossible to describe the sort of squalidness and filth with which these mansions are distinguished. I have seen dirty faces in dirty apartments, which have nevertheless borne the impression of health, and spoke carelessness and levity rather than distress. But the dirt of a prison speaks sadness to the heart, and appears to be already in a state of putridity and infection.

I was detained for more than an hour in the apartment of the keeper, one turnkey after another coming in, that they might make themselves familiar with my person. As I was already considered as guilty of felony to a considerable amount, I underwent a rigorous search, and they took from me a penknife, a pair of scissars and that part of my money which was in gold. It was debated whether or not these should be sealed up, to be returned to me, as they said, as soon as I should be acquitted; and had I not displayed an unexpected firmness of manner and vigour of expostulation, such was probably the conduct that would have been pursued. Having undergone these ceremonies, I was thrust into a day room in which all the persons then under confinement for felony were assembled, to the number of eleven. Each of them was too much engaged in his own reflections to take notice of me. Of these two were imprisoned for horse stealing, and three for having stolen a sheep, one for shop lifting, one for coining, two for highway robbery and two for burglary.

The horse stealers were engaged in a game at cards, which was presently interrupted by a difference of opinion, attended with great vociferation, they calling upon one and another to decide it to no purpose, one paying no attention to their summons, and another leaving them in the midst of their story, being no longer able to endure his own internal anguish in the midst of their mummery.

It is a custom among thieves to constitute a sort of mock tribunal of their own body, from whose decision every one is informed whether he shall be acquitted, respited or pardoned, as well as respecting the supposed most skilful way of conducting his defence. One of the housebreakers who had already passed this ordeal was stalking up and down the room with a forced bravery, exclaimed to his companion that he was as rich as the duke of Bedford himself. He had five guineas and a half, which was as much as he could possibly spend in the course of the ensuing month, and what happened after that it was Jack Ketch's[1] business to see to, not his. As he uttered these words he threw himself abruptly upon a bench that was near him, and seemed to be asleep in a moment. But his sleep was uneasy and disturbed, his breathing was hard, and at intervals had rather the nature of a groan. A young fellow from the other side of the room came softly to the place where he lay with a large knife in his hand, and pressed the back of it with such violence upon his neck, the head hanging over the side of the bench, that it was not till after several efforts that he was able to rise. Oh, Jack! cried this manual jester, I had almost done your business for you! The other expressed no marks of resentment, but sullenly answered, Damn you, why did not you take the edge? It would have been the best thing you have done this many a day*!

The case of one of the persons committed for highway robbery was not a little extraordinary. He was a common soldier, of a most engaging physiognomy, and two and twenty years of age. The prosecutor, who had been robbed one evening as he returned late from the alehouse, of the sum of three shillings, swore positively to his person. The character of the prisoner was such as has seldom been equalled. He had been ardent in the pursuit of intellectual cultivation; and was accustomed to draw his favourite amusement from the works of Virgil and Horace. The humbleness of his situation, combined with his ardour for literature, only served to give an inexpressible heightening to the interestingness of his character. He was plain and unaffected; he assumed nothing; he was capable, when occasion demanded, of firmness, but, in his ordinary deportment, he seemed unarmed and unresisting, unsuspicious of guile in others, as he was totally free from guile in himself. His integrity was proverbially great. In one instance he had been intrusted by a lady to convey a sum of a thousand pounds to a person at some miles distance: in another he was employed by a gentleman during his absence in the care of his house and furniture to the value of at least five times that sum. His habits of thinking were strictly his own, full of justice, simplicity, and wisdom. He from time to time earned money of his officers by his peculiar excellence in furbishing arms; but he declined offers that had been made him to become a serjeant or a corporal, saying, that he did not want money, and that in a new situation he should have less leisure for study. He was equally constant in refusing presents that were offered him by persons who had been struck with his merit: not that he was under the influence of false delicacy and pride, but that he had no inclination to accept that, the want

* An incident exactly similar to this, was witnessed by a friend of the author, a few years since, in a visit to the prison of Newgate.

of which he did not feel to be an evil. This man died while I was in prison. I received his last breath*.

The whole day I was obliged to spend in the company of these men, some of them having really committed the actions laid to their charge, others whom their ill fortune had rendered the victims of suspicion. The whole was a scene of misery such as nothing short of actual observation can suggest to the mind. Some were noisy and obstreperous, endeavouring by a false bravery to keep at bay the remembrance of their condition; while others, incapable even of this effort, had the torment of their thoughts aggravated by the perpetual noise and confusion that prevailed around them. In the faces of those who assumed the most courage you might trace the furrows of anxious care, and in the midst of their laboured hilarity dreadful ideas would ever and anon intrude, convulsing their features and working every line into an expression of the keenest agony. To these men the sun brought no return of joy. Day after day rolled on, but their state was immutable. Existence was to them a scene of invariable melancholy; every moment was a moment of anguish, yet did they wish to prolong that moment, fearful that the coming period would bring a severer fate. They thought of the past with insupportable repentance, each man contented to give his right hand, to have again the choice of that peace and liberty which he had unthinkingly bartered away. We talk of instruments of torture; Englishmen take credit to themselves for having banished the use of them from their happy shore! Alas, he that has observed the secrets of a prison, well knows that there is more torture in the lingering existence of a criminal, in the silent, intolerable minutes that he spends, than in the tangible misery of whips and racks!

Such were our days. At sun set our jailors appeared, and ordered each man to come away, and be locked into his dungeon. It was a bitter aggravation of our fate to be under the arbitrary control of these fellows. They felt no man's sorrow; they were of all men least capable of any sort of feeling. They had a barbarous and sullen pleasure in issuing their detested mandates, and observing the mournful reluctance with which they were obeyed. Whatever they directed, it was in vain to expostulate; fetters and bread and water were the sure consequences of resistance. Their tyranny had no

* A story extremely similar to this is to be found in the Newgate Calendar, Vol. I. p. 382.[1]

other limit than their own caprice; to whom shall the unfortunate felon appeal? To what purpose complain, when his complaints are sure to be received with incredulity? A tale of mutiny and necessary precaution is the unfailing refuge of the keeper, and this tale is an everlasting bar against redress.

Our dungeons were cells, $7\frac{1}{2}$ feet by $6\frac{1}{2}$, below the surface of the ground, damp, without window, light or air, except from a few holes worked for that purpose in the door. In some of these miserable receptacles three persons were put to sleep together*. I was fortunate enough to have one to myself. It was now the approach of winter. We were not allowed to have candles; and, as I have already said, were thrust in here at sun set and not liberated till the returning day. This was our situation for fourteen or fifteen hours out of the four and twenty. I had never been accustomed to sleep more than six or seven hours, and my inclination to sleep was now less than ever. Thus was I reduced to spend half my day in this dreary abode and in complete darkness. This was no trifling aggravation of my lot.

Among my melancholy reflections I tasked my memory, and counted over the doors, the locks, the bolts, the chains, the massy walls and grated windows that were between me and liberty. These, said I, are the engines that tyranny sits down in cold and serious meditation to invent. This is the empire that man exercises over man. Thus is a being, formed to expatiate, to act, to smile and enjoy, restricted and benumbed. How great must be his depravity or heedlessness who vindicates this scheme for changing health and gaiety and serenity, into the wanness of a dungeon and the deep furrows of agony and despair!

Thank God, exclaims the Englishman, we have no Bastille! Thank God, with us no man can be punished without a crime! Unthinking wretch! Is that a country of liberty where thousands languish in dungeons and fetters? Go, go, ignorant fool! and visit the scenes of our prisons! witness their unwholesomeness, their filth, the tyranny of their governors, the misery of their inmates! After that show me the man shameless enough to triumph, and say, England has no Bastille! Is there any charge so frivolous upon which men are not consigned to those detested abodes? Is there any villainy that is not practised by justices and prosecutors? But against all this, perhaps you have been told, there is redress. Yes,

* See Howard on Prisons.[1]

a redress, that it is the consummation of insult so much as to name! Where shall the poor wretch, reduced to the last despair, and to whom acquittal perhaps comes just time enough to save him from perishing,—where shall this man find leisure, and much less money, to see counsel and officers, and purchase the tedious, dear bought remedy of the law? No, he is too happy to leave his dungeon and the memory of his dungeon behind him; and the same tyranny and wanton oppression become the inheritance of his successor.

For myself I looked round upon my walls, and forward upon the premature death I had too much reason to expect; I consulted my own heart that whispered nothing but innocence; and I said, This is society. This is the object, the distribution of justice, which is the end of human reason. For this sages have toiled, and the midnight oil has been wasted. This!

The reader will forgive this digression from the immediate subject of my story. If it should be said, these are general remarks; let it be remembered that they are the dear bought result of experience. It is from the fulness of a bursting heart that reproach thus flows to my pen. These are not the declamations of a man desirous to be eloquent. I have felt the iron of slavery grating upon my soul.

I believed that misery, more pure than that which I now endured, had never fallen to the lot of a human being. I recollected with astonishment my puerile eagerness to be brought to the test and have my innocence examined. I execrated it as the vilest and most insufferable pedantry. I exclaimed in the bitterness of my heart, Of what value is a fair fame? It is the jewel of men formed to be amused with baubles. Without it I might have had serenity of heart and chearfulness of occupation, peace and liberty; why should I consign my happiness to other men's arbitration? But, if a fair fame were of the most inexpressible value, is this the method which common sense would prescribe to retrieve it? The language which these institutions hold out to the unfortunate is, Come, and be shut out from the light of day, be the associate of those whom society has marked out for her abhorrence, be the slave of jailers, be loaded with fetters; thus shall you be cleared from every unworthy asper-sion, and restored to reputation and honour! This is the consolation she affords to those whom malignity or folly, private pique or unfounded positiveness have without the smallest foundation loaded with calumny. For myself I felt my own innocence, and I soon found upon enquiry that three fourths of those who are regularly subjected to a similar treatment are persons whom even with all the superciliousness and precipitation of our courts of justice no evidence can be found sufficient to convict. How slender then must be that man's portion of information and discernment, who is willing to commit his character and welfare to such guardianship!

But my case was even worse than this. I intimately felt that a trial, such as our institutions have hitherto been able to make it, is only the worthy sequel of such a beginning. What chance was there, after the purgation I was now suffering, that I should come out acquitted at last? What probability was there that the trial I had endured in the house of Mr. Falkland was not just as fair as any that might be expected to follow? No, I anticipated my own condemnation.

Thus was I cut off for ever from all that existence has to bestow, from all the high hopes I had so often conceived, from all the future excellence my soul so much delighted to imagine, to spend a few weeks in a miserable prison, and then to perish by the hand of the public executioner.[1] No language can do justice to the indignant and soul-sickening loathing that these ideas excited. My resentment was not restricted to my prosecutor, but extended itself to the whole machine of society. I could never believe that all this was the fair result of institutions inseparable from the general good. I regarded the whole human species as so many hangmen and torturers. I considered them as confederated to tear me to pieces; and this wide scene of inexorable persecution inflicted upon me inexpressible agony. I looked on this side and on that; I was innocent; I had a right to expect assistance; but every heart was steeled against me; every hand was ready to lend its force to make my ruin secure. No man that has not felt in his own most momentous concerns justice, eternal truth, unalterable equity engaged in his behalf, and on the other side brute force, impenetrable obstinacy and unfeeling insolence, can imagine the sensations that then passed through my mind. I saw treachery triumphant and enthroned; I saw the sinews of innocence crumbled into dust by the gripe of almighty guilt.

What relief had I from these sensations? Was it relief that I spent the day in the midst of profligacy and execrations, that I saw reflected from every countenance agonies only inferior to my own? He that would form a lively idea of the regions of the damned,

need only to witness for six hours a scene to which I was confined
for many months. Not for one hour could I withdraw myself from
this complexity of horrors, or take refuge in the calmness of
meditation. Air, exercise, series, contrast, those grand enliveners
of the human frame, I was for ever debarred by the inexorable
tyranny under which I was fallen. Nor did I find the solitude of
my nightly dungeon less insupportable. Its only furniture was the
straw that served me for my repose. It was narrow, damp and
unwholesome. The slumbers of a mind, wearied like mine with
the most detestable uniformity, to whom neither amusement nor
occupation ever offered themselves to beguile the painful hours,
were short, disturbed and unrefreshing. My sleeping, still more
than my waking thoughts, were full of perplexity, deformity and
disorder. To these slumbers succeeded the hours which by the
regulations of our prison I was obliged though awake to spend in
solitary and chearless darkness. Here I had neither books, nor pens,
nor any thing upon which to engage my attention; all was a sight-
less blank. How was a mind, active and indefatigable like mine, to
endure this misery? I could not sink it in lethargy; I could not
forget my woes; they haunted me with unintermitted and demoniac
malice. Cruel, inexorable policy of human affairs, that condemns
a man to torture like this; that sanctions it and knows not what is
done under its sanction; that is too supine and unfeeling to enquire
into these petty details; that calls this the ordeal of innocence and
the protector of freedom! A thousand times I could have dashed
my brains against the walls of my dungeon; a thousand times I
longed for death, and wished with inexpressible ardour for an end
to what I suffered; a thousand times I meditated suicide, and
ruminated in the bitterness of my soul upon the different means of
escaping from the load of existence. What had I to do with life?
I had seen enough to make me regard it with detestation. Why
should I wait the lingering process of legal despotism, and not dare
so much as to die but when and how its instruments decreed? Still
some inexplicable suggestion withheld my hand. I clung with
desperate fondness to this shadow of existence, its mysterious
attractions and its hopeless prospects.

SUCH were the reflections that haunted the first days of my imprisonment, in consequence of which they were spent in perpetual anguish. But after a time nature, wearied with distress, would no longer stoop to the burthen; thought, which is incessantly varying, introduced a series of reflections totally different.

My fortitude revived. I had always been accustomed to chearfulness, good humour and serenity, and this habit now returned to visit me at the bottom of my dungeon. No sooner did my contemplations take this turn, than I saw the reasonableness and possibility of tranquillity and peace, and my mind whispered to me the propriety of showing in this forlorn condition that I was superior to all my persecutors. Blessed state of innocence and self approbation! The sunshine of conscious integrity pierced through all the barriers of my cell, and spoke ten thousand times more joy to my heart, than the accumulated splendours of nature and art can communicate to the slaves of vice.

I found out the secret of employing my mind. I said, I am shut up for half the day in total darkness without any external source of amusement; the other half I spend in the midst of noise, turbulence and confusion. What then? Can I not draw amusement from the stores of my own mind? Is it not freighted with various knowledge? Have I not been employed from my infancy in gratifying an insatiable curiosity? When should I derive benefit from these superior advantages, if not at present? Accordingly I tasked the stores of my memory and my powers of invention. I amused myself with recollecting the history of my life. By degrees I called to mind a number of minute circumstances which but for this exercise would have been for ever forgotten. I repassed in my thoughts whole conversations, I recollected their subjects, their arrangement, their incidents and frequently their very words. I mused upon these ideas till I was totally absorbed in thought. I repeated them till my mind glowed with enthusiasm. I had my different employments fitted for the solitude of the night in which I could give full scope to the impulses of my mind, and the uproar of the day in which my chief object was to be insensible to the disorder with which I was surrounded.

By degrees I quitted my own story, and employed myself with

imaginary adventures. I figured to myself every situation in which
I could be placed, and conceived the conduct to be observed in
each. Thus scenes of insult and danger, of tenderness and oppression became familiar to me. In fancy I often passed the awful hour
of dissolving nature. In some of my reveries I boiled with impetuous
indignation, and in others patiently collected the whole force of
my mind for some fearful encounter. I cultivated the powers of
oratory suited to these different states, and improved more in
eloquence in the solitude of my dungeon, than perhaps I should
have done in the busiest and most crowded scenes. At length
I proceeded to as regular a disposition of my time as the man in his
study who passes from mathematics to poetry, and from poetry to
the law of nations in the different parts of each single day; and I as
seldom infringed upon my plan. Nor were my subjects of disquisition less numerous than his. I went over, by the assistance of
memory only, a considerable part of Euclid during my confinement, and revived day after day the series of facts and incidents in
some of the most celebrated historians. I became myself a poet;
and while I described the sentiments cherished by the view of
natural objects, recorded the characters and passions of men, and
partook with a burning zeal in the generosity of their determina-
tions, I eluded the squalid solitude of my dungeon, and wandered
in idea through all the varieties of human society. I easily found
expedients, such as the mind seems always to require, and which
books and pens supply to the man at large, to record from time to
time the progress that had been made.

While I was thus employed I reflected with exultation upon the
degree in which man is independent of the smiles and frowns of
fortune. I was beyond her reach, for I could fall no lower. To an
ordinary eye I might seem destitute and miserable, but in reality
I wanted for nothing. My fare was coarse; but I was in health. My
dungeon was noisome; but I felt no inconvenience. I was shut up
from the usual means of exercise and air; but I found the method
of exercising myself even to perspiration in my dungeon. I had no
power of withdrawing my person from a disgustful society in the
most chearful and valuable part of the day; but I soon brought to
perfection the art of withdrawing my thoughts, and saw and heard
the people about me for just as short a time and as seldom as
I pleased.

Such is man in himself considered; so simple his nature; so few his wants. How different from the man of artificial society! Palaces are built for his reception, a thousand vehicles provided for his exercise, provinces are ransacked for the gratification of his appetite, and the whole world traversed to supply him with apparel and furniture. Thus vast is his expenditure, and the purchase slavery. He is dependent on a thousand accidents for tranquillity and health, and his body and soul are at the devotion of whoever will satisfy his imperious cravings.

In addition to the disadvantages of my present situation, I was reserved for an ignominious death. What then? Every man must die. No man knows how soon. It surely is not worse to encounter the king of terrors in health and with every advantage for the collection of fortitude, than to encounter him already half subdued by sickness and suffering. I was resolved at least fully to possess the days I had to live, and this is peculiarly in the power of the man who preserves his health to the last moment of his existence. Why should I suffer my mind to be invaded by unavailing regrets? Every sentiment of vanity, or rather of independence and justice within me, instigated me to say to my persecutor, You may cut off my existence, but you cannot disturb my serenity.

CHAPTER XIII

IN the midst of these reflections another thought, which had not before struck me, occurred to my mind. I exult, said I, and reasonably, over the impotence of my persecutor. Is not that impotence greater than I have yet imagined? I say, he may cut off my existence, but cannot disturb my serenity. It is true: my mind, the clearness of my spirit, the firmness of my temper, are beyond his reach; is not my life equally so, if I please? What are the material obstacles that man never subdued? What is the undertaking so arduous that by some has not been accomplished? And, if by others, why not by me? Had they stronger motives than I? Was existence more variously endeared to them, or had they more numerous methods by which to animate and adorn it? Many of those who have exerted most perseverance and intrepidity were obviously my inferiors in that respect. Why should not I be as daring as they? Adamant and steel have a ductility like water to a mind sufficiently bold and contemplative. The mind is master of itself; and is endowed with powers that might enable it to laugh at the tyrant's vigilance. I passed and repassed these ideas in my mind; and, heated with the contemplation, I said, No, I will not die!

My reading in early youth had been extremely miscellaneous. I had read of housebreakers to whom locks and bolts were a jest, and who, vain of their art, exhibited the experiment of entering a house the most strongly barricaded, with as little noise and almost as little trouble as other men would lift up a latch. There is nothing so interesting to the juvenile mind as the wonderful; there is no power that it so eagerly covets as that of astonishing spectators by its miraculous exertions. Mind appeared to my untutored reflections vague, airy and unfettered, the susceptible perceiver of reasons, but never intended by nature to be the slave of force. Why should it be in the power of man to overtake and hold me by violence? Why, when I chuse to withdraw myself, should I not be capable of eluding the most vigilant search? These limbs and this trunk are a cumbrous and unfortunate load for the power of thinking to drag along with it; but why should not the power of thinking be able to lighten the load till it shall be no longer felt?—These early modes of reflection were by no means indifferent to my present enquiries.

Our next-door neighbour at my father's house had been a carpenter. Fresh from the sort of reading I have mentioned, I was eager to examine his tools, their powers and their uses. This carpenter was a man of a strong and vigorous mind; and, his faculties having been chiefly confined to the range of his profession, he was fertile in experiments and ingenious in reasoning upon these particular topics. I therefore obtained from him considerable satisfaction; and, my mind being set in action, I sometimes even improved upon the hints he furnished. His conversation was particularly agreeable to me; I at first worked with him sometimes for my amusement, and afterwards occasionally for a short time as his journeyman. I was constitutionally vigorous; and by the experience thus attained I added to the abstract possession of power the skill of applying it, when I pleased, in such a manner as that no part should be inefficient.

It is a strange, but no uncommon feature in the human mind, that the very resource of which we stand in greatest need in a critical situation, though already accumulated it may be by preceding industry, fails to present itself at the time when it should be called into action. Thus my mind had passed through two very different stages since my imprisonment, before this means of liberation suggested itself. My faculties were overwhelmed in the first instance, and raised to a pitch of enthusiasm in the second, while in both I took it for granted in a manner that I must passively submit to the good pleasure of my persecutors.

During the period in which my mind had been thus undecided, and when I had been little more than a month in durance, the assizes, which were held twice a year in the town in which I was a prisoner, came on. Upon this occasion my case was not brought forward, but was suffered to stand over six months longer. It would have been just the same, if I had had as strong reason to expect acquittal, as I had conviction. If I had been apprehended upon the most frivolous reasons upon which any justice of the peace ever thought proper to commit a naked beggar for trial, I must still have waited about two hundred and seventeen days, before my innocence could be cleared. So imperfect are the effects of the boasted laws of a country whose legislators hold their assembly from four to six months in every year! I could never discover with certainty, whether this delay were owing to any interference on the part of my prosecutor, or whether it fell out in the regular administration of justice, which is too solemn and dignified to accommodate itself to the rights or benefit of an insignificant individual.

But this was not the only incident that occurred to me during my confinement for which I could find no satisfactory solution. It was nearly at the same time, that the keeper began to alter his behaviour to me. He sent for me one morning into the part of the building which was appropriated for his own use, and after some hesitation told me he was sorry my accommodations had been so indifferent, and asked whether I should like to have a chamber in his family? I was struck with the unexpectedness of this question, and desired to know whether any body had employed him to ask it. No, he replied; but, now the assizes were over, he had fewer felons on his hands, and more time to look about him: He believed I was a good kind of a young man; and he had taken a sort of a liking to me. I fixed my eye upon his countenance as he said this. I could discover none of the usual symptoms of kindness; he appeared to me to be acting a part, unnatural and that sat with aukwardness upon him. He went on however to offer me the liberty of eating at

his table, which, if I chose it, he said would make no difference to
him, and he should not think of charging me any thing for it. He
had always indeed as much upon his hands as one person could
see to; but his wife and his daughter Peggy would be woundily
pleased to hear a person of learning talk, as he understood I was;
and perhaps I might not feel myself unpleasantly circumstanced
in their company.

I reflected on this proposal, and had little doubt, notwithstanding
what the keeper had affirmed to the contrary, that it did not proceed from any spontaneous humanity in him, but that he had, to
speak the language of persons of his cast, good reasons for what he
did. I busied myself in conjectures as to who could be the author
of this sort of indulgence and attention. The two most likely persons
were Mr. Falkland and Mr. Forester. The latter I knew to be a man
austere and inexorable towards those whom he deemed vicious.
He piqued himself upon being insensible to those softer emotions,
which he believed answered no other purpose than to seduce us
from our duty. Mr. Falkland on the contrary was a man of the
acutest sensibility; hence arose his pleasures and his pains, his
virtues and his vices. Though he were the bitterest enemy to whom
I could possibly be exposed, and though no sentiments of humanity
could divert or control the bent of his mind, I yet persuaded
myself that he was more likely than his kinsman to visit in idea
the scene of my dungeon, and to feel impelled to alleviate my
sufferings.

This conjecture was by no means calculated to serve as balm to
my mind. My thoughts were full of irritation against my persecutor.
How could I think kindly of a man, in competition with the gratification of whose ruling passion my good name or my life was deemed
as of no consideration? I saw him crushing the one and bringing
the other into jeopardy with a quietness and composure on his
part, that I could not recollect without horror. I knew not what
were his plans respecting me. I knew not whether he troubled
himself so much as to form a barren wish for the preservation of
one, whose future prospects he had so iniquitously tarnished. I had
hitherto been silent as to my principal topic of recrimination. But
I was by no means certain that I should consent to go out of the
world in silence, the victim of this man's obduracy and art. In
every view I felt my heart ulcerated with a sense of his injustice;
and my very soul spurned these pitiful indulgences at a time that

he was grinding me into dust with the inexorableness of his vengeance.

I was influenced by these sentiments in my reply to the jailor; and I found a secret pleasure in pronouncing them in all their bitterness. I viewed him with a sarcastic smile, and said, I was glad to find him of a sudden become so humane: I was not however without some penetration as to the humanity of a jailor, and could guess at the circumstances by which it was produced. But he might tell his employer that his cares were fruitless; I would accept no favours from a man that held a halter about my neck, and had courage enough to endure the worst both in time to come and now.—The jailor looked at me with astonishment, and, turning upon his heel, exclaimed, Well done, my cock! You have not had your learning for nothing I see. You are set upon not dying dung-hil. But that is to come, lad: you had better by half keep your courage till you shall find it wanted.

The assizes, which passed over without influence to me, produced a great revolution among my fellow-prisoners. I lived long enough in the jail to witness a general mutation of its inhabitants. One of the housebreakers (the rival of the duke of Bedford) and the coiner were hanged. Two more were cast for transportation, and the rest acquitted. The transports remained with us; and, though the prison was thus lightened of nine of its inhabitants, there were, at the next half-yearly period of assizes, as many persons on the felons' side, within three, as I had found on my first arrival.

The soldier, whose story I have already recorded, died, on the evening of the very day on which the judges arrived, of a disease the consequence of his confinement. Such was the justice that resulted from the laws of his country to an individual who would have been the ornament of any age, one who of all the men I ever knew was perhaps the kindest, of the most feeling heart, of the most engaging and unaffected manners, and the most unblemished life. The name of this man was Brightwel. Were it possible for my pen to consecrate him to never dying fame, I could undertake no task more grateful to my heart. His judgment was penetrating and manly, totally unmixed with imbecility and confusion, while at the same time there was such an uncontending frankness in his countenance, that a superficial observer would have supposed he must have been the prey of the first plausible knavery that was practised against him. Great reason have I to remember him with affection! He was the most ardent, and I had almost said the last of my friends. Nor did I remain in this respect in his debt. There was indeed a great congeniality, if I may presume to say so, in our characters, except that I cannot pretend to rival the originality and self-created vigour of his mind, or to compare with, what the world has scarcely surpassed, the correctness and untainted purity of his conduct. He heard my story, as far as I thought proper to disclose it, with interest, he examined it with sincere impartiality, and, if at first any doubt remained upon his mind, a frequent observation of me in my most unguarded moments taught him in no long time to place an unreserved confidence in my innocence.

He talked of the injustice of which we were mutual victims without bitterness, and delighted to believe that the time would come when the possibility of such intolerable oppression would be extirpated. But this, he said, was a happiness reserved for posterity; it was too late for us to reap the benefit of it. It was some consolation to him that he could not tell the period in his past life which the best judgment of which he was capable would teach him to spend better. He could say, with as much reason as most men, he had discharged his duty. But he foresaw that he should not survive his present calamity. This was his prediction, while yet in health. He might be said in a certain sense to have a broken heart. But, if that phrase were in any way applicable to him, sure never was despair more calm, more full of resignation and serenity.

At no time in the whole course of my adventures was I exposed to a shock more severe than I received from this man's death. The circumstances of his fate presented themselves to my mind in their full complication of iniquity. From him and the execrations with which I loaded the government that could be the instrument of his tragedy, I turned to myself. I beheld the catastrophe of Brightwel with envy. A thousand times I longed that my corse had laid in death, instead of his. I was only reserved, as I persuaded myself, for unutterable woe. In a few days he would have been acquitted, his liberty, his reputation restored; mankind perhaps, struck with the injustice he had suffered, would have shown themselves eager to balance his misfortunes and obliterate his disgrace. But this man died; and I remained alive! I, who, though not less wrongfully treated than he, had no hope of reparation, must be marked as long as I lived for a villain, and in my death probably held up to the scorn and detestation of my species!

Such were some of the immediate reflections which the fate of this unfortunate martyr produced in my mind. Yet my intercourse with Brightwel was not in the review without its portion of comfort. I said, This man has seen through the veil of calumny that overshades me; he has understood, and has loved me. Why should I despair? May I not meet hereafter with men ingenuous like him, who shall do me justice and sympathise with my calamity? With that consolation I will be satisfied. I will rest in the arms of friendship, and forget the malignity of the world. Henceforth I will be contented with tranquil obscurity, with the cultivation of sentiment and wisdom, and the exercise of benevolence within a narrow circle. It was thus that my mind became excited to the project I was about to undertake.

I had no sooner meditated the idea of an escape, than I determined upon the following method of facilitating the preparations for it. I undertook to ingratiate myself with my keeper. In the world I have generally found such persons as had been acquainted with the outline of my story, regarding me with a sort of loathing and abhorrence, which made them avoid me with as much care as if I had been spotted with the plague. The idea of my having first robbed my patron, and then endeavouring to clear myself by charging him with subornation against me, placed me in a class distinct from and infinitely more guilty than that of common felons. But this man was too good a master of his profession to entertain aversion against a fellow creature upon such a score. He considered the persons committed to his custody merely as so many human bodies for whom he was responsible that they should be forthcoming in time and place; and the difference of innocence and guilt he looked down upon as an affair beneath his attention. I had not therefore the prejudices to encounter in recommending myself to him, that I have found so peculiarly obstinate in many other cases. Add to which, the same motive, whatever it was, that had made him so profuse in his offers a little before, had probably its influence on the present occasion.

I informed him of my skill in the profession of a joiner, and offered to make him half a dozen handsome chairs, if he would facilitate my obtaining the tools necessary for carrying on my profession in my present confinement; for, without his consent previously obtained, it would have been in vain for me to expect that I could quietly exert an industry of this kind, even if my existence had depended upon it. He looked at me first as asking himself what he was to understand by this novel proposal, and then, his countenance most graciously relaxing, said, he was glad I was come off a little of my high notions and my buckram, and he would see what he could do. Two days after he signified his compliance. He said that, as to the matter of the present I had offered him, he thought nothing of that, I might do as I pleased in it; but I might depend upon every civility from him that he could show with safety to himself, if so be as, when he was civil, I did not offer a second time for to snap and take him up short.

Having thus gained my preliminary, I gradually accumulated tools of various sorts, gimlets, piercers, chissels, *et cetera*. I immediately set myself to work. The nights were long, and the sordid eagerness of my keeper notwithstanding his ostentatious generosity was great; I therefore petitioned and was indulged with a bit of candle that I might amuse myself for an hour or two with my work after I was locked up in my dungeon. I did not however by any means apply constantly to the work I had undertaken, and my jailor betrayed various tokens of impatience. Perhaps he was afraid I should not have finished it before I was hanged. I however insisted upon working at my leisure as I pleased, and this he did not venture expressly to dispute. In addition to the advantages thus obtained, I procured secretly from miss Peggy, who now and then came into the jail to make her observations of the prisoners, and who seemed to have conceived some partiality for my person, the implement of an iron crow.

In these proceedings it is easy to trace the vice and duplicity that must be expected to grow out of injustice. I know not whether my readers will pardon the sinister advantage I extracted from the mysterious concessions of my keeper. But I must acknowledge my weakness in that respect; I am writing my adventures and not my apology; and I was not prepared to maintain the unvaried sincerity of my manners, at the expence of a speedy close of my existence.

My plan was now digested. I believed that by means of the crow I could easily and without much noise force the door of my dungeon from its hinges, or, if not, that I could, in case of necessity, cut away the lock. This door led into a narrow passage, bounded on one side by the range of dungeons, and on the other by the jailor's and turnkey's apartments, through which was the usual entrance from the street. This outlet I dared not attempt for fear of disturbing the persons close to whose very door I should in that case have found it necessary to pass. I determined therefore upon another door at the farther end of the passage, which was well barricaded, and which led to a sort of a garden in the occupation of the keeper. This garden I had never entered, but I had had an opportunity of observing it from the window of the felons' day room, which looked that way, the room itself being immediately over the range of dungeons. I perceived that it was bounded by a wall of considerable height, which I was told by my fellow prisoners was the extremity of the jail on that side, and beyond which was a back-lane of some length that terminated in the skirts of the town. Upon an accurate observation and much reflection upon the subject I found that I should be able, if once I got into the garden, with my gimlets and piercers inserted at proper distances to make a sort of ladder, by means of which I could clear the wall, and once more take possession of the sweets of liberty. I preferred this wall to that which immediately skirted my dungeon, on the other side of which was a populous street.

I suffered about two days to elapse from the period at which I had thoroughly digested my project, and then in the very middle of the night began to set about its execution. The first door was attended with considerable difficulty, but at length this obstacle was happily removed. The second door was fastened on the inside. I was therefore able with perfect ease to push back the bolts. But the lock, which of course was depended upon for the principal security, and was therefore strong, was double shot, and the key taken away. I endeavoured with my chissel to force back the bolt of the lock, but to no purpose. I then unscrewed the box of the lock; and, that being taken away, the door was no longer opposed to my wishes.

Thus far I had proceeded with the happiest success, but close on the other side of the door there was a kennel with a large mastiff dog, of which I had not the smallest previous knowledge. Though I stepped along in the most careful manner, this animal was disturbed, and began to bark. I was extremely disconcerted, but immediately applied myself to soothe the animal, in which I presently succeeded. I then returned along the passage to listen whether any body had been disturbed by the noise of the dog;

resolved, if that were the case, that I would return to my dungeon, and endeavour to replace every thing in its former state. But the whole appeared perfectly quiet, and I was encouraged to proceed in my operation.

I now got to the wall, and had nearly gained half the ascent, when I heard a voice at the garden door, crying, Hulloa! who is there? who opened the door? The man received no answer, and the night was too dark for him to distinguish objects at any distance. He therefore returned, as I judged, into the house for a light. Meantime the dog, understanding the key in which these interrogations were uttered, began barking again more violently than ever. I had now no possibility of retreat, and I was not without hopes that I might yet accomplish my object, and clear the wall. Meanwhile a second man came out, while the other was getting his lanthorn, and, by that time I had got to the top of the wall, was able to perceive me. He immediately set up a shout, and threw a large stone which grazed me in its flight. Alarmed at my situation, I was obliged to descend on the other side without taking the necessary precautions, and in my fall nearly dislocated my ancle.

There was a door in the wall, of which I was not previously apprised; and, this being opened, the two men with the lanthorn were on the other side in an instant. They had then nothing to do but to run along the lane to the place from which I had descended. I endeavoured to rise after my fall, but the pain was so intense that I was scarcely able to stand, and, after having limped a few paces, I twisted my foot under me, and fell down again. I had now no remedy, and quietly suffered myself to be retaken.

CHAPTER XIV

I WAS conducted to the keeper's room for that night, and the two men sat up with me. I was accosted with many interrogatories, to which I gave little answer, but complained of the hurt in my leg. To this I could obtain no reply except, Curse you, my lad! if that be all, we will give you some ointment for that; we will anoint it with a little cold iron. They were indeed excessively sulky with me, for having broken their night's rest and given them all this trouble. In the morning they were as good as their word, fixing a pair of fetters upon both my legs, regardless of the ancle which was now swelled to a considerable size, and then fastening me with a padlock to a staple in the floor of my dungeon. I expostulated with warmth upon this treatment, told them that I was a man upon whom the law had as yet passed no censure, and who therefore in the eye of the law was innocent. But they bid me keep such fudge for people who knew no better; that they knew what they did, and would answer it to any court in England.

The pain of the fetter was intolerable. I endeavoured in various ways to relieve it, and even privily to free my leg; but the more it was swelled, the more was this rendered impossible. I then resolved to bear it with patience; still the longer it continued, the worse it grew. After two days and two nights I intreated the turnkey to go and ask the surgeon who usually attended the prison to look at it, for, if it continued longer as it was, I was convinced it would mortify. But he glared surlily at me, and said, Damn my blood! I should like to see that day. To die of a mortification is too good an end for such a rascal! At the time that he thus addressed me, the whole mass of my blood was already severed by the anguish I had undergone, my patience was wholly exhausted, and I was silly enough to be irritated beyond bearing by his impertinence and vulgarity. Look you, Mr. turnkey, said I, there is one thing that such fellows as you are set over us for, and another thing that you are not. You are to take care we do not escape, but it is no part of your office to call us names and abuse us. If I were not chained to the floor, you dare as well eat your fingers as use such language; and, take my word for it, you shall yet live to repent of your insolence.

While I thus spoke, the man stared at me with astonishment. He was so little accustomed to such retorts that at first he could scarcely believe his ears; and such was the firmness of my manner that he seemed to forget for a moment that I was not at large. But, as soon as he had time to recollect himself, he did not deign even to be angry. His face relaxed into a smile of contempt, he snapped his fingers at me, and, turning upon his heel, exclaimed, Well said, my cock! Crow away! Have a care you do not burst! and, as he shut the door upon me, mimicked the voice of the animal he mentioned.

This rejoinder brought me to myself in a moment, and showed me the impotence of the resentment I was expressing. But, though he thus put an end to the violence of my speech, the torture of my body continued as great as ever. I was determined to change my mode of attack. The same turnkey returned in a few minutes; and, as he approached me to put down some food he had brought, I slipped a shilling into his hand, saying at the same time, My good fellow, for God's sake, go to the surgeon: I am sure you do not wish me to perish for want of assistance. The fellow put the shilling in his pocket, looked hard at me, and then with one nod of his head, and without uttering a single word, went away. The surgeon presently after made his appearance; and, finding the part in a high state of inflammation, ordered certain applications, and gave peremptory directions that the fetter should not be replaced upon that leg, till a cure had been effected. It was a full month before the leg was perfectly healed, and made equally strong and flexible with the other.

The condition in which I was now placed was totally different from that which had preceded this attempt. I was chained all day in my dungeon, with no other mitigation, except that the door was regularly opened for a few hours, at which time some of the prisoners occasionally came and spoke to me, particularly one, who, though he could ill replace my beloved Brightwel, was not deficient in excellent qualities. This was no other than the individual whom Mr. Falkland had some months before dismissed upon an accusation of murder. His courage was gone, his garb was squalid, and the comeliness and clearness of his countenance utterly obliterated. He was innocent, worthy, brave and benevolent. He was, I believe, afterwards acquitted, and turned loose to wander a desolate and perturbed spectre through the world. My manual labours were now at an end; my dungeon was searched every night, and every kind of tool carefully kept from me. The straw which had been hitherto allowed me was removed, under pretence that it was adapted for concealment; and the only conveniences with which I was indulged were a chair and a blanket.

A prospect of some alleviation in no long time opened upon me; but this my usual ill fortune rendered abortive. The keeper once more made his appearance, and with his former constitutional and ambiguous humanity. He pretended to be surprised at my want of every accommodation. He reprehended in strong terms my attempt to escape, and observed that there must be an end of civility from people in his situation, if gentlemen after all would not know when they were well. It was necessary in cases the like of this to let the law take its course, and it would be ridiculous in me to complain, if after a regular trial things should go hard with me. He was desirous of being in every respect my friend if I would let him.—In the midst of this circumlocution and preamble, he was called away from me for something relating to the business of his office. In the mean time I ruminated upon his overtures; and, detesting as I did the source from which I conceived them to flow, I could not help reflecting how far it would be possible to extract from them the means of escape.—But my meditations in this case were vain. The keeper returned no more during the remainder of that day, and on the next an incident occurred which put an end to all expectations from his kindness.

An active mind, which has once been forced into any particular train, can scarcely be persuaded to desert it as hopeless. I had studied my chains during the extreme anguish that I endured from the pressure of the fetter upon the ancle which had been sprained; and, though from the swelling and acute sensibility of the part I had found all attempts at relief in that instance impracticable, I obtained from the coolness of my investigation another and apparently superior advantage. During the night my dungeon was in a complete state of darkness; but, when the door was open the case was somewhat different. The passage indeed into which it opened was so narrow, and the opposite dead wall so near, that it was but a glimmering and melancholy light that entered my apartment, even at full noon, and when the door was at its widest extent. But my eyes, after a practice of two or three weeks, accommodated themselves to this circumstance, and I learned to distinguish the minutest objects. One day, as I was alternately meditating and examining the objects around me, I chanced to observe a nail trodden into the mud floor at no great distance from me. I immediately conceived the desire of possessing myself of this implement; but, for fear of surprise, people passing perpetually to and fro, I contented myself for the present with remarking its situation so accurately that I might easily find it again in the dark. Accordingly, as soon as my door was shut, I seized upon this new treasure, and having contrived to fashion it to my purpose, found that I could unlock with it the padlock that fastened me to the staple in the floor. This I regarded as no inconsiderable advantage, separately from the use I might derive from it in relation to my principal object. My chain permitted me to move only about eighteen inches to the right or left; and, having borne this confinement for several weeks, my very heart leaped at the pitiful consolation of being able to range without constraint, the miserable coop in which I was immured. This incident had occurred several days previously to the last visit of my keeper.

From this time it had been my constant practice to liberate myself every night, and not to replace things in their former situation, till I awoke in the morning, and expected shortly to perceive the entrance of the turnkey. Security breeds negligence. On the morning succeeding my conference with the jailor, it so happened, whether I overslept myself, or the turnkey went his round earlier than usual, that I was roused from my sleep by the noise he made in opening the cell next to my own; and, though I exerted the utmost diligence, yet having to grope for my materials in the dark, I was unable to fasten the chain to the staple, before he entered as usual with his lanthorn. He was extremely surprised to find me disengaged, and immediately summoned the principal keeper. I was questioned respecting my method of proceeding; and, as I believed concealment could lead to nothing but a severer search and a more accurate watch, I readily acquainted them with the exact truth. The illustrious personage whose function it was to control the inhabitants of these walls was by this last instance completely exasperated against me. Artifice and fair speaking were at an end. His eyes sparkling with fury, he exclaimed, that he was now convinced of the folly of showing kindness to rascals, the scum of the earth, such as I was; and, damn him, if any body should catch him at that again towards any one. I had cured him effectually! He was astonished that the laws had not provided some terrible retaliation for thieves that attempted to deceive their jailors. Hanging was a thousand times too good for me!

Having vented his indignation, he proceeded to give such orders as the united instigations of anger and alarm suggested to his mind. My apartment was changed. I was conducted to a room called the strong room, the door of which opened into the middle cell of the range of dungeons. It was underground as they were, and had also the day room for felons, already described, immediately over it. It was spacious and dreary. The door had not been opened for years; the air was putrid; and the walls hung round with damps and mildew. The fetters, the padlock and the staple were employed as in the former case, in addition to which they put on me a pair of hand cuffs. For my first provision the keeper sent me nothing but a bit of bread, mouldy and black, and some dirty and stinking water. I know not indeed whether this is to be regarded as gratuitous tyranny on the part of the jailor, the law having providently directed in certain cases, that the water to be administered to the prisoners, shall be taken from 'the next sink[1] or puddle nearest to the jail*.' It was farther ordered that one of the turnkeys should sleep in the cell that formed a sort of antichamber to my apartment. Though every convenience was provided to render this chamber fit for the reception of a personage of a dignity so superior to the felon he was appointed to guard, he expressed much dissatisfaction at the mandate: but there was no alternative.

The situation to which I was thus removed was apparently the most undesirable that could be imagined; but I was not discouraged. I had for some time learned not to judge by appearances. The apartment was dank and unwholesome; but I had acquired the secret of counteracting these influences. My door was kept continually shut, and the other prisoners were debarred access to me. But, if the intercourse of our fellow men has its pleasures, solitude on the other hand is not without its advantages. In solitude we can pursue our own thoughts undisturbed; and I was able to call up at will the most pleasing avocations. Beside which, to one who meditated such designs as now filled my mind, solitude had peculiar recommendations. I was scarcely left to myself before I tried an experiment the idea of which I conceived while they were fixing my hand cuffs; and, with my teeth only, disengaged myself from this restraint. The hours at which I was visited by the keepers were regular, and I took care to be provided for them. Add to which, I had a narrow grated window near the ceiling, about nine inches in perpendicular, and a foot and a half horizontally, which, though small, admitted a much stronger light, than that to which I had been accustomed for several weeks. Thus circumstanced, I scarcely ever found myself in total darkness, and was better provided against surprises, than I had been in my preceding situation. Such were the sentiments which this change of abode immediately suggested.

I had been a very little time removed, when I received an unexpected visit from Thomas, Mr. Falkland's footman, whom

* In the case of the *peine forte et dure*. See State Trials, Vol. I, *anno* 1615.[2]

I have already mentioned in the course of my narrative. A servant of Mr. Forester happened to come to the town where I was imprisoned, a few weeks before, while I was confined with the hurt in my ancle, and had called in to see me. The account he gave of what he observed had been the source of many an uneasy sensation to Thomas. The former visit was a matter of mere curiosity, but Thomas was of the better order of servants. He was considerably struck at the sight of me. Though my mind was now serene, and my health sufficiently good, yet the floridness of my complexion was gone, and there was a rudeness in my physiognomy, the consequence of hardship and fortitude, extremely unlike the sleekness of my better days. Thomas looked alternately in my face, at my hands and my feet; and then fetched a deep sigh. After a pause:

Lord bless us! said he, in a voice in which commiseration was sufficiently perceptible, is this you?

Why not, Thomas? You knew I was sent to prison, did not you?

Prison! and must people in prison be shackled and bound of that fashion?—And where do you lay of nights?

Here.

Here? Why there is no bed!

No, Thomas, I am not allowed a bed. I had straw formerly, but that is taken away.

And do they take off them there things of nights?

No; I am expected to sleep just as you see.

Sleep? Why I thought this was a Christian country; but this usage is too bad for a dog.

You must not say so, Thomas. It is what the wisdom of government has thought fit to provide.

Zounds, how I have been deceived! They told me what a fine thing it was to be an Englishman, and about liberty and property, and all that there; and I find it is all a flam. Lord, what fools we be! Things are done under our very noses, and we know nothing of the matter; and a parcel of fellows with grave faces swear to us that such things never happen but in France, and other countries the like of that. Why, you han't been tried, ha' you?

No.

And what signifies being tried, when they do worse than hang a man, and all beforehand? Well, master Williams, you have been very wicked to be sure, and I thought it would have done me good to see you hanged. But, I do not know how it is, one's heart melts, and pity comes over one, if we take time to cool. I know that ought not to be; but, damn it, when I talked of your being hanged, I did not think of your suffering all this into the bargain.

Soon after this conversation Thomas left me. The idea of the long connexion of our families rushed upon his memory, and he felt more for my sufferings at the moment than I did for myself. In the afternoon I was surprised to see him again. He said, that he could not get the thought of me out of his mind, and therefore he hoped I would not be displeased at his coming once more to take leave of me. I could perceive that he had something upon his mind, which he did not know how to discharge. One of the turnkeys had each time come into the room with him, and continued as long as he staid. Upon some avocation however, a noise I believe in the passage, the turnkey went as far as the door to satisfy his curiosity; and Thomas, watching the opportunity, slipt into my hand a chissel, a file and a saw, exclaiming at the same time with a sorrowful tone, I know I am doing wrong; but, if they hang me too, I cannot help it: I cannot do no other. For Christ's sake, get out of this place; I cannot bear the thoughts of it!—I received the implements with great joy, and thrust them into my bosom; and, as soon as he was gone, concealed them in the rushes of my chair. For himself he had accomplished the object for which he came, and presently after bade me farewell.

The next day the keepers, I know not for what reason, were more than usually industrious in their search, saying, though without assigning any ground for their suspicion, that they were sure I had some tool in my possession that I ought not; but the depository I had chosen escaped them.

I waited from this time the greater part of a week that I might have the benefit of a bright moon light. It was necessary that I should work in the night; it was necessary that my operations should be performed between the last visit of the keepers at night and their first in the morning, that is, between nine in the evening and seven. In my dungeon, as I have already said, I passed fourteen or fifteen hours of the four and twenty undisturbed; but, since I had acquired a character for mechanical ingenuity, a particular exception with respect to me was made from the general rules of the prison.

It was ten o'clock when I entered on my undertaking. The room in which I was confined was secured with a double door. This was totally superfluous for the purpose of my detention, since there was a centinel planted on the outside. But it was very fortunate for my plan, because these doors prevented the easy communication of sound, and afforded me tolerable satisfaction that with a little care in my mode of proceeding I might be secure against the danger of being overheard. I first took off my hand cuffs. I then filed through my fetters; and next performed the same service to three of the iron bars that secured my window, to which I climbed partly by the assistance of my chair and partly by means of certain irregularities in the wall. All this was the work of more than two hours. When the bars were filed through, I easily forced them a little from the perpendicular, and then drew them one by one out of the wall, into which they were sunk about three inches, perfectly strait, and without any precaution to prevent their being removed. But the space thus obtained was by no means wide enough to admit the passing of my body. I therefore applied myself partly with my chissel, and partly with one of the iron bars, to the loosening the brick work; and, when I had thus disengaged four or five bricks, I got down, and piled them upon the floor. This operation I repeated three or four times. The space was now sufficient for my purpose, and, having crept through the opening, I stepped upon a sort of shed on the outside.

I was now in a kind of rude area between two dead walls, that south of the felons' day room the windows of which were at the east end, and the wall of the prison. But I had not, as formerly, any instruments to assist me in scaling the wall which was of a considerable height. There was of consequence no resource for me but that of effecting a practicable breach in the lower part of the wall, which was of no contemptible strength, being of stone on the outside, with a facing of brick within. The rooms for the debtors were at right angles with the building from which I had just escaped; and, as the night was extremely bright, I was in momentary danger, particularly in case of the least noise, of being discovered by them, several of their windows commanding the area. Thus circumstanced, I determined to make the shed answer the purpose of concealment. It was locked; but, with the broken link of my fetters, which I had had the precaution to bring with me, I found no great difficulty in opening the lock. I had now got a sufficient means of hiding my person while I proceeded in my work, attended with no other disadvantage than that of being obliged to leave the door through which I had thus broken, a little open for the sake of light. After some time I had removed a considerable part of the brick work of the outer wall; but, when I came to the stone, I found the undertaking infinitely more difficult. The mortar, which bound together the building, was by length of time nearly petrified, and appeared to my first efforts one solid rock of the hardest adamant. I had now been six hours incessantly engaged in incredible labour; my chissel broke in the first attempt upon this new obstacle, and, between fatigue already endured, and the seemingly invincible difficulty before me, I concluded that I must remain where I was, and gave up the idea of further effort as useless. At the same time the moon, whose light had till now been of the greatest use to me, set, and I was left in total darkness. After a respite of ten minutes however, I returned to the attack with new vigour. It could not be less than two hours before the first stone was loosened from the edifice. In one hour more the space was sufficient to admit of my escape. The pile of bricks I had left in the strong room was considerable. But it was a mole hill compared with the ruins I had forced from the outer wall. I am fully assured that the work I had thus performed would have been to a common labourer with every advantage of tools the business of two or three days.

But my difficulties, instead of being ended, seemed to be only begun. The day broke before I had completed the opening, and in ten minutes more the keepers would probably enter my apartment, and perceive the devastation I had left. The lane, which connected the side of the prison through which I had escaped with the adjacent country, was formed chiefly by two dead walls, with here and there a stable, a few warehouses and some mean habitations tenanted by the lower order of people. My best security lay in clearing the town as soon as possible, and depending upon the open country for protection. My arms were intolerably swelled and bruised with my labour, and my strength seemed wholly exhausted with fatigue. Speed I was nearly unable to exert for any continuance; and, if I could, with the enemy so close at my heels, speed would too probably have been useless. It appeared as if I were now in almost the same situation as that in which I had been placed five or six weeks before, in which after having completed my escape I was obliged to yield myself up without resistance to my pursuers. I was not however disabled as then; I was capable of exertion to what precise extent I could not ascertain; and I was well aware that every instance in which I should fail of my purpose would contribute to enhance the difficulty of any future attempt. Such were the considerations that presented themselves in relation to my escape; and, even if that were effected, I had to reckon among my difficulties that, at the time I quitted my prison, I was destitute of every resource, and had not a shilling remaining in the world.

END OF VOLUME II

VOLUME III

CHAPTER I

I PASSED along the lane I have described without perceiving or being observed by a human being. The doors were shut, the window-shutters closed, and all was still as night. I reached the extremity of the lane unmolested. My pursuers, if they immediately followed, would know that the likelihood was small of my having in the interval found shelter in this place; and would proceed without hesitation, as I on my part was obliged to do, from the end nearest to the prison to its farthest termination.

The face of the country, in the spot to which I had thus opened myself a passage, was rude and uncultivated. It was overgrown with brushwood and furze; the soil was for the most part of a loose sand; and the surface extremely irregular. I climbed a small eminence, and could perceive not very remote in the distance a few cottages thinly scattered. This prospect did not altogether please me; I conceived that my safety would for the present be extremely assisted by keeping myself from the view of any human being.

I therefore came down again into the valley, and upon a careful examination perceived that it was interspersed with cavities, some deeper than others, but all of them so shallow as neither to be capable of hiding a man, nor of exciting suspicion as places of possible concealment. Meanwhile the day had but just begun to dawn; the morning was lowering and drizzly; and, though the depth of these caverns was of course well known to the neighbouring inhabitants, the shadows they cast were so black and impenetrable as might well have produced wider expectations in the mind of a stranger. Poor therefore as was the protection they were able to afford, I thought it right to have recourse to it for the moment as the best the emergency would supply. It was for my life; and, the greater was the jeopardy to which it was exposed, the more dear did that life seem to become to my affections. The recess I chose as most secure was within little more than a hundred yards of the end of the lane and the extreme buildings of the town.

I had not stood up in this manner two minutes, before I heard the sound of feet, and presently saw the ordinary turnkey and another pass by the place of my retreat. They were so close to me that, if I had stretched out my hand, I believe I could have caught hold of their clothes without so much as changing my posture. As no part of the overhanging earth intervened between me and them, I could see them entire, though the deepness of the shade rendered me almost completely invisible. I heard them say to each other, in tones of vehement asperity, Curse the rascal! which way can he be gone? The reply was, Damn him! I wish we had him but safe once again! Never fear! rejoined the first, he cannot have above half a mile the start of us. They were presently out of hearing; for, as to sight, I dared not advance my body so much as an inch to look after them, lest I should be discovered by my pursuers in some other direction. From the very short time that elapsed between my escape and the appearance of these men I concluded that they had made their way through the same outlet as I had done, it being impossible that they could have had time to come from the gate of the prison and so round a considerable part of the town, as they must otherwise have done.

I was so alarmed at this instance of diligence on the part of the enemy, that for some time I scarcely ventured to proceed an inch from my place of concealment, or almost to change my posture. The morning, which had been bleak and drizzly, was succeeded by a day of heavy and incessant rain; and the gloomy state of the air and surrounding objects, together with the extreme nearness of my prison, and a total want of food, caused me to pass the hours in no very agreeable sensations. This inclemency of the weather however, which generated a feeling of stilness and solitude, encouraged me by degrees to change my retreat, for another of the same nature, but of somewhat greater security. I hovered with little variation about a single spot as long as the sun continued above the horizon.

Towards evening the clouds began to disperse, and the moon shone, as on the preceding night, in full brightness. I had perceived no human creature during the whole day, except in the instance already mentioned. This had perhaps been owing to the nature of the day; at all events I considered it as too hazardous an experiment to venture from my hiding place in so clear and fine a night. I was therefore obliged to wait for the setting of this luminary, which was not till near five o'clock in the morning. My only relief during this interval was to allow myself to sink to the bottom of my cavern, it being scarcely possible for me to continue any longer on my feet. Here I fell into an interrupted and unrefreshing doze, the consequence of a laborious night and a tedious, melancholy day; though I rather sought to avoid sleep, which, co-operating with the coldness of the season, would tend more to injury than advantage.

The period of darkness which I had determined to use for the purpose of removing to a greater distance from my prison was in its whole duration something less than three hours. When I rose from my seat, I was weak with hunger and fatigue, and, which was worse, I seemed between the dampness of the preceding day, and the sharp, clear frost of the night, to have lost the command of my limbs. I stood up and shook myself; I leaned against the side of the hill, impelling in different directions the muscles of the extremities; and at length recovered in some degree the sense of feeling. This operation was attended with an incredible aching pain, and required no common share of resolution to encounter and prosecute it. Having quitted my retreat, I at first advanced with weak and tottering steps; but, as I proceeded, increased my pace. The barren heath which reached to the edge of the town was at least on this side without a path; but the stars shone, and guiding myself by them I determined to steer as far as possible from the hateful scene where I had been so long confined. The line I pursued was of irregular surface, sometimes obliging me to climb a steep ascent, and at others to go down into a dark and impenetrable dell. I was often compelled by the dangerousness of the way to deviate considerably from the direction I wished to pursue. In the mean time I advanced with as much rapidity, as these and similar obstacles would permit me to do. The swiftness of the motion and the thinness of the air restored to me my alacrity. I forgot the inconveniences under which I laboured, and my mind became lively, spirited and enthusiastic.

I had now reached the border of the heath and entered upon what is usually termed the forest. Strange as it may seem, it is nevertheless true, that, in this conjecture, exhausted with hunger, destitute of

all provision for the future, and surrounded with the most alarming
dangers, my mind suddenly became glowing, animated and chearful. I thought that by this time the most formidable difficulties of
my undertaking were surmounted; and I could not believe that,
after having effected so much, I should find any thing invincible in
what remained to be done. I recollected the confinement I had
undergone and the fate that had impended over me with horror.
Never did man feel more vividly than I felt at that moment the
sweets of liberty. Never did man more strenuously prefer poverty
with independence to the artificial allurements of a life of slavery.
I stretched forth my arms with rapture, I clapped my hands one
upon the other, and exclaimed, Ah, this is indeed to be a man!
These wrists were lately galled with fetters; all my motions,
whether I rose up or sat down, were echoed to with the clanking of
chains; I was tied down like a wild beast, and could not move but
in a circle of a few feet in circumference. Now I can run, fleet as a
greyhound; and leap like a young roe upon the mountains. Oh,
God! (if God there be, that condescends to record the lonely
beatings of an anxious heart) thou only canst tell with what delight
a prisoner, just broke forth from his dungeon, hugs the blessings
of new found liberty! Sacred and indescribable moment, when man
regains his rights! But lately I held my life in jeopardy, because one
man was unprincipled enough to assert what he knew to be false;
I was destined to suffer an early and inexorable death from the
hands of others, because none of them had penetration enough to
distinguish from falshood what I uttered with the entire conviction
of a full fraught heart! Strange, that men from age to age should
consent to hold their lives at the breath of another, merely that
each in his turn may have a power of acting the tyrant according to
law! Oh, God! give me poverty! shower upon me all the imaginary
hardships of human life! I will receive them all with thankfulness.
Turn me a prey to the wild beasts of the desert, so I be never again
the victim of man dressed in the gore-dripping robes of authority!
Suffer me at least to call life and the pursuits of life my own! Let
me hold it at the mercy of elements, of the hunger of beasts or the
revenge of barbarians, but not of the cold blooded prudence of
monopolists and kings!——How enviable was the enthusiasm
which could thus furnish me with energy, in the midst of hunger,
poverty and universal desertion!

I had now walked at least six miles. At first I carefully avoided the habitations that lay in my way, and feared to be seen by any of the persons to whom they belonged, lest it should in any degree furnish a clue to the researches of my pursuers. As I went forward, I conceived it might be proper to relax a part of my precaution. At this time I perceived several persons coming out of a thicket close to me. I immediately considered this circumstance as rather favourable than the contrary. It was necessary for me to avoid entering any of the towns and villages in the vicinity. It was however full time that I should procure for myself some species of refreshment; and by no means improbable that these men might be in some way assisting to me in that respect. In my situation it appeared to me indifferent what might be their employment or profession. I had little to apprehend from thieves, and I believed that they, as well as honest men, could not fail to have some compassion for a person under my circumstances. I therefore rather threw myself in their way than avoided them.

They were thieves. One of the company cried out, Who goes there? stand! I accosted them. Gentlemen, said I, I am a poor traveller, almost——While I spoke, they came round me, and he that had first hailed me said, Damn me, tip us none of your palaver; we have heard that story of a poor traveller any time these five years. Come, down with your dust! let us see what you have got! Sir, I replied, I have not a shilling in the world, and am more than half starved beside. Not a shilling! answered my assailant, what, I suppose you are as poor as a thief? But, if you have not money, you have clothes, and those you must resign.

My clothes! rejoined I with indignation, you cannot desire such a thing. Is it not enough that I am pennyless? I have been all night upon the open heath. It is now the second day that I have not eaten a morsel of bread. Would you strip me naked to the weather in the midst of this depopulated forest? No, no, you are men! The same hatred of oppression that arms you against the insolence of wealth, will teach you to relieve those who are perishing like me. For God's sake, give me food! do not strip me of the benefits I still possess!

While I uttered this apostrophe, the unpremeditated eloquence of sentiment, I could perceive by their gestures, though the day had not yet begun to dawn, that the feelings of one or two of the company appeared to take my part. The man, who had already undertaken to be their spokesman, perceived the same thing; and excited either by the brutality of his temper or the love of command,

hastened to anticipate the disgrace of a defeat. He brushed suddenly
up to me, and by main force pushed me several feet from the place
where I stood. The shock I received drove me upon a second of the
gang, not one of those who had listened to my expostulation; and
he repeated the same brutality. My indignation was strongly
excited by this treatment; and, after being thrust backward and
forward two or three times in this manner, I broke through my
assailants, and turned round to defend myself. The first that
advanced within my reach was my original enemy. In the present
moment I listened to nothing but the dictates of passion, and I laid
him at his length on the earth. I was immediately assailed with
sticks and bludgeons on all sides, and presently received a blow
that almost deprived me of my senses. The man I had knocked
down was now upon his feet again, and aimed a stroke at me with
a cutlass as I fell, which took place in a deep wound upon my neck
and shoulder. He was going to repeat his blow. The two who had
seemed to waver at first in their animosity, afterwards appeared to
me to join in the attack, urged either by animal sympathy or the
spirit of imitation. One of them however, as I afterwards understood, seized the arm of the man who was going to strike me a
second time with his cutlass, and who would otherwise probably
have put an end to my existence. I could hear the words, Damn it,
enough, enough! that is too bad, Gines! How so? replied a second
voice; he will but pine here upon the forest, and die by inches: it
will be an act of charity to put him out of his pain.—It will be
imagined that I was not uninterested in this sort of debate. I made
an effort to speak; my voice failed me. I stretched out one hand
with a gesture of intreaty. You shall not strike, by God! said one
of the voices; why should we be murderers?—The side of forbearance at length prevailed. They therefore contented themselves
with stripping me of my coat and waistcoat, and rolling me into a
dry ditch. They then left me, totally regardless of my distressed
condition, and the plentiful effusion of blood which streamed from
my wound.

IN this woful situation, though extremely weak, I was not deprived of sense. I tore my shirt from my naked body, and with it endeavoured with some success to make a bandage to stanch the flowing of the blood. I then exerted myself to crawl up the side of the ditch. I had scarcely effected the latter, when with equal surprise and joy I perceived a man advancing at no great distance. I called for help as well as I could. The man came towards me with evident signs of compassion, and the appearance I exhibited was indeed sufficiently calculated to excite it. I had no hat. My hair was disheveled, and the ends of the locks clotted with blood. My shirt was wrapped about my neck and shoulder, and was plentifully stained with red. My body which was naked to my middle was variegated with streams of blood, nor had my lower garments which were white by any means escaped.

For God's sake, my poor fellow! said he, with a tone of the greatest imaginable kindness, how came you thus? And, saying this, he lifted me up, and set me on my feet. Can you stand? added he doubtfully. Oh, yes, very well, I replied. Having received this answer, he quitted me, and began to take off his own coat, that he might cover me from the cold. I had however overrated my strength, and was no sooner left to myself, than I reeled, and fell almost at my length upon the ground. But I broke my fall by stretching out my sound arm, and again raised myself upon my knees. My benefactor now covered me, raised me, and bidding me lean upon him told me he would presently conduct me to a place where I should be taken care of. Courage is a capricious property; and, though while I had no one to depend upon but myself, I possessed a mine of seemingly inexhaustible fortitude, yet no sooner did I find this unexpected sympathy on the part of another, than my resolution appeared to give way, and I felt ready to faint. My charitable conductor perceived this, and every now and then encouraged me in a manner so chearful, so good humoured and benevolent, equally free from the torture of droning expostulation, and the weakness of indulgence, that I thought myself under the conduct of an angel rather than a man. I could perceive that his behaviour had in it nothing of boorishness, and that he was thoroughly imbued with the principles of affectionate civility.

We walked about three quarters of a mile, and that not towards the open, but the most uncouth and unfrequented part of the forest. We crossed a place which had once been a moat, but which was now in some parts dry and in others contained a little muddy and stagnated water. Within the inclosure of this moat, I could only discover a pile of ruins, and several walls, the upper part of which seemed to overhang their foundations, and to totter to their ruin. After having entered however with my conductor through an arch-way, and passed along a winding passage that was perfectly dark, we came to a stand.

At the upper end of this passage was a door which I was unable to perceive. My conductor knocked at the door, and was answered by a voice from within, which for body and force might have been the voice of a man, but with a sort of female sharpness and acidity, enquiring, Who is there? Satisfaction was no sooner given on this point, than I heard two bolts pushed back and the door unlocked. The apartment opened, and we entered. The interior of this habitation by no means corresponded with the appearance of my protector, but on the contrary wore a face of discomfort, carelessness and dirt. The only person I saw within was a woman, rather advanced in life, and whose appearance had I know not what of extraordinary and loathsome. Her eyes were red and blood-shot; her hair was pendent in matted and shaggy tresses about her shoulders; her complexion swarthy, and of the consistency of parchment; her form spare, and her whole body, her arms in particular, uncommonly vigorous and muscular. Not the milk of human kindness, but the feverous blood of savage ferocity seemed to flow from her heart; and her whole figure suggested an idea of unmitigable energy and an appetite gorged in malevolence. This infernal Thalestris[1] had no sooner cast her eyes upon us as we entered, than she exclaimed in a discordant and discontented voice, What have we got here? this is not one of our people! My conductor, without answering this apostrophe, bade her push an easy chair which stood in one corner, and set it directly before the fire. This she did with apparent reluctance, muttering, Ah, you are at your old tricks; I wonder what such folks as we have to do with charity! It will be the ruin of us at last, I can see that! Hold your tongue, beldam! said he, with a stern significance of manner, and fetch one of my best shirts, a waistcoat and some dressings. Saying this, he at the same time put into her hand a small bunch of keys. In a word, he treated me with as much kindness as if he had been my father. He examined my wound, washed and dressed it; at the same time that the old woman by his express order prepared for me such nourishment as he thought most suitable to my weak and languid condition.

These operations were no sooner completed, than my benefactor recommended to me to retire to rest, and preparations were making for that purpose, when suddenly a trampling of feet was heard, succeeded by a knock at the door. The old woman opened the door with the same precautions as had been employed upon our arrival, and immediately six or seven persons tumultuously entered the apartment. Their appearance was different, some having the air of mere rustics, and others that of a tarnished sort of gentry. All had a feature of boldness, inquietude and disorder, extremely unlike any thing I had before observed in such a groupe. But my astonishment was still increased, when upon a second glance I perceived something in the general air of several of them, and of one in particular, that persuaded me they were the gang from which I had just escaped, and this one the antagonist by whose animosity I was so near having been finally destroyed. I imagined they had entered our hovel with a hostile intention, that my benefactor was upon the point of being robbed, and I probably murdered.

This suspicion however was soon removed. They addressed my conductor with respect under the appellation of captain. They were boisterous and noisy in their remarks and exclamations, but their turbulence was tempered by a certain deference to his opinion and authority. I could observe in the person who had been my active opponent some aukwardness and irresolution as he first perceived me, which he dismissed with a sort of effort, exclaiming, Who the devil is here? There was something in the tone of this apostrophe that roused the attention of my protector. He looked at the speaker with a fixed and penetrating glance, and then said, Nay, Gines, do you know? Did you ever see the person before? Curse it, Gines! interrupted a third, you are damnably out of luck. They say dead men walk, and you see there is some truth in it. Truce with your impertinence, Jeckols! replied my protector, this is no proper occasion for a joke. Answer me, Gines, were you the cause of this young man being left naked and wounded this bitter morning upon the forest?

Mayhap I was. What then?

What provocation could induce you to so cruel a treatment?
Provocation enough. He had no money.

What, did you use him thus without so much as being irritated
by any resistance on his part?

Yes, he did resist. I only hustled him; and he had the impudence
to strike me.

Gines! you are an incorrigible fellow.

Pooh, what signifies what I am? You with your compassion and
your fine feelings will bring us all to the gallows.

I have nothing to say to you; I have no hopes of you! Comrades,
it is for you to decide upon the conduct of this man as you think
proper. You know how repeated his offences have been; you know
what pains I have taken to mend him. Our profession is the profession of justice. [It is thus that the prejudices of men universally
teach them to colour the most desperate cause, to which they have
determined to adhere.] We, who are thieves without a licence, are
at open war with another set of men, who are thieves according to
law.—A thief is of course a man living among his equals; I do not
pretend therefore to assume any authority among you; act as you
think proper; but, so far as relates to myself, I vote that Gines be
expelled from among us as a disgrace to our society.

This proposition seemed to meet the general sense. It was easy
to perceive that the opinion of the rest coincided with that of their
leader; notwithstanding which a few of them hesitated as to the
conduct to be pursued. In the mean time Gines muttered something
in a surly and irresolute way about taking care how they provoked
him. This insinuation instantly roused the courage of my protector,
and his eyes flashed with contempt.

Rascal! said he, do you menace us? Do you think we will be your
slaves? No, no, do your worst! Go to the next justice of the peace
and impeach us; I can easily believe you are capable of it. Sir, when
we entered into this gang, we were not such fools as not to know
that we entered upon a service of danger. One of its dangers consists in the treachery of fellows like you. But we did not enter at
first, to flinch now. Did you believe that we would live in hourly
fear of you, tremble at your threats, and compromise, whenever
you should so please, with your insolence? That would be a blessed
life indeed! I would rather see my flesh torn piecemeal from my
bones! Go, sir! I defy you! You dare not do it! You dare not
sacrifice these gallant fellows to your rage, and publish yourself

to all the world a traitor and a scoundrel! If you do, you will punish yourself, not us! Begone!

The intrepidity of the leader communicated itself to the rest of the company. Gines easily saw that there was no hope of bringing them over to a contrary sentiment. After a short pause, he answered, I did not mean—No, damn it! I will not snivel neither. I was always true to my principles and a friend to you all. But, since you are resolved to turn me out, why,—good bye to you!

The expulsion of this man produced a remarkable improvement in the whole gang. Those who were before inclined to humanity assumed new energy in proportion as they saw such sentiments likely to prevail. They had before suffered themselves to be overborne by the boisterous insolence of their antagonists; but now they adopted and with success a different conduct. Those who envied the ascendancy of their comrade and therefore imitated his conduct began to hesitate in their career. Stories were brought forward of the cruelty and brutality of Gines both to men and animals which had never before reached the ear of the leader. These stories I shall not repeat. They could excite only emotions of abhorrence and disgust, and some of them argued a mind of such a stretch of depravity as to many readers would appear utterly incredible. And yet this man had his virtues. He was enterprising, persevering and faithful.

His removal was a considerable benefit to me. It would have been no small hardship to have been turned adrift immediately under my unfavourable circumstances, with the additional disadvantage of the wound I had received; and yet I could scarcely have ventured to remain under the same roof with a man to whom my appearance was as a guilty conscience, perpetually reminding him of his own offence and the counteraction of his leader. His profession accustomed him to a certain degree of indifference to consequences and indulgence to the sallies of passion, and he might easily have found his opportunity to insult or injure me when I should have had nothing but my own debilitated exertions to protect me.

Freed from this danger, I found my situation sufficiently fortunate for a man under my circumstances. It was attended with all the advantages for concealment my fondest imagination could have hoped; and it was by no means destitute of the benefits which arise from kindness and humanity. Nothing could be more unlike

than the thieves I had seen in —— jail and the thieves of my new
residence. The latter were generally full of chearfulness and merriment. They could expatiate freely wherever they thought proper.
They could form plans and execute them. They consulted their
inclinations. They did not impose upon themselves the task, as is
too often the case in human society, of seeming tacitly to approve
that from which they suffered most; or, which is worse, of persuading themselves that all the wrongs they suffered were right;
but were at open war with their oppressors. On the contrary the
imprisoned felons I had lately seen were shut up like wild beasts in
a cage, deprived of activity and palsied with indolence. The
occasional demonstrations that still remained of their former enterprising life, were the starts and convulsions of disease, not the
meditated and consistent exertions of a mind in health. They had
no more of hope, of project, of golden and animated dreams, but
were reserved to the most dismal prospects, and forbidden to
think upon any other topic. It is true that these two scenes were
parts of one whole, the one the consummation, the hourly to be
expected successor of the other. But the men I now saw were
wholly inattentive to this, and in that respect appeared to hold no
commerce with reflection or reason.

I might in one view, as I have said, congratulate myself upon my
present residence; it answered completely the purposes of concealment. It was the seat of merriment and hilarity; but the hilarity
that characterised it produced no correspondent feelings in my
bosom. The persons who composed this society had each of them
cast off all control from established principle; their trade was terror,
and their constant object to elude the vigilance of the community.
The influence of these circumstances was visible in their character.
I found among them benevolence and kindness; they were strongly
susceptible of emotions of generosity. But, as their situation was
precarious, their dispositions were proportionably fluctuating.
Inured to the animosity of their species, they were irritable and
passionate. Accustomed to exercise harshness towards the subject
of their depredations, they did not always confine their brutality
within that scope. They were habituated to consider wounds, and
bludgeons and stabbing, as the obvious mode of surmounting
every difficulty. Uninvolved in the debilitating routine of human
affairs, they frequently displayed an energy, which from every
impartial observer would have extorted veneration. Energy is

perhaps of all qualities the most valuable; and a just political system would possess the means of extracting from it thus circumstanced its beneficial qualities, instead of consigning it as now to indiscriminate destruction. We act like the chymist who should reject the finest ore, and employ none but what was sufficiently debased to fit it immediately for the vilest uses. But the energy of these men, such as I beheld it, was in the highest degree misapplied, unassisted by liberal and enlightened views, and directed only to the most narrow and contemptible purposes.

The residence I have been describing might to many persons have appeared attended with intolerable inconveniences. But, exclusively of its advantages as a field for speculation, it was Elysium compared with that from which I had just escaped. Displeasing company, incommodious apartments, filthiness and riot, lost the circumstance by which they could most effectually disgust, when I was not compelled to remain with them. All hardships I could patiently endure, in comparison with the menace of a violent and untimely death. There was no suffering that I could not persuade myself to consider as trivial, except that which flowed from the tyranny, the frigid precaution, or the inhuman revenge of my own species.

My recovery advanced in the most favourable manner. The attention and kindness of my protector were incessant, and the rest caught the spirit from his example. The old woman who superintended the houshold, still retained her animosity. She considered me as the cause of the expulsion of Gines from the fraternity; Gines had been the object of her particular partiality; and, zealous as she was for the public concern, she thought an old and experienced sinner for a raw probationer but an ill exchange. Add to which, that her habits inclined her to moroseness and discontent, and that persons of her complexion seem unable to exist without some object upon which to employ the superfluity of their gall. She lost no opportunity upon the most trifling occasion of displaying her animosity, and ever and anon eyed me with a furious glance of canine hunger for my destruction. Nothing was more evidently mortifying to her than the procrastination of her malice; nor could she bear to think that a fierceness so gigantic and uncontrolable should show itself in nothing more terrific than the pigmy spite of a chambermaid. For myself, I had been accustomed to the warfare of formidable adversaries and the encounter of alarming dangers; and what I saw of her spleen had not power sufficient to disturb my tranquillity.

As I recovered, I told my story, except so far as related to the detection of Mr. Falkland's eventful secret, to my protector. That particular I could not as yet prevail upon myself to disclose even in a situation like this, which seemed to preclude the possibility of its being made use of to the disadvantage of my persecutor. My present auditor however, whose habits of thinking were extremely opposite to those of Mr. Forester, did not from the obscurity which flowed from this reserve, deduce any unfavourable conclusion. His penetration was such as to afford little room for an impostor to hope to mislead him by a fictitious statement, and he confided in that penetration. So confiding, the simplicity and integrity of my manner carried conviction to his mind and insured his good opinion and friendship.

He listened to my story with eagerness, and commented on the several parts as I related them. He said that this was only one fresh instance of the tyranny and perfidiousness exercised by the powerful members of the community against those who were less privileged than themselves. Nothing could be more clear than their readiness to sacrifice the human species at large to their meanest interest or wildest caprice. Who that saw the situation in its true light would wait till their oppressors thought fit to decree their destruction, and not take arms in their defence while it was yet in their power? Which was most meritorious, the unresisting and dastardly submission of a slave, or the enterprise and gallantry of the man who dared to assert his claims? Since by the partial administration of our laws innocence, when power was armed against it, had nothing better to hope for than guilt, what man of true courage would fail to set these laws at defiance, and, if he must suffer by their injustice, at least take care that he had first shown his contempt of their yoke? For himself he should certainly never have embraced his present calling, had he not been stimulated to it by these cogent and irresistible reasons; and he hoped, as experience had so forcibly brought a conviction of this sort to my mind, that he should for the future have the happiness to associate me to his pursuits.—It will presently be seen with what event these hopes were attended.

Numerous were the precautions exercised by the gang of thieves with whom I now resided to elude the vigilance of the satellites of justice. It was one of their rules to commit no depredations but at a considerable distance from the place of their residence, and Gines had transgressed this regulation in the attack to which I was indebted for my present asylum. After having possessed themselves of any booty, they took care in the sight of the persons whom they had robbed to pursue a route as nearly as possible opposite to that which led to their true haunts. The appearance of their place of residence together with its environs was peculiarly desolate and forlorn, and it had the reputation of being haunted. The old woman I have described had long been its inhabitant, and was commonly supposed to be its only inhabitant; and her person well accorded with the rural ideas of a witch. Her lodgers never went out or came in but with the utmost circumspection and generally by night. The lights which were occasionally seen from various parts of her habitation were by the country people regarded with horror as supernatural; and, if the noise of revelry at any time saluted their ears, it was imagined to proceed from a carnival of devils. With all these advantages the thieves did not venture to reside here but by intervals: they frequently absented themselves for months, and removed to a different part of the country. The old woman sometimes attended them in these transportations, and sometimes remained; but in all cases her decampment took place either sooner or later than theirs, so that the nicest observer could scarcely have traced any connection between her reappearance and the alarms of depredation that were frequently given; and the festival of demons seemed to the terrified rustics indifferently to take place whether she were present or absent.

CHAPTER III

ONE day, while I continued in this situation, a circumstance occurred, which involuntarily attracted my attention. Two of our people had been sent to a town at some distance for the purpose of procuring us the things of which we were in want. After having delivered these to our landlady, they retired to one corner of the room, and, one of them pulling a printed paper from his pocket, they mutually occupied themselves in examining its contents. I was sitting in an easy chair by the fire, being considerably better than

I had been, though still in a weak and languid state. Having read for a considerable time, they looked at me, and then at the paper, and then at me again. They then went out of the room together, as if to consult without interruption upon something which that paper suggested to them. Some time after they returned, and my protector, who had been absent upon the former occasion, entered the room at the same instant.

Captain! said one of them with an air of pleasure, look here! we have found a prize! I believe it is as good as a bank note of a hundred guineas.

Mr. Raymond (that was his name) took the paper and read. He paused for a moment. He then crushed the paper in his hand; and, turning to the person from whom he had received it, said with the tone of a man confident in the success of his reasons,

What use have you for these hundred guineas? Are you in want? Are you in distress? Can you be contented to purchase them at the price of treachery? of violating the laws of hospitality?

Faith, captain, I do not very well know. After having violated other laws, I do not see why we should be frightened at an old saw. We pretend to judge for ourselves, and ought to be above shrinking from a bugbear of a proverb. Beside, this is a good deed, and I should think no more harm of being the ruin of such a thief, than of getting my dinner.

A thief! You talk of thieves!——

Not so fast, captain. God defend that I should say a word against thieving as a general occupation! But one man steals in one way, and another in another. For my part, I go upon the highway, and take from any stranger I meet what it is a hundred to one he can very well spare. I see nothing to be found fault with in that. But I have as much conscience as another man. Because I laugh at assizes and great wigs and the gallows, and because I will not be frightened from an innocent action when the lawyers say me nay, does it follow that I am to have a fellow feeling for pilferers, and rascally servants, and people that have neither justice nor principle? No: I have too much respect for the trade, not to be a foe to interlopers and people that so much the more deserve my hatred because the world calls them by my name.

You are wrong, Larkins! You certainly ought not to employ against people that you hate, supposing your hatred to be reasonable, the instrumentality of that law which in your practice you defy.

Be consistent. Either be the friend of law, or its adversary. Depend upon it that, wherever there are laws at all, there will be laws against such people as you and me. Either therefore we all of us deserve the vengeance of the law, or law is not the proper instrument of correcting the misdeeds of mankind. I tell you this, because I would fain have you aware that an informer or a king's evidence, a man who takes advantage of the confidence of another in order to betray him, who sells the life of his neighbour for money, or, coward like, upon any pretence calls in the law to do that for him which he cannot or dares not do for himself, is the vilest of rascals. But in the present case, if your reasons were the best in the world, they do not apply.

While Mr. Raymond was speaking, the rest of the gang came into the room. He immediately turned to them and said,

My friends, here is a piece of intelligence that Larkins has just brought in, which with his leave I will lay before you.

Then unfolding the paper he had received, he continued: This is the description of a felon with the offer of a hundred guineas for his apprehension. Larkins picked it up at ——. By the time and other circumstances, but particularly by the minute description of his person, there can be no doubt but the object of it is our young friend, whose life I was a while ago the instrument of saving. He is charged here with having taken advantage of the confidence of his patron and benefactor, to rob him of property to a large amount. Upon this charge he was committed to the county jail, from whence he made his escape about a fortnight ago without venturing to stand his trial, a circumstance which is stated by the advertiser as tantamount to a confession of his guilt.

My friends, I was acquainted with the particulars of this story some time before. This lad let me into his history at a time that he could not possibly foresee that he should stand in need of that precaution as an antidote against danger. He is not guilty of what is laid to his charge. Which of you is so ignorant as to suppose that his escape is any confirmation of his guilt? Who ever thinks, when he is apprehended for trial, of his innocence or guilt as being at all material to the issue? Who ever was fool enough to volunteer a trial, where those who are to decide think more of the horror of the thing of which he is accused than whether he were the person that did it, and where the nature of our motives is to be collected from a set of ignorant witnesses that no wise man would trust for a fair representation of the most indifferent action of his life?

The poor lad's story is a long one, and I will not trouble you with it now. But from that story it is as clear as the day, that, because he wished to leave the service of his master, because he had been perhaps a little too inquisitive in his master's concerns, and because, as I suspect, he had been trusted with some important secrets, his master conceived an antipathy against him. This antipathy gradually proceeded to such a length, as to induce the master to forge this vile accusation. He seems willing to hang the lad out of the way, rather than suffer him to go where he pleases or get beyond the reach of his power. Williams has told me the story with such ingenuousness that I am as sure that he is guiltless of what they lay to his charge as that I am so myself. Nevertheless the man's servants who were called in to hear the accusation, and his relation, who as justice of the peace made out the mittimus, and who had the folly to think he could be impartial, gave it on his side with one voice, and thus afforded Williams a sample of what he had to expect in the sequel.

Larkins, who when he received this paper had no previous knowledge of particulars, was for taking advantage of it for the purpose of earning the hundred guineas. Are you of that mind, now you have heard them? Will you for so paltry a consideration deliver up the lamb into the jaws of the wolf? Will you abet the purposes of this sanguinary rascal who, not contented with driving his late dependent from house and home, depriving him of character and all the ordinary means of subsistence, and leaving him almost without a refuge, still thirsts for his blood? If no other person have the courage to set limits to the tyranny of courts of justice, shall not we? Shall we, who earn our livelihood by generous daring, be indebted for a penny to the vile artifices of the informer? Shall we, against whom the whole species is in arms, refuse our protection to an individual, more exposed to, but still less deserving of their persecution than ourselves?

The representation of the captain produced an instant effect upon the whole company. They all exclaimed, Betray him! No, not for worlds! He is safe. We will protect him at the hazard of our lives. If fidelity and honour be banished from thieves, where shall they find refuge upon the face of the earth*? Larkins in particular

* This seems to be the parody of a celebrated saying of John King of France, who was taken prisoner by the Black Prince at the battle of Poitiers.[1]

thanked the captain for his interference, and swore that he would rather part with his right hand, than injure so worthy a lad, or assist such an unheard-of villainy. Saying this, he took me by the hand, and bade me fear nothing. Under their roof no harm should ever befal me; and, even if the understrappers of the law should discover my retreat, they would to a man die in my defence, sooner than a hair of my head should be hurt. I thanked him most sincerely for his good will; but I was principally struck with the fervent benevolence of my benefactor. I told them, I found that my enemies were inexorable, and would never be appeased but with my blood; and I assured them with the most solemn and earnest veracity, that I had done nothing to deserve the persecution which was exercised against me.

The spirit and energy of Mr. Raymond had been such, as to leave no part for me to perform in repelling this unlooked-for danger. Nevertheless, it left a very serious impression upon my mind. I had always placed some confidence in the returning equity of Mr. Falkland. Though he persecuted me with bitterness, I could not help believing that he did it unwillingly, and I was persuaded it would not be for ever. A man, whose original principles had been so full of rectitude and honour, could not fail at some time or other to recollect the injustice of his conduct, and to remit his asperity. This idea had been always present to me, and had in no small degree conspired to instigate my exertions. I said, I will convince my persecutor that I am of more value than that I should be sacrificed purely by way of precaution. These expectations on my part had been encouraged by Mr. Falkland's behaviour upon the question of my imprisonment and by various particulars which had occurred since.

But this new incident gave to the subject a totally different appearance. I saw him, not contented with blasting my reputation, confining me for a period in jail, and reducing me to the situation of a houseless vagabond, still continuing his pursuit under these forlorn circumstances with unmitigable cruelty. Indignation and resentment seemed now for the first time to penetrate my mind. I knew his misery so well, I was so fully acquainted with its cause, and so strongly impressed with the idea of its being unmerited, that, while I suffered so deeply, I still continued to pity, rather than hate my persecutor. But this incident introduced some change into my feelings. I said, Surely he might now believe that he had sufficiently disarmed me, and might at length suffer me to be at peace. At least ought he not to be contented to leave me to my fate, the perilous and uncertain condition of an escaped felon, instead of thus whetting the animosity and vigilance of my country-men against me? Were his interference on my behalf in opposition to the stern severity of Mr. Forester, and his various acts of kind-ness since, a mere part that he played in order to lull me into patience? Was he perpetually haunted with the fear of an ample retaliation, and for that purpose did he personate remorse at the very moment that he was secretly keeping every engine at play that could secure my destruction? The very suspicion of such a fact filled me with inexpressible horror, and struck a sudden chill through every fibre of my frame.

My wound was by this time completely healed, and it became absolutely necessary that I should form some determination respecting the future. My habits of thinking were such as gave me an uncontrolable repugnance to the vocation of my hosts. I did not indeed feel that aversion and abhorrence to the men which are commonly entertained. I saw and respected their good qualities and their virtues. I was by no means inclined to believe them worse men, or more inimical in their dispositions to the welfare of their species, than the generality of those that look down upon them with most censure. But, though I did not cease to love them as individuals, my eyes were perfectly opened to their mistakes. If I should otherwise have been in danger of being misled, it was my fortune to have studied felons in a jail, before I studied them in their state of comparative prosperity; and this was an infallible antidote to the poison. I saw that in this profession were exerted uncommon energy, ingenuity and fortitude, and I could not help recollecting how admirably beneficial such qualities might be made in the great theatre of human affairs; while in their present direction they were thrown away upon purposes diametrically at war with the first interests of human society. Nor were their proceedings less injurious to their own interest, than incompatible with the general welfare. The man who risks or sacrifices his life for the public cause is rewarded with the testimony of an approving conscience; but persons who wantonly defy the necessary, though atrociously exaggerated precautions of government in the matter of property, at the same time that they commit an alarming hos-tility against the whole, are as to their own concerns scarcely less

absurd and self-neglectful, than the man who should set himself
up as a mark for a file of musqueteers to shoot at.

Viewing the subject in this light, I not only determined that I
would have no share in their occupation myself, but thought I
could not do less in return for the benefits I had received from
them, than endeavour to dissuade them from an employment in
which they must themselves be the greatest sufferers. My expostulation met with a various reception. All the persons to whom it was
addressed had been tolerably successful in persuading themselves
of the innocence of their calling; and what remained of doubt in
their mind was smothered and, so to speak, laboriously forgotten.
Some of them laughed at my arguments as a ridiculous piece of
missionary quixotism. Others, and particularly our captain, repelled them with the boldness of a man that knows he has got the
strongest side. But this sentiment of ease and self-satisfaction did
not long remain. They had been used to arguments derived from
religion and the sacredness of law. They had long ago shaken these
from them as so many prejudices. But my view of the subject
appealed to principles which they could not contest, and had by
no means the air of that customary reproof which is for ever
dinned in our ears, without finding one responsive chord in our
hearts. Urged, as they now were, with objections unexpected and
cogent, some of those to whom I addressed them began to grow
peevish and impatient of the intrusive remonstrance. But this was
by no means the case with Mr. Raymond. He was possessed of a
candour that I have seldom seen equalled. He was surprised to
hear objections so powerful to that which as a matter of speculation
he believed he had examined on all sides. He revolved them with
impartiality and care. He admitted them slowly, but he at length
fully admitted them. He had now but one rejoinder in reserve.

Alas, Williams, said he, it would have been fortunate for me if
these views had been presented to me previously to my embracing
my present profession. It is now too late. Those very laws, which
by a perception of their iniquity drove me to what I am, preclude
my return. God, we are told, judges of men by what they are at the
period of arraignment, and, whatever be their crimes, if they have
seen and abjured the folly of those crimes, receives them to favour.
But the institutions of countries that profess to worship this God,
admit no such distinctions. They leave no room for amendment,
and seem to have a brutal delight in confounding the demerits of

offenders. It signifies not what is the character of the individual at the hour of trial. How changed, how spotless and how useful avails him nothing. If they discover at the distance of fourteen* or of forty years† an action for which the law ordains that his life shall be the forfeit, though the interval should have been spent with the purity of a saint and the devotedness of a patriot, they disdain to enquire into it. What then can I do? Am I not compelled to go on in folly, having once begun?

CHAPTER IV

I was extremely affected by this plea. I could only answer that Mr. Raymond must himself be the best judge of the course it became him to hold; I trusted the case was not so desperate as he imagined. This subject was pursued no farther, and was in some degree driven from my thoughts by an incident of a very extra-ordinary nature. I have already mentioned the animosity that was entertained against me by the infernal portress of this solitary mansion. Gines, the expelled member of the gang, had been her particular favourite. She submitted to his exile indeed, because her genius felt subdued by the energy and inherent superiority of Mr. Raymond; but she submitted with murmuring and discontent. Not daring to resent the conduct of the principal in this affair, she collected all the bitterness of her spirit against me. To the un-pardonable offence I had thus committed in the first instance, were added the reasonings I had lately offered against the profession of robbery. Robbery was a fundamental article in the creed of this hoary veteran, and she listened to my objections with the same unaffected astonishment and horror, that an old woman of other habits would listen to one who objected to the agonies and dis-solution of the creator of the world, or to the garment of imputed righteousness prepared to envelop the souls of the elect. Like the religious bigot, she was sufficiently disposed to avenge a hostility against her opinions with the weapons of sublunary warfare. Meanwhile I had smiled at the impotence of her malice, as an object of contempt, rather than alarm. She perceived, as I imagine,

* Eugene Aram.[1] See Annual Register for 1759.
† William Andrew Horne.[2] Ibid.

the slight estimation in which I held her, and this did not a little increase the perturbation of her thoughts.

One day I was left alone with no other person in the house than this swarthy sybil. The thieves had set out upon an expedition about two hours after sunset on the preceding evening, and had not returned, as they were accustomed to do, before day break the next morning. This was a circumstance that sometimes occurred, and therefore did not produce any extraordinary alarm. At one time the scent of prey would lead them beyond the bounds they had prescribed themselves, and at another the fear of pursuit; the life of a thief is always uncertain. The old woman had been preparing during the night for the meal to which they would expect to sit down, as soon as might be after their return.

For myself I had learned from their habits to be indifferent to the regular return of the different parts of the day, and in some degree to turn day into night, and night into day. I had been now several weeks in this residence, and the season was considerably advanced. I had passed some hours during the night in ruminating on my situation. The character and manners of the men among whom I lived were disgusting to me. Their brutal ignorance, their ferocious habits and their coarse behaviour, instead of becoming more tolerable by custom, hourly added force to my original aversion. The uncommon vigour of their minds and acuteness of their invention in the business they pursued, compared with the odiousness of that business and their habitual depravity, awakened in me sensations too painful to be endured. Moral disapprobation, at least in a mind unsubdued by philosophy, I found to be one of the most fertile sources of disquiet and uneasiness. From this pain the society of Mr. Raymond by no means relieved me. He was indeed eminently superior to the vices of the rest; but I did not less exquisitely feel how much he was out of his place, how disproportionably associated, or how contemptibly employed. I had attempted to counteract the errors under which he and his companions laboured; but I had found the obstacles that presented themselves, greater than I had imagined.

What was I to do? Was I to wait the issue of this my missionary undertaking, or was I to withdraw myself immediately? When I withdrew, ought that to be done privately, or with an open avowal of my design, and an endeavour to supply by the force of example what was deficient in my arguments? It was certainly improper, as

I declined all participation in the pursuits of these men, did not pay my contribution of hazard to the means by which they subsisted, and had no congeniality with their habits, that I should continue to reside with them longer than was absolutely necessary. There was one circumstance that rendered this deliberation particularly pressing. They intended in a few days removing from their present habitation, to a haunt to which they were accustomed in a distant county. If I did not propose to continue with them, it would perhaps be wrong to accompany them in this removal. The state of calamity to which my inexorable prosecutor had reduced me, had made the encounter even of a den of robbers a fortunate adventure. But the time that had since elapsed, had probably been sufficient to relax the keenness of the quest that was made after me. I sighed for that solitude and obscurity, that retreat from the vexations of the world and the voice even of common fame, which I had proposed to myself when I broke my prison.

Such were the meditations which now occupied my mind. At length I grew fatigued with continued contemplation, and to relieve myself I pulled out a pocket Horace, the legacy of my beloved Brightwel! I read with avidity the epistle in which he so beautifully describes to Fuscus the grammarian, the pleasures of rural tranquillity and independence. By this time the sun rose from behind the eastern hills, and I opened my casement to contemplate it. The day commenced with peculiar brilliancy, and was accompanied with all those charms, which the poets of nature, as they have been styled, have so much delighted to describe. There was something in this scene, particularly as succeeding to the active exertions of intellect, that soothed the mind to composure. Insensibly a confused reverie invaded my faculties, I withdrew from the window, threw myself upon the bed, and fell asleep.

I do not recollect the precise images which in this situation passed through my thoughts, but I know that they concluded with the idea of some person, the agent of Mr. Falkland, approaching to assassinate me. This thought had probably been suggested, by the project I meditated of entering once again into the world, and throwing myself within the sphere of his possible vengeance. I imagined that the design of the murderer was to come upon me by surprise, that I was aware of his design, and yet by some fascination had no thought of evading it. I heard the steps of the murderer as he cautiously approached. I seemed to listen to his constrained, yet audible breathings. He came up to the corner where I was placed, and then stopped. The idea became too terrible, I started, opened my eyes, and beheld the execrable hag before mentioned standing over me with a butcher's cleaver. I shifted my situation with a speed that seemed too swift for volition, and the blow already aimed at my scull, sunk impotent upon the bed. Before she could wholly recover her posture I sprung upon her, seized hold of the weapon, and had nearly wrested it from her. But in a moment she resumed her strength and her desperate purpose, and we had a furious struggle, she impelled by inveterate malice, and I resisting for my life. Her vigour was truly Amazonian, and at no time had I ever occasion to contend with a more formidable opponent. Her glance was sudden and exact, and the shock with which from time to time she impelled her whole frame, inconceivably vehement. At length I was victorious, took from her the instrument of death, and threw her upon the ground. Till now the earnestness of her exertions had curbed her rage; but now she gnashed with her teeth, her eyes seemed as if starting from their sockets, and her body heaved with uncontrolable insanity.

Rascal! devil! she exclaimed, what do you mean to do to me?

Till now the scene had passed uninterrupted by a single word.

Nothing, I replied: begone, infernal witch! and leave me to myself.

Leave you! No: I will thrust my fingers through your ribs, and drink your blood!—You conquer me?—Ha, ha!—Yes, yes! you shall!—I will sit upon you, and press you to hell! I will roast you with brimstone, and dash your entrails into your eyes!—Ha, ha!—ha!

Saying this, she sprung up, and prepared to attack me with redoubled fury. I seized her hands, and compelled her to sit upon the bed. Thus restrained, she continued to express the tumult of her thoughts by grinning, by certain furious motions of her head, and by occasional vehement efforts to disengage herself from my grasp. These contortions and starts were of the nature of those fits, in which the patients are commonly supposed to need three or four persons to hold them. But I found by experience that, under the circumstances in which I was placed, my single strength was sufficient. The spectacle of her emotions was inconceivably frightful. Her violence at length however began to abate, and she became convinced of the hopelessness of the contest.

Let me go! said she. Why do you hold me? I will not be held!

I wanted you gone from the first, replied I. Are you contented to go now?

Yes, I tell you, misbegotten villain! Yes, rascal!

I immediately loosed my hold. She flew to the door, and, holding it in her hand, said, I will be the death of you yet: you shall not be your own man twenty four hours longer! With these words she shut the door, and locked it upon me. An action so totally unexpected startled me. Whither was she gone? What was it she intended? To perish by the machinations of such a hag as this, was a thought not to be endured. Death in any form, brought upon us by surprise, and for which the mind has had no time to prepare, is inexpressibly terrible. My thoughts wandered in breathless horror and confusion, and all within was uproar. I endeavoured to break the door, but in vain. I went round the room in search of some tool to assist me. At length I rushed against it with a desperate effort, to which it yielded, and had nearly thrown me from the top of the stairs to the bottom.

I descended with all possible caution and vigilance. I entered the room which served us for a kitchen, but it was deserted. I searched every other apartment in vain. I went out among the ruins; still I discovered nothing of my late assailant. It was extraordinary: what could be become of her? what was I to conclude from her disappearance? I reflected on her parting menace. 'I should not be my own man twenty four hours longer.' It was mysterious; it did not seem to be the menace of assassination.

Suddenly the recollection of the hand bill brought to us by Larkins rushed upon my memory. Was it possible that she alluded to that in her parting words? Would she set out upon such an expedition by herself? Was it not dangerous to the whole fraternity, if without the smallest precaution she should bring the officers of justice in the midst of them? It was perhaps improbable she would engage in an undertaking thus desperate. It was not however easy to answer for the conduct of a person in her state of mind. Should I wait, and risk the preservation of my liberty upon the issue?

To this question I returned an immediate negative. I had resolved in a very short time to quit my present situation, and the difference of a little sooner or a little later could not be very material. It promised to be neither agreeable nor prudent, for

me to remain under the same roof with a person who had manifested such a fierce and inexpiable hostility. But the consideration which had inexpressibly the most weight with me belonged
to the ideas of imprisonment, trial and death. The longer they
had formed the subject of my contemplation, the more forcibly
was I impelled to avoid them. I had entered upon a system of
action for that purpose; I had already made many sacrifices;
and I believed that I would never miscarry in this project through
any neglect of mine. The thought of what was reserved for me
by my persecutors sickened my very soul; and the more intimately I was acquainted with oppression and injustice, the more
deeply was I penetrated with the abhorrence to which they are
entitled.

Such were the reasons that determined me, instantly, abruptly,
without leave-taking or acknowledgment for the peculiar and
repeated favours I had received, to quit a habitation to which
for six weeks I had apparently been indebted for protection
from trial, conviction and an ignominious death. I had come
hither pennyless; I quitted my abode with the sum of a few
guineas in my possession, Mr. Raymond having insisted upon
my taking a share, at the time that each man received his dividend
from the common stock. Though I had reason to suppose that
the heat of the pursuit against me would be somewhat remitted
by the time that had elapsed, the magnitude of the mischief
that in an unfavourable event might fall on me, determined me
to neglect no imaginable precaution. I recollected the hand bill
which was the source of my present alarm, and conceived that
one of the principal dangers which threatened me was the recognition of my person either by such as had previously known me
or even by strangers. It seemed prudent therefore to disguise
it as effectually as I could. For this purpose I had recourse to a
parcel of tattered garments that lay in a neglected corner of our
habitation. The disguise I chose was that of a beggar. Upon
this plan I threw off my shirt. I tied a handkerchief about my
head, with which I took care to cover one of my eyes. Over this
I drew a piece of an old woollen nightcap. I selected the worst
apparel I could find, and this I reduced to a still more deplorable
condition by rents that I purposely made in various places.
Thus equipped, I surveyed myself in a looking glass. I had
rendered my appearance complete, nor would any one have

suspected that I was not one of the fraternity to which I assumed
to belong. I said, This is the form in which tyranny and injustice
oblige me to seek for refuge; but better, a thousand times better,
is it, thus to incur contempt with the dregs of mankind, than to
trust to the tender mercies of our superiors!

CHAPTER V

THE only rule that I laid down to myself in traversing the forest
was to take a direction as opposite as possible to that which led to
the scene of my late imprisonment. After about two hours walking
I arrived at the termination of this ruder scene, and reached that
part of the county which is inclosed and cultivated. Here I sat down
by the side of a brook, and, pulling out a crust of bread which I had
brought away with me, rested and refreshed myself. While I continued in this place, I began to ruminate upon the plan I should
lay down for my future proceedings; and my propensity now led
me, as it had done in a former instance, to fix upon the capital,
which I believed beside its other recommendations would prove
the safest place for concealment. During these thoughts I saw a
couple of peasants passing at a small distance, and enquired of
them respecting the London road. By their description I understood that the most immediate way would be to repass a part of
the forest, and that it would be necessary to approach considerably
nearer to the county town, than I was at the spot which I had at
present reached. I did not imagine that this could be a circumstance
of considerable importance. My disguise appeared to be a sufficient
security against momentary danger; and I therefore took a path,
though not the most direct one, which led towards the point they
suggested.

Some of the occurrences of the day are deserving to be mentioned. As I passed along a road which lay in my way for a few
miles, I saw a carriage advancing in the opposite direction. I
debated with myself for a moment, whether I should pass it
without notice, or should take this occasion by voice or gesture of
making an essay of my trade. This idle disquisition was however
speedily driven from my mind when I perceived that the carriage
was Mr. Falkland's. The suddenness of the encounter struck me

with terror, though perhaps it would have been difficult for calm reflection to have discovered any considerable danger. I withdrew from the road, and skulked behind a hedge till it should have completely gone by. I was too much occupied with my own feelings to venture to examine whether or no the terrible adversary of my peace were in the carriage. I persuaded myself that he was. I looked after the equipage, and exclaimed, There you may see the luxurious accommodations and appendages of guilt, and here the forlornness that waits upon innocence!—I was to blame to imagine that my case was singular in that respect. I only mention it to show how the most trivial circumstance contributes to embitter the cup to the man of adversity. The thought however was a transient one. I had learned this lesson from my sufferings, not to indulge in the luxury of discontent. As my mind recovered its tranquillity, I began to enquire whether the phenomenon I had just seen could have any relation to myself. But, though my mind was extremely inquisitive and versatile in this respect, I could discover no sufficient ground upon which to build a judgment.

At night I entered a little public house at the extremity of a village, and, seating myself in a corner of the kitchen, asked for some bread and cheese. While I was sitting at my repast, three or four labourers came in for a little refreshment after their work. Ideas respecting the inequality of rank pervade every order in society; and, as my appearance was meaner and more contemptible than theirs, I found it expedient to give way to these gentry of a village alehouse, and remove to an obscurer station. I was surprised and not a little startled to find them fall almost immediately into conversation about my history, whom with a slight variation of circumstances they styled the notorious housebreaker, Kit Williams.

Damn the fellow, said one of them, one never hears of any thing else. O' my life, I think he makes talk for the whole county.

That is very true, replied another. I was at the market town today to sell some oats for my master, and there was a hue and cry, some of them thought they had got him, but it was a false alarm.

That hundred guineas is a fine thing, rejoined the first. I should be glad if so be as how it fell in my way.

For the matter of that, said the traveller, I should like a hundred guineas as well as another. But I cannot be of your mind for all that. I should never think money would do me any good, that had been the means of bringing a Christian creature to the gallows.

Poh, that is all my granny! Some folks must be hanged to keep the wheels of our state folks a-going. Beside, I could forgive the fellow all his other robberies, but that he should have been so hardened as to break the house of his own master at last, that is too bad.

Lord, lord, replied the other, I see you know nothing of the matter! I will tell you how it was, as I learned it at the town. I question whether he ever robbed his master at all. But, hark you! you must know as how that squire Falkland was once tried for murder——

Yes, yes, we know that.

Well, he was as innocent as the child unborn. But I supposes as how he is a little soft or so. And so Kit Williams—Kit is a devilish cunning fellow, you may judge that from his breaking prison no less than five times,——so, I say, he threatened to bring his master to trial at the 'size all over again, and so frightened him, and got money from him at divers times. Till at last one squire Forester, a relation of t'other, found it all out. And he made the hell of a rumpus, and sent away Kit to prison in a twinky, and I believe he would have been hanged; for when two squires lay their heads together, they do not much matter law, you know; or else they twist the law to their own ends, I cannot exactly say which; but it is much at one, when the poor fellow's breath is out of his body.

Though this story was very circumstantially told and with a sufficient detail of particulars, it did not pass unquestioned. Each man maintained the justness of his own statement, and the dispute was long and obstinately pursued. Historians and commentators at length withdrew together. The terrors with which I was seized when this conversation began, were extreme. I stole a sidelong glance to one quarter and another, to observe if any man's attention were turned upon me. I trembled as if in an ague fit; and at first felt continual impulses to quit the house and take to my heels. I drew closer in my corner, held aside my head, and seemed from time to time to undergo a total revolution of the animal economy.

At length the tide of ideas turned. Perceiving they paid no attention to me, the recollection of the full security my disguise afforded recurred strongly to my thoughts, and I began inwardly to exult, though I did not venture to obtrude myself to examination.

By degrees I began to be amused at the absurdity of their tales, and the variety of the falsehoods I heard asserted around me. My soul seemed to expand; I felt a pride in the self possession and lightness of heart with which I could listen to the scene; and I determined to prolong and heighten the enjoyment. Accordingly, when they were withdrawn, I addressed myself to our hostess, a buxom, bluff, good humoured widow, and asked what sort of a man this Kit Williams might be? She replied that, as she was informed, he was as handsome, likely a lad, as any in four counties round; and that she loved him for his cleverness, by which he outwitted all the keepers they could set over him, and made his way through stone walls, as if they were so many cobwebs. I observed that the country was so thoroughly alarmed, that I did not think it possible he should escape the pursuit that was set up after him. This idea excited her immediate indignation; she said, she hoped he was far enough away by this time, but, if not, she wished the curse of God might light on them that betrayed so noble a fellow to an ignominious end!—Though she little thought that the person of whom she spoke was so near her, yet the sincere and generous warmth with which she interested herself in my behalf, gave me considerable pleasure. With this sensation to sweeten the fatigues of the day and the calamities of my situation, I retired from the kitchen to a neighbouring barn, laid myself down upon some straw, and fell into a profound sleep.

The next day about noon as I was pursuing my journey, I was overtaken by two men on horse back who stopped me to enquire respecting a person that they supposed might have passed along that road. As they proceeded in their description I perceived with astonishment and terror that I was myself the person to whom their questions related. They entered into a tolerably accurate detail of the various characteristics by which my person might best be distinguished. They said, they had good reason to believe that I had been seen at a place in that county the very day before. While they were speaking, a third person who had fallen behind came up, and my alarm was greatly increased upon seeing that this person was the servant of Mr. Forester, who had visited me in prison about a fortnight before my escape. My best resource in this crisis was composure and apparent indifference. It was fortunate for me that my disguise was so complete, that the eye of Mr. Falkland itself could scarcely have penetrated it. I had been aware for some time before that this was a refuge which events might make necessary, and had endeavoured to arrange and methodise my ideas upon the subject. From my youth I had possessed a considerable facility in the art of imitation; and, when I quitted my retreat in the habitation of Mr. Raymond, I adopted along with my beggar's attire a peculiar slouching and clownish gait to be used whenever there should appear the least chance of my being observed, together with an Irish brogue which I had had an opportunity of studying in my prison. Such are the miserable expedients and so great the studied artifice, which man, who never deserves the name of manhood but in proportion as he is erect and independent, may find it necessary to employ for the purpose of eluding the inexorable animosity and unfeeling tyranny of his fellow man! I had made use of this brogue, though I have not thought it necessary to write it down in my narrative, in the conversation of the village alehouse. Mr. Forester's servant as he came up observed that his companions were engaged in conversation with me; and, guessing at the subject, asked whether they had gained any intelligence. He added to the information at which they had already hinted, that a resolution was taken to spare neither diligence nor expence for my discovery and apprehension, and that they were satisfied that, if I were above ground and in the kingdom, it would be impossible for me to escape them.

Every new incident that had occurred to me, thus tended to impress upon my mind the extreme danger to which I was exposed. I could almost have imagined that I was the sole subject of general attention, and that the whole world was in arms to exterminate me. The very idea tingled through every fibre of my frame. But, terrible as it appeared to my imagination, it did but give new energy to my purpose; and I determined that I would not voluntarily resign the field, that is literally speaking my neck to the cord of the executioner, notwithstanding the greatest superiority in my assailants. But the incidents which had befallen me, though they did not change my purpose, induced me to examine over again the means by which it might be effected. The consequence of this revisal was to determine me to bend my course to the nearest sea port on the west side of the island, and transport myself to Ireland. I cannot now tell what it was that inclined me to prefer this scheme to that which I had originally formed. Perhaps the latter, which had been for some time present to my imagination, for that reason appeared the more obvious of the two; and I found an appearance of complexity, which the mind did not stay to explain, in substituting the other in its stead.

I arrived without farther impediment at the place from which I intended to sail, enquired for a vessel which I found ready to put to sea in a few hours, and agreed with the captain for my passage. Ireland had to me the disadvantage of being a dependency of the British government, and therefore a place of less security than most other countries which are divided from it by the ocean. To judge from the diligence with which I seemed to be pursued in England, it was not improbable that the zeal of my persecutors might follow me to the other side of the channel. It was however sufficiently agreeable to my mind that I was upon the point of being removed one step farther from the danger which was so grievous to my imagination.

Could there be any peril in the short interval that was to elapse before the vessel was to weigh anchor, and quit the English shore? Probably not. A very short time had intervened between my determination for the sea and my arrival at this place; and, if any new alarm had been given to my persecutors, it proceeded from the old woman a very few days before. I hoped I had anticipated their diligence. Meanwhile that I might neglect no reasonable precaution, I went instantly on board, resolved that I would not unnecessarily, by walking the streets of the town, expose myself to any untoward accident. This was the first time I had upon any occasion taken leave of my native country.

CHAPTER VI

THE time was now nearly elapsed that was prescribed for our stay, and orders for weighing anchor were every moment expected, when we were hailed by a boat from the shore with two other men in it beside those that rowed. They entered our vessel in an instant. They were officers of justice. The passengers, five persons beside myself, were ordered upon deck for examination. I was inexpressibly disturbed at the occurrence of such a circumstance in so unseasonable a moment. I took it for granted that it was of me that they were in search. Was it possible that by any unaccountable

accident they should have got an intimation of my disguise? It was
infinitely more distressing to encounter them upon this narrow
stage and under these pointed circumstances, than, as I had before
encountered my pursuers, under the appearance of an indifferent
person. My recollection however did not forsake me. I confided in
my conscious disguise and my Irish brogue, as a rock of dependence against all accidents.

No sooner did we appear upon deck than to my great consternation I could observe the attention of our guests principally turned
upon me. They asked a few frivolous questions of such of my
fellow passengers as happened to be nearest to them; and then
turning to me enquired my name, who I was, whence I came, and
what had brought me there? I had scarcely opened my mouth to
reply, when with one consent they laid hold of me, said I was their
prisoner, and declared that my accent, together with the correspondence of my person, would be sufficient to convict me before
any court in England. I was hurried out of the vessel into the boat
in which they came, and seated between them, as if by way of
precaution lest I should spring overboard and by any means
escape them.

I now took it for granted that I was once more in the power of
Mr. Falkland, and the idea was insupportably mortifying and
oppressive to my imagination. Escape from his pursuit, freedom
from his tyranny, were objects upon which my whole soul was
bent; could no human ingenuity and exertion effect them? Did
his power reach through all space, and his eye penetrate every
concealment? Was he like that mysterious being, to protect us
from whose fierce revenge mountains and hills we are told might
fall on us in vain? No idea is more heart-sickening and tremendous
than this. But in my case it was not a subject of reasoning or of
faith; I could derive no comfort either directly from the unbelief
which, upon religious subjects, some men avow to their own minds,
or secretly from the remoteness and incomprehensibility of the
conception; it was an affair of sense; I felt the fangs of the tyger
striking deep into my heart.

But, though this impression was at first exceedingly strong, and
accompanied with its usual attendants of dejection and pusillanimity, my mind soon began as it were mechanically, to turn
upon the consideration of the distance between this sea port and
my county prison, and the various opportunities of escape that

might offer themselves in the interval. My first duty was to avoid betraying myself more than it might afterwards appear I was betrayed already. It was possible that, though apprehended, my apprehension might have been determined on upon some slight score, and that by my dexterity I might render my dismission as sudden as my arrest had been. It was even possible that I had been seized through a mistake, and that the present measure might have no connection with Mr. Falkland's affair. Upon every supposition it was my business to gain information. In my passage from the ship to the town I did not utter a word. My conductors commented on my sulkiness, but remarked that it would avail me nothing, I should infallibly swing, as it was never known that any body got off, who was tried for robbing his majesty's mail. It is difficult to conceive the lightness of heart which was communicated to me by these words: I persisted however in the silence I had meditated. From the rest of their conversation, which was sufficiently voluble, I learned that the mail from Edinburgh to London had been robbed about ten days before by two Irishmen, that one of them was already secured, and that I was taken up upon suspicion of being the other. They had a description of his person which, though, as I afterwards found, it disagreed from mine in several material articles, appeared to them to tally to the minutest tittle. The intelligence that the whole proceeding against me was founded in a mistake, took an oppressive load from my mind. I believed that I should immediately be able to establish my innocence to the satisfaction of any magistrate in the kingdom; and, though crossed in my plans, and thwarted in my design of quitting the island even after I was already at sea, this was but a trifling inconvenience compared with what I had had but too much reason to fear.

As soon as we came ashore I was conducted to the house of a justice of peace, a man who had formerly been the captain of a collier, but who, having been successful in the world, had quitted this wandering life, and for some years had had the honour to represent his majesty's person. We were detained for some time in a sort of anti-room, waiting his reverence's leisure. The persons by whom I had been taken up were experienced in their trade, and insisted upon employing this interval in searching me, in presence of two of his worship's servants. They found upon me fifteen guineas and some silver. They required me to strip myself perfectly naked, that they might examine whether I had bank notes concealed any where about my person. They took up the detached parcels of my miserable attire as I threw it from me, and felt them one by one to discover whether the articles of which they were in search might by any device be sewn up in them. To all this I submitted without murmuring. It might probably come to the same thing at last, and summary justice was sufficiently coincident with my views, my principal object being to get as soon as possible out of the clutches of the respectable persons who now had me in custody.

This operation was scarcely completed, before we were directed to be ushered into his worship's apartment. My accusers opened the charge, and told him that they had been ordered to this town upon an intimation that one of the persons who robbed the Edinburgh mail was to be found here; and that they had taken me on board a vessel which was by this time under sail for Ireland. Well, says his worship, that is your story; now let us hear what account the gentleman gives of himself. What is your name, ha, sirrah? and from what part of Tipperary are you pleased to come? I had already taken my determination upon this article; and, the moment I learned the particulars of the charge against me, resolved, for the present at least, to lay aside my Irish accent, and speak my native tongue. This I had done in the very few words I had spoken to my conductors in the anti-room: they stared at the metamorphosis, but they had gone too far for it to be possible they should retract in consistence with their honour. I now told the justice that I was no Irishman, nor had ever been in that country: I was a native of England. This occasioned a consulting of the deposition, in which my person was supposed to be described, and which my conductors had brought along with them for their direction. To be sure that required that the offender should be an Irishman.

Observing his worship hesitate, I thought this was the time to push the matter a little farther. I referred to the paper, and showed him that the description neither tallied as to height nor complexion. But then it did as to years and the colour of the hair; and it was not this gentleman's habit, as he informed me, to squabble about trifles, or to let a man's neck out of the halter for a pretended flaw of a few inches in his stature. If a man were too short, he said, there was no remedy like a little stretching. The miscalculation in my case happened to be the opposite way, but his reverence did not think proper to lose his jest. Upon the whole he was somewhat at a loss how to proceed.

My conductors observed this, and began to tremble for the reward, which two hours ago they thought as good as in their own pocket. To retain me in custody they judged to be a safe speculation; if it turned out a mistake at last, they felt little apprehension of a suit for false imprisonment from a poor man accoutred as I was in rags. They therefore urged his worship to comply with their views. They told him, that to be sure the evidence against me did not prove so strong, as for their part they heartily wished it had, but that there were a number of suspicious circumstances respecting me. When I was brought up to them upon the deck of the vessel, I spoke as fine an Irish brogue as one shall hear on a summer's day; and now all at once there was not the least particle of it left. In searching me they had found upon me fifteen guineas; how should a poor beggar lad, such as I appeared, come honestly by fifteen guineas? Besides, when they had stripped me naked, though my dress was so shabby, my skin had all the sleekness of a gentleman. In fine, for what purpose could a poor beggar, who had never been in Ireland in his life, want to transport himself to that country? It was as clear as the sun that I was no better than I should be. This reasoning, together with some significant winks and gestures between the justice and the plaintiffs, brought him over to their way of thinking. He said, I must go to Warwick, where it seems the other robber was at present in custody, and be confronted with him; and, if then every thing appeared fair and satisfactory, I should be discharged.

No intelligence could be more terrible than that which was contained in these words. That I, who had found the whole country in arms against me, who was exposed to a pursuit so peculiarly vigilant and penetrating, should now be dragged to the very centre of the kingdom, without power of accommodating myself to circumstances, and under the immediate custody of the officers of justice, seemed to my ears almost the same thing as if they had pronounced upon me a sentence of death! I strenuously urged the injustice of this proceeding. I observed to the magistrate that it was impossible I should be the person at whom the description pointed. It required an Irishman; I was no Irishman. It described a person shorter than I; a circumstance of all others the least capable of being counterfeited. There was not the slightest reason for detaining me in custody. I had been already disappointed of my voyage and lost the money I had paid down through the officiousness of these gentlemen in apprehending me. I assured his worship that every delay under my circumstances was of the utmost importance to me. It was impossible to devise a greater injury to be inflicted on me, than the proposal that, instead of being permitted to proceed upon my voyage, I should be sent under arrest into the heart of the kingdom.

My remonstrances were in vain. The justice was by no means inclined to digest the being expostulated with in this manner by a person in the habiliments of a beggar. In the midst of my address he would have silenced me for my impertinence, but that I spoke with an earnestness with which he was wholly unable to contend. When I had finished, he told me that it was all to no purpose, and that it might have been better for me if I had shown myself less insolent. It was clear that I was a vagabond and a suspicious person. The more earnest I showed myself to get off, the more reason there was he should keep me fast. Perhaps after all I should turn out to be the felon in question. But, if I was not that, he had no doubt I was worse; a poacher, or for what he knew a murderer. He had a kind of a notion that he had seen my face before about some such affair; out of all doubt I was an old offender. He had it in his choice to send me to hard labour as a vagrant upon the strength of my appearance and the contradictions in my story, or to order me to Warwick; and out of the spontaneous goodness of his disposition he chose the milder side of the alternative. He could assure me I should not slip through his fingers. It was of more benefit to his majesty's government to hang one such fellow as he suspected me to be, than out of mistaken tenderness to concern oneself for the good of all the beggars in the nation.

Finding it was impossible to work, in the way I desired, on a man, so fully impressed with his own dignity and importance and my utter insignificance, I claimed that at least the money taken from my person should be restored to me. This was granted. His worship perhaps suspected that he had stretched a point in what he had already done, and was therefore the less unwilling to relax in this incidental circumstance. My conductors did not oppose themselves to this indulgence, for a reason that will appear in the sequel. The justice however enlarged upon his clemency in this proceeding. He did not know whether he was not exceeding the spirit of his commission in complying with my demand. So much money in my possession could not be honestly come by. But it was his temper to soften, as far as could be done with propriety, the strict letter of the law.

There were cogent reasons why the gentlemen who had originally taken me into custody, chose that I should continue in their custody when my examination was over. Every man is in his different mode susceptible to a sense of honour; and they did not choose to encounter the disgrace that would accrue to them if justice had been done. Every man is in some degree influenced by the love of power; and they were willing I should owe any benefit I received, to their sovereign grace and benignity, and not to the mere reason of the case. It was not however an unsubstantial honour and barren power that formed the objects of their pursuit: no, their views were deeper than that. In a word, though they chose that I should retire from the seat of justice as I had come before it, a prisoner, yet the tenour of my examination had obliged them in spite of themselves to suspect, that I was innocent of the charge they alleged against me. Apprehensive therefore that the hundred guineas which had been offered as a reward for taking the robber, was completely out of the question in the present business, they were contented to strike at smaller game. Having conducted me to an inn, and given directions respecting a vehicle for the journey, they took me aside, while one of them addressed me in the following manner:

You see, my lad, how the case stands; heigh for Warwick is the word! and, when we are got there, what may happen then I will not pretend for to say. Whether you are innocent or no is no business of mine; but you are not such a chicken as to suppose, if so be as you are innocent, that that will make your game altogether sure. You say, your business calls you another way, and as how you are in haste: I scorns to cross any man in his concerns, if I can help it. If therefore you will give us them there fifteen shiners, why snug is the word. They are of no use to you; a beggar, you know, is always at home. For the matter of that we could have had them in the way of business as you saw at the justice's. But I am a man of principle; I loves to do things above board, and scorns to extort a shilling from any man.

He who is tinctured with principles of moral discrimination, is apt upon occasion to be run away with by his feelings in that respect, and to forget the immediate interest of the moment. I confess that the first sentiment excited in my mind by this overture was that of indignation. I was irresistibly impelled to give utterance to this feeling, and postpone for a moment the consideration of the future. I replied with the severity which so base a proceeding appeared to deserve. My bear-leaders were considerably surprised with my firmness, but seemed to think it beneath them to contest with me the principles I delivered. He who had made the overture contented himself with replying, Well, well, my lad, do as you will; you are not the first man that has been hanged rather than part with a few guineas. His words did not pass unheeded by me. They were strikingly applicable to my situation, and I was determined not to suffer the occasion to escape me unimproved.

The pride of these gentlemen however was too great to admit of farther parley for the present. They left me abruptly, having first ordered an old man, the father of the landlady, to stay in the room with me while they were absent. The old man they ordered for security to lock the door and put the key in his pocket, at the same time mentioning below stairs the station in which they had left me, that the people of the house might have an eye upon what went forward, and not suffer me to escape. What was the intention of this manœuvre I am unable certainly to pronounce. Probably it was a sort of compromise between their pride and their avarice, being desirous for some reason or other to drop me as soon as convenient, and therefore determining to wait the result of my private meditations on the proposal they had made.

CHAPTER VII

THEY were no sooner withdrawn than I cast my eye upon the old man, and found something extremely venerable and interesting in his appearance. His form was above the middle size. It indicated that his strength had once been considerable; nor was it at this time by any means annihilated. His hair was in considerable quantity, and was as white as the drifted snow. His complexion was healthful and ruddy, at the same time that his face was furrowed with wrinkles. In his eye there was remarkable vivacity, and his whole countenance was strongly expressive of good nature. The boorishness of his rank in society was lost, in the cultivation his mind had derived from habits of sensibility and benevolence.

The view of his figure immediately introduced a train of ideas into my mind respecting the advantage to be drawn from the presence of such a person. The attempt to take any step without his consent was hopeless, for, though I should succeed with regard to him, he could easily give the alarm to other persons who would no doubt be within call. Add to which, I could scarcely have prevailed on myself to offer any offence, to a person whose first appearance so strongly engaged my affection and esteem. In reality my thoughts were turned into a different channel. I was impressed with an ardent wish, to be able to call this man my benefactor. Pursued by a train of ill fortune, I could no longer consider myself as a member of society. I was a solitary being cut off from the expectation of sympathy, kindness and the good will of mankind. I was strongly impelled by the situation in which the present moment placed me, to indulge in a luxury which my destiny seemed to have denied. I could not conceive of the smallest comparison between the idea of deriving my liberty from the spontaneous kindness of a worthy and excellent mind, and that of being indebted for it to the selfishness and baseness of the worst members of society. It was thus that I allowed myself in the wantonness of refinement even in the midst of destruction.

Guided by these sentiments, I requested his attention to the circumstances by which I had been brought into my present situation. He immediately signified his assent, and said he would chearfully listen to any thing I thought proper to communicate. I told him the persons who had just left me in charge with him, had come to this town for the purpose of apprehending some person who had been guilty of robbing the mail; that they had chosen to take me up under this warrant, and had conducted me before a justice of the peace; that they had soon detected their mistake, the person in question being an Irishman, and differing from me both in country and stature; but that by collusion between them and the justice they were permitted to retain me in custody, and pretended to undertake to conduct me to Warwick to confront me with my accomplice; that in searching me at the justice's they had found a sum of money in my possession which excited their cupidity, and that they had just been proposing to me to give me my liberty upon condition of my surrendering this sum into their hands. Under these circumstances I requested him to consider whether he would wish to render himself the instrument of their extortion. I put

myself into his hands, and solemnly averred the truth of the facts
I had just stated. If he would assist me in my escape, it could have
no other effect than to disappoint the base passions of my conductors. I would upon no account expose him to any real inconvenience; but I was well assured that the same generosity that
prompted him to a good deed, would enable him effectually to
vindicate it when done; and that those who detained me, when they
had lost sight of their prey, would feel covered with confusion, and
not dare to take another step in the affair.

The old man listened to what I related with curiosity and
interest. He said that he had always felt an abhorrence to the sort of
people who had me in their hands, that he had an aversion to the
task they had just imposed upon him, but that he could not refuse
some little disagreeable offices to oblige his daughter and son in
law. He had no doubt, from my countenance and manner, of the
truth of what I had asserted to him. It was an extraordinary request
I had made, and he did not know what had induced me to think
him the sort of person to whom, with any prospect of success, it
might be made. In reality however his habits of thinking were
uncommon, and he felt more than half inclined to act as I desired.
One thing at least he would ask of me in return, which was to be
faithfully informed in some degree respecting the person he was
desired to oblige. What was my name?

The question came upon me unprepared. But, whatever might
be the consequence, I could not bear to deceive the person by
whom it was put, and in the circumstances under which it was put.
The practice of perpetual falshood is too painful a task. I replied
that my name was Williams.

He paused. His eye was fixed upon me. I saw his complexion
alter at the repetition of that word. He proceeded with visible
anxiety.

My christian name?

Caleb.

Good God! it could not be——? He conjured me by every thing
that was sacred to answer him faithfully to one question more. I
was not?—no, it was impossible—the person who had formerly
lived servant with Mr. Falkland of ——?

I told him that, whatever might be the meaning of his question,
I would answer him truly. I was the individual he mentioned.

As I uttered these words, the old man rose from his seat. He was sorry that fortune had been so unpropitious to him, as for him ever to have set eyes upon me! I was a monster with whom the very earth groaned!

I intreated that he would suffer me to explain this new misapprehension, as he had done in the former instance. I had no doubt that I should do it equally to his satisfaction.

No! no! no! he would upon no consideration admit that his ears should suffer such contamination. This case and the other were very different. There was no criminal upon the face of the earth, no murderer, half so detestable, as the person who could prevail upon himself to utter the charges I had done by way of recrimination against so generous a master.—The old man was in a perfect agony with the recollection.

At length he calmed himself enough to say he should never cease to grieve that he had held a moment's parley with me. He did not know what was the conduct that severe justice required of him; but, since he had come into the knowledge of who I was only by my own confession, it was irreconcilably repugnant to his feelings to make use of that knowledge to my injury. Here therefore all relation between us ceased; as indeed it would be an abuse of words to consider me in the light of a human creature. He would do me no mischief; but on the other hand he would not for the world be in any way assisting and abetting me.

I was inexpressibly affected at the abhorrence this good and benevolent creature expressed against me. I could not be silent; I endeavoured once and again to prevail upon him to hear me. But his determination was unalterable. Our contest lasted for some time, and he at length terminated it by ringing the bell, and calling up the waiter. A very little while after this my conductors entered, and the other persons withdrew.

It was a part of the singularity of my fate, that it hurried me from one species of anxiety and distress to another, too rapidly to suffer any one of them to sink deeply into my mind. I am apt to believe in the retrospect that half the calamities I was destined to endure would infallibly have overwhelmed and destroyed me. But, as it was, I had no leisure to chew the cud upon misfortunes as they befel me, but was under the necessity of forgetting them to guard against peril that the next moment seemed ready to crush me. The behaviour of this incomparable and amiable old man cut me to the heart. It was a dreadful prognostic for all my future life. But, as I

have just observed, my conductors entered, and another subject
called imperiously upon my attention. I could have been content,
mortified as I was at this instant, to have been shut up in some
impenetrable solitude, and to have wrapped myself up in inconsolable misery. But the grief I endured had not such power over me,
as that I could be content to risk the being led to the gallows. The
love of life, and still more a hatred against oppression, steeled my
heart against that species of inertness. In the scene that had just
passed I had indulged, as I have said, in a wantonness and luxury of
refinement. It was time that that indulgence should be brought to
a period. It was dangerous to trifle any more upon the brink of
fate; and, penetrated as I was with sadness by the result of my last
attempt, I was little disposed to unnecessary circumambulation.
I was exactly in the temper in which the gentlemen who had me in
their power, would have desired to find me. Accordingly we entered
immediately upon business; and, after some chaffering, they
agreed to accept eleven guineas as the price of my freedom. To
preserve however the chariness of their reputation, they insisted
upon conducting me with them for a few miles on the outside of
a stage coach. They then pretended that the road they had to
travel lay in a cross-country direction; and, having quitted the
vehicle, they suffered me, almost as soon as it was out of sight, to
shake off this troublesome association, and follow my own inclinations. It may be worth remarking by the way, that these fellows
outwitted themselves at their own trade. They had laid hold of me
at first under the idea of a prize of a hundred guineas; they had
since been glad to accept a composition of eleven; but, if they had
retained me a little longer in their possession, they would have
found the possibility of acquiring the sum that had originally
excited their pursuit, upon a different score.

The mischances that had befallen me in my late attempt to
escape from my pursuers by sea, deterred me from the thought of
repeating that experiment. I therefore once more returned to the
suggestion of hiding myself, at least for the present, amidst the
crowds of the metropolis. Meanwhile I by no means thought proper
to venture by the direct route, and the less so as that was the course
which would be steered by my late conductors; but took my road
along the borders of Wales. The only incident worth relating in
this place, occurred in an attempt to cross the Severn in a particular
point. The mode was by a ferry; but by some strange inadvertence

I lost my way so completely as to be wholly unable that night to reach the ferry, and arrive at the town which I had destined for my repose.

This may seem a petty disappointment, in the midst of the overwhelming considerations that might have been expected to engross every thought of my mind. Yet it was borne by me with singular impatience. I was that day uncommonly fatigued. Previously to the time that I mistook, or at least was aware of the mistake of the road, the sky had become black and lowering, and soon after the clouds burst down in sheets of rain. I was in the midst of a heath, without a tree or covering of any sort to shelter me. I was thoroughly drenched in a moment. I pushed on with a sort of sullen determination. By and by the rain gave place to a storm of hail. The hail-stones were large and frequent. I was ill defended by the miserable covering I wore, and they seemed to cut me in a thousand directions. The hail-storm subsided, and was again succeeded by a heavy rain. By this time it was that I had perceived I was wholly out of my road. I could discover neither man, nor beast, nor habitation of any kind. I walked on, measuring at every turn the path it would be proper to pursue, but in no instance finding a sufficient reason to reject one or prefer another. My mind was bursting with depression and anguish. I muttered imprecations and murmuring, as I passed along. I was full of loathing and abhorrence of life, and all that life carries in its train. After wandering without any certain direction for two hours, I was overtaken by the night. The scene was nearly pathless, and it was vain to think of proceeding any further.

Here I was, without comfort, without shelter and without food. There was not a particle of my covering that was not as wet, as if it had been fished from the bottom of the ocean. My teeth chattered. I trembled in every limb. My heart burned with universal fury. At one moment I stumbled and fell over some unseen obstacle. At another I was turned back by an impediment I could not overcome.

There was no strict connection between these casual inconveniencies, and the persecution under which I laboured. But my distempered thoughts confounded them together. I cursed the whole system of human existence. I said, Here I am an outcast, destined to perish with hunger and cold. All men desert me. All men hate me. I am driven with mortal threats from the sources of comfort and existence. Accursed world! that hates without a cause, that overwhelms innocence with calamities which ought to be spared even to guilt! Accursed world! dead to every manly sympathy; with eyes of horn, and hearts of steel! Why do I consent to live any longer? Why do I seek to drag on an existence which, if protracted, must be protracted amidst the lairs of these human tygers?

This paroxysm at length exhausted itself. Presently after I discovered a solitary shed which I was contented to resort to for shelter. In a corner of the shed I found some clean straw. I threw off my rags, placed them in a situation where they would best be dried, and buried myself amidst this friendly warmth. Here I forgot, by degrees, the anguish that had racked me. A wholsome shed and fresh straw may seem but scanty benefits; but they offered themselves when least expected, and my whole heart was lightened by the encounter. Through fatigue of mind and body it happened in this instance, though in general my repose was remarkably short, that I slept till almost noon of the next day. When I rose, I found that I was at no great distance from the ferry, which I crossed, and entered the town where I intended to have rested the preceding night.

It was market day. As I passed near the cross,[1] I observed two people look at me with great earnestness, after which one of them exclaimed, I will be damned, if I do not think that this is the very fellow those men were enquiring for, who set off an hour ago by the coach for ——. I was extremely alarmed at this information; and, quickening my pace, turned sharp down a narrow lane. The moment I was out of sight I ran with all the speed I could exert, and did not think myself safe till I was several miles distant from the place where this information had reached my ears. I have always believed that the men to whom it related were the very persons who had apprehended me on board the ship in which I had embarked for Ireland, that by some accident they had met with the description of my person as published on the part of Mr. Falkland, and that from putting together the circumstances they had been led to believe that this was the very individual who had lately been in their custody. Indeed it was a piece of infatuation in me for which I am now unable to account, that, after the various indications which had occurred in that affair proving to them that I was a man in very critical and peculiar circumstances, I should have persisted in wearing the same disguise without the smallest alteration. My escape in the present case was eminently fortunate. If I had not lost my way in consequence of the hail-storm of the preceding night, or if I had not so greatly overslept myself this very morning, I must almost infallibly have fallen into the hands of these infernal blood hunters.

The town they had chosen for their next stage, the name of which I had thus caught in the market-place, was the town to which, but for this intimation, I should have immediately proceeded. As it was, I determined to take a road as wide of it as possible. In the first place to which I came, in which it was practicable to do so, I bought a great coat which I drew over my beggar's weeds, and a better hat. The hat I slouched over my face, and covered one of my eyes with a green silk shade. The handkerchief, which I had hitherto worn about my head, I now tied about the lower part of my visage, so as to cover my mouth. By degrees I discarded every part of my former dress, and wore for my upper garment a kind of carman's frock, which, being of the better sort, made me look like the son of a reputable farmer of the lower class. Thus equipped, I proceeded on my journey, and, after a thousand alarms, precautions, and circuitous deviations from the direct path, arrived safely in London.

CHAPTER VIII

HERE then was the termination of an immense series of labours, upon which no man could have looked back without astonishment, or forward without a sentiment bordering on despair. It was at a price which defies estimation that I had purchased this resting place; whether we consider the efforts it had cost me to escape from the walls of my prison, or the dangers and anxieties to which I had been a prey from that hour to the present.

But why do I call the point at which I was now arrived a resting place? Alas, it was diametrically the reverse! It was my first and immediate business, to review all the projects of disguise I had hitherto conceived, to derive every improvement I could invent from the practice to which I had been subjected, and to manufacture a veil of concealment more impenetrable than ever. This

was an effort to which I could see no end. In ordinary cases the
hue and cry after a supposed offender is a matter of temporary
operation; but ordinary cases formed no standard for the colossal
intelligence of Mr. Falkland. For the same reason, London, which
appears an inexhaustible reservoir of concealment to the majority
of mankind, brought no such consolatory sentiment to my mind.
Whether life were worth accepting on such terms I cannot pronounce. I only know that I persisted in this exertion of my faculties,
through a sort of parental love that men are accustomed to entertain for their intellectual offspring; the more thought I had
expended in rearing it to its present perfection, the less did I find
myself disposed to abandon it. Another motive not less strenuously
exciting me to perseverance, was the ever-growing repugnance I
felt to injustice and arbitrary power.

   The first evening of my arrival in town I slept at an obscure inn
in the borough of Southwark, choosing that side of the metropolis
on account of its lying entirely wide of the part of England from
which I came. I entered the inn in the evening in my countryman's
frock; and, having paid for my lodging before I went to bed,
equipped myself next morning as differently as my wardrobe would
allow, and left the house before day. The frock I made up into a
small packet; and, having carried it to a distance as great as I
thought necessary, I dropped it in the corner of an alley through
which I passed. My next care was to furnish myself with another
suit of apparel totally different from any to which I had hitherto
had recourse. The exterior which I was now induced to assume was
that of a Jew. One of the gang of thieves upon —— forest had been
of that race; and, by the talent of mimicry which I have already
stated myself to possess, I could copy their pronunciation of the
English language, sufficiently to answer such occasions as were
likely to present themselves. One of the preliminaries I now adopted
was to repair to a quarter of the town in which great numbers of
this people reside, and study their complexion and countenance.
Having made such provision as my prudence suggested to me, I
retired for that night to an inn in the midway between Mile End
and Wapping. Here I accoutred myself in my new habiliments;
and, having employed the same precautions as before, retired from
my lodging at a time least exposed to observation. It is unnecessary
to describe the particulars of my new equipage. Suffice it to say, that
one of my cares was to discolour my complexion, and give it the

dun and sallow hue which is in most instances characteristic of the tribe to which I assumed to belong; and that, when my meta-morphosis was finished, I could not upon the strictest examination conceive, that any one could have traced out the person of Caleb Williams in this new disguise.

Thus far advanced in the execution of my project, I deemed it advisable to procure a lodging, and change my late wandering life for a stationary one. In this lodging I constantly secluded myself from the rising to the setting of the sun; the periods I allowed for exercise and air were few, and those few by night. I was even cautious of so much as approaching the window of my apartment, though upon the attic story; a principle I laid down to myself was, not wantonly and unnecessarily to expose myself to risk, however slight that risk might appear.

Here let me pause for a moment, to bring before the reader, in the way in which it was impressed upon my mind, the nature of my situation. I was born free: I was born healthy, vigorous and active, complete in all the lineaments and members of a human body. I was not born indeed to the possession of hereditary wealth; but I had a better inheritance, an enterprising mind, an inquisitive spirit, a liberal ambition. In a word, I accepted my lot with willing-ness and content; I did not fear but I should make my cause good in the lists of existence. I was satisfied to aim at small things; I was pleased to play at first for a slender stake; I was more willing to grow, than to descend, in my individual significance.

The free spirit and the firm heart with which I commenced, one circumstance was sufficient to blast. I was ignorant of the power which the institutions of society give to one man over others; I had fallen unwarily into the hands of a person, who held it as his fondest wish, to oppress and destroy me.

I found myself subjected, undeservedly on my part, to all the disadvantages which mankind, if they reflected upon them, would hesitate to impose on acknowledged guilt. In every human coun-tenance I feared to find the countenance of an enemy. I shrunk from the vigilance of every human eye. I dared not open my heart to the best affections of our nature. I was shut up a deserted, solitary wretch in the midst of my species. I dared not look for the consolations of friendship; but, instead of seeking to identify myself with the joys and sorrows of others, and exchanging the delicious gifts of confidence and sympathy, was compelled to centre my thoughts and my vigilance in myself. My life was all a lie. I had a counterfeit character to support. I had counterfeit manners to assume. My gait, my gestures, my accents were all of them to be studied. I was not free to indulge, no not one, honest sally of the soul. Attended with these disadvantages, I was to procure myself a subsistence, a subsistence, to be acquired with infinite precautions, and to be consumed without the hope of enjoyment.

This, even this, I was determined to endure; to put my shoulder to the burthen, and support it with unshrinking firmness. Let it not however be supposed, that I endured it without repining and abhorrence. My time was divided, between the terrors of an animal that skulks from its pursuers, the obstinacy of unshrinking firmness, and that elastic revulsion that from time to time seems to shrivel the very hearts of the miserable. If at one moment I fiercely defied all the rigours of my fate, at others, and those of frequent recurrence, I sunk into helpless despondence, I looked forward without hope through the series of my existence, tears of anguish rushed from my eyes, my courage became extinct, and I cursed the conscious life that was reproduced with every returning day.

Why, upon such occasions I was accustomed to exclaim,—why am I overwhelmed with the load of existence? Why are all these engines at work to torment me? I am no murderer; yet, if I were, what worse could I be fated to suffer? How vile, squalid and disgraceful is the state to which I am condemned! This is not my place in the roll of existence, the place for which either my temper or my understanding has prepared me! To what purpose serve the restless aspirations of my soul, but to make me, like a frighted bird, beat myself in vain against the inclosure of my cage? Nature, barbarous nature, to me thou hast proved indeed the worst of step-mothers; endowed me with wishes insatiate, and sunk me in never-ending degradation!

I might have thought myself more secure, if I had been in possession of money upon which to subsist. The necessity of earning for myself the means of existence, evidently tended to thwart the plan of secrecy to which I was condemned. Whatever labour I adopted, or deemed myself qualified to discharge, it was first to be considered how I was to be provided with employment, and where I was to find an employer or purchaser for my commodities. In the mean time I had no alternative. The little money with which I had escaped from the blood hunters was almost wholly expended.

After the minutest consideration I was able to bestow upon this question, I determined that literature should be the field of my first experiment. I had read of money being acquired in this way, and of prices given by the speculators in this sort of ware to its proper manufacturers. My qualifications I estimated at a slender valuation. I was not without a conviction that experience and practice must pave the way to excellent production. But, though of these I was utterly destitute, my propensities had always led me in this direction; and my early thirst of knowledge had conducted me to a more intimate acquaintance with books, than could perhaps have been expected under my circumstances. If my literary pretensions were slight, the demand I intended to make upon them was not great. All I asked was a subsistence, and I was persuaded few persons could subsist upon slenderer means than myself. I also considered this as a temporary expedient, and hoped that accident or time might hereafter place me in a less precarious situation. The reasons that principally determined my choice, were that this employment called upon me for the least preparation, and could, as I thought, be exercised with least observation.

There was a solitary woman of middle age, who tenanted a chamber in this house upon the same floor with my own. I had no sooner determined upon the destination of my industry, than I cast my eye upon her as the possible instrument for disposing of my productions. Excluded as I was from all intercourse with my species in general, I found pleasure in the occasional exchange of a few words with this inoffensive and good-humoured creature, who was already of an age to preclude scandal. She lived upon a very small annuity allowed her by a distant relation, a woman of quality, who, possessed of thousands herself, had no other anxiety with respect to this person, than that she should not contaminate her alliance by the exertion of honest industry. This humble creature was of a uniformly chearful and active disposition, unacquainted alike with the cares of wealth, and the pressure of misfortune. Though her pretensions were small, and her information slender, she was by no means deficient in penetration. She remarked the faults and follies of mankind with no contemptible discernment; but her temper was of so mild and forgiving a cast, as would have induced most persons to believe that she perceived nothing of the matter. Her heart overflowed with the milk of kindness. She was sincere and ardent in her attachments, and never did she omit a service which she perceived herself able to render to a human being.

Had it not been for these qualifications of temper, I should probably have found that my appearance, that of a deserted, solitary lad of Jewish extraction, effectually precluded my demands upon her kindness. But I speedily perceived, from her manner of receiving and returning civilities of an indifferent sort, that her heart was too noble, to have its effusions checked by any base and unworthy considerations. Encouraged by these preliminaries, I determined to select her as my agent. I found her willing and alert in the business I proposed to her. That I might anticipate occasions of suspicion, I frankly told her that, for reasons which I wished to be excused from relating, but which, if related, I was sure would not deprive me of her good opinion, I found it necessary for the present to keep myself private. With this statement she readily acquiesced, and told me that she had no desire for any farther information than I found it expedient to give.

My first productions were of the poetical kind. After having finished two or three, I directed this generous creature to take them to the office of a newspaper; but they were rejected with contempt by the Aristarchus[1] of that place, who, having bestowed on them a superficial glance, told her that such matters were not in his way. I cannot help mentioning in this place that the countenance of Mrs. Marney (that was the name of my ambassadress) was in all cases a perfect indication of her success, and rendered explanation by words wholly unnecessary. She interested herself so unreservedly in what she undertook, that she felt either miscarriage or good fortune much more exquisitely than I did. I had an unhesitating confidence in my own resources, and, occupied as I was in meditations more interesting and more painful, I regarded these matters as altogether trivial.

I quietly took the pieces back, and laid them upon my table. Upon revisal I altered and transcribed one of them, and, joining it with two others, dispatched them together to the editor of a magazine. He desired they might be left with him till the day after tomorrow. When that day came, he told my friend they should be inserted; but, Mrs. Marney asking respecting the price, he replied, it was their constant rule to give nothing for poetical compositions, the letter-box being always full of writings of that sort; but, if the gentleman would try his hand in prose, a short essay or a tale, he would see what he could do for him.

With the requisition of my literary dictator I immediately complied. I attempted a paper in the style of Addison's Spectators, which was accepted. In a short time I was upon an established footing in this quarter. I however distrusted my resources in the way of moral disquisition, and soon turned my thoughts to his other suggestion, a tale. His demands upon me were now frequent, and to facilitate my labour I bethought myself of the resource of translation. I had scarcely any convenience with respect to the procuring of books; but, as my memory was retentive, I frequently translated or modelled my narratives upon a reading of some years before. By a fatality for which I did not exactly know how to account, my thoughts frequently led me to the histories of celebrated robbers; and I retailed from time to time incidents and anecdotes of Cartouche, Gusman d'Alfarache and other memorable worthies, whose carreer was terminated upon the gallows or the scaffold.

In the mean time a retrospect to my own situation, rendered a perseverance even in this industry, difficult to be maintained. I often threw down my pen in an extacy of despair. Sometimes, for whole days together I was incapable of action, and sunk into a sort of partial stupor too wretched to be described. Youth and health however enabled me, from time to time, to get the better of my dejection; and to rouse myself to something like a gaiety, which, if it had been permanent, might have made this interval of my story tolerable to my reflections.

CHAPTER IX

WHILE I was thus endeavouring to occupy and provide for the intermediate period till the violence of the pursuit after me might be abated, a new source of danger opened upon me of which I had no previous suspicion. Gines, the thief who had been expelled from captain Raymond's gang, had fluctuated during the last years of his life, between the two professions of a violator of the laws and a retainer to their administration. He had originally devoted himself to the first, and probably his initiation in the mysteries of thieving qualified him to be peculiarly expert in the profession of a thief-taker, a profession he had adopted not from choice, but necessity. In this employment his reputation was great, though perhaps not equal to his merits; for it happens here, as in other departments of human society, that, however the subalterns may furnish wisdom and skill, the principals exclusively possess the eclat. He was exercising this art in a very prosperous manner, when it happened by some accident, that one or two of his atchievements, previous to his having shaken off the dregs of unlicensed depredation, were in danger of becoming subjects of public attention. Having had repeated intimations of this, he thought it prudent to decamp, and it was during this period of his retreat that he entered into the —— gang.

Such was the history of this man antecedently to his being placed in the situation in which I had first encountered him. At the time of that encounter he was a veteran of captain Raymond's gang; for, thieves being a short lived race, the character of veteran costs the less time in acquiring. Upon his expulsion from this community he returned once more to his lawful profession, and by his old comrades was received with congratulation as a lost sheep. In the vulgar classes of society no length of time is sufficient to expiate a crime; but among the honorable fraternity of thief-takers it is a rule never to bring one of their own brethren to a reckoning, when it can with any decency be avoided. Another rule observed by those who have passed through the same gradation as Gines had done, and which was adopted by Gines himself, is always to reserve such as have been the accomplices of their depredations to the last, and on no account to assail them without great necessity or powerful temptation. For this reason, according to Gines's system of tactics, captain Raymond and his confederates were, as he would have termed it, safe from his retaliation.

But, though Gines was in this sense of the term a man of strict honour, my case unfortunately did not fall within the laws of honour he acknowledged. Misfortune had overtaken me, and I was on all sides without protection or shelter. The persecution to which I was exposed was founded upon the supposition of my having committed felony to an immense amount. But in this Gines had had no participation; he was careless whether the supposition were true or false, and hated me as much as if my innocence had been established beyond the reach of suspicion. The blood hunters who had taken me into custody at ——, related, as usual, among their fraternity a part of their adventure, and told of the reason which inclined them to suppose, that the individual who had passed through their custody, was the very Caleb Williams for whose apprehension a reward had been offered of a hundred guineas. Gines, whose acuteness was eminent in the way of his profession, by comparing facts and dates was induced to suspect in his own mind that Caleb Williams was the person he had hustled and wounded upon —— forest. Against that person he entertained the bitterest aversion. I had been the innocent occasion of his being expelled with disgrace from captain Raymond's gang; and Gines, as I afterwards understood, was intimately persuaded that there was no comparison between the liberal and manly profession of a robber, from which I had driven him, and the sordid and mechanical occupation of a blood hunter, to which he was obliged to return. He no sooner received the information I have mentioned, than he vowed revenge. He determined to leave all other objects, and consecrate every faculty of his mind to the unkenneling me from my hiding place. The offered reward, which his vanity made him consider as assuredly his own, appeared as the complete indemnification of his labour and expence. Thus I had to encounter the sagacity he possessed in the way of his profession, whetted and stimulated by a sentiment of vengeance in a mind that knew no restraint from conscience or humanity.

When I drew to myself a picture of my situation soon after having fixed on my present abode, I foolishly thought, as the unhappy are accustomed to do, that my calamity would admit of no aggravation. The aggravation which, unknown to me, at this time occurred, was the most fearful that any imagination could have devised. Nothing could have happened more critically hostile to my future peace, than my fatal encounter with Gines upon —— forest. By this means, as it now appears, I had fastened upon myself a second enemy, of that singular and dreadful sort, that is determined never to dismiss its animosity, as long as life shall endure. While Falkland was the hungry lion whose roarings astonished and appalled me, Gines was a noxious insect, scarcely less formidable and tremendous, that hovered about my goings, and perpetually menaced me with the poison of his sting.

The first step pursued by him in execution of his project, was

to set out for the seaport town where I had formerly been apprehended. From thence he traced me to the banks of the Severn, and
from the banks of the Severn to London. It is scarcely necessary to
observe that this is always practicable, provided the pursuer have
motives strong enough to excite him to perseverance, unless the
precautions of the fugitive be in the highest degree both judicious
in the conception and fortunate in the execution. Gines indeed in
the course of his pursuit was often obliged to double his steps; and,
like the harrier, whenever he was at a fault, return to the place
where he had last perceived the scent of the animal whose death he
had decreed. He spared neither pains nor time in the gratification
of the passion which choice had made his ruling one.

Upon my arrival in town he for a moment lost all trace of me,
London being a place in which, on account of the magnitude of its
dimensions, it might well be supposed that an individual could
remain hidden and unknown. But no difficulty could discourage
this new adversary. He went from inn to inn, reasonably supposing
that there was no private house to which I could immediately
repair, till he found, by the description he gave, and the recollec-
tions he excited, that I had slept for one night in the borough of
Southwark. But he could get no farther information. The people
of the inn had no knowledge what had become of me the next
morning. This however did but render him more eager in the
pursuit. The describing me was now more difficult, on account of
the partial change of my dress I had made the second day of my
being in town. But Gines at length overcame the obstacle from that
quarter. Having traced me to my second inn, he was here furnished
with a more copious information. I had been a subject of speculation
for the leisure hours of some of the persons belonging to this inn.
An old woman of a most curious and loquacious disposition who
lived opposite to it, and who that morning rose early to her washing, had espied me from her window by the light of a large lamp
which hung over the inn, as I issued from the gate. She had but a
very imperfect view of me, but she thought there was something
Jewish in my appearance. She was accustomed to hold a conference
every morning with the landlady of the inn, some of the waiters
and chambermaids occasionally assisting at it. In the course of the
dialogue of this morning she asked some questions about the Jew
who had slept there the night before. No Jew had slept there. The
curiosity of the landlady was excited in her turn. By the time of the

morning it could be no one but me. It was very strange! They compared notes respecting my appearance and dress. No two things could be more dissimilar. The Jew-Christian, upon any dearth of subjects of intelligence, repeatedly furnished matter for their discourse.

The information thus afforded to Gines, appeared exceedingly material. But the performance did not for some time keep pace with the promise. He could not enter every private house into which lodgers were ever admitted, in the same manner that he had treated the inns. He walked the streets, and examined with a curious and inquisitive eye the countenance of every Jew about my stature; but in vain. He repaired to Duke's Place¹ and the synagogues. It was not here that in reality he could calculate upon finding me; but he resorted to these means in despair and as a last hope. He was more than once upon the point of giving up the pursuit; but he was recalled to it by an insatiable and restless appetite for revenge.

It was during this perturbed and fluctuating state of his mind that he chanced to pay a visit to a brother of his who was the head-workman of a printing office. There was little intercourse between these two persons, their dispositions and habits of life being extremely dissimilar. The printer was industrious, sober, inclined to methodism, and of a propensity to accumulation. He was extremely dissatisfied with the character and pursuits of his brother, and had made some ineffectual attempts to reclaim him. But, though they by no means agreed in their habits of thinking, they sometimes saw each other. Gines loved to boast of as many of his atchievements, as he dared venture to mention; and his brother was one more hearer, in addition to the set of his usual associates. The printer was amused, with the blunt sagacity of remark and novelty of incident that characterised Gines's conversation. He was secretly pleased, in spite of all his sober and church-going prejudices, that he was brother to a man of so much ingenuity and fortitude.

After having listened for some time upon this occasion to the wonderful stories which Gines in his rugged way condescended to tell, the printer felt an ambition to entertain his brother in his turn. He began to retail some of my stories of Cartouche and Gusman d'Alfarache. The attention of Gines was excited. His first emotion was wonder; his second was envy and aversion. Where did the printer get these stories? This question was answered. I will tell you what, said the printer, we none of us know what to make of the writer of these articles. He writes poetry and morality and history: I am a printer and corrector of the press, and may pretend without vanity to be a tolerably good judge of these matters: he writes them all to my mind extremely fine, and yet he is no more than a Jew. [To my honest printer this seemed as strange as if they had been written by a Cherokee chieftain at the falls of the Missisippi.]

A Jew! How do you know? Did you ever see him?

No; the matter is always brought to us by a woman. But my master hates all mysteries; he likes to see his authors themselves. So he plagues and plagues the old woman; but he can never get any thing out of her, except that one day she happened to drop that the young gentleman was a Jew.

A Jew! a young gentleman! a person who did every thing by proxy, and made a secret of all his motions! Here was abundant matter for the speculations and suspicions of Gines. He was confirmed in them, without adverting to the process of his own mind, by the subject of my lucubrations, men who died by the hands of the executioner. He said little more to his brother, except asking, as if casually, what sort of an old woman this was? of what age she might be? and whether she often brought him materials of this kind? and soon after took occasion to leave him.

It was with vast pleasure that Gines had listened to this unhoped for information. Having collected from his brother sufficient hints relative to the person and appearance of Mrs. Marney, and understanding that he expected to receive something from me the next day, Gines took his stand in the street early that he might not risk miscarriage by negligence. He waited several hours but not without success. Mrs. Marney came; he watched her into the house; and after about twenty minutes delay saw her return. He dogged her from street to street; observed her finally enter the door of a private house; and congratulated himself upon having at length arrived at the consummation of his labours.

The house she entered was not her own habitation. By a sort of miraculous accident she had observed Gines following her in the street. As she went home, she saw a woman who had fallen down in a fainting fit. Moved by the compassion that was ever alive in her, she approached her in order to render her assistance. Presently a crowd collected round them. Mrs. Marney, having done what she was able, once more proceeded homewards. Observing the crowd round her, the idea of pickpockets occurred to her mind; she put her hands to her sides, and at the same time looked round upon the populace. She had left the circle somewhat abruptly; and Gines, who had been obliged to come nearer lest he should lose her in the confusion, was at that moment standing exactly opposite to her. His visage was of the most extraordinary kind; habit had written the characters of malignant cunning and dauntless effrontery in every line of his face; and Mrs. Marney, who was neither philosopher nor physiognomist, was nevertheless struck. This good woman, like most persons of her notable character, had a peculiar way of going home, not through the open streets, but by narrow lanes and alleys, with intricate insertions and sudden turnings. In one of these by some accident she once again caught a glance of her pursuer. This circumstance, together with the singularity of his appearance, awakened her conjectures. Could he be following her? It was the middle of the day, and she could have no fears for herself. But could this circumstance have any reference to me? She recollected the precautions and secrecy I practised, and had no doubt that I had reasons for what I did. She recollected that she had always been upon her guard respecting me; but had she been sufficiently so? She thought that, if she should be the means of any mischief to me, she should be miserable for ever. She determined therefore by way of precaution in case of the worst, to call at a friend's house, and send me word of what had occurred. Having instructed her friend, she went out immediately upon a visit to a person in the exactly opposite direction, and desired her friend to proceed upon the errand to me, five minutes after she left the house. By this prudence she completely extricated me from the present danger.

Meantime the intelligence that was brought me by no means ascertained the greatness of the danger. For any thing I could discover in it, the circumstance might be perfectly innocent, and the fear solely proceed from the over caution and kindness of this benevolent and excellent woman. Yet such was the misery of my situation, I had no choice. For this menace or no menace, I was obliged to desert my habitation at a minute's warning, taking with me nothing but what I could carry in my hand; to see my generous benefactress no more; to quit my little arrangements and provision; and to seek once again in some forlorn retreat new projects and, if of that I could have any rational hope, a new friend: I descended into the street with a heavy, not an irresolute heart. It was broad day. I said, Persons are at this moment supposed to be roaming the street in search of me: I must not trust to the chance of their pursuing one direction, and I another. I traversed half a dozen streets, and then dropped into an obscure house of entertainment for persons of small expence. In this house I took some refreshment, passed several hours of active, but melancholy thinking, and at last procured a bed. As soon however as it was dark, I went out (for this was indispensible) to purchase the materials of a new disguise. Having adjusted it as well as I could during the night, I left this asylum with the same precautions that I had employed in former instances.

CHAPTER X

I PROCURED a new lodging. By some bias of the mind it may be, gratifying itself with images of peril, I inclined upon the whole to believe that Mrs. Marney's alarm had not been without foundation. I was however unable to conjecture through what means danger had approached me; and had therefore only the unsatisfactory remedy of redoubling my watch upon all my actions. Still I had the joint considerations pressing upon me of security and subsistence. I had some small remains of the produce of my former industry; but this was but small, for my employer was in arrear with me, and I did not chuse in any method to apply to him for payment. The anxieties of my mind in spite of all my struggles preyed upon my health. I did not consider myself as in safety for an instant. My appearance was wasted to a shadow; and I started at every sound that was unexpected. Sometimes I was half tempted to resign myself into the hands of the law, and brave its worst; but resentment and indignation at those times speedily flowed back upon my mind, and reanimated my perseverance.

I knew no better resource with respect to subsistence, than that I had employed in the former instance, of seeking some third person to stand between me and the disposal of my industry. I might find an individual ready to undertake this office in my behalf, but where should I find the benevolent soul of Mrs.

Marney? The person I fixed upon was a Mr. Spurrel, a man who took in work from the watch-makers, and had an apartment upon our second floor. I examined him two or three times with irresolute glances, as we passed upon the stairs, before I would venture to accost him. He observed this, and at length kindly invited me into his apartment.

Being seated, he condoled with me upon my seeming bad health, and the solitary mode of my living, and wished to know whether he could be of any service to me. From the first moment he saw me, he had conceived an affection for me. In my present disguise I appeared twisted and deformed, and in other respects by no means an object of attraction. But it seemed, Mr. Spurrel had lost an only son about six months before, and I was the very picture of him. If I had put off my counterfeited ugliness, I should probably have lost all hold upon his affections. He was now an old man, as he observed, just dropping into the grave, and this son had been his only consolation. The poor lad was always ailing, but he had been a nurse to him; and the more tending he required while he was alive, the more he missed him now he was dead. Now he had not a friend, nor any body that cared for him in the whole world. If I pleased, I should be instead of that son to him, and he would treat me in all respects with the same attention and kindness.

I expressed my sense of these benevolent offers; but told him that I should be sorry to be in any way burthensome to him. My ideas at present led me to a private and solitary life, and my chief difficulty was to reconcile this with some mode of earning necessary subsistence. If he would condescend to lend me his assistance in smoothing this difficulty, it would be the greatest benefit he could confer on me. I added, that my mind had always had a mechanical and industrious turn, and that I did not doubt of soon mastering any craft to which I seriously applied myself. I had not been brought up to any trade; but, if he would favour me with his instructions, I would work with him as long as he pleased for a bare subsistence. I knew that I was asking of him an extraordinary kindness, but I was urged on the one hand by the most extreme necessity, and encouraged on the other by the persuasiveness of his friendly professions.

The old man dropped some tears over my apparent distress, and readily consented to every thing I proposed. Our agreement was soon made, and I entered upon my functions accordingly. My new friend was a man of a singular turn of mind. Love of money and a charitable officiousness of demeanour were his leading characteristics. He lived in the most penurious manner, and denied himself every indulgence. I entitled myself almost immediately as he frankly acknowledged, to some remuneration for my labours, and accordingly he insisted upon my being paid. He did not however, as some persons would have done under the circumstance, pay me the whole amount of my earnings, but professed to subtract from them twenty per cent, as an equitable consideration for instruction and commission-money in procuring me a channel for my industry. Yet he frequently shed tears over me, was uneasy in every moment of our indispensible separation, and exhibited perpetual tokens of attachment and fondness. I found him a man of excellent mechanical contrivance, and received considerable pleasure from his communications. My own sources of information were various; and he frequently expressed his wonder and delight, in the contemplation of my powers, as well of amusement, as exertion.

Thus I appeared to have attained a situation, not less eligible, than in my connection with Mrs. Marney. I was however still more unhappy. My fits of despondence were deeper, and of more frequent recurrence. My health every day grew worse; and Mr. Spurrel was not without apprehensions that he should lose me, as he before lost his only son.

I had not been long however in this new situation, before an incident occurred which filled me with greater alarm and apprehension than ever. I was walking out one evening, after a long visitation of langour, for an hour's exercise and air, when my ears were struck with two or three casual sounds from the mouth of a hawker who was bawling his wares. I stood still to inform myself more exactly, when to my utter astonishment and confusion I heard him deliver himself nearly in these words. 'Here you have the most wonderful and surprising history, and miraculous adventures of Caleb Williams; you are informed how he first robbed, and then brought false accusations against his master; as also of his attempting divers times to break out of prison, till at last he effected his escape in the most wonderful and uncredible manner; as also of his travelling the kingdom in various disguises, and the robberies he committed with a most desperate and daring gang of thieves; and of his coming up to London, where it is supposed he now lies concealed; with a true and faithful copy of the hue and cry printed and published by one of his majesty's most principal secretaries of state, offering a reward of one hundred guineas for apprehending him. All for the price of one halfpenny.'

Petrified as I was at these amazing and dreadful sounds, I had the temerity to go up to the man and purchase one of his papers. I was desperately resolved to know the exact state of the fact, and what I had to depend upon. I carried it with me a little way, till, no longer able to endure the tumult of my impatience, I contrived to make out the chief part of its contents by the help of a lamp, at the upper end of a narrow passage. I found it contain a greater number of circumstances than could have been expected in this species of publication. I was equalled to the most notorious house-breaker in the art of penetrating through walls and doors, and to the most accomplished swindler in plausibleness, duplicity and disguise. The hand-bill which Larkins had first brought to us upon the forest, was printed at length. All my disguises, previously to the last alarm that had been given me by the providence of Mrs. Marney, were faithfully enumerated; and the public was warned to be upon their watch against a person of an uncouth and extra-ordinary appearance, and who lived in a recluse and solitary manner. I also learned from this paper that my former lodgings had been searched on the very evening of my escape, and that Mrs. Marney had been sent to Newgate upon a charge of misprision of felony.—This last circumstance affected me deeply. In the midst of my own sufferings, my sympathies flowed undiminished. It was a most cruel and intolerable idea, if I were not only myself to be an object of unrelenting persecution, but my very touch were to be infectious, and every one that succoured me was to be involved in the common ruin. My instant feeling was that of a willingness to undergo the utmost malice of my enemies, could I by that means have saved this excellent woman from alarm and peril.—I after-wards learned that Mrs. Marney was delivered from confinement, by the interposition of her noble relation.

My sympathy for Mrs. Marney however was at this moment a transient one. A more imperious and irresistible consideration demanded to be heard.

With what sensations did I ruminate upon this paper? Every word of it carried despair to my heart. The actual apprehension that I dreaded, would perhaps have been less horrible. It would have put an end to that lingering terror to which I was a prey.

Disguise was no longer of use. A numerous class of individuals, through every department, almost every house of the metropolis, would be induced to look with a suspicious eye upon every stranger, especially every solitary stranger, that fell under their observation. The prize of one hundred guineas was held out to excite their avarice, and sharpen their penetration. It was no longer Bow-Street,[1] it was a million of men, in arms against me. Neither had I the refuge, which few men have been so miserable as to want, of one single individual with whom to repose my alarms, and who might shelter me from the gaze of indiscriminate curiosity.

What could exceed the horrors of this situation? My heart knocked against my ribs, my bosom heaved, I gasped and panted for breath. There is no end then, said I, to my persecutors! My unwearied and long continued labours lead to no termination! Termination! No! the lapse of time, that cures all other things, makes my case more desperate! Why then, exclaimed I, a new train of thought suddenly rushing into my mind,—Why should I sustain the contest any longer? I can at least elude my persecutors in death. I can bury myself, and the traces of my existence together, in friendly oblivion; and thus bequeath eternal doubt, and ever new alarm, to those who have no peace but in pursuing me!

In the midst of the horrors with which I was now impressed, this idea gave me pleasure, and I hastened to the Thames to put it in instant execution. Such was the paroxysm of my mind, that my powers of vision became partially suspended. I was no longer conscious to the feebleness of disease, but rushed along with fervent impetuosity. I passed from street to street, without observing what direction I pursued. After wandering I know not how long, I arrived at London-Bridge. I hastened to the stairs, and saw the river covered with vessels.

No human being must see me, said I, at the instant that I vanish for ever.—This thought required some consideration. A portion of time had elapsed since my first desperate purpose. My understanding began to return. The sight of the vessels suggested to me the idea of once more attempting to leave my native country.

I enquired, and speedily found that the cheapest passage I could procure was in a vessel, moored near the Tower, and which was to sail in a few days for Middleburg in Holland. I would have gone instantly on board and have endeavoured to prevail with the captain to let me remain there till he sailed; but unfortunately I had not money enough in my pocket to defray my passage. It was worse than this. I had not money enough in the world. I however paid the captain half his demand, and promised to return with the rest. I knew not in what manner it was to be procured, but I believed that I should not fail in it. I had some idea of applying to Mr. Spurrel. Surely he would not refuse me? He appeared to love me with parental affection, and I thought I might trust myself for a moment in his hands.

I approached my place of residence with a heavy and foreboding heart. Mr. Spurrel was not at home; and I was obliged to wait for his return. Worn out with fatigue, disappointment, and the ill state of my health, I sunk upon a chair. Speedily however I recollected myself. I had work of Mr. Spurrel's in my trunk, which had been delivered out to me that very morning, to five times the amount I wanted. I canvassed for a moment whether I should make use of this property as if it were my own; but I rejected the idea with disdain. I had never in the smallest degree merited the reproaches that were cast upon me; and I was determined I never would merit them. I sat gasping, anxious, full of the blackest forebodings. My terrors appeared, even to my own mind, greater and more importunate than the circumstances authorised.

It was extraordinary that Mr. Spurrel should be abroad at this hour; I had never known it happen before. His bed-time was between nine and ten. Ten o'clock came, eleven o'clock, but not Mr. Spurrel. At midnight I heard his knock at the door. Every soul in the house was in bed. Mr. Spurrel, on account of his regular hours, was unprovided with a key to open for himself. A gleam, a sickly gleam! of the social spirit came over my heart. I flew nimbly down the stairs, and opened the door.

I could perceive by the little taper in my hand something extraordinary written in his countenance. I had not time to speak, before I saw two other men follow him. At the first glance I was sufficiently assured what sort of persons they were. At the second I perceived that one of them was no other than Gines himself. I had understood formerly that he had been of this profession, and I was not surprised to find him in it again. Though I had for three hours endeavoured, as it were, to prepare myself for the unavoidable necessity of falling once again into the hands of the officers of law, the sensation I felt at their entrance was undescribably agonizing. I was beside not a little astonished at the time and manner of their entrance, and

I felt anxious to know whether Mr. Spurrel could be base enough to have been their introducer.

I was not long held in perplexity. He no sooner saw his followers within the door, than he exclaimed with convulsive eagerness, There, there, that is your man! thank God! thank God! Gines looked eagerly in my face, with a countenance expressive alternately of hope and doubt, and answered, By God, and I do not know whether it be or no! I am afraid we are in the wrong box! then recollecting himself, We will go into the house, and examine farther however. We all went up stairs into Mr. Spurrel's room; I set down the candle upon the table. I had hitherto been silent; but I determined not to desert myself, and was a little encouraged to exertion by the skepticism of Gines. With a calm and deliberate manner therefore, in my feigned voice, one of the characteristics of which was lisping, I asked, Pray, gentlemen, what may be your pleasure with me? Why, said Gines, our errand is with one Caleb Williams, and a precious rascal he is! I ought to know the chap well enough; but they say he has as many faces as there are days in the year. So you please to pull off your face; or if you cannot do that, at least you can pull off your clothes, and let us see what your hump is made of.

I remonstrated, but in vain. I stood detected in part of my artifice; and Gines, though still uncertain, was every moment more and more confirmed in his suspicions. Mr. Spurrel perfectly gloted, with eyes that seemed ready to devour every thing that passed. As my imposture gradually appeared more palpable, he repeated his exclamation, Thank God! thank God! At last, tired with this scene of mummery, and disgusted beyond measure with the base and hypocritical figure I seemed to exhibit, I exclaimed, Well, I am Caleb Williams; conduct me wherever you please! And now, Mr. Spurrel!—He gave a violent start. The instant I declared myself, his transport had been at the highest, and was, to any power he was able to exert, absolutely uncontrolable. But the unexpectedness of my address, and the tone in which I spoke, electrified him.——Is it possible, continued I, that you should have been the wretch to betray me? What had I done to deserve this treatment? Is this the kindness you professed? the affection that was perpetually in your mouth? to be the death of me!

My poor boy! my dear creature! cried Spurrel, whimpering, and in a tone of the humblest expostulation, indeed I could not help it! I would have helped it, if I could! I hope they will not hurt my darling! I am sure, I shall die if they do!

Miserable driveller! interrupted I, with a stern voice, do you betray me into the remorseless fangs of the law, and then talk of my not being hurt? I know my sentence, and am prepared to meet it! You have fixed the halter upon my neck, and at the same price would have done so to your only son! Go, count your accursed guineas! My life would have been safer in the hands of one I had never seen, than in yours, whose mouth and whose eyes for ever ran over with crocodile affection!

I have always believed that my sickness, and, as he apprehended, approaching death, contributed its part to the treachery of Mr. Spurrel. He predicted to his own mind the time when I should no longer be able to work. He recollected with agony the expence that attended his son's illness and death. He was determined to afford me no assistance of a similar kind. He feared however the reproach of deserting me. He feared the tenderness of his nature. He felt, that I was growing upon his affections, and that, in a short time, he could not have deserted me. He was driven by a sort of implicit impulse, for the sake of avoiding one ungenerous action, to take refuge in another, the basest and most diabolical. This motive, conjoining with the prospect of the proffered reward, was an incitement too powerful for him to resist.

CHAPTER XI

HAVING given vent to my resentment, I left Mr. Spurrel, motionless, and unable to utter a word. Gines and his companion attended me. It is unnecessary to repeat all the insolence of this man. He alternately triumphed in the completion of his revenge, and regretted the loss of the reward to the shrivelled old curmudgeon we had just quitted, whom however he swore he would cheat of it, by one means or another. He claimed to himself the ingenuity of having devised the halfpenny legend, the thought of which was all his own, and was an expedient that was impossible to fail. There was neither law nor justice, he said, to be had, if Hunks,[1] who had done nothing, were permitted to pocket the cash, and his merit were left undistinguished and pennyless.

I paid but little attention to his story. It struck upon my sense, and I was able to recollect it at my nearest leisure, though I thought not of it at the time. For the present I was busily employed reflecting on my new situation, and the conduct to be observed in it. The thought of suicide had twice, in moments of uncommon despair, suggested itself to my mind; but it was far from my habitual meditations. At present, and in all cases where death was immediately threatened me from the injustice of others, I felt myself disposed to contend to the last.

My prospects were indeed sufficiently gloomy and discouraging. How much labour had I exerted, first to extricate myself from prison, and next to evade the diligence of my pursuers; and the result of all, to be brought back to the point from which I began! I had gained fame indeed, the miserable fame to have my story bawled forth by hawkers and ballad-mongers, to have my praises as an active and enterprising villain celebrated among footmen and chambermaids; but I was neither an Erostratus nor an Alexander, to die contented with that species of eulogium. With respect to all that was solid, what chance could I find in new exertions of a similar nature? Never was a human creature pursued by enemies more inventive or envenomed. I could have small hope that they would ever cease their persecution, or that my future attempts could be crowned with a more desirable issue.

They were considerations like these that dictated my resolution. My mind had been gradually weaning from Mr. Falkland, till its feelings rose to something like abhorrence. I had long cherished a reverence for him, which not even animosity and subordination on his part could readily destroy. But I now ascribed a character so inhumanly sanguinary to his mind; I saw something so fiend-like in the thus hunting me round the world, and determining to be satisfied with nothing less than my blood, while at the same time he knew my innocence, my indisposition to mischief, nay I might add my virtues; that henceforth I trampled reverence and the recollection of former esteem under my feet. I lost all regard to his intellectual greatness, and all pity for the agonies of his soul. I also would abjure forbearance. I would show myself bitter and inflexible as he had done. Was it wise in him to drive me into extremity and madness? Had he no fears for his own secret and atrocious offences?

I had been obliged to spend the remainder of the night upon

which I had been apprehended in prison. During the interval I had thrown off every vestige of disguise, and appeared the next morning in my own person. I was of course easily identified; and, this being the whole with which the magistrates before whom I now stood thought themselves concerned, they were proceeding to make out an order for my being conducted back to my own county. I suspended the dispatch of this measure by observing that I had something to disclose. This is an overture to which men appointed for the administration of criminal justice never fail to attend.

I went before the magistrates to whose office Gines and his comrade conducted me, fully determined to publish those astonishing secrets, of which I had hitherto been the faithful depository; and once for all to turn the tables upon my accuser. It was time that the real criminal should be the sufferer, and not that innocence should for ever labour under the oppression of guilt.

I said that I had always protested my innocence, and must now repeat the protest.

In that case, retorted the senior magistrate abruptly, what can you have to disclose? If you are innocent, that is no business of ours! We act officially.

I always declared, continued I, that I was the perpetrator of no guilt, but that the guilt wholly belonged to my accuser. He privately conveyed these effects among my property, and then charged me with the robbery. I now declare more than that, that this man is a murderer, that I detected his criminality, and that for that reason he is determined to deprive me of life. I presume, gentlemen, that you do consider it as your business to take this declaration. I am persuaded you will be by no means disposed actively or passively to contribute to the atrocious injustice under which I suffer, to the imprisonment and condemnation of an innocent man in order that a murderer may go free. I suppressed this story as long as I could. I was extremely averse to be the author of the unhappiness or the death of a human being. But all patience and submission have their limits.

Give me leave, sir, rejoined the magistrate with an air of affected moderation, to ask you two questions. Were you any way aiding, abetting or contributing to this murder?

No.

And pray, sir, who is this Mr. Falkland, and what may have been the nature of your connection with him?

Mr. Falkland is a gentleman of six thousand per annum. I lived with him as his secretary.

In other words you were his servant?

As you please.

Very well, sir, that is quite enough for me. First I have to tell you as a magistrate, that I can have nothing to do with your declaration. If you had been concerned in the murder you talk of, that would alter the case. But it is out of all reasonable rule, for a magistrate to take an information from a felon, except against his accomplices. Next I think it right to observe to you in my own proper person, that you appear to me to be the most impudent rascal I ever saw. Why, are you such an ass as to suppose, that the sort of story you have been telling, can be of any service to you, either here, or at the assizes, or any where else? A fine time of it indeed it would be, if, when gentlemen of six thousand a year take up their servants for robbing them, those servants could trump up such accusations as these, and could get any magistrate or court of justice to listen to them! Whether or no the felony with which you stand charged would have brought you to the gallows, I will not pretend to say. But I am sure this story will. There would be a speedy end to all order and good government, if fellows that trample upon ranks and distinctions in this atrocious sort, were upon any consideration suffered to get off.

And do you refuse, sir, to attend to the particulars of the charge I allege?

Yes, sir, I do.—But, if I did not, pray what witnesses have you of the murder?

This question staggered me.

None.—But I believe I can make out a circumstantial proof of a nature to force attention from the most indifferent hearer.

I thought so.—Officers, take him from the bar!

Such was the success of this ultimate resort on my part, upon which I had built with such undoubting confidence. Till now I had conceived that the unfavourable situation in which I was placed was prolonged by my own forbearance; and I had determined to endure all that human nature could support, rather than have recourse to this extreme recrimination. That idea secretly consoled me under all my calamities: it was a voluntary sacrifice, and was chearfully made. I thought myself allied to the army of martyrs and confessors; I applauded my fortitude and self-denial; and I pleased myself with the idea, that I had the power, though I hoped never to employ it, by an unrelenting display of all my resources to put an end at once to my sufferings and persecutions.

And this at last was the justice of mankind! A man under certain circumstances shall not be heard in the detection of a crime, because he has not been a participator of it! The story of a flagitious murder shall be listened to with indifference, while an innocent man is hunted like a wild beast to the farthest corners of the earth! Six thousand a year shall protect a man from accusation; and the validity of an impeachment shall be superseded, because the author of it is a servant!

I was conducted back to the very prison from which a few months before I had made my escape. With a bursting heart I entered those walls, compelled to feel that all my more than Herculean labours served for my own torture, and for no other end. Since my escape from prison, I had acquired some knowledge of the world; I had learned by bitter experience by how many links society had a hold upon me, and how closely the snares of despotism beset me. I no longer beheld the world, as my youthful fancy had once induced me to do, as a scene in which to hide or to appear, and to exhibit the freaks of a wanton vivacity. I saw my whole species as ready, in one mode or other, to be made the instruments of the tyrant. Hope died away in the bottom of my heart. Shut up for the first night in my dungeon, I was seized at intervals with temporary frenzy. From time to time I rent the universal silence with the roarings of unsupportable despair. But this was a transient distraction. I soon returned to the sober recollection of myself and my miseries.

My prospects were more gloomy, and my situation apparently more irremediable than ever. I was exposed again, if that were of any account, to the insolence and tyranny that are uniformly exercised within those walls. Why should I repeat the loathsome tale of all that was endured by me, and is endured by every man who is unhappy enough to fall under the government of these consecrated ministers of national jurisprudence? The sufferings I had already experienced, my anxieties, my flight, the perpetual expectation of being discovered, worse than the discovery itself, would perhaps have been enough to satisfy the most insensible individual in the court of his own conscience, if I had even been the felon I was pretended to be. But the law has neither eyes, nor ears, nor bowels of humanity; and it turns into marble the hearts of all those that are nursed in its principles.

I however once more recovered my spirit of determination. I resolved that, while I had life, I would never be deserted by this spirit. Oppressed, annihilated I might be; but, if I died, I would die resisting. What use, what advantage, what pleasurable sentiment could arise from a tame surrender? There is no man that is ignorant, that to humble yourself at the feet of the law is a bootless task; in her courts there is no room for amendment and reformation.

My fortitude may to some persons appear above the standard of human nature. But, if I draw back the veil from my heart, they will readily confess their mistake. My heart bled at every pore. My resolution was not the calm sentiment of philosophy and reason. It was a gloomy and desperate purpose; the creature, not of hope, but of a mind austerely held to its design, that felt, as it were, satisfied with the naked effort, and prepared to give success or miscarriage to the winds. It was to this miserable condition, which might awaken sympathy in the most hardened bosom, that Mr. Falkland had reduced me.

In the mean time, strange as it may seem, here, in prison, subject to innumerable hardships, and in the assured expectation of a sentence of death, I recovered my health. I ascribe this to the state of my mind, which was now changed, from perpetual anxiety, terror, and alarm, the too frequent inmates of a prison, but which I, upon this occasion, did not seem to bring along with me, to a desperate firmness.

I anticipated the event of my trial. I determined once more to escape from my prison, nor did I doubt of my ability to effect at least this first step towards my future preservation. The assizes however were near, and there were certain considerations unnecessary to be detailed that persuaded me there might be benefit in waiting till my trial should actually be terminated before I made my attempt. It stood upon the list as one of the latest to be brought forward. I was therefore extremely surprised to find it called out of its order early on the morning of the second day. But, if this were unexpected, how much greater was my astonishment, when my prosecutor was called, to find neither Mr. Falkland, nor Mr. Forester, nor a single individual of any description appear against me! The recognizances into which my prosecutors had entered were declared to be forfeited, and I was dismissed without farther impediment from the bar.

The effect which this incredible reverse produced upon my mind it is impossible to express. I, who had come to that bar with the sentence of death already in idea ringing in my ears, to be told that I was free to transport myself whithersoever I pleased! Was it for this that I had broken through so many locks, and bolts, and the adamantine walls of my prison; that I had passed so many anxious days, and sleepless, spectre-haunted nights; that I had racked my invention for expedients of evasion and concealment; that my mind had been roused to an energy of which I could scarcely have believed it capable; that my existence had been enthralled to an ever-living torment such as I could scarcely have supposed it in man to endure? Great God! What is man? Is he thus blind to the future, thus totally unsuspecting of what is to occur in the next moment of his existence? I have somewhere read that heaven in mercy hides from us the future incidents of our life. My own experience does not well accord with this assertion. In this instance at least I should have been saved from insupportable labour and undescribable anguish, could I have foreseen the catastrophe of this most interesting transaction.

CHAPTER XII

IT was not long before I took my everlasting leave of this detested and miserable scene. My heart was for the present too full of astonishment and exultation in this unexpected deliverance, to admit of anxiety about the future. I withdrew from the town. I rambled with a slow and thoughtful pace, now bursting with exclamation, and now buried in profound and undefinable reverie. Accident led me towards the very heath which had first sheltered me, when upon a former occasion I broke out of my prison. I wandered among its cavities and its vallies. It was a forlorn and desolate solitude. I continued here I know not how long. Night at length overtook me unperceived, and I prepared to return for the present to the town I had quitted.

It was now perfectly dark when two men whom I had not previously observed sprung upon me from behind. They seized me by the arms, and threw me upon the ground. I had no time for resistance or recollection. I could however perceive that one of them was the diabolical Gines. They blindfolded, gagged me, and hurried me I knew not whither. As we passed along in silence, I endeavoured to conjecture what could be the meaning of this extraordinary violence. I was strongly impressed with the idea that, after the event of this morning, the most severe and painful part of my history was past; and, strange as it may seem, I could not persuade myself to regard with alarm this unexpected attack. It might however be some new project suggested by the brutal temper and unrelenting animosity of Gines.

I presently found that we were returned into the town I had just quitted. They led me into a house, and, as soon as they had taken possession of a room, freed me from the restraints they had before imposed. Here Gines informed me with a malicious grin, that no harm was intended me, and therefore I should show most sense in keeping myself quiet. I perceived that we were in an inn; I overheard company in a room at no great distance from us, and therefore was now as thoroughly aware as he could be, that there was at present little reason to stand in fear of any species of violence, and that it would be time enough to resist when they attempted to conduct me from the inn in the same manner that they had brought me into it. I was not without some curiosity to see the conclusion that was to follow upon so extraordinary a commencement.

The preliminaries I have described were scarcely completed, before Mr. Falkland entered the room. I remember Collins, when he first communicated to me the particulars of our patron's history, observed that he was totally unlike the man he had once been. I had no means of ascertaining the truth of that observation. But it was strikingly applicable to the spectacle which now presented itself to my eyes, though, when I last beheld this unhappy man, he had been a victim to the same passions, a prey to the same undying remorse as now. Misery was at that time inscribed in legible characters upon his countenance. But now he appeared like nothing that had ever been visible in human shape. His visage was haggard, emaciated and fleshless. His complexion was a dun and tarnished red, the colour uniform through every region of the face, and suggested the idea of its being burnt and parched by the eternal fire that burned within him. His eyes were red, quick, wandering, full of suspicion and rage. His hair was neglected, ragged and

floating. His whole figure was thin to a degree that suggested the
idea rather of a skeleton than a person actually alive. Life seemed
hardly to be the capable inhabitant of so woe-be-gone and ghost-
like a figure. The taper of wholesome life was expired; but passion
and fierceness and frenzy were able for the present to supply its
place.

I was to the utmost degree astonished and shocked at the sight
of him.—He sternly commanded my conductors to leave the room.

Well, sir, I have this day successfully exerted myself to save your
life from the gallows. A fortnight ago you did what you were able
to bring my life to that ignominious close.

Were you so stupid and undistinguishing as not to know that
the preservation of your life was the uniform object of my exertions?
Did not I maintain you in prison? Did not I endeavour to prevent
your being sent thither? Could you mistake the bigoted and
obstinate conduct of Forester in offering a hundred guineas for
your apprehension, for mine?

I had my eye upon you in all your wanderings. You have taken
no material step through their whole course with which I have not
been acquainted. I meditated to do you good. I have spilled no
blood but that of Tyrrel: that was in the moment of passion, and
it has been the subject of my uninterrupted and hourly remorse.
I have connived at no man's fate but that of the Hawkinses: they
could no otherwise have been saved than by my acknowledging
myself a murderer. The rest of my life has all been spent in acts of
benevolence.

I meditated to do you good. For that reason I was willing to
prove you. You pretended to act towards me with consideration
and forbearance. If you had persisted in that to the end, I would
yet have found a way to reward you. I left you to your own discretion. You might show the impotent malignity of your own heart,
but in the circumstances in which you were then placed I knew
you could not hurt me. Your forbearance has proved, as I all along
suspected, empty and treacherous. You have attempted to blast
my reputation. You have sought to disclose the select and eternal
secret of my soul. Because you have done that, I will never forgive
you. I will remember it to my latest breath. The memory shall
survive me, when my existence is no more. Do you think you are
out of the reach of my power, because a court of justice has
acquitted you?

While Mr. Falkland was speaking, a sudden distemper came over his countenance, his whole frame was shaken by an instantaneous convulsion, and he staggered to a chair. In about three minutes he recovered.

Yes, said he, I am still alive. I shall live for days and months and years, the power that made me, of whatever kind it be, can only determine how long. I live the guardian of my reputation. That, and to endure a misery such as man never endured, are the only ends to which I live. But, when I am no more, my fame shall still survive. My character shall be revered as spotless and unimpeachable by all posterity, as long as the name of Falkland shall be repeated in the most distant regions of the many-peopled globe.

Having said this, he returned to the discourse which more immediately related to my future condition and happiness.

There is one condition, said he, upon which you may obtain some mitigation of your future calamity. It is for that purpose that I have sent for you. Listen to my proposal with deliberation and sobriety! Remember, that the insanity is not less to trifle with the resolved determination of my soul, than it would be to pull a mountain upon your head that hung trembling upon the edge of the mighty Appenine!

I insist then upon your signing a paper declaring in the most solemn manner that I am innocent of murder, and that the charge you alleged at the office in Bow Street is false, malicious and groundless. Perhaps you may scruple out of a regard to truth. Is truth then entitled to adoration for its own sake, and not for the sake of the happiness it is calculated to produce? Will a reasonable man sacrifice to barren truth, when benevolence, humanity and every consideration that is dear to the human heart require that it should be superseded? It is probable that I may never make use of this paper, but I require it as the only practicable reparation to the honour you have assailed. This is what I had to propose. I expect your answer.

Sir, answered I, I have heard you to an end, and I stand in need of no deliberation to enable me to answer you in the negative. You took me up a raw and inexperienced boy, capable of being moulded to any form you pleased. But you have communicated to me volumes of experience in a very short period. I am no longer irresolute and pliable. What is the power you retain over my fate I am unable to discover. You may destroy me; but you cannot make me tremble. I am not concerned to enquire whether what I have suffered flowed from you by design or otherwise, whether you were the author of my miseries or only connived at them. This I know, that I have suffered too exquisitely on your account, for me to feel the least remaining claim on your part to my making any voluntary sacrifice.

You say that benevolence and humanity require this sacrifice of me. No. It would only be a sacrifice to your mad and misguided love of fame, to that passion which has been the source of all your miseries, of the most tragical calamities to others, and of every misfortune that has happened to me. I have no forbearance to exercise towards that passion. If you be not yet cured of this tremendous and sanguinary folly, at least I will do nothing to cherish it. I know not whether from my youth I was destined for a hero; but I may thank you for having taught me a lesson of insurmountable fortitude.

What is it that you require of me? That I should sign away my own reputation for the better maintaining of yours. Where is the equality of that? What is it that casts me at such an immense distance below you, as to make every thing that relates to me wholly unworthy of consideration? You have been educated in the prejudice of birth. I abhor that prejudice. You have made me desperate, and I utter what that desperation suggests.

You will tell me perhaps that I have no reputation to lose, that, while you are esteemed faultless and unblemished, I am universally reputed a thief, a suborner and a calumniator. Be it so. I will never do any thing to countenance those imputations. The more I am destitute of the esteem of mankind, the more careful I will be to preserve my own. I will never from fear or any other mistaken motive do any thing of which I ought to be ashamed.

You are determined to be for ever my enemy. I have in no degree deserved this eternal abhorrence. I have always esteemed and pitied you. For a considerable time I rather chose to expose myself to every kind of misfortune, than disclose the secret that was so dear to you. I was not deterred by your menaces (What could you make me suffer more than I actually suffered?), but by the humanity of my own heart; in which, and not in means of violence, you ought to have reposed your confidence. What is the mysterious vengeance that you can yet execute against me? You menaced me before; you can menace no worse now. You are wearing out the

springs of terror. Do with me as you please! You teach me to hear
you with an unshrinking and desperate firmness. Recollect yourself! I did not proceed to the step with which you reproach me till
I was apparently urged to the very last extremity. I had suffered
as much as human nature can suffer; I had lived in the midst of
eternal alarm and unintermitted watchfulness; I had twice been
driven to purposes of suicide. I am now sorry however that the
step of which you complain, was ever adopted. But, urged to
exasperation by an unintermitted rigour, I had no time to cool or
to deliberate. Even at present I cherish no vengeance against you.
All that is reasonable, all that can really contribute to your security,
I will readily concede; but I will not be driven to an act repugnant
to all reason, integrity and justice.

Mr. Falkland listened to me with astonishment and impatience.
He had entertained no previous conception of the firmness I
displayed. Several times he was convulsed with the fury that
laboured in his breast. Once and again he betrayed an intention to
interrupt; but he was restrained by the collectedness of my manner, and perhaps by a desire to be acquainted with the entire state
of my mind. Finding that I had concluded, he paused for a moment;
his passion seemed gradually to enlarge, till it was no longer
capable of control.

It is well! said he, gnashing his teeth, and stamping upon the
ground. You refuse the composition I offer! I have no power to
persuade you to compliance! You defy me! At least I have a power
respecting you, and that power I will exercise; a power that shall
grind you into atoms. I condescend to no more expostulation.
I know what I am, and what I can be! I know what you are, and
what fate is reserved for you!

Saying this, he quitted the room.

Such were the particulars of this memorable scene. The impression it has left upon my understanding is indelible. The figure and
appearance of Mr. Falkland, his death-like weakness and decay,
his more than mortal energy and rage, the words that he spoke, the
motives that animated him, produced one compounded effect upon
my mind that nothing of the same nature could ever parallel. The
idea of his misery thrilled through my frame. How weak in comparison of it is the imaginary hell, which the great enemy of mankind is represented as carrying every where about with him!

From this consideration my mind presently turned to the

menaces he had vented against myself. They were all mysterious and undefined. He had talked of power, but had given no hint from which I could collect in what he imagined it to consist. He had talked of misery, but had not dropped a syllable respecting the nature of the misery to be inflicted.

I sat still for some time ruminating on these thoughts. Neither Mr. Falkland, nor any other person appeared, to disturb my meditations. I rose, went out of the room, and from the inn into the street. No one offered to molest me. It was strange! What was the nature of this power from which I was to apprehend so much, yet which seemed to leave me at perfect liberty? I began to imagine that all I had heard from this dreadful adversary was mere madness and extravagance, that he was at length deprived of the use of reason, which had long served him only as a medium of torment. Yet was it likely in that case that he should be able to employ Gines and his associate, who had just been his instruments of violence upon my person?

I proceeded along the streets with considerable caution. I looked before me and behind me, as well as the darkness would allow me to do, that I might not again be hunted in sight by some man of stratagem and violence without my perceiving it. I was not as before beyond the limits of the town, but considered the streets, the houses and the inhabitants as affording some degree of security. I was still walking with my mind thus full of suspicion and forecast, when I discovered Thomas, that servant of Mr. Falkland whom I have already more than once had occasion to mention. He advanced towards me with an air so blunt and direct, as instantly to remove from me the idea of any thing insidious in his purpose; beside that I had always felt the character of Thomas, rustic and uncultivated as it was, to be entitled to a more than common portion of esteem.

Thomas, said I, as he advanced, I hope you are willing to give me joy, that I am at length delivered from the dreadful danger which for many months haunted me so unmercifully.

No, rejoined Thomas roughly, I be not at all willing. I do not know what to make of myself in this affair. While you were in prison in that miserable fashion, I felt all at one almost as if I loved you: and, now that that is over, and you are turned out loose in the world to do your worst, my blood rises at the very sight of you. To look at you, you are almost that very lad Williams for whom I could

with pleasure as it were have laid down my life; and yet behind that
smiling face there lie robbery, and lying, and every thing that is
ungrateful and murderous. Your last action was worse than all the
rest. How could you find in your heart to revive that cruel story
about Mr. Tyrrel, which every body had agreed out of regard to
the squire never to mention again, and of which I know and you
know he is as innocent as the child unborn? There are causes and
reasons, or else I could have wished from the bottom of my soul
never to have set eyes on you again!

And you still persist in your hard thoughts of me!

Worse! I think worse of you than ever! Before, I thought you as
bad as man could be. I wonder from my soul what you are to do
next. But you make good the old saying, Needs must go, that the
devil drives.

And so there is never to be an end of my misfortunes. What can
Mr. Falkland contrive for me worse than the ill opinion and
enmity of all mankind?

Mr. Falkland contrive? He is the best friend you have in the
world, though you are the basest traitor to him. Poor man! it makes
one's heart ache to look at him; he is the very image of grief. And
it is not clear to me that it is not all owing to you. At least you have
given the finishing lift to the misfortune that was already destroying him. There have been the devil and all to pay between him and
squire Forester. The squire is right raving mad with my master,
for having outwitted him in the matter of the trial, and saved your
life. He swears that you shall be taken up and tried all over again at
the next assizes; but my master is resolute, and I believe will carry
it his own way. He says indeed, that the law will not allow squire
Forester to have his will in this. To see him ordering every thing
for your benefit, and taking all your maliciousness as mild and
innocent as a lamb, and to think of your vile proceedings against
him, is a sight one shall not see again, go all the world over. For
God's sake, repent of your reprobate doings, and make what little
reparation is in your power! Think of your poor soul, before you
awake, as to be sure one of these days you will, in fire and brimstone
everlasting!

Saying this, he held out his hand, and took hold of mine. The
action seemed strange, but I at first thought it the unpremeditated
result of his solemn and well-intentioned adjuration. I felt however that he put something into my hand. The next moment he

quitted his hold, and hastened from me with the swiftness of an arrow. What he had thus given me was a bank-note of twenty pounds. I had no doubt that he had been charged to deliver it to me from Mr. Falkland.

What was I to infer? What light did it throw upon the intentions of my inexorable persecutor? His animosity against me was as great as ever; that I had just had confirmed to me from his own mouth. Yet his animosity appeared to be still tempered with the remains of humanity. He prescribed to it a line wide enough to embrace the gratification of his views, and within the boundaries of that line it stopped. But this discovery carried no consolation to my mind. I knew not what portion of calamity I was fated to endure, before his jealousy of dishonour and inordinate thirst of fame would deem themselves satisfied.

Another question offered itself. Was I to receive the money which had just been put into my hands? The money of a man, who had inflicted upon me injuries, less than those which he had entailed upon himself, but the greatest that one man can inflict upon another? who had blasted my youth, who had destroyed my peace, who had held me up to the abhorrence of mankind, and rendered me an outcast upon the face of the earth? who had forged the basest and most atrocious falsehoods, and urged them with a seriousness and perseverance which produced universal belief? who an hour before had vowed against me inexorable enmity, and sworn to entail upon me misery without end? Would not this conduct on my part betray a base and abject spirit, that crouched under tyranny, and kissed the hands that were embrued in my blood?

If these reasons appeared strong, neither was the other side without reasons in reply. I wanted the money: not for any purpose of vice or superfluity, but for those purposes without which life cannot subsist. Man ought to be able, wherever placed, to find for himself the means of existence; but I was to open a new scene of life, to remove to some distant spot, to be prepared against the ill-will of mankind, and the unexplored projects of hostility of a most accomplished foe. The actual means of existence are the property of all. What should hinder me from taking that of which I was really in want, when in taking it I risked no vengeance and perpetrated no violence? The property in question will be beneficial to me, and the voluntary surrender of it is accompanied with no injury to its late proprietor; what other condition can be necessary to render the use of it on my part a duty? He that lately possessed it has injured me; does that alter its value as a medium of exchange? He will boast perhaps of the imaginary obligation he has conferred on me: Surely, to shrink from a thing in itself right, from any such apprehension, can be the result only of pusillanimity and cowardice.

CHAPTER XIII

INFLUENCED by these reasonings, I determined to retain what had thus been put into my hands. My next care was in regard to the scene I should choose as the retreat of that life which I had just saved from the grasp of the executioner. The danger to which I was exposed of forcible interruption in my pursuits was probably in some respects less now, than it had been previously to this crisis. Besides, that I was considerably influenced in this deliberation by the strong loathing I conceived for the situations in which I had lately been engaged. I knew not in what mode Mr. Falkland in-tended to exercise his vengeance against me; but I was seized with so unconquerable an aversion to disguise and the idea of spending my life in the personating a fictitious character, that I could not for the present at least reconcile my mind to any thing of that nature. The same kind of disgust I had conceived for the metropolis, where I had spent so many hours of artifice, sadness, and terror. I therefore decided in favour of the project which had formerly proved amusing to my imagination, of withdrawing to some distant, rural scene, a scene of calmness and obscurity, where for a few years at least, perhaps during the life of Mr. Falkland, I might be hidden from the world, recover the wounds my mind had received in this fatal connexion, methodise and improve the experience which had been accumulated, cultivate the faculties I in any degree possessed, and employ the intervals of these occupations in simple industry and the intercourse of guileless, uneducated, kind-intentioned minds. The menaces of my persecutor seemed to forebode the inevitable interruption of this system. But I deemed it wise to put these menaces out of my consideration. I compared them to death, which must infallibly overtake us, we know not when; but the possibility of whose arrival next year, next week, tomorrow, must be left out of the calculation of him who would enter upon any important or well concerted undertaking.

Such were the ideas that determined my choice. Thus did my youthful mind delineate the system of distant years, even when the threats of instant calamity still sounded in my ears. I was inured to the apprehension of mischief, till at last the hoarse roarings of the beginning tempest had lost their power of annihilating my peace. I however thought it necessary, while I was most palpably within the sphere of the enemy, to exert every practicable degree of vigilance. I was careful not to incur the hazards of darkness and solitude. When I left the town, it was with the stage-coach, an obvious source of protection against glaring and enormous violence. Meanwhile I found myself no more exposed to molestation in my progress, than the man in the world who should have had the least reason for apprehensions of this nature. As the distance increased, I relaxed something in my precaution, though still awake to a sense of danger, and constantly pursued with the image of my foe. I fixed upon an obscure market-town in Wales as the chosen seat of my operations. This place recommended itself to my observation, as I was wandering in quest of an abode. It was clean, chearful and of great simplicity of appearance. It was at a distance from any public and frequented road, and had nothing which could deserve the name of trade. The face of nature around it was agreeably diversified, being partly wild and romantic, and partly rich and abundant in production.

Here I solicited employment in two professions; the first that of a watchmaker, in which though the instructions I had received were few, they were eked out and assisted by a mind fruitful in mechanical invention; the other that of an instructor in mathematics and its practical application, geography, astronomy, land-surveying and navigation. Neither of these was a very copious source of emolument in the obscure retreat I had chosen for myself: but, if my receipts were slender, my disbursements were still fewer. In this little town I became acquainted with the vicar, the apothecary, the lawyer, and the rest of the persons who time out of mind had been regarded as the top gentry of the place. Each of these centred in himself a variety of occupations. There was little in the appearance of the vicar that reminded you of his profession except on the recurring Sunday. At other times he condescended with his evangelical hand to guide the plough, or to drive the cows from the field to the farm-yard for the milking. The apothecary occasionally officiated as a barber, and the lawyer was the village schoolmaster.

By all these persons I was received with kindness and hospitality. Among people thus remote from the bustle of human life there is an open spirit of confidence, by means of which, a stranger easily finds access to their benevolence and goodwill. My manners had never been greatly debauched from the simplicity of rural life by the scenes through which I had passed; and the hardships I had endured had given additional mildness to my character. In the theatre upon which I was now placed I had no rival. My mechanical occupation had hitherto been a non-resident; and the schoolmaster, who did not aspire to the sublime heights of science I professed to communicate, was willing to admit me as a partner in the task of civilizing the unpolished manners of the inhabitants. For the parson, civilisation was no part of his trade; his business was with the things of a better life, not with the carnal concerns of this material scene; in truth, his thoughts were principally occupied with his oatmeal and his cows.

These however were not the only companions, which this remote retirement afforded me. There was a family of a very different description, of which I gradually became the chosen intimate. The father was a shrewd, sensible, rational man, but who had turned his principal attention to subjects of agriculture. His wife was a truly admirable and extraordinary woman. She was the daughter of a Neapolitan nobleman, who, after having visited, and made a considerable figure in every country of Europe, had at length received the blow of fate in this village. He had been banished his country upon suspicion of religious and political heresy, and his estates confiscated. With this only child, like Prospero in the Tempest, he had withdrawn himself to one of the most obscure and uncultivated regions of the world. Very soon however after his arrival in Wales, he had been siezed with a malignant fever, which carried him off in three days. He died possessed of no other property, than a few jewels, and a bill of credit, to no considerable amount, upon an English banker.

Here then was the infant Laura, left in a foreign country, and without a single friend. The father of her present husband, was led, by motives of pure humanity, to seek to mitigate the misfortunes of the dying Italian. Though a plain, uninstructed man, with no extraordinary refinement of intellect, there was something in his countenance, that determined the stranger, in his present forlorn and melancholy situation, to make him his executor, and the guardian of his daughter. The Neapolitan understood enough of English, to explain his wishes to this friendly attendant of his death-bed. As his circumstances were narrow, the servants of the stranger, two Italians, a male and a female, were sent back to their own country, soon after the death of their master.

Laura was at this time eight years of age. At these tender years she had been susceptible of little direct instruction; and, as she grew up, even the memory of her father, became, from year to year, more vague and indistinct in her mind. But there was something she derived from her father, whether along with the life he bestowed, or as the consequence of his instruction and manners, which no time could efface. Every added year of her life, contributed to develop the fund of her accomplishments. She read, she observed, she reflected. Without instructors, she taught herself to draw, to sing, and to understand the more polite European languages. As she had no society, in this remote situation, but that of peasants, she had no idea of honour or superiority to be derived from her acquisitions; but pursued them from a secret taste, and as the sources of personal enjoyment.

A mutual attachment gradually arose, between her and the only son of her guardian. His father led him, from early youth, to the labours and the sports of the field, and there was little congeniality between his pursuits and those of Laura. But this was a defect that she was slow to discover. She had never been accustomed to society in her chosen amusements, and habit, at that time, even made her conceive, that they were indebted to solitude for an additional relish. The youthful rustic had great integrity, great kindness of heart, and was a lad of excellent sense. He was florid, well-proportioned, and the goodness of his disposition made his manners amiable. Accomplishments greater than these she had never seen in human form, since the death of her father. In fact she is scarcely to be considered as a sufferer in this instance; since, in her forlorn and destitute condition, it is little probable, when we consider the habits and notions that now prevail, that her accomplishments, unassisted by fortune, would have procured her an equal alliance in marriage.

When she became a mother, her heart opened to a new affection.

The idea now presented itself, which had never occurred before, that, in her children at least, she might find the partners and companions of her favourite employments. She was, at the time of my arrival, mother of four, the eldest of which was a son. To all of them she had been a most assiduous instructor. It was well for her perhaps, that she obtained this sphere for the exercise of her mind. It came, just at the period when the charm which human life derives from novelty, is beginning to wear off. It gave her new activity and animation. It is perhaps impossible, that the refinements of which human nature is capable, should not, after a time, subside into sluggishness, if they be not aided by the influence of society and affection.

The son of the Welch farmer by this admirable woman, was about seventeen years of age, at the time of my settlement in their neighbourhood. His eldest sister was one year younger than himself. The whole family composed a groupe, with which a lover of tranquillity and virtue would have delighted to associate in any situation. It is easy therefore to conceive how much I rejoiced in their friendship, in this distant retirement, and suffering, as I felt myself, from the maltreatment and desertion of my species. The amiable Laura had a wonderful quickness of eye, and rapidity of apprehension; but this feature in her countenance was subdued by a sweetness of disposition, such as I never, in any other instance, saw expressed in the looks of a human being. She soon distinguished me by her kindness and friendship; for, living as she had done, though familiar with the written productions of a cultivated intellect, she had never seen the thing itself realised in a living being, except in the person of her father. She delighted to converse with me upon subjects of literature and taste, and she eagerly invited my assistance in the education of her children. The son, though young, had been so happily improved and instructed by his mother, that I found in him nearly all the most essential qualities we require in a friend. Engagement and inclination equally led me to pass a considerable part of every day in this agreeable society. Laura treated me as if I had been one of the family, and I sometimes flattered myself that I might one day become such in reality. What an enviable resting-place for me, who had known nothing but calamity, and had scarcely dared to look for sympathy and kindness in the countenance of a human being!

The sentiments of friendship which early disclosed themselves between me and the members of this amiable family, daily became stronger. At every interview, the confidence reposed in me by the mother, increased. While our familiarity gained in duration, it equally gained in that subtlety of communication, by which it seemed to shoot forth its roots in every direction. There are a thousand little evanescent touches in the development of a growing friendship, that are neither thought of, nor would be understood, between common acquaintances. I honoured and esteemed the respectable Laura like a mother; for, though the difference of our ages was by no means sufficient to authorise the sentiment, it was irresistibly suggested to me, by the fact of her always being presented to my observation under the maternal character. Her son was a lad of great understanding, generosity, and feeling, and of no contemptible acquirements; while his tender years, and the uncommon excellence of his mother, subtracted something from the independence of his judgment, and impressed him with a sort of religious deference for her will. In the eldest daughter I beheld the image of Laura; for that I felt attached to her for the present; and I sometimes conceived it probable, that hereafter I might learn to love her for her own sake.—Alas, it was thus that I amused myself with the visions of distant years, while I stood in reality on the brink of the precipice!

It will perhaps be thought strange, that I never once communicated the particulars of my story to this amiable matron, or to my young friend, for such I may almost venture to call him, her son. But in truth I abhorred the memory of this story; I placed all my hopes of happiness in the prospect of its being consigned to oblivion. I fondly flattered myself that such would be the event; in the midst of my unlooked-for happiness, I scarcely recollected, or, recollecting, was disposed to yield but a small degree of credit to, the menaces of Mr. Falkland.

One day, that I was sitting alone with the accomplished Laura, she repeated his all-dreadful name. I started with astonishment, amazed that a woman like this, who knew nobody, who lived as it were alone, in a corner of the universe, who had never, in a single instance, entered into any fashionable circle, this admirable and fascinating hermit, should by some unaccountable accident, have become acquainted with this fatal and tremendous name. Astonishment however was not my only sensation. I became pale with terror; I rose from my seat; I attempted to sit down again; I reeled

out of the room, and hastened to bury myself in solitude. The
unexpectedness of the incident, took from me all precaution, and
overwhelmed my faculties. The penetrating Laura observed my
behaviour; but nothing further occurring to excite her attention to
it at that time, and concluding from my manner that enquiry would
be painful to me, she humanely suppressed her curiosity.

I afterwards found that Mr. Falkland had been known to the
father of Laura; that he had been acquainted with the story of count
Malvesi, and with a number of other transactions, redounding in
the highest degree to the credit of the gallant Englishman. The
Neapolitan had left letters in which these transactions were recorded, and which spoke of Mr. Falkland in the highest terms of
panegyric. Laura had been used to regard every little relic of her
father with a sort of religious veneration; and, by this accident, the
name of Mr. Falkland was connected in her mind, with the sentiments of unbounded esteem.

The scene by which I was surrounded was perhaps more grateful
to me, than it would have been to most other persons with my
degree of intellectual cultivation. Sore with persecution and distress, and bleeding at almost every vein, there was nothing I so
much coveted as rest and tranquillity. It seemed as if my faculties
were, at least for the time, exhausted by the late preternatural
intensity of their exertions, and that they stood indispensibly in
need of a period of comparative suspension.

This was however but a temporary feeling. My mind had always
been active, and I was probably indebted to the sufferings I had
endured, and the exquisite and increased susceptibility they produced, for new energies. I soon felt the desire of some additional
and vigorous pursuit. In this state of mind, I met by accident, in a
neglected corner of the house of one of my neighbours, with a
general dictionary of four of the northern languages. This incident
gave a direction to my thoughts. In my youth I had not been
inattentive to languages. I determined to attempt, at least for my
own use, an etymological analysis of the English language. I easily
perceived that this pursuit had one advantage to a person in my
situation, and that a small number of books, consulted with this
view, would afford employment for a considerable time. I procured
other dictionaries. In my incidental reading, I noted the manner in
which words were used, and applied these remarks to the illustra-
tion of my general enquiry. I was unintermitted in my assiduity,

and my collections promised to accumulate. Thus I was provided with sources both of industry and recreation, the more completely to divert my thoughts from the recollection of my past misfortunes.

In this state, so grateful to my feelings, week after week glided away without interruption and alarm. The situation in which I was now placed, had some resemblance to that in which I had spent my earlier years, with the advantage of a more attractive society, and a riper judgment. I began to look back upon the intervening period as upon a distempered and tormenting dream; or rather perhaps my feelings were like those of a man recovered from an interval of raging delirium, from ideas of horror, confusion, flight, persecution, agony and despair! When I recollected what I had undergone, it was not without satisfaction as the recollection of a thing that was past; every day augmented my hope that it was never to return. Surely the dark and terrific menaces of Mr. Falkland were rather the perturbed suggestions of his angry mind, than the final result of a deliberate and digested system! How happy should I feel beyond the ordinary lot of man, if, after the terrors I had undergone, I should now find myself unexpectedly restored to the immunities of a human being!

While I was thus soothing my mind with fond imaginations, it happened that a few bricklayers and their labourers came over from a distance of five or six miles, to work upon some additions to one of the better sort of houses in the town which had changed its tenant. No incident could be more trivial than this, had it not been for a strange coincidence of time between this circumstance and a change which introduced itself into my situation. This first manifested itself in a sort of shyness with which I was treated first by one person and then another of my new-formed acquaintance. They were backward to enter into conversation with me, and answered my enquiries with an aukward and embarrassed air. When they met me in the street or the field, their countenances contracted a cloud, and they endeavoured to shun me. My scholars quitted me one after another, and I had no longer any employment in my mechanical profession. It is impossible to describe the sensations which the gradual, but uninterrupted progress of this revolution produced in my mind. It seemed as if I had some contagious disease, from which every man shrunk with alarm, and left me to perish unassisted and alone. I asked one man and another to explain to me the meaning of these appearances; but every one avoided the task, and answered in an evasive and ambiguous manner. I sometimes supposed that it was all a delusion of the imagination; till the repetition of the sensation brought the reality too painfully home to my apprehension. There are few things that give a greater shock to the mind than a phenomenon in the conduct of our fellow men, of great importance to our concerns, and for which we are unable to assign any plausible reason. At times I was half inclined to believe that the change was not in other men, but that some alienation of my own understanding generated the horrid vision. I endeavoured to awake from my dream, and return to my former state of enjoyment and happiness; but in vain. To the same consideration it may be ascribed, that unacquainted with the source of the evil, observing its perpetual increase, and finding it so far as I could perceive entirely arbitrary in its nature, I was unable to ascertain its limits, or the degree in which it would finally overwhelm me.

In the midst however of the wonderful and seemingly inexplicable nature of this scene, there was one idea that instantly obtruded itself, and that I could never after banish from my mind. It is Falkland! In vain I struggled against the seeming improbability of the supposition. In vain I said, Mr. Falkland, wise as he is and pregnant in resources, acts by human and not by supernatural means. He may overtake me by surprise and in a manner of which I have no previous expectation; but he cannot produce a great and notorious effect without some visible agency, however difficult it may be to trace that agency to its absolute author. He cannot, like those invisible personages who are supposed from time to time to interfere in human affairs, ride in the whirlwind, shroud himself in clouds and impenetrable darkness, and scatter destruction upon the earth from his secret habitation. Thus it was that I bribed my imagination, and endeavoured to persuade myself that my present unhappiness originated in a different source from my former. All evils appeared trivial to me, in comparison of the recollection and perpetuation of my parent misfortune. I felt like a man distracted by the incoherence of my ideas to my present situation excluding from it the machinations of Mr. Falkland, on the one hand; and on the other by the horror I conceived at the bare possibility of again encountering his animosity, after a suspension of many weeks, a suspension as I had hoped for ever. An interval like this was an age to a person in the calamitous situation I had so long experienced. But, in spite of my efforts, I could not banish from my mind the dreadful idea. My original conceptions of the genius and perseverance of Mr. Falkland had been such, that I could with difficulty think any thing impossible to him. I knew not how to set up my own opinions of material causes and the powers of the human mind as the limits of existence. Mr. Falkland had always been to my imagination an object of wonder, and that which excites our wonder we scarcely suppose ourselves competent to analyse.

It may well be conceived, that one of the first persons to whom I applied for an explanation of this dreadful mystery, was the accomplished Laura. My disappointment here cut me to the heart. I was not prepared for it. I recollected the ingenuousness of her nature, the frankness of her manners, the partiality with which she had honoured me. If I were mortified with the coldness, the ruggedness, and the cruel mistake of principles, with which the village inhabitants repelled my enquiries, the mortification I suffered, only drove me more impetuously to seek the cure of my griefs from this object of my admiration. In Laura, said I, I am secure from these vulgar prejudices. I confide in her justice. I am sure she will not cast me off unheard, nor without strictly examining a question on all sides, in which every thing that is valuable to a person she once esteemed, may be involved.

Thus encouraging myself, I turned my steps to the place of her residence. As I passed along, I called up all my recollection, I summoned my faculties. I may be made miserable, said I, but it shall not be for want of any exertion of mine that promises to lead to happiness. I will be clear, collected, simple in narrative, ingenuous in communication. I will leave nothing unsaid that the case may require. I will not volunteer any thing that relates to my former transactions with Mr. Falkland; but, if I find that my present calamity is connected with those transactions, I will not fear but that by an honest explanation I shall remove it.

I knocked at the door. A servant appeared, and told me that her mistress hoped I would excuse her; she must really beg to dispense with my visit.

I was thunderstruck. I was rooted to the spot. I had been carefully preparing my mind for every thing that I supposed likely to happen, but this event had not entered into my calculations. I roused myself in a partial degree, and walked away without uttering a word.

I had not gone far, before I perceived one of the workmen following me, who put into my hands a billet. The contents were these.

Mr. Williams,

LET me see you no more. I have a right at least to expect your compliance with this requisition; and, upon that condition, I pardon the enormous impropriety and guilt, with which you have conducted yourself to me and my family.

Laura Denison.

The sensations with which I read these few lines, are indescribable. I found in them a dreadful confirmation of the calamity that on all sides invaded me. But what I felt most, was the unmoved coldness with which they appeared to be written. This coldness from Laura, my comforter, my friend, my mother! To dismiss, to cast me off, for ever, without one thought of compunction!

I determined however, in spite of her requisition, and in spite of her coldness, to have an explanation with her. I did not despair of conquering the antipathy she harboured. I did not fear, that I should rouse her from the vulgar and unworthy conception, of condemning a man, in points the most material to his happiness, without stating the accusations that are urged against him, and without hearing him in reply.

Though I had no doubt, by means of resolution, of gaining access to her in her house, yet I preferred taking her unprepared, and not warmed against me by any previous contention. Accordingly, the next morning, at the time she usually devoted to half an hour's air and exercise, I hastened to her garden, leaped the paling, and concealed myself in an arbour. Presently I saw, from my retreat, the younger part of the family, strolling through the garden, and from thence into the fields; but it was not my business to be seen by them. I looked after them however with earnestness, unobserved; and I could not help asking myself, with a deep and heart-felt sigh, whether it were possible that I saw them now for the last time?

They had not advanced far into the fields, before their mother made her appearance. I observed in her her usual serenity and sweetness of countenance. I could feel my heart knocking against my ribs. My whole frame was in a tumult. I stole out of the arbour; and, as I advanced nearer, my pace became quickened.

For God's sake, madam, exclaimed I, give me a hearing! Do not avoid me!

She stood still. No, sir, she replied, I shall not avoid you. I wished you to dispense with this meeting. But, since I cannot obtain that,—I am conscious of no wrong; and therefore, though the meeting gives me pain, it inspires me with no fear.

Oh, madam, answered I, my friend! the object of all my reverence! whom I once ventured to call, my mother! Can you wish not to hear me? Can you have no anxiety for my justification, whatever may be the unfavourable impression you may have received against me?

Not an atom. I have neither wish nor inclination to hear you. That tale which, in its plain and unadorned state, is destructive of the character of him to whom it relates, no colouring can make an honest one.

Good God! Can you think of condemning a man, when you have heard only one side of his story?

Indeed I can, replied she, with dignity. The maxim of hearing both sides may be very well in some cases; but it would be ridiculous to suppose that there are not cases, that, at the first mention, are too clear to admit the shadow of a doubt. By a well-concerted defence you may give me new reason to admire your abilities; but I am acquainted with them already. I can admire your abilities, without tolerating your character.

Madam! Amiable, exemplary Laura! whom, in the midst of all your harshness and inflexibility, I honour! I conjure you, by every thing that is sacred, to tell me what it is that has filled you with this sudden aversion to me.

No, sir: that you shall never obtain from me. I have nothing to say to you. I stand still and hear you: because virtue disdains to appear abashed and confounded in the presence of vice. Your conduct even at this moment, in my opinion, condemns you. True virtue refuses the drudgery of explanation and apology. True virtue shines by its own light, and needs no art to set it off. You have the first principles of morality as yet to learn.

And can you imagine, that the most upright conduct, is always superior to the danger of ambiguity?

Exactly so. Virtue, sir, consists in actions, and not in words. The good man and the bad, are characters precisely opposite, not characters distinguished from each other by imperceptible shades.

The Providence that rules us all, has not permitted us to be left without a clue in the most important of all questions. Eloquence may seek to confound it; but it shall be my care to avoid its deceptive influence. I do not wish to have my understanding perverted, and all the differences of things concealed from my apprehension.

Madam, madam! It would be impossible for you to hold this language, if you had not always lived in this obscure retreat, if you had ever been conversant with the passions and institutions of men.

It may be so. And, if that be the case, I have great reason to be thankful to my God, who has thus enabled me, to preserve the innocence of my heart, and the integrity of my understanding.

Can you believe then, that ignorance is the only, or the safest, preservative of integrity?

Sir, I told you at first, and I repeat to you again, that all your declamation is in vain. I wish you would have saved me and yourself, that pain which is the only thing that can possibly result from it. But let us suppose that virtue could ever be the equivocal thing you would have me believe. Is it possible, if you had been honest, that you would not have acquainted me with your story? Is it possible, that you would have left me to have been informed of it by a mere accident, and with all the shocking aggravations you well knew that accident would give it? Is it possible you should have violated the most sacred of all trusts, and have led me unknowingly to admit to the intercourse of my children, a character, which if, as you pretend, it is substantially honest, you cannot deny to be blasted and branded in the face of the whole world? Go, sir, I despise you. You are a monster, and not a man. I cannot tell whether my personal situation misleads me, but, to my thinking, this last action of yours is worse than all the rest. Nature has constituted me the protector of my children. I shall always remember and resent the indelible injury you have done them. You have wounded me to the very heart, and have taught me to what a pitch the villainy of man can extend.

Madam, I can be silent no longer. I see that you have by some means come to a hearing of the story of Mr. Falkland.

I have. I am astonished you have the effrontery to pronounce his name. That name has been a denomination, as far back as my memory can reach, for the most exalted of mortals, the wisest and most generous of men.

Madam, I owe it to myself to set you right on this subject. Mr. Falkland——

Mr. Williams, I see my children returning from the fields, and coming this way. The basest action you ever did, was the obtruding yourself upon them as an instructor. I insist that you see them no more. I command you to be silent. I command you to withdraw. If you persist in your absurd resolution of expostulating with me, you must take some other time.

I could continue no longer. I was in a manner heart broken through the whole of this dialogue. I could not think of protracting the pain of this admirable woman, upon whom, though I was innocent of the crimes she imputed to me, I had inflicted so much pain already. I yielded to the imperiousness of her commands, and withdrew.

I hastened, without knowing why, from the presence of Laura, to my own habitation. Upon entering the house, an apartment of which I occupied, I found it totally deserted of its usual inhabitants. The woman and her children were gone to enjoy the freshness of the breeze. The husband was engaged in his usual out-door occupations. The doors of persons of the lower order in this part of the country, are secured, in the day-time, only with a latch. I entered, and went into the kitchen of the family. Here, as I looked round, my eyes accidentally glanced upon a paper lying in one corner, which by some association I was unable to explain, roused in me a strong sensation of suspicion and curiosity. I eagerly went towards it, caught it up, and found it to be the very paper of the Wonderful and Surprising History of Caleb Williams, the discovery of which towards the close of my residence in London had produced in me such inexpressible anguish.

This encounter at once cleared up all the mystery that hung upon my late transactions. Abhorred and intolerable certainty, succeeded to the doubts which had haunted my mind. It struck me with the rapidity of lightning. I felt a sudden torpor and sickness that pervaded every fibre of my frame.

Was there no hope that remained for me? Was acquittal useless? Was there no period, past or in prospect, that could give relief to my sufferings? Was the odious and atrocious falshood that had been invented against me, to follow me wherever I went, to strip me of character, to deprive me of the sympathy and good will of mankind, to wrest from me the very bread by which life must be sustained?

For the space perhaps of half an hour the agony I felt from this termination to my tranquillity, and the expectation it excited of the enmity which would follow me through every retreat, was such as to bereave me of all consistent thinking, much more of the power of coming to any resolution. As soon as this giddiness and horror of the mind subsided, and the deadly calm that invaded my faculties was no more, one stiff and master gale gained the ascendancy, and drove me to an instant desertion of this late cherished retreat. I had no patience to enter into further remonstrance and explanation with the inhabitants of my present residence. I believed that it was in vain to hope to recover that favourable prepossession and tranquillity I had lately enjoyed. In encountering the prejudices that were thus armed against me, I should have to deal with a variety of dispositions, and, though I might succeed with some, I could not expect to succeed with all. I had seen too much of the reign of triumphant falshood, to have that sanguine confidence in the effects of my innocence, which would have suggested itself to the mind of any other person of my propensities and my age. The recent instance which had occurred in my conversation with Laura, might well contribute to discourage me. I could not endure the thought of opposing the venom that was thus scattered against me, in detail and through its minuter particles. If ever it should be necessary to encounter it, if I were pursued like a wild beast till I could no longer avoid turning upon my hunters, I would then turn upon the true author of this unprincipled attack. I would encounter the calumny in its strong hold, I would rouse myself to an exertion hitherto unessayed, and, by the firmness, intrepidity and unalterable constancy I should display, would yet compel mankind to believe Mr. Falkland a suborner and a murderer!

CHAPTER XIV

I HASTEN to the conclusion of my melancholy story. I began to write soon after the period to which I have now conducted it. This was another resource that my mind, ever eager in inventing means to escape from my misery, suggested. In my haste to withdraw myself from the retreat in Wales, where first the certainty of Mr. Falkland's menaces was confirmed to me, I left behind me the apparatus of my etymological enquiries, and the papers I had written upon the subject. I have never been able to persuade myself to resume this pursuit. It is always discouraging, to begin over again a laborious task, and exert one's self to recover a position we had already occupied. I knew not how soon or how abruptly I might be driven from any new situation; the appendages of the study in which I had engaged, were too cumbrous for this state of dependence and uncertainty; they only served to give new sharpness to the enmity of my foe, and new poignancy to my hourly-renewing distress.

But what was of greatest importance, and made the deepest impression upon my mind, was my separation from the family of Laura. Fool that I was, to imagine that there was any room for me in the abodes of friendship and tranquillity! It was now first that I felt, with the most intolerable acuteness, how completely I was cut off from the whole human species. Other connections I had gained, comparatively without interest; and I saw them dissolved, without the consummation of agony. I had never experienced the purest refinements of friendship, but in two instances, that of Collins, and this of the family of Laura. Solitude, separation, banishment! These are words often in the mouths of human beings; but few men, except myself, have felt the full latitude of their meaning. The pride of philosophy has taught us to treat man as an individual. He is no such thing. He holds, necessarily, indispensibly, to his species. He is like those twin-births, that have two heads indeed, and four hands; but, if you attempt to detach them from each other, they are inevitably subjected to miserable and lingering destruction.

It was this circumstance, more than all the rest, that gradually gorged my heart with abhorrence of Mr. Falkland. I could not think of his name, but with a sickness and a loathing, that seemed more than human. It was by his means, that I suffered the loss of one consolation after another, of every thing that was happiness, or that had the resemblance of happiness.

The writing of these memoirs served me as a source of avocation for several years. For some time I had a melancholy satisfaction in writing. I was better pleased to retrace the particulars of calamities that had formerly afflicted me, than to look forward, as at other times I was too apt to do, to those by which I might hereafter be overtaken. I conceived that my story faithfully digested would

carry in it an impression of truth that few men would be able to
resist; or at worst that, by leaving it behind me when I should no
longer continue to exist, posterity might be induced to do me
justice, and, seeing in my example what sort of evils are entailed
upon mankind by society as it is at present constituted, might be
inclined to turn their attention upon the fountain from which such
bitter waters have been accustomed to flow. But these motives
have diminished in their influence. I have contracted a disgust for
life and all its appendages. Writing, which was at first a pleasure,
is changed into a burthen. I shall compress into a small compass
what remains to be told.

I discovered not long after the period of which I am speaking the
precise cause of the reverse I had experienced in my residence in
Wales, and included in that cause what it was I had to look for in
my future adventures. Mr. Falkland had taken the infernal Gines
into his pay, a man critically qualified for the service in which he
was now engaged; by the unfeeling brutality of his temper, by his
habits of mind at once audacious and artful, and by the peculiar
animosity and vengeance he had conceived against me. The
employment to which this man was hired was that of following me
from place to place blasting my reputation, and preventing me from
the chance, by continuing long in one residence, of acquiring a
character for integrity that should give new weight to any accusation I might at a future time be induced to prefer. He had come to
the seat of my residence with the bricklayers and labourers I have
mentioned; and, while he took care to keep out of sight so far as
related to me, was industrious in disseminating that which in the
eye of the world seemed to amount to a demonstration of the
profligacy and detestableness of my character. It was, no doubt,
from him that the detested scroll had been procured, which I had
found in my habitation immediately prior to my quitting it. In all
this Mr. Falkland, reasoning upon his principles, was only employing a necessary precaution. There was something in the temper of
his mind that impressed him with aversion to the idea of violently
putting an end to my existence; at the same time that unfortunately
he could never deem himself sufficiently secured against my
recrimination, so long as I remained alive. As to the fact of Gines
being retained by him for this tremendous purpose, he by no means
desired that it should become generally known; but neither did
he look upon the possibility of its being known with terror. It was

already too notorious for his wishes, that I had advanced the most odious charges against him. If he regarded me with abhorrence as the adversary of his fame, those persons who had had occasion to be in any degree acquainted with our history, did not entertain less abhorrence against me for my own sake. If they should at any time know the pains he exerted in causing my evil reputation to follow me, they would consider it as an act of impartial justice, perhaps as a generous anxiety to prevent other men from being imposed upon and injured, as he had been.

What expedient was I to employ for the purpose of counter-acting the meditated and barbarous prudence, which was thus destined in all changes of scene to deprive me of the benefits and consolations of human society? There was one expedient against which I was absolutely determined, disguise. I had experienced so many mortifications and such intolerable restraint when I formerly had recourse to it, it was associated in my memory with sensations of such acute anguish, that my mind was thus far entirely convinced: Life was not worth purchasing at so high a price! But, though in this respect I was wholly resolved, there was another point that did not appear so material, and in which therefore I was willing to accommodate myself to circumstances. I was contented, if that would insure my peace, to submit to the otherwise unmanly expedient of passing by a different name.

But the change of my name, the abruptness with which I removed from place to place, the remoteness and the obscurity which I proposed to myself in the choice of my abode, were all insufficient to elude the sagacity of Gines, or the unrelenting constancy with which Mr. Falkland incited my tormentor to pursue me. Whithersoever I removed myself, it was not long before I had occasion to perceive this detested adversary in my rear. No words can enable me to do justice to the sensations which this circumstance produced in me. It was like what has been described of the eye of omniscience pursuing the guilty sinner, and darting a ray that awakens him to new sensibility, at the very moment that, otherwise, exhausted nature would lull him into a temporary oblivion of the reproaches of his conscience. Sleep fled from my eyes. No walls could hide me from the discernment of this hated foe. Every where his industry was unwearied to create for me new distress. Rest I had none: relief I had none: never could I count upon an instant's security: never could I wrap myself for a moment in the shroud of oblivion. The minutes in which I did not actually perceive him, were contaminated and blasted with the certain expectation of his speedy interference. In my first retreat I had passed a few weeks of delusive tranquillity, but never after was I happy enough to attain so much as that shadowy gratification. I spent some years in this dreadful vicissitude of pain. My sensations at certain periods amounted to insanity.

I pursued in every succeeding instance the conduct I had adopted at first. I determined never to enter into a contest of accusation and defence with the execrable Gines. If I could have submitted to it in other respects, what purpose would it answer? I should have but an imperfect and mutilated story to tell. This story had succeeded with persons already prepossessed in my favour by personal intercourse; but could it succeed with strangers? It had succeeded so long as I was able to hide myself from my pursuers; but could it succeed, now that this appeared impracticable, and that they proceeded by arming against me a whole vicinity at once?

It is inconceivable the mischiefs that this kind of existence included. Why should I insist upon such aggravations as hunger, beggary and external wretchedness? These were an inevitable consequence. It was by the desertion of mankind that, in each successive instance, I was made acquainted with my fate. Delay in such a moment served but to increase the evil; and, when I fled, meagreness and penury were the ordinary attendants of my course. But this was a small consideration. Indignation at one time, and unconquerable perseverance at another, sustained me where humanity, left to itself, would probably have sunk.

It has already appeared that I was not of a temper to endure calamity without endeavouring by every means I could devise to elude and disarm it. Recollecting, as I was habituated to do, the various projects by which my situation could be meliorated, the question occurred to me: Why should I be harassed by the pursuit of this Gines; why, man to man, may I not by the powers of my mind attain the ascendancy over him? at present he appears to be the persecutor and I the persecuted: is not this difference the mere creature of the imagination? may I not employ my ingenuity to vex him with difficulties and laugh at the endless labour to which he will be condemned?

Alas, this is a speculation for a mind at ease! It is not the persecution, but the catastrophe which is annexed to it, that makes the difference between the tyrant and the sufferer! In mere corporal exertion the hunter perhaps is upon a level with the miserable animal he pursues! But could it be forgotten by either of us, that at every stage Gines was to gratify his malignant passions by disseminating charges of the most infamous nature and exciting against me the abhorrence of every honest bosom, while I was to sustain the still repeated annihilation of my peace, my character and my bread? Could I by any refinement of reason convert this dreadful series into sport? I had no philosophy that qualified me for so extraordinary an effort. If under other circumstances I could even have entertained so strange an imagination, I was restrained in the present instance by the necessity of providing for myself the means of subsistence, and the fetters which through that necessity the forms of human society imposed upon my exertions.

In one of those changes of residence to which my miserable fate repeatedly compelled me, I met, upon a road which I was obliged to traverse, the friend of my youth, my earliest and best beloved friend, the venerable Collins. It was one of those misfortunes which served to accumulate my distress, that this man had quitted the island of Great Britain only a very few weeks before that fatal reverse of fortune which had ever since pursued me with unrelenting eagerness. Mr. Falkland, in addition to the large estate he possessed in England, had a very valuable plantation in the West Indies. This property had been greatly mismanaged by the person who had the direction of it on the spot; and, after various promises and evasions on his part, which, however they might serve to beguile the patience of Mr. Falkland, had been attended with no salutary fruits, it was resolved that Mr. Collins should go over in person to rectify the abuses which had so long prevailed. There had even been some idea of his residing several years, if not settling finally, upon the plantation. From that hour to the present I had never received the smallest intelligence respecting him.

I had always considered the circumstance of his critical absence as one of my severest misfortunes. Mr. Collins had been one of the first persons even in the period of my infancy to conceive hopes of me as of something above the common standard, and had contributed more than any other to encourage and assist my juvenile studies. He had been the executor of the little property of my father,

who had fixed upon him for that purpose in consideration of the
mutual affection that existed between us; and I seemed on every
account to have more claim upon his protection than upon that of
any other human being. I had always believed that, had he been
present in the crisis of my fortune, he would have felt conviction
of my innocence; and, convinced himself, would by means of the
venerableness and energy of his character have interposed so
effectually, as to have saved me the greater part of my subsequent
misfortunes.

There was yet another idea in my mind relative to this subject,
which had more weight with me, than even the substantial exertions of friendship I should have expected from him. The greatest
aggravation of my present lot, was, that I was cut off from the
friendship of mankind. I can safely affirm, that poverty and hunger,
that endless wanderings, that a blasted character and the curses
that clung to my name, were all of them slight misfortunes compared to this. I endeavoured to sustain myself by the sense of my
integrity, but the voice of no man upon earth echoed to the voice
of my conscience. 'I called aloud; but there was none to answer;
there was none that regarded.' To me the whole world was as
unhearing as the tempest, and as cold as the torpedo. Sympathy,
the magnetic virtue, the hidden essence of our life, was extinct.
Nor was this the sum of my misery. This food, so essential to an
intelligent existence, seemed perpetually renewing before me in its
fairest colours, only the more effectually to elude my grasp, and to
mock my hunger. From time to time I was prompted to unfold
the affections of my soul, only to be repelled with the greater
anguish, and to be baffled in a way the most intolerably mortifying.

No sight therefore could give me a purer delight than that which
now presented itself to my eyes. It was some time however before
either of us recognised the person of the other. Ten years had
elapsed since our last interview. Mr. Collins looked much older
than he had done at that period; in addition to which he was in
his present appearance pale, sickly and thin. These unfavourable
effects had been produced by the change of climate, particularly
trying to persons in an advanced period of life. Add to which,
I supposed him to be at that moment in the West Indies. I was
probably as much altered in the period that had elapsed as he had
been. I was the first to recollect him. He was on horseback; I on
foot. I had suffered him to pass me. In a moment the full idea of

who he was rushed upon my mind; I ran; I called with an impetuous voice; I was unable to restrain the vehemence of my emotions.

The ardour of my feelings disguised my usual tone of speaking,
which otherwise Mr. Collins would infallibly have recognised.
His sight was already dim; he pulled up his horse till I should
overtake him; and then said, Who are you? I do not know you.

My father! exclaimed I, embracing one of his knees with fervour
and delight, I am your son! once your little Caleb, whom you a
thousand times loaded with your kindness!

The unexpected repetition of my name gave a kind of shuddering emotion to my friend, which was however checked by his age,
and the calm and benevolent philosophy that formed one of his
most conspicuous habits.

I did not expect to see you! replied he.—I did not wish it!

My best, my oldest friend! answered I, respect blending itself
with my impatience, Do not say so! I have not a friend any where
in the whole world, but you! In you at least let me find sympathy
and reciprocal affection! If you knew how anxiously I have thought
of you during the whole period of your absence, you would not
thus grievously disappoint me in your return!

How is it, said Mr. Collins gravely, that you have been reduced
to this forlorn condition? Was it not the inevitable consequence of
your own actions?

The actions of others, not mine! Does not your heart tell you
that I am innocent?

No. My observation of your early character taught me that you
would be extraordinary. But unhappily all extraordinary men are
not good men; that seems to be a lottery, dependent on circumstances apparently the most trivial.

Will you hear my justification? I am as sure as I am of my
existence that I can convince you of my purity.

Certainly, if you require it, I will hear you. But that must not be
just now. I could have been glad to decline it wholly. At my age
I am not fit for the storm, and I am not so sanguine as you in my
expectation of the result. Of what would you convince me? That
Mr. Falkland is a suborner and murderer?

I made no answer. My silence was an affirmative to the question.

And what benefit will result from this conviction? I have known
you a promising boy, whose character might turn to one side or the
other as events should decide. I have known Mr. Falkland in his

maturer years, and have always admired him as the living model of
liberality and goodness. If you could change all my ideas, and show
me that there was no criterion by which vice might be prevented
from being mistaken for virtue, what benefit would arise from that?
I must part with all my interior consolation, and all my external
connections. And for what? What is it you propose? The death of
Mr. Falkland by the hands of the hangman?

No. I will not hurt a hair of his head, unless compelled to it by
a principle of defence. But surely you owe me justice?

What justice? The justice of proclaiming your innocence? You
know what consequences are annexed to that. But I do not believe
I shall find you innocent. If you even succeed in perplexing my
understanding, you will not succeed in enlightening it. Such is the
state of mankind, that innocence when involved in circumstances
of suspicion can scarcely ever make out a demonstration of its
purity, and guilt can often make us feel an insurmountable reluctance to the pronouncing it guilt. Meanwhile for the purchase of this
uncertainty I must sacrifice all the remaining comforts of my life.
I believe Mr. Falkland to be virtuous, but I know him to be pre-
judiced. He would never forgive me even this accidental parley, if
by any means he should come to be acquainted with it.

Oh, argue not the consequences that are possible to result!
answered I impatiently. I have a right to your kindness; I have a
right to your assistance!

You have them. You have them to a certain degree; and it is not
likely that by any process of examination you can have them entire.
You know my habits of thinking. I regard you as vicious; but I do
not consider the vicious as proper objects of indignation and scorn.
I consider you as a machine: you are not constituted, I am afraid,
to be greatly useful to your fellow men; but you did not make
yourself; you are just what circumstances irresistibly compelled
you to be. I am sorry for your ill properties; but I entertain no
enmity against you, nothing but benevolence. Considering you in
the light in which I at present consider you, I am ready to contribute every thing in my power to your real advantage, and would
gladly assist you, if I knew how, in detecting and extirpating the
errors that have misled you. You have disappointed me, but I have
no reproaches to utter: it is more necessary for me to feel compassion for you, than that I should accumulate your misfortune by
my censures.

What could I say to such a man as this? Amiable, incomparable man! Never was my mind more painfully divided than at that moment. The more he excited my admiration, the more imperiously did my heart command me, whatever were the price it should cost, to extort his friendship. I was persuaded that severe duty required of him, that he should reject all personal considerations, that he should proceed resolutely to the investigation of the truth, and that, if he found the result terminating in my favour, he should resign all his advantages, and, deserted as I was by the world, make a common cause, and endeavour to compensate the general injustice. But was it for me to force this conduct upon him, if, now in his declining years, his own fortitude shrunk from it? Alas, neither he nor I foresaw the dreadful catastrophe that was so closely impending! Otherwise I am well assured, that no tenderness for his remaining tranquillity would have withheld him from a compliance with my wishes! On the other hand, could I pretend to know what evils might result to him from his declaring himself my advocate? Might not his integrity be brow-beaten and defeated as mine had been? Did the imbecility of his grey hairs afford no advantage to my terrible adversary in the contest? Might not Mr. Falkland reduce him to a condition as wretched and low as mine? After all, was it not vice in me to desire to involve another man in my sufferings? If I regarded them as intolerable, this was still an additional reason why I should bear them alone.

Influenced by these considerations, I assented to his views. I assented to be thought hardly of by the man in the world whose esteem I most ardently desired, rather than involve him in possible calamity. I assented to the resigning what appeared to me at that moment as the last practicable comfort of my life, a comfort upon the thought of which, while I surrendered it, my mind dwelt with undescribable longings. Mr. Collins was deeply affected with the apparent ingenuousness with which I expressed my feelings. The secret struggle of his mind was, Can this be hypocrisy? The individual with whom I am conferring, if virtuous, is one of the most disinterestedly virtuous persons in the world. We tore ourselves from each other. Mr. Collins promised, as far as he was able, to have an eye upon my vicissitudes, and to assist me in every respect that was at all consistent with a just recollection of consequences. Thus I parted as it were with the last expiring hope of my mind; and voluntarily consented, thus

maimed and forlorn, to encounter all the evils that were yet in
store for me.

This is the latest event, which at present I think it necessary to
record. I shall doubtless hereafter have further occasion to take
up the pen. Great and unprecedented as my sufferings have been,
I feel intimately persuaded that there are worse sufferings that
await me. What mysterious cause is it, that enables me to write
this, and not to perish under the horrible apprehension!

CHAPTER XV

It is as I foreboded. The presage with which I was visited was
prophetic. I am now to record a new and terrible revolution of my
fortune and my mind.

Having made experiment of various situations with one uniform
result, I at length determined to remove myself, if possible, from
the reach of my persecutor, by going into voluntary banishment
from my native soil. This was my last resource for tranquillity, for
honest fame, for those privileges to which human life is indebted
for the whole of its value. In some distant climate, said I, surely I
may find that security which is necessary to persevering pursuit;
surely I may lift my head erect, associate with men upon the footing of a man, acquire connections, and preserve them! It is inconceivable, with what ardent reachings of the soul I aspired to this
termination.

This last consolation was denied me by the inexorable Falkland.

At the time the project was formed, I was at no great distance
from the east coast of the island, and I resolved to take ship at
Harwich, and pass immediately into Holland. I accordingly
repaired to that place, and went almost as soon as I arrived to the
port. But there was no vessel perfectly ready to sail. I left the port,
and withdrew to an inn, where after some time I retired to a
chamber. I was scarcely there, before the door of the room was
opened, and the man, whose countenance was the most hateful to
my eyes, Gines, entered the apartment. He shut the door as soon
as he entered.

Youngster, said he, I have a little private intelligence to communicate to you. I come as a friend, and that I may save you a

labour-in-vain trouble. If you consider what I have to say in that light, it will be the better for you. It is my business now, do you see, for want of a better, to see that you do not break out of bounds. Not that I much matter having one man for my employer, or dancing attendance after another's heels; but I have a special kindness for you, for some good turns that you wot of, and therefore I do not stand upon ceremonies! You have led me a very pretty round already; and, out of the love I bear you, you shall lead me as much farther, if you will. But beware the salt seas! They are out of my orders. You are a prisoner at present, and I believe all your life will remain so. Thanks to the milk-and-water softness of your former master! If I had the ordering of these things, it should go with you in another fashion. As long as you think proper, you are a prisoner within the rules; and the rules with which the soft-hearted squire indulges you are all England, Scotland and Wales. But you are not to go out of these climates. The squire is determined you shall never pass the reach of his disposal. He has therefore given orders that, whenever you attempt so to do, you shall be converted from a prisoner at large to a prisoner in good earnest. A friend of mine followed you just now to the harbour; I was within call; and, if there had been any appearance of your setting your foot from land, we should have been with you in a trice, and laid you fast by the heels. I would advise you for the future to keep at a proper distance from the sea, for fear of the worst. You see I tell you all this for your good. For my part I should be better satisfied, if you were in limbo, with a rope about your neck, and a comfortable bird's-eye prospect to the gallows: but I do as I am directed; and so, good night to you!

The intelligence thus conveyed to me occasioned an instantaneous revolution in both my intellectual and animal system. I disdained to answer or take the smallest notice of the fiend by whom it was delivered. It is now three days since I received it, and from that moment to the present my blood has been in a perpetual ferment. My thoughts wander from one idea of horror to another with incredible rapidity. I have had no sleep. I have scarcely remained in one posture for a minute together. It has been with the utmost difficulty that I have been able to command myself far enough to add a few pages to my story. But, uncertain as I am of the events of each succeeding hour, I determined to force myself to the performance of this task. All is not right within me.

How it will terminate God knows. I sometimes fear that I shall be wholly deserted of my reason.

What—dark, mysterious, unfeeling, unrelenting tyrant!—is it come to this?—When Nero and Caligula swayed the Roman sceptre, it was a fearful thing to offend these bloody rulers. The empire had already spread itself from climate to climate, and from sea to sea. If their unhappy victim fled to the rising of the sun, where the luminary of day seems to us first to ascend from the waves of the ocean, the power of the tyrant was still behind him. If he withdrew to the west, to Hesperian darkness, and the shores of barbarian Thule, still he was not safe from his gore-drenched foe.—Falkland! art thou the offspring in whom the lineaments of these tyrants are faithfully preserved? Was the world with all its climates made in vain for thy helpless, unoffending victim?

Tremble!

Tyrants have trembled surrounded with whole armies of their Janissaries![1] What should make thee inaccessible to my fury?—No, I will use no daggers! I will unfold a tale—! I will show thee for what thou art, and all the men that live shall confess my truth!—Didst thou imagine that I was altogether passive, a mere worm, organized to feel sensations of pain, but no emotion of resentment? Didst thou imagine that there was no danger in inflicting on me pains however great, miseries however dreadful? Didst thou believe me impotent, imbecil and idiot-like, with no understanding to contrive thy ruin, and no energy to perpetrate it?

I will tell a tale—! The justice of the country shall hear me! The elements of nature in universal uproar shall not interrupt me! I will speak with a voice more fearful than thunder!—Why should I be supposed to speak from any dishonourable motive? I am under no prosecution now! I shall not now appear to be endeavouring to remove a criminal indictment from myself, by throwing it back on its author!—Shall I regret the ruin that will overwhelm thee? Too long have I been tender-hearted and forbearing! What benefit has ever resulted from my mistaken clemency? There is no evil thou hast scrupled to accumulate upon me! Neither will I be more scrupulous! Thou hast shown no mercy; and thou shalt receive none!—I must be calm! Bold as a lion, yet collected!

This is a moment pregnant with fate. I know—I think I know—that I will be triumphant, and crush my seemingly omnipotent foe.

But, should it be otherwise, at least he shall not be every way successful. His fame shall not be immortal, as he thinks. These papers shall preserve the truth: they shall one day be published, and then the world shall do justice on us both. Recollecting that, I shall not die wholly without consolation. It is not to be endured that falshood and tyranny should reign for ever.

How impotent are the precautions of man against the eternally existing laws of the intellectual world? This Falkland has invented against me every species of foul accusation. He has hunted me from city to city. He has drawn his lines of circumvallation round me that I may not escape. He has kept his scenters of human prey for ever at my heels. He may hunt me out of the world.—In vain! With this engine, this little pen I defeat all his machinations; I stab him in the very point he was most solicitous to defend!

Collins! I now address myself to you. I have consented that you should yield me no assistance in my present terrible situation. I am content to die rather than do any thing injurious to your tranquillity.—But, remember,—you are my father still!—I conjure you, by all the love you ever bore me, by the benefits you have conferred on me, by the forbearance and kindness towards you that now penetrates my soul, by my innocence—for, if these be the last words I shall ever write, I die protesting my innocence!—by all these or whatever tie more sacred has influence on your soul, I conjure you, listen to my last request! Preserve these papers from destruction, and preserve them from Falkland! It is all I ask! I have taken care to provide a safe mode of conveying them into your possession; and I have a firm confidence which I will not suffer to depart from me, that they will one day find their way to the public!

The pen lingers in my trembling fingers!—Is there any thing I have left unsaid?—The contents of the fatal trunk from which all my misfortunes originated, I have never been able to ascertain. I once thought it contained some murderous instrument or relique connected with the fate of the unhappy Tyrrel. I am now persuaded that the secret it incloses is a faithful narrative of that and its concomitant transactions, written by Mr. Falkland, and reserved in case of the worst, that, if by any unforeseen event his guilt should come to be fully disclosed, it might contribute to redeem the wreck of his reputation. But the truth or the falshood of this conjecture is of little moment. If Falkland shall never be detected to the satisfaction of the world, such a narrative will probably never see the light. In that case this story of mine may amply, severely perhaps, supply its place.

I know not what it is that renders me thus solemn. I have a secret foreboding as if I should never again be master of myself. If I succeed in what I now meditate respecting Falkland, my precaution in the disposal of these papers will have been unnecessary; I shall no longer be reduced to artifice and evasion. If I fail, the precaution will appear to have been wisely chosen.

POSTSCRIPT

ALL is over. I have carried into execution my meditated attempt. My situation is totally changed; I now sit down to give an account of it. For several weeks after the completion of this dreadful business, my mind was in too tumultuous a state to permit me to write. I think I shall now be able to arrange my thoughts sufficiently for that purpose. Great God! how wondrous, how terrible are the events that have intervened since I was last employed in a similar manner! It is no wonder that my thoughts were solemn, and my mind filled with horrible forebodings!

Having formed my resolution I set out from Harwich for the metropolitan town of the county in which Mr. Falkland resided. Gines I well knew was in my rear. That was of no consequence to me. He might wonder at the direction I pursued, but he could not tell with what purpose I pursued it. My design was a secret carefully locked up in my own breast. It was not without a sentiment of terror that I entered a town which had been the scene of my long imprisonment. I proceeded to the house of the chief magistrate the instant I arrived, that I might give no time to my adversary to counterwork my proceeding.

I told him who I was, and that I was come from a distant part of the kingdom for the purpose of rendering him the medium of a charge of murder against my former patron. My name was already familiar to him. He answered that he could not take cognizance of my deposition, that I was an object of universal execration in that part of the world, and he was determined upon no account to be the vehicle of my depravity

I warned him to consider well what he was doing. I called upon him for no favour; I only applied to him in the regular exercise of his function. Would he take upon him to say that he had a right at his pleasure to suppress a charge of this complicated nature? I had to accuse Mr. Falkland of repeated murders. The perpetrator knew that I was in possession of the truth upon the subject; and, knowing that, I went perpetually in danger of my life from his malice and revenge. I was resolved to go through with the business, if justice were to be obtained from any court in England. Upon what pretence did he refuse my deposition? I was in every respect a competent witness. I was of age to understand the nature of an oath; I was in my perfect senses; I was untarnished by the verdict of any jury, or the sentence of any judge. His private opinion of my character could not alter the law of the land. I demanded to be confronted with Mr. Falkland, and I was well assured I should substantiate the charge to the satisfaction of the whole world. If he did not think proper to apprehend him upon my single testimony, I should be satisfied if he only sent him notice of the charge and summoned him to appear.

The magistrate finding me thus resolute, thought proper a little to lower his tone. He no longer absolutely refused to comply with my requisition, but condescended to expostulate with me. He represented to me Mr. Falkland's health which had for some years been exceedingly indifferent, his having been once already brought to the most solemn examination upon this charge, the diabolical malice in which alone my proceeding must have originated, and the tenfold ruin it would bring down upon my own head. To all these representations my answer was short. I was determined to go on, and would abide the consequences. A summons was at length granted, and notice sent to Mr. Falkland of the charge preferred against him.

Three days elapsed before any farther step could be taken in this business. This interval in no degree contributed to tranquillise my mind. The thought of preferring a capital accusation against, and hastening the death of such a man as Mr. Falkland, was by no means an opiate to reflection. At one time I commended the action, either as just revenge (for the benevolence of my nature was in a great degree turned to gall), or as necessary self-defence, or as that which in an impartial and philanthropical estimate included the smallest evil. At another time I was haunted with doubts. But, spite of these variations of sentiment, I uniformly determined to persist; I felt as if impelled by a tide of unconquerable impulse. The consequences were such as might well appal the stoutest heart. Either the ignominious execution of a man whom I had once so deeply venerated, and whom now I sometimes suspected not to be without his claims to veneration; or a confirmation, perhaps an increase, of the calamities I had so long endured. Yet these I preferred to a state of uncertainty. I desired to know the worst; to put an end to the hope, however faint, which had been so long my torment; and above all to exhaust and finish the catalogue of expedients that were at my disposition. My mind was worked up to a state little short of frenzy. My body was in a burning fever with the agitation of my thoughts. When I laid my hand upon my bosom or my head, it seemed to scorch them with the fervency of its heat. I could not sit still for a moment. I panted with incessant desire that the dreadful crisis I had so eagerly invoked were come, and were over.

After an interval of three days I met Mr. Falkland in the presence of the magistrate to whom I had applied upon the subject. I had only two hours notice to prepare myself, Mr. Falkland seeming as eager as I to have the question brought to a crisis, and laid at rest for ever. I had an opportunity before the examination to learn that Mr. Forester was drawn by some business on an excursion to the continent, and that Collins, whose health when I saw him was in a very precarious state, was at this time confined with alarming illness. His constitution had been wholly broken with his West Indian voyage. The audience I met at the house of the magistrate consisted of several gentlemen and others selected for the purpose, the plan being, in some respects as in the former instance, to find a medium between the suspicious air of a private examination, and the indelicacy as it was styled of an examination exposed to the remark of every casual spectator.

I can conceive of no shock greater than that I received from the sight of Mr. Falkland. His appearance on the last occasion on which we met had been haggard, ghost-like and wild, energy in his gestures and frenzy in his aspect. It was now the appearance of a corpse. He was brought in in a chair unable to stand, fatigued and almost destroyed by the journey he had just taken. His visage was colourless; his limbs destitute of motion, almost of life. His head reclined upon his bosom, except that now and then he lifted it up and opened his eyes with a languid glance, immediately after which he sunk back into his former apparent insensibility. He seemed not to have three hours to live. He had kept his chamber for several weeks; but the summons of the magistrate had been delivered to him at his bed-side; his orders respecting letters and written papers being so peremptory that no one dared to disobey them. Upon reading the paper he was seized with a very dangerous fit; but, as soon as he recovered, he insisted upon being conveyed with all practicable expedition to the place of appointment. Falkland in the most helpless state was still Falkland, firm in command, and capable to extort obedience from every one that approached him.

What a sight was this to me! Till the moment that Falkland was presented to my view, my breast was steeled to pity. I thought that I had coolly entered into the reason of the case (passion in a state of solemn and omnipotent vehemence always appears to be coolness to him in whom it domineers); and that I had determined impartially and justly. I believed that, if Mr. Falkland were permitted to persist in his schemes, we must both of us be completely wretched. I believed that it was in my power by the resolution I had formed to throw my share of this wretchedness from me, and that his could scarcely be increased. It appeared therefore to my mind to be a mere piece of equity and justice, such as an impartial spectator would desire, that one person should be miserable in preference to two, that one person rather than two should be incapacitated from acting his part, and contributing his share to the general welfare. I thought that in this business I had risen superior to personal considerations, and judged with a total neglect of the suggestions of self-regard. It is true, Mr. Falkland was mortal: but, notwithstanding his apparent decay, he might live long. Ought I to submit to waste the best years of my life in my present wretched situation? He had declared that his reputation should be for ever inviolate; this was his ruling passion, the thought that worked his soul to madness. He would probably therefore leave a legacy of persecution to be received by me from the hands of Gines or some other villain equally atrocious, when he should himself be no more. Now or never was the time for me to redeem my future life from endless woe.

But all these fine-spun reasonings vanished before the object that was now presented to me. Shall I trample upon a man thus dreadfully reduced? Shall I point my animosity against one whom the system of nature has brought down to the grave? Shall I poison with sounds the most intolerable to his ears the last moments of a man like Falkland? It is impossible. There must have been some dreadful mistake in the train of argument that persuaded me to be the author of this hateful scene. There must have been a better and more magnanimous remedy to the evils under which I groaned.

It was too late. The mistake I had committed was now gone past all power of recal. Here was Falkland solemnly brought before a magistrate to answer a charge of murder. Here I stood, having already declared myself the author of the charge, gravely and sacredly pledged to support it. This was my situation; and, thus situated, I was called upon immediately to act. My whole frame shook. I would eagerly have consented that that moment should have been the last of my existence. I however believed that the conduct now most indispensibly incumbent on me, was to lay the emotions of my soul naked before my hearers. I looked first at Mr. Falkland, and then at the magistrate and attendants, and then at Mr. Falkland again. My voice was suffocated with agony. I began:

Why cannot I recal the four last days of my life? How was it possible for me to be so eager, so obstinate in a purpose so diabolical? Oh, that I had listened to the expostulations of the magistrate that hears me, or submitted to the well meant despotism of his authority! Hitherto I have only been miserable; henceforth I shall account myself base! Hitherto, though hardly treated by mankind, I stood acquitted at the bar of my own conscience. I had not filled up the measure of my wretchedness!

Would to God it were possible for me to retire from this scene without uttering another word! I would brave the consequences —I would submit to any imputation of cowardice, falshood and profligacy, rather than add to the weight of misfortune with which Mr. Falkland is overwhelmed. But the situation and the demands of Mr. Falkland himself forbid me. He, in compassion for whose fallen state I would willingly forget every interest of my own, would compel me to accuse, that he might enter upon his justification.—I will confess every sentiment of my heart.

No penitence, no anguish can expiate the folly and the cruelty of this last act I have perpetrated. But Mr. Falkland well knows— I affirm it in his presence—how unwillingly I have proceeded to this extremity. I have reverenced him; he was worthy of reverence:

I have loved him; he was endowed with qualities that partook of divine.

From the first moment I saw him, I conceived the most ardent admiration. He condescended to encourage me; I attached myself to him with the fulness of my affection. He was unhappy; I exerted myself with youthful curiosity to discover the secret of his woe. This was the beginning of misfortune.

What shall I say?—He was indeed the murderer of Tyrrel; he suffered the Hawkinses to be executed, knowing that they were innocent, and that he alone was guilty. After successive surmises, after various indiscretions on my part and indications on his, he at length confided to me at full the fatal tale!

Mr. Falkland! I most solemnly conjure you to recollect yourself! Did I ever prove myself unworthy of your confidence? The secret was a most painful burthen to me; it was the extremest folly that led me unthinkingly to gain possession of it; but I would have died a thousand deaths rather than betray it. It was the jealousy of your own thoughts, and the weight that hung upon your mind, that led you to watch my motions, and conceive alarm from every particle of my conduct.

You began in confidence; why did you not continue in confidence? The evil that resulted from my original imprudence, would then have been comparatively little. You threatened me: did I then betray you? A word from my lips at that time would have freed me from your threats for ever. I bore them for a considerable period, and at last quitted your service, and threw myself a fugitive upon the world in silence. Why did you not suffer me to depart? You brought me back by stratagem and violence, and wantonly accused me of an enormous felony; did I then mention a syllable of the murder, the secret of which was in my possession?

Where is the man that has suffered more from the injustice of society than I have done? I was accused of a villainy that my heart abhorred. I was sent to jail. I will not enumerate the horrors of my prison, the lightest of which would make the heart of humanity shudder. I looked forward to the gallows! Young, ambitious, fond of life, innocent as the child unborn, I looked forward to the gallows! I believed that one word of resolute accusation against my patron would deliver me, yet I was silent, I armed myself with patience, uncertain whether it were better to accuse or to die. Did this show me a man unworthy to be trusted?

I determined to break out of prison. With infinite difficulty and repeated miscarriages I at length effected my purpose. Instantly a proclamation with a hundred guineas reward was issued for apprehending me. I was obliged to take shelter among the refuse of mankind, in the midst of a gang of thieves. I encountered the most imminent peril of my life when I entered into this retreat, and when I quitted it. Immediately after I travelled almost the whole length of the kingdom in poverty and distress, in hourly danger of being retaken and manacled like a felon. I would have fled my country; I was prevented. I had recourse to various disguises; I was innocent, and yet was compelled to as many arts and subterfuges as could have been entailed on the worst of villains. In London I was as much harrassed and as repeatedly alarmed, as I had been in my flight through the country. Did all these persecutions persuade me to put an end to my silence? No: I suffered them with patience and submission; I did not make one attempt to retort them upon their author. I fell at last into the hands of the miscreants that are nourished with human blood. In this terrible situation I for the first time attempted by turning informer to throw the weight from myself. Happily for me the London magistrate listened to my tale with insolent contempt.

I soon and long repented of my rashness and rejoiced in my miscarriage. I acknowledge that in various ways Mr. Falkland showed humanity towards me during this period. He would have prevented my going to prison at first; he contributed to my subsistence during my detention; he had no share in the pursuit that had been set on foot against me; he at length procured my discharge when brought forward for trial. But a great part of his forbearance was unknown to me; I supposed him to be my unrelenting pursuer. I could not forget that, whoever heaped calamities on me in the sequel, they all originated in his forged accusation.

The prosecution against me for felony was now at end. Why were not my sufferings permitted to terminate then, and I allowed to hide my weary head in some obscure yet tranquil retreat? Had I not sufficiently proved my constancy and fidelity? Would not a compromise in this situation have been most wise and most secure? But the restless and jealous anxiety of Mr. Falkland would not permit him to repose the least atom of confidence. The only compromise that he proposed was that with my own hand I should sign myself a villain. I refused this proposal, and have ever since been driven from place to place, deprived of peace, of honest fame, even of bread. For a long time I persisted in the resolution that no emergency should convert me into the assailant. In evil hour I at last listened to my resentment and impatience, and the hateful mistake into which I fell has produced the present scene.

I now see that mistake in all its enormity. I am sure that, if I had opened my heart to Mr. Falkland, if I had told to him privately the tale that I have now been telling, he could not have resisted my reasonable demand. After all his precautions, he must ultimately have depended upon my forbearance. Could he be sure that, if I were at last worked up to disclose every thing I knew and to inforce it with all the energy I could exert, I should obtain no credit? If he must in every case be at my mercy, in which mode ought he to have sought his safety, in conciliation or in inexorable cruelty?

Mr. Falkland is of a noble nature. Yes; in spite of the catastrophe of Tyrrel, of the miserable end of the Hawkinses, and of all that I have myself suffered, I affirm that he has qualities of the most admirable kind. It is therefore impossible that he could have resisted a frank and fervent expostulation, the frankness and the fervour in which the whole soul was poured out. I despaired, while it was yet time to have made the just experiment; but my despair was criminal, was treason against the sovereignty of truth.

I have told a plain and unadulterated tale. I came hither to curse, but I remain to bless. I came to accuse, but am compelled to applaud. I proclaim to all the world that Mr. Falkland is a man worthy of affection and kindness, and that I am myself the basest and most odious of mankind! Never will I forgive myself the iniquity of this day. The memory will always haunt me, and embitter every hour of my existence. In thus acting I have been a murderer, a cool, deliberate, unfeeling murderer.—I have said what my accursed precipitation has obliged me to say. Do with me as you please! I ask no favour. Death would be a kindness, compared to what I feel!

Such were the accents dictated by my remorse. I poured them out with uncontrolable impetuosity, for my heart was pierced, and I was compelled to give vent to its anguish. Every one that heard me was petrified with astonishment. Every one that heard me was melted into tears. They could not resist the ardour with which I praised the great qualities of Falkland; they manifested their sympathy in the tokens of my penitence.

How shall I describe the feelings of this unfortunate man? Before I began, he seemed sunk and debilitated, incapable of any strenuous impression. When I mentioned the murder, I could perceive in him an involuntary shuddering, though it was counteracted partly by the feebleness of his frame, and partly by the energy of his mind. This was an allegation he expected, and he had endeavoured to prepare himself for it. But there was much of what I said, of which he had had no previous conception. When I expressed the anguish of my mind, he seemed at first startled and alarmed lest this should be a new expedient to gain credit to my tale. His indignation against me was great for having retained all my resentment towards him thus, as it might be, to the last hour of his existence. It was increased, when he discovered me, as he supposed, using a pretence of liberality and sentiment, to give new edge to my hostility. But, as I went on, he could no longer resist. He saw my sincerity; he was penetrated with my grief and compunction. He rose from his seat supported by the attendants, and —to my infinite astonishment—threw himself into my arms!

Williams, said he, you have conquered! I see too late the greatness and elevation of your mind. I confess that it is to my fault and not yours, that it is to the excess of jealousy that was ever burning in my bosom, that I owe my ruin. I could have resisted any plan of malicious accusation you might have brought against me. But I see that the artless and manly story you have told, has carried conviction to every hearer. All my prospects are concluded. All that I most ardently desired is for ever frustrated. I have spent a life of the basest cruelty to cover one act of momentary vice and to protect myself against the prejudices of my species. I stand now completely detected. My name will be consecrated to infamy, while your heroism, your patience and your virtues will be for ever admired. You have inflicted on me the most fatal of all mischiefs, but I bless the hand that wounds me. And now,—turning to the magistrate—and now, do with me as you please. I am prepared to suffer all the vengeance of the law. You cannot inflict on me more than I deserve. You cannot hate me more than I hate myself. I am the most execrable of all villains. I have for many years (I know not how long) dragged on a miserable existence in insupportable pain. I am at last, in recompense for all my labours and my crimes, dismissed from it, with the disappointment of my only remaining hope, the destruction of that for the sake of which alone I consented to exist. It was worthy of such a life, that it should continue just long enough to witness this final overthrow. If however you wish to punish me, you must be speedy in your justice; for, as reputation was the blood that warmed my heart, so I feel that death and infamy must seize me together.

I record the praises bestowed on me by Falkland, not because I deserve them, but because they serve to aggravate the baseness of my cruelty. He survived this dreadful scene but three days. I have been his murderer. It was fit that he should praise my patience, who has fallen a victim, life and fame, to my precipitation! It would have been merciful in comparison, if I had planted a dagger in his heart. He would have thanked me for my kindness. But, atrocious, execrable wretch that I have been! I wantonly inflicted on him an anguish a thousand times worse than death. Meanwhile I endure the penalty of my crime. His figure is ever in imagination before me. Waking or sleeping I still behold him. He seems mildly to expostulate with me for my unfeeling behaviour. I live the devoted victim of conscious reproach. Alas! I am the same Caleb Williams that, so short a time ago, boasted, that, however great were the calamities I endured, I was still innocent.

Such has been the result of a project I formed for delivering myself from the evils that had so long attended me. I thought that, if Falkland were dead, I should return once again to all that makes life worth possessing. I thought that, if the guilt of Falkland were established, fortune and the world would smile upon my efforts. Both these events are accomplished; and it is only now that I am truly miserable.

Why should my reflections perpetually centre upon myself? self, an overweening regard to which has been the source of my errors! Falkland, I will think only of thee, and from that thought will draw ever fresh nourishment for my sorrows! One generous, one disinterested tear I will consecrate to thy ashes! A nobler spirit lived not among the sons of men. Thy intellectual powers were truly sublime, and thy bosom burned with a godlike ambition. But of what use are talents and sentiments in the corrupt wilderness of human society? It is a rank and rotten soil from which every finer shrub draws poison as it grows. All that in a happier field and a purer air would expand into virtue and germinate into general usefulness, is thus converted into henbane and deadly nightshade.

Falkland! thou enteredst upon thy carreer with the purest and most laudable intentions. But thou imbibedst the poison of chivalry with thy earliest youth; and the base and low-minded envy that met thee on thy return to thy native seats, operated with this poison to hurry thee into madness. Soon, too soon, by this fatal coincidence were the blooming hopes of thy youth blasted for ever! From that moment thou only continuedst to live to the phantom of departed honour. From that moment thy benevolence was in a great part turned into rankling jealousy and inexorable precaution. Year after year didst thou spend in this miserable project of imposture; and only at last continuedst to live long enough to see, by my misjudging and abhorred intervention, thy closing hope disappointed, and thy death accompanied with the foulest disgrace!

I began these memoirs with the idea of vindicating my character. I have now no character that I wish to vindicate: but I will finish them that thy story may be fully understood; and that, if those errors of thy life be known which thou so ardently desiredst to conceal, the world may at least not hear and repeat a half-told and mangled tale.

FINIS

APPENDIX I

MANUSCRIPT ENDING OF *CALEB WILLIAMS*

Godwin originally concluded Caleb Williams *with an entirely different denouement than that found in the novel as it has always been
published. His diary indicates that he finished the first version of the
novel on 30 April 1794, but he was apparently dissatisfied with it,
had a better idea, and on 4 to 8 May wrote the published version.[1]
The original ending consists of nine manuscript pages, two of which
are lost. The action begins with the final trial scene, immediately after
Falkland enters the court-room to face Caleb's accusations. It was
intended to follow the sentence on p. 319 of this edition: 'Falkland in
the most helpless state was still Falkland, firm in command, and
capable to extort obedience from every one that approached him.'*

WHAT a sight was this to me? It harmonised with the madness of
my soul, and gave double vehemence to the tide of my fury. Could
I allow my tongue to accuse a man thus deplorably circumstanced,
and impel the stroke of death which was ready to fall on him? Yes:
how knew I that this was not a new expedient of my hundred-
handed foe, merely to evade the blow, and prolong my misery?
Yes: he had declared that his reputation should be for ever inviolate, and therefore would probably leave a legacy of persecution
to be received by me from the hand of Jones[2] or some other villain
equally atrocious, whom his ingenious animosity could easily
raise up against me. Yes: for I had no longer the liberty of choice.
I must either suffer the penalties of a false accuser; or go on, resolute
and unaltered, in the prosecution I had begun.

As soon as I entered, the magistrate addressed me with a stern
voice, and asked me, Whether what I saw there did not make me
repent my villainy? Had I the heart under these circumstances to
perpetrate the miserable scheme I had contrived?—The peculiarity of the scene before him deprived the magistrate of all power to
control this burst of his indignation.

[1] For a description of the manuscript of *Caleb Williams*, see the article by
D. Gilbert Dumas cited in the Select Bibliography.

[2] After the first edition of the novel, Godwin changed 'Jones' to 'Gines' throughout.

Mr. Falkland motioned to speak. His voice was [?], and with difficulty audible. He begged them upon no account to interpose and endeavour to alter my design. It was necessary to his vindication that I should be invited to say all that I had meditated. He was thankful that his life had been spared long enough to meet this last essay of the malice of his fate.

I collected myself for the awful minute that was now before me; and the sense of its inestimable importance seemed to put to instant flight the tumult of contending passions that had till then possessed me. In a moment I recovered from a state little short of frenzy, and found myself perfectly self-possessed. My mind reviewed with ease the successive parts of the transaction I had to explain. I was varied, perspicuous and forcible. My confidence every instant increased, till I felt all the satisfaction of undoubting certainty.

I described how much I was at present exempt from that state of retort and recrimination, which formerly, while I was myself under prosecution, had rendered my evidence, perhaps reasonably arguing upon general principles, though unjustly in my particular instance, a subject of suspicion. I now came forward voluntarily, when all was over; and was as well entitled to be heard as another man.

I expressed my sorrow for the apparent state of Mr. Falkland's health. I did not thirst for his blood. But I could no longer be easy to confine within my own bosom the knowledge I had upon this terrible subject.

I related to them a variety of particulars with which the reader is already acquainted. I entered with minuteness into some parts of the story. I depended for my success upon the consistency and probability of my narrative. In several places I pointed it expressly to Mr. Falkland, and I could perceive the shuddering which was partly counteracted by the firmness of his mind, and partly by the general relaxation of his frame incapable either to receive or to convey strong impressions. In several places I could discern in my audience feelings exactly such as I intended to excite. Upon the effect now to be produced depended my future character, my liberty and my peace. I remembered this. I spoke with energy, fervour and conscious truth.

When I had finished, Mr. Falkland begged leave to answer me. He appeared to bring out his words with great difficulty. He observed that he was not able, as he could have wished to have done, to follow me through the particulars of my story. He acknowledged that it was told with great artifice and appearance of consistency. To as much of it as related to Mr. Tyrrel he had already answered upon solemn occasion in the face of his country. This charge I had accumulated with the accusation of his being in the eye of reason the murderer also of the Hawkinses; and I had added to all the rest the unparallelled effrontery of pretending to have received a confession of these facts from his own mouth.

To these allegations he would offer under the present circumstances only one short answer. The character of neither of the parties, the accuser or the accused, was wholly unknown. He had lived in the face of his country and in the face of Europe. His life had been irreproachable; it had been more than this; he must say it, it had been uniformly benevolent and honourable. I also was known, notwithstanding the meanness of my origin, as extensively as he was. My history was notorious; first a thief; then a breaker of prisons; and last a consummate adept in every species of disguise. The question under discussion by its very nature depended upon the veracity of the parties. I affirmed that I had had the confession from his own mouth; he that he had made no such confession, for he had had no such confession to make. Which of the two would they believe? What credit was due to the palpable mockery of oaths and asseverations, when put into competition with a life of unimpeachable virtue?

He added that he might safely risk the question upon another issue. He would consent that they should believe every tittle of my deposition, if I could assign any probable reason for making it. I pretended that I did not thirst for his blood, and that I should be contented to drop the business in its present stage, if the facts to which I swore were fully admitted for true. What an absurd declaration? I said that my conscience was uneasy, and I was anxious to disburthen it. That sentiment, if it existed, would render me either desirous to see my deposition followed up by the exemplary punishment of the party accused, or would make me contented to relate what I knew, without being anxious as to the reception it experienced. No: it was plain that my motive was either revenge for his having brought me to shame, though he had generously remitted to me the penalty annexed; or a weak hope of retrieving my character by retaliating upon my prosecutor the disgrace I had suffered.

I listened with impatience to the animadversions of Mr. Falkland. They did not appear to my inflamed mind to have any considerable force; yet I was anxious to destroy their possible effect. The moment he ceased, I began again; without waiting till I was called upon, without waiting to see whether it was likely I should be called upon.

I said, I stood there for justice. I observed that it was of consequence, in a degree beyond any thing they could suspect, that justice should be done. I intreated them by every thing that was honourable, I conjured them by every thing that was tremendous, to deal impartially and truly. I spoke with a rapidity, perturbation and vehemence that were absolutely alarming to my hearers. I offered to produce witnesses of the symptoms of guilt which Mr. Falkland had long continued to display, of the early date of my accusations against him, and of the mischiefs I was every day suffering from his unremitting jealousy.

Having spoken for some time with incredible eagerness, and at length gasping and panting for breath, the magistrate sternly interposed. Be silent! said he. What is it you intend by thus continuing to intrude yourself? Do you believe you can overbear and intimidate us? We will hear none of your witnesses. We have heard you too long. Never was the dignity of administrative justice in any instance insulted with so bare faced and impudent a forgery!

Great God! with what an effect did these words[1]

[Postscript
No. I]

vicissitude of my fortune may be styled pleasure, in comparison with what I underwent in this situation. Wild and incoherent visions perpetually succeeded each other, dragged my attention this way and that, and allowed me not a moment's respite. I had no sleep; day and night it was still the same; the same torture and racking of the faculties. If at any time the pictures that glided along before my terrified imagination moved with a slower pace, the idea then occurred of mystery, of something which the understanding was incessantly anxious to penetrate, it turned it on this side and on that, it tried to enter by a thousand paths, but always returned

[1] Two manuscript pages are missing. Caleb next appears in prison.

empty, wearied, dissatisfied and unrewarded. His keeper is to a madman something infinitely terrible, a being that delights to thwart him, that endures no expostulation, and whose authority is uncontrolable and omnipotent. But Jones was no common keeper. He stood connected in my mind with other detestable associations, beside those which belonged to his present office. Jones also, habituated to cruelty and revenge, reserved all the refinement and luxury of these passions to be exercised on me. He would continue with me for hours still inventing new methods of exasperation. I have no distinct conception of what he practised on me during the period of my insanity; but I am persuaded that no distracted slave of superstition ever annexed such painful ideas to his dreaded Beelzebub, as I annexed to the figure and appearance of this man.

By what strange cause it has happened that under the discipline of this man I have ever recovered any portion of reason, I am unable to pronounce. How long I shall retain the degree of composure I at present feel, or what will be the fate of my remaining life, I have no materials to judge. It would be better at once to cease to exist, than remain for ever in this horrible situation. But hope still clings to my heart. I may escape. Why should I, who have broken fetters, and made my way through walls of stone, doubt of my deliverance from this new confinement? I dare not attempt this at present. It is my duty to wait till I can be more sure of my faculties, both that I may contrive more wisely the methods of escape, and that I may have less reason to fear the afterwards betraying myself through any sudden impulse of absurdity. At present I by no means find myself satisfied with the state of my intellects. I am subject to wanderings in which the imagination seems to refuse to obey the curb of judgment. I dare not attempt to think long and strenuously on any one subject. In writing these pages I obtain in the first place a means of essaying the force of my new found understanding; and I am able, writing them as I do, uncertainly and by short snatches, to proportion my essay to the strength of which I am conscious. Above all, I must reserve strength enough to counteract the malignity of Jones, and not suffer him again to irritate me into madness.

One of the thoughts that first presented itself to my mind with the dawn of returning reason, was that of recording these recent and tragical transactions which had occurred subsequently to my putting out of my possession the body of my memoirs. Surely, said I, such a story is worth recording! Surely incidents so extraordinary and so terrible cannot fail to be pregnant with instruction to mankind! It is not necessary that I should trouble the reader with a detail of the expedients by which I enabled myself to reduce this design into practice in my present forlorn situation. I have seen but two persons, Jones and a woman whose business it is to do the drudgery of my apartment. The woman I have seldom seen, it was intended I should have never seen, apart. But the man that watches his opportunity with a quick and eager eye, and who is ardently solicitous to accomplish his purpose, will seldom be long frustrated in an attempt of this sort. The woman has not a heart of flint.

I understand that Mr. Falkland contrary to all previous appearances still lives, nay, that he is considerably better in his health. Alas! alas! it too plainly appears in my history that persecution and tyranny can never die!

I am still in the highest degree perplexed, whenever it recurs to my mind, to account for the entire and ignominious miscarriage of my last [?] accusation before the chief magistrate at ——. Mr. Falkland to have so little to say! I so ardent, so impassioned, so full of my subject, so confident in the justice of my cause! It must surely have been with the persons that heard me an affair of the senses rather than the understanding. They were seduced by the forlorn and deplorable appearance of my adversary; yet how formidable [it is dishonour and madness so much as to think of that!] in the midst of ruin!

Am I not deceiving myself while I thus explain my defeat? Am I not applying an imaginary balm to the gaping wounds of my mind? Perhaps all men will reason upon my story as these men reasoned. Perhaps I am beguiling myself during all this time, merely for want of strength to put myself in the place of an unprepossessed auditor, and to conceive how the story will impress every one that hears it. My innocence will then die with me! The narrative I have taken the pains to digest will then only perpetuate my shame and spread more widely the persuasion of my nefarious guilt! How excruciating so much as to suspect the possibility of such an issue to the scene! This is the bitterest aggravation of all my sufferings! I cannot endure to think it!

I just now feel a sensation unexperienced before. During the whole of my restraint sleep has been a stranger to me; its visits have been rare and of short duration. I feel now a benumbing heaviness, that I conceive to have something in it more than natural. I have tried again and again to shake it off. I can scarcely hold my pen. Surely—surely there is no foul play in all this! My mind misgives me. I will send away these papers, while I am yet able to do so.

Postscript
No. II

Dear Mr. Collins, I have a thousand things to tell you—I do not know what is the matter with me, but I am very ill—My head throbs, and my pulses flutter, and yet I am so heavy—Indeed, if you were to see me, you would pity me now—and you would not refuse to take my part as you did at a certain time!—Well, I had something to say—but I cannot think of it—and I cannot hold up my head.

There was once a poor traveller—he was very good natured—and very innocent—and meant no ill to any living soul—he met with a wild beast—the creature seemed to be in great distress, and moaned most piteously—I forget whether it had hurt itself—but the traveller came up to it, and asked it what it wanted, and would have assisted it—but the cries of the beast were only an imposition! —It was a CROCODILE!

I wonder how long I have slept—sometimes it seems to have been so long—and sometimes it seems a very little while—As soon as I eat, and drink, I fall asleep again—is not that strange?

I should like to recollect something—it would make an addition to my history—but it is all a BLANK!—sometimes it is day, and sometimes it is night—but nobody does any thing, and nobody says any thing—It would be an odd kind of a history!

Once I had an enemy—oh! two or three enemies!—and they drove me about, and menaced me, and tormented me!—and now nobody disturbs me—I am so quiet—I have not an enemy in the world—*nor a* FRIEND!

So you tell me Mr. Falkland is dead?—Very likely—it was high time—I believe—was not it?

They do nothing but tell me over and over again that Mr. Falkland is dead—What is that to me?—Heaven rest his soul!—I wonder who that Mr. Falkland was, for every body to think so much about him?—Do you know?

If I could once again be thoroughly myself, I should tell such tales!—Some folks are afraid of that, do you see, and so—But I never shall—never—never!—I sit in a chair in a corner, and never move hand or foot—I am like a log—I know all that very well, but I cannot help it!—I wonder which is the man, I or my chair?

I have dreams—they are strange dreams—I never know what they are about—No, not while I am dreaming—they are about nothing at all—and yet there is one thing first, and then another thing, and there is so much of them, and it is all nothing—when I am awake it is just the same!—I used to have dreams of quite a different kind—and to talk in my dreams—and some folks said I disturbed them—and so, I believe they have given me something to quiet me.

Well, it is all one at last—I believe there was nothing in life worth making such a bustle about—no, nor in SECRETS—nor in MURDERS neither, for the matter of that—when people are dead, you know, one cannot bring them to life again!—dead folks tell no tales—ghosts do not walk these days—I never saw Mr. Tyrrel's —Only once!

Well then,—It is wisest to be quiet, it seems—Some people are ambitious—other people talk of sensibility—but it is all folly! —I am sure I am not one of those—was I ever?—True happiness lies in being like a stone—Nobody can complain of me—all day long I do nothing—am a stone—a GRAVE-STONE!—an obelisk to tell you, HERE LIES WHAT WAS ONCE A MAN!

APPENDIX II

GODWIN'S ACCOUNT OF THE COMPOSITION
OF *CALEB WILLIAMS*

Quoted from Godwin's preface to the 'Standard Novels' edition (1832) of Fleetwood

London, November 20. 1832.

'CALEB WILLIAMS' has always been regarded by the public with an unusual degree of favour. The proprietor of 'THE STANDARD NOVELS' has therefore imagined, that even an account of the concoction and mode of writing of the work would be viewed with some interest.

I finished the 'Enquiry concerning Political Justice,' the first work which may be considered as written by me in a certain degree in the maturity of my intellectual powers, and bearing my name, early in January, 1793; and about the middle of the following month the book was published. It was my fortune at that time to be obliged to consider my pen as the sole instrument for supplying my current expenses. By the liberality of my bookseller, Mr. George Robinson, of Pasternoster Row, I was enabled then, and for nearly ten years before, to meet these expenses, while writing different things of obscure note, the names of which though innocent, and in some degree useful, I am rather inclined to suppress. In May, 1791, I projected this, my favourite work, and from that time gave up every other occupation that might interfere with it. My agreement with Robinson was, that he was to supply my wants at a specified rate, while the book was in the train of composition. Finally, I was very little beforehand with the world on the day of its publication, and was therefore obliged to look round and consider to what species of industry I should next devote myself.

I had always felt in myself some vocation towards the composition of a narrative of fictitious adventure; and among the things of obscure note, which I have above referred to, were two or three pieces of this nature.[1] It is not therefore extraordinary that some project of the sort should have suggested itself on the present occasion.

But I stood now in a very different situation from that in which I had been placed at a former period. In past years, and even almost from boyhood, I was perpetually prone to exclaim with Cowley,—

> What shall I do to be for ever known,
> And make the age to come my own?[2]

But I had endeavoured for ten years, and was as far from approaching my object as ever. Every thing I wrote fell dead-born from the press. Very often I was disposed to quit the enterprise in despair. But still I felt ever and anon impelled to repeat my effort.

At length I conceived the plan of Political Justice. I was convinced that my object of building to myself a name would never be attained, by merely repeating and refining a little upon what other men had said, even though I should imagine that I delivered things of this sort with a more than usual point and elegance. The world, I believed, would accept nothing from me with distinguishing favour, that did not bear upon the face of it the undoubted stamp of originality. Having long ruminated upon the principles of Political Justice, I persuaded myself that I could offer to the public, in a treatise on this subject, things at once new, true and important. In the progress of the work I became more sanguine and confident. I talked over my ideas with a few familiar friends during its progress, and they gave me every generous encouragement. It happened that the fame of my book, in some inconsiderable degree, got before its publication, and a certain number of persons were prepared to receive it with favour. It would be false modesty in me to say, that its acceptance, when published, did not early come up to every thing that could soberly have been expected by me. In consequence of this, the tone of my mind, both during the period in which I was engaged in the work, and afterwards, acquired a certain elevation, and made me now unwilling to stoop to what was insignificant.

I formed a conception of a book of fictitious adventure, that

---

[1] Among his early, obscure works are three short novels, *Damon and Delia*, *Italian Letters*, and *Imogen*, all published in 1784.
[2] Quoted from Abraham Cowley's *Miscellanies*, 'The Motto', ll. 1-2.

should in some way be distinguished by a very powerful interest. Pursuing this idea, I invented first the third volume of my tale, then the second, and last of all the first. I bent myself to the conception of a series of adventures of flight and pursuit; the fugitive in perpetual apprehension of being overwhelmed with the worst calamities, and the pursuer, by his ingenuity and resources, keeping his victim in a state of the most fearful alarm. This was the project of my third volume.

I was next called upon to conceive a dramatic and impressive situation adequate to account for the impulse that the pursuer should feel, incessantly to alarm and harass his victim, with an inextinguishable resolution never to allow him the least interval of peace and security. This I apprehended could best be effected by a secret murder, to the investigation of which the innocent victim should be impelled by an unconquerable spirit of curiosity. The murderer would thus have a sufficient motive to persecute the unhappy discoverer, that he might deprive him of peace, character and credit, and have him for ever in his power. This constituted the outline of my second volume.

The subject of the first volume was still to be invented. To account for the fearful events of the third, it was necessary that the pursuer should be invested with every advantage of fortune, with a resolution that nothing could defeat or baffle, and with extraordinary resources of intellect. Nor could my purpose of giving an overpowering interest to my tale be answered, without his appearing to have been originally endowed with a mighty store of amiable dispositions and virtues, so that his being driven to the first act of murder should be judged worthy of the deepest regret, and should be seen in some measure to have arisen out of his virtues themselves. It was necessary to make him, so to speak, the tenant of an atmosphere of romance, so that every reader should feel prompted almost to worship him for his high qualities. Here were ample materials for a first volume.

I felt that I had a great advantage in thus carrying back my invention from the ultimate conclusion to the first commencement of the train of adventures upon which I purposed to employ my pen. An entire unity of plot would be the infallible result; and the unity of spirit and interest in a tale truly considered, gives it a powerful hold on the reader, which can scarcely be generated with equal success in any other way.

I devoted about two or three weeks to the imagining and putting down hints for my story, before I engaged seriously and methodically in its composition. In these hints I began with my third volume, then proceeded to my second, and last of all grappled with the first. I filled two or three sheets of demy writing-paper, folded in octavo, with these memorandums. They were put down with great brevity, yet explicitly enough to secure a perfect recollection of their meaning, within the time necessary for drawing out the story at full, in short paragraphs of two, three, four, five, or six lines each.

I then sat down to write my story from the beginning. I wrote for the most part but a short portion in any single day. I wrote only when the afflatus was upon me. I held it for a maxim, that any portion that was written when I was not fully in the vein, told for considerably worse than nothing. Idleness was a thousand times better in this case, than industry against the grain. Idleness was only time lost; and the next day, it may be, was as promising as ever. It was merely a day perished from the calendar. But a passage written feebly, flatly, and in a wrong spirit, constituted an obstacle that it was next to impossible to correct and set right again. I wrote therefore by starts; sometimes for a week or ten days not a line. Yet all came to the same thing in the sequel. On an average, a volume of 'Caleb Williams' cost me four months, neither less, nor more.

It must be admitted however, that, during the whole period, bating a few intervals, my mind was in a high state of excitement. I said to myself a thousand times, 'I will write a tale, that shall constitute an epoch in the mind of the reader, that no one, after he has read it, shall ever be exactly the same man that he was before.' —I put these things down just as they happened, and with the most entire frankness. I know that it will sound like the most pitiable degree of self-conceit. But such perhaps ought to be the state of mind of an author, when he does his best. At any rate, I have said nothing of my vain-glorious impulse for nearly forty years.

When I had written about seven-tenths of the first volume, I was prevailed upon by the extreme importunity of an old and intimate friend[1] to allow him the perusal of my manuscript. On the second day he returned it with a note to this purpose: 'I return you your manuscript, because I promised to do so. If I had obeyed the impulse of my own mind, I should have thrust it in the fire. If you

---

[1] James Marshal, Godwin's secretary.

persist, the book will infallibly prove the grave of your literary fame.'

I doubtless felt no implicit deference for the judgment of my friendly critic. Yet it cost me at least two days of deep anxiety, before I recovered the shock. Let the reader picture to himself my situation. I felt no implicit deference for the judgment of my friendly critic. But it was all I had for it. This was my first experiment of an unbiased decision. It stood in the place of all the world to me. I could not, and I did not feel disposed to, appeal any further. If I had, how could I tell that the second and third judgment would be more favourable than the first? Then what would have been the result? No; I had nothing for it but to wrap myself in my own integrity. By dint of resolution I became invulnerable. I resolved to go on to the end, trusting as I could to my own anticipations of the whole, and bidding the world wait its time, before it should be admitted to the consult.

I began my narrative, as is the more usual way, in the third person. But I speedily became dissatisfied. I then assumed the first person, making the hero of my tale his own historian; and in this mode I have persisted in all my subsequent attempts at works of fiction. It was infinitely the best adapted, at least, to my vein of delineation, where the thing in which my imagination revelled the most freely, was the analysis of the private and internal operations of the mind, employing my metaphysical dissecting knife in tracing and laying bare the involutions of motive, and recording the gradually accumulating impulses, which led the personages I had to describe primarily to adopt the particular way of proceeding in which they afterwards embarked.

When I had determined on the main purpose of my story, it was ever my method to get about me any productions of former authors that seemed to bear on my subject. I never entertained the fear, that in this way of proceeding I should be in danger of servilely copying my predecessors. I imagined that I had a vein of thinking that was properly my own, which would always preserve me from plagiarism. I read other authors, that I might see what they had done, or more properly, that I might forcibly hold my mind and occupy my thoughts in a particular train, I and my predecessors travelling in some sense to the same goal, at the same time that I struck out a path of my own, without ultimately heeding the direction they pursued, and disdaining to enquire whether by any chance it for a few steps coincided or did not coincide with mine.

Thus, in the instance of 'Caleb Williams,' I read over a little old book, entitled 'The Adventures of Mademoiselle de St. Phale,'[1] a French Protestant in the times of the fiercest persecution of the Huguenots, who fled through France in the utmost terror, in the midst of eternal alarms and hair-breadth escapes, having her quarters perpetually beaten up, and by scarcely any chance finding a moment's interval of security. I turned over the pages of a tremendous compilation, entitled 'God's Revenge against Murder,'[2] where the beam of the eye of Omniscience was represented as perpetually pursuing the guilty, and laying open his most hidden retreats to the light of day. I was extremely conversant with the 'Newgate Calendar,'[3] and the 'Lives of the Pirates.'[4] In the mean time no works of fiction came amiss to me, provided they were written with energy. The authors were still employed upon the same mine as myself, however different was the vein they pursued: we were all of us engaged in exploring the entrails of mind and motive, and in tracing the various rencontres and clashes that may occur between man and man in the diversified scene of human life.

I rather amused myself with tracing a certain similitude between the story of Caleb Williams and the tale of Bluebeard,[5] than derived any hints from that admirable specimen of the terrific. Falkland was my Bluebeard, who had perpetrated atrocious crimes, which if discovered, he might expect to have all the world roused to revenge against him. Caleb Williams was the wife, who in spite of warning, persisted in his attempts to discover the forbidden secret; and, when he had succeeded, struggled as fruitlessly to

---

[1] *The History of Mademoiselle de St. Phale: Giving a Full Account of the Miraculous Conversion of a Noble French Lady and her Daughter to the Reformed Religion, with the Defeat of the Intrigues of a Jesuit their Confessor.* Translated out of the French, 1690 (9th edition, 1787).

[2] John Reynolds, *The Triumphs of God's Revenge against the Crying and Execrable Sin of Murder*, 1621–35 (published in altered form in 1770 as *God's Revenge against Murder and Adultery*).

[3] A collection of histories of notorious criminals. See note to p. 180.

[4] Charles Johnson, *A General History of the Robberies and Murders of the Most Notorious Pirates*, 1724.

[5] In Charles Perrault's collection of fairy tales, *Histoires et contes du temps passé* (1697), Bluebeard's young wife, overcome by curiosity, opens a forbidden closet and finds the bodies of Bluebeard's former wives.

escape the consequences, as the wife of Bluebeard in washing the key of the ensanguined chamber, who, as often as she cleared the stain of blood from the one side, found it showing itself with frightful distinctness on the other.

When I had proceeded as far as the early pages of my third volume, I found myself completely at a stand. I rested on my arms from the 2d of January, 1794, to the 1st of April following, without getting forward in the smallest degree. It has ever been thus with me in works of any continuance. The bow will not be for ever bent.

Opere in longo fas est obrepere somnum. [1]

I endeavoured however to take my repose to myself in security, and not to inflict a set of crude and incoherent dreams upon my readers. In the mean time, when I revived, I revived in earnest, and in the course of that month carried on my work with unabated speed to the end. [2]

Thus I have endeavoured to give a true history of the concoction and mode of writing of this mighty trifle. When I had done, I soon became sensible that I had done in a manner nothing. How many flat and insipid parts does the book contain! How terribly unequal does it appear to me! From time to time the author plainly reels to and fro like a drunken man. And, when I had done all, what had I done? Written a book to amuse boys and girls in their vacant hours, a story to be hastily gobbled up by them, swallowed in a pusillanimous and unanimated mood, without chewing and digestion. I was in this respect greatly impressed with the confession of one of the most accomplished readers and excellent critics that any author could have fallen in with (the unfortunate Joseph Gerald[3]). He told me that he had received my book late one evening, and had read through the three volumes before he closed his eyes. Thus, what had cost me twelve months' labour, ceaseless heart-aches and industry, now sinking in despair, and now roused and sustained in unusual energy, he went over in a few hours, shut the book, laid himself on his pillow, slept and was refreshed, and cried,

To-morrow to fresh woods and pastures new. [4]

[1] Horace, *The Art of Poetry*, l. 360. 'When a work is long, a drowsy mood may well creep over it' (Loeb Classical Library trans.).

[2] Godwin chooses not to mention his false ending and revision. See Appendix I.

[3] Joseph Gerald (or Gerrald) was a political reformer who urged universal suffrage and annual parliaments. He was convicted of sedition in 1794, transported to Botany Bay, and died soon after at the age of 33.   [4] Milton, *Lycidas*, l. 193.

TEXTUAL NOTES

ABBREVIATIONS: *1* first edition, 1794; *2* second edition, 1796; *3* third edition, 1797; *4* fourth edition, 1816; *5* Bentley's 'Standard Novels, No. II', 1831.

This list includes all substantive variants between *MS* and *1*, all additions of more than one sentence made by Godwin after *1* (except in existing scenes which he rewrote extensively), and other *selected* revisions in *2* through *5*. For comment on the extent and kind of revisions not listed here, see Note on the Text. The *MS* reading is cited below only when it differs from *1*.

Title-page. CALEB WILLIAMS *5*: THINGS AS THEY ARE; OR, THE ADVENTURES OF CALEB WILLIAMS. *1–4*

Title-page of the first edition.

> *Amidst the woods the leopard knows his kind;*
> *The tyger preys not on the tyger brood:*
> *Man only is the common foe of man.* Not in *3–5*

Preface, 1. 1–2. *5.* PREFACE . . . OCTOBER 29, 1795. *Not in 1.*

VOLUME I

4. 3–19 There are other circumstances . . . invention. *Not in 1* 4. 20–36 The spring . . . dormant. *Not in 1, 2*

9. 40–10. 2 To avoid . . . patron. *Not in 1, 2*

13. 31 frenzy *3–5*: hell *1*: frensy *2*

16. 33–17. 1 The only . . . proprietors. *Not in 1*

17. 22 five feet ten inches in height *3–5*: six feet *1, 2*

19. 1–3 A form eminently . . . protector. *Not in 1, 2* 19. 13–20 Such was the rival . . . abhorrence. *Not in 1, 2*

20. 28 in spite to] in spite of *5* 20. 33 for contempt] of contempt *5*

21. 4 before we *1–5*: we before *MS* 21. 19 chivalry *3–5*: Venus *1, 2*

22. 1–5 Though the manners . . . election-borough. *Not in 1*

25. 28 consent. *2-5*: consent. If their kindness led them to expect too much, the loss, he said, was theirs. What he ought most to desire was to be set right, and he hoped he had fortitude enough tranquilly to abide the verdict of justice. *1*

27. 7 felt *1-5*: received *MS*

28. 13-29 Well, sir, . . . to offer. *Not in 1*

29. 32-4 Mr. Falkland . . . himself. *Not in 1*

32. 18 therefore was *1-5*: was therefore *MS*   32. 24 given directions *1-5*: taken precautions *MS*

33. 3 better. *3-5*: better. These strange seeds of distemper seem to float in the air, and to fasten upon the frame without its being possible for us to tell what was the method of their approach. *1, 2*   33. 36 yet at least *2-5*: yet *1*

34. 4-5 mine has been . . . existence. *3-5*: mine. *1, 2*   34. 11-12 They might . . . disturb. *Not in 1, 2*   34. 34-5 Think *2-5*: Would to God you would think *1*

35. 6-7 I have a . . . quarter. *Not in 1, 2*

37. 36 The vices of Mr. Tyrrel . . . *In MS, 1, and 2 this is the beginning of Chap. vii and is preceded by the Hawkins story which Godwin transposed to Chap. ix in 3-5. Therefore, there is some difference in chapter numbering between early and later editions. Chaps. vi, vii, viii, and ix in MS, 1, and 2 later appear as Chaps. ix, vi, vii, and viii, respectively, in 3-5*

38. 2-3 the young lady . . . occasion, *2-5*: miss Emily Melvile, *1*   38. 19 equivocal *4-5*: amphibious *1-3*

39. 5-7 Force . . . conception. *Not in 1, 2*   39. 33 more *5*: other *1-4*   39. 34 one *5*: a *1-4*

40. 19 whom *1-5*: which *MS*   40. 21 approach *5*: handle *1-4*

41. 4 the other *1-5*: our *MS*

44. 5-15 He found her . . . in his arms. *Not in 1*   44. 14-15 half-naked *Not in 1, 2*   44. 21-2 Emily, who by . . . fire. *3-5*: Emily. *1, 2*   44. 30-3 She had a confused . . . intoxicating. *Not in 1*

45. 33 She sometimes flattered *2-5*: She flattered, *1*

47. 8 thrust her from *1-5*: thrust from *MS*

53. 28 is *1-5*: are *MS*

58. 23 had rode *1-5*: was rode *MS*

59. 5-13 Between one . . . as they were accustomed to do every inferior that resisted their will. *3-5*: *Not in 1*: Between one . . . as poor Hawkins had been ruined before. *2*

60. 7 character *1-5*: mind *MS*

63. 33 come *MS*] comed *1–5*

66. 13–22 Mr. Falkland . . . of Mr. Tyrrel. *Not in 1, 2*

68. 20 stamp *1–5*: temper *MS*

71. 30 law for poor folk, as well as rich. *4, 5*: law for rich folk, as well as for poor ones. *1, 2*: law for rich folk, as well as for poor. *3*

72. 3 get out *MS*] get you out *1*

74. 24–75. 5 Mr. Tyrrel was . . . its strictness. *Not in 1*

76. 21 has *MS*] have *1–5*   76. 23 has *MS*] have *1–5*

77. 31 plague *1–5*: torment *MS*

79. 9 shall shortly have occasion *MS*] shall have occasion shortly *1*   79. 14 of the tragedy *1–5*: of tragedy *MS*   79. 16–19 It may easily . . . Emily. *Not in 1, 2*

80. 10–13 [In the bitterness . . . malice.] *Not in 1, 2*

82. 18 owed you *1–5*: owed you the money *MS*

91. 30–1 is not dead!— *1–5*: is not!— *MS*   91. 31 only been *1–5*: been only *MS*

97. 2 narrative *1*: history *MS*

101. 16 me *4, 5*: my character *1–3*

VOLUME II

112. 18 instant *1–5*: moment *MS*

116. 19 how to introduce *1–5*: how introduce *MS*

129. 2–4 In each case . . . career. *Not in 1*

130. 21 persons *1–5*: people *MS*

137. 39 such as *1–5*: those whom *MS*

144. 8 but I *1–5*: but then I *MS*

147. 6 one *1–5*: a road *MS*

150. 18 ache *4, 5*: quake *1, 2*: ake *3*   150. 31–2 ingenuousness and consistency *1–5*: ingenuity and firmness *MS*

153. 13 I had not been here three minutes *1–5*: I had been here about an hour *MS*

155. 1–12 In searching . . . had previously chosen, *Not in 1, 2*   155. 25 result *1–5*: event *MS*

156. 1–6 I was destitute . . . safety. *Not in 1*   156. 38–9 day after tomorrow *4, 5*: following day *1–3*

157. 34 impulse *1–5*: dictate *MS*

160. 14 reprehensible *1-5*: irregular *MS*

164. 25 contending *1-5*: appearing *MS*   164. 29 disorder *1-5*: confusion *MS*   164. 36 overcome *1-5*: confused *MS*

166. 30 impression in his favour *1-5*: blow with you *MS*

167. 2-3 was so struck with my appearance *Not in 5*   167. 23-4 and proposed searching my boxes, *Not in 5*   167. 31-6 I listened to . . . enquired for. *Not in 1, 2*

168. 39 loss to conceive through *1-5*: loss through *MS*

170. 11-13 Should I have dared . . . penance? *1-5*: Should I have said that after this letter I was convinced you would not desire to retain me in your employment? *MS*

182. 21 believed *1-5*: conceived *MS*   182. 30 the most inexpressible value *1-5*: ever so great a value *MS*

183. 19 hand *1-5*: hands *MS*

186. 18-26 I became myself a poet . . . had been made. *Not in 1*

190. 29 was *1-5*: were *MS*

192. 14 delighted to believe *3-5*: predicted *1, 2*

198. 24-8 His courage . . . world. *Not in 1*   198. 34 A prospect of *1-5*: A prospect indeed of *MS*

199. 2 and it *1-5*: and *MS*

200. 12-13 went his round *1-5*: went round *MS*   200. 24-5 Artifice . . . an end. *1-5*: *Not in MS*   200. 28 any one *1-5*: me or any person *MS*

201. 7 sink or *Not in MS*   201n. State . . . 1615. *Not in MS*   201n. *In the case. . . . See *Not in 1*   201. 15-16 I was not discouraged. *Not in MS*   201. 17 The apartment *1-5*: It *MS*   201. 32 much stronger light, than *1-5*: pure and cheerful light, compared with *MS*   201. 34 and was *1-5*: and by this means was *MS*   201. 36-7 Such were . . . suggested. *Not in MS*

202. 26-7 this usage is *1-5*: this is usage *MS*

203. 7 at the moment than *1-5*: than at the moment *MS*   203. 24 bade *1-5*: bid *MS*

204. 2 since there *1-5*: since, as I have already said, there *MS*   204. 25 south *1-5*: north *MS*

209. 6 continue *1-5*: support myself *MS*   209. 25 edge of the town *1-5*: foot of the wall, *MS*

211. 14 could *1-5*: would *MS*

218. 36 habituated *1–5*: accustomed *MS*

221. 19 they frequently *3–5*: sometimes they *1, 2*   221. 20 removed to
4, 5: resided in *1, 2, 3*   221. 22 decampment *5*: removal *1–4*

224. 38 they *1–5*: it *MS*   224n. *This seems . . . Poitiers. *Not in 1, 2*

227. 22 Urged, as they now were, *5*: Finding themselves urged *1–4*

230. 10 prosecutor *5*: persecutor *1–4*

231. 17 earnestness *5*: sobriety *1*: accuracy *2*: studiedness *3, 4*   231. 36
persons *1–5*: people *MS*

238. 32 superiority in my assailants *1–5*: superiority *MS*

239. 25–6 This was . . . country. *Not in 1*   239. 35 that *1–5*: who *MS*

240. 22 the *1–5*: this *MS*

241. 9 information. *5*: information, and not to communicate it. [*new para-
graph*] I soon found the benefits of this resolution. *1–4*   241. 18
before *1–5*: ago *MS*   241. 33 had had *1–5*: had *MS*

245. 2 strict letter *1–5*: rigid dictates *MS*   245. 30 I scorns *3–5*: I have not
the heart *1, 2*

251. 17 heavy *1–5*: violent *MS*   251. 28–252. 7 Here I was . . . these human
tygers? *Not in 1*

254. 31 I now adopted *MS*] I adopted *1–5*

255. 15–256. 32 Here let me pause . . . never-ending degradation! *Not
in 1, 2*

256. 38 employment *1–5*: implements *MS*

258. 5–12 Had it not been . . . my agent. *Not in 1, 2*

259. 20–8 In the mean time . . . reflections. *Not in 1, 2*

261. 26–39 When I drew . . . sting. *Not in 1, 2*

266. 19 lodging. *2–5*: lodging. I became more cautious, and went out sel-
domer than ever. *1*   266. 26 remains *1–5*: remain *MS*

268. 12 exhibited *1–5*: betrayed *MS*   268. 13–23 I found him . . . his only
son. *Not in 1*

271. 19–21 I sat gasping . . . authorised. *Not in 1, 2*

272. 2 to have been *1–5*: to be *MS*

273. 4 remorseless *2–5*: gore-dripping *1*   273. 11–23 I have always . . .
resist. *Not in 1, 2*

277. 13–29 With a bursting heart . . . my miseries. *Not in 1*

278. 16 prepared to give *1–5*: gave *MS*   278. 20–6 In the mean time . . .
firmness. *Not in 1, 2*

289. 31-2 was . . . source *1-5*: were sources *MS*   289. 37 these *1-5*: these persons *MS*

290. 20-294. 16 These however were not . . . unbounded esteem. *Not in 1, 2*

294. 25-295. 3 This was however . . . my past misfortunes. *Not in 1*

297. 9-301. 16 It may well be conceived . . . my own habitation. *Not in 1, 2*

302. 29-31 The recent instance . . . discourage me. *Not in 1, 2*   302. 36-303. 34 This was another resource . . . of happiness. *Not in 1, 2*

306. 8-28 I pursued . . . have sunk. *Not in 1, 2*

308. 10-28 There was yet another . . . mortifying. *Not in 1, 2*

312. 3-16 This is the latest . . . of my mind. *Not in 1*   312. 20-7 This was my last . . . termination. *Not in 1*

316. 9 to have been *MS*] to be *1, 2*

318. 7 so long endured *MS*] so endured *1*

323. 29-30 basest and most odious of mankind! *3-5*: worst of villains! *1, 2*

326. 4 enteredst upon *2-5*: settedst out in *1*

EXPLANATORY NOTES

Page 1. While one party pleads, etc.: Godwin refers to the debate in England instigated by the French Revolution. The most memorable product of the debate was Edmund Burke's *Reflections on the Revolution in France* (1790), but over one hundred books and pamphlets appeared between 1790 and 1793 contributing to the debate, largely in answer to Burke's *Reflections* (see Appendix to J. T. Boulton, *The Language of Politics in the Age of Wilkes and Burke*, 1963). Burke was the undisputed leader of those who 'in warmest terms' (his impassioned style was often attacked by opponents like Thomas Paine) extolled 'the existing constitution of society' as a way of combating the pro-revolutionary party. The *Reflections* was ostensibly written in answer to Richard Price's Old Jewry Sermon of 4 November 1789, which urged each man to shun prejudice, 'think of all things as they are, and not suffer any partial affections to blind his understanding' while he strives for greater political freedom (*A Discourse on the Love of Our Country*, 6th ed., 1790, p. 4). The pleaders of 'reformation and change' included Godwin, Price, Paine, Joseph Priestley, Horne Tooke, and the parliamentary followers of Charles James Fox.

Page 11. Bayard: Pierre du Terrail, Chevalier de Bayard (*c.* 1473–1524), a French captain, distinguished for his bravery and called *le chevalier sans peur et sans reproche* (the knight without fear or blame).

Page 18. Antæus: in Greek mythology, a mighty giant and wrestler of Libya. All strangers to the country were compelled to wrestle with him, and to his father, Poseidon, he built a house of their skulls.

Page 30. senna and valerian: two plants used medicinally: senna as a purgative and valerian as a sedative.

Page 53. Orson in the story-book: Valentine and Orson, an early French romance. The queen of Constantinople and her two sons are banished from the kingdom. One of them, Orson, is carried away by a bear and reared as a wild man.

Page 72. impropriator of the great tithes: Tyrrel had the privilege of receiving from his farmers a tithe of their produce, such as grain, fruit, or wood, which had formerly been given to the church.

Page 74. The Black Act: passed in 1723 to suppress a gang called the 'Waltham Blacks', who, with blackened faces for disguise, had been taking deer, fish, and wood from Waltham Forest. The law was repealed in 1827.

Page 98. *Themistocles*: an Athenian soldier and statesman of the fifth century B.C.; *Eurybiades*, his ally, a Spartan.

Page 110. (1) *Doctor Prideaux says in his Connections*: Humphrey Prideaux (1648-1724), Anglican clergyman and author of *The Old and New Testament Connected in the History of the Jews and Neighbouring Nations*, 1716-18.

(2) *the author of Tom Jones*: Henry Fielding. Caleb refers to *The Life of Mr. Jonathan Wild the Great*, 1743, published six years before *Tom Jones*.

(3) *a Westminster justice*: Fielding was justice of the peace for Westminster as well as a novelist.

Page 111. *the Seleucidæ, the Antiochuses and the Ptolomies*: ruling dynasties of ancient Syria and Egypt.

Page 113. *Clitus*: one of Alexander's generals and friends. He saved Alexander's life in battle, but was slain by Alexander at a banquet when Clitus provoked the king's resentment by a taunt.

Page 134. *Roscius*: the greatest Roman actor of his time (*c*. 126-62 B.C.).

Page 164. *three gold repeaters*: a repeater is a clock or watch which, when a spring is pressed, sounds the hour, quarter hour, and sometimes minute.

Page 178. *Jack Ketch*: the name of a seventeenth-century hangman, perpetuated in the eighteenth century.

Page 180. *A story extremely similar*, etc.: In 1724 Francis and Benjamin Brightwell were imprisoned for highway robbery, tried, and acquitted. Shortly after the trial Francis Brightwell died from a disease contracted in prison. Many of the details about Caleb's friend, including his name, his reading of Virgil and Horace, his being entrusted with a thousand pounds and a horse, and his excellence at furbishing arms, were taken from this account. *The Malefactor's Register; or, the Newgate and Tyburn Calendar . . . from the Year 1700 to Lady-Day 1779* (n.d.), i. 382-7.

Page 181. *Howard on Prisons*: John Howard, *The State of the Prisons in England and Wales*, 1777-80, 4th ed. (1792).

Page 183. *perish by the hand of the public executioner*: Caleb's fear of the executioner is by no means exaggerated. Throughout the eighteenth century Parliament added statute after statute to the 'bloody code' of English law, so that by the end of the century there were two hundred offences punishable by death. Among them were stealing a horse or sheep, snatching any property from a man's hands, stealing to the amount of forty shillings from a house or five shillings from a shop, slitting a man's nose, and picking a man's pocket of more than twelve pence.

Page 201. (1) *sink*: cesspool.

(2) *See State Trials, Vol. I, anno 1615*: Godwin's note refers to the trial of Richard Weston, a gaoler at the Tower of London, charged with

poisoning Sir Thomas Overbury, a prisoner in the Tower. Weston refused to plead either guilty or not guilty, making an ordinary legal trial impossible, whereupon the Lord Chief Justice (Sir Edward Coke) threatened him with the threefold *peine forte et dure* (the strong and hard pain): 'For the first, he was to receive his Punishment by the Law, to be extended, and then to have Weights laid upon him, no more than he was able to bear, which were by little and little to be increased.

'For the second, that he was to be exposed in an open Place, near to the Prison, in the open Air, being naked.

'And lastly, that he was to be preserved with the coarsest Bread that could be got, and water out of the next Sink or Puddle to the Place of Execution, and that Day he had Water he should have no Bread, and that Day he had Bread he should have no Water; and in this Torment he was to linger as long as Nature could linger out, so that oftentimes Men lived in that Extremity eight or nine Days: Adding further, that as Life left him, so Judgment should find him.' Weston then consented to the usual legal trial, was convicted and hanged at Tyburn. (*A Complete Collection of State Trials*, 4th ed., 1776, i. 323-4.)

Page 214. *Thalestris*: Queen of the Amazons, the legendary tribe of female warriors.

Page 224. *a celebrated saying of John King of France*: see Godwin's *Life of Chaucer* (1803), i. 474-5: 'It was on this occasion [when King John revisited England in 1364] that he is said to have uttered that laudable sentiment, a sentiment which, if acted on, would have saved to mankind a world of woe, that, "if truth were banished from all other mortals, it ought still to find refuge in the breast of a king."'

Page 228. (1) *Eugene Aram*: a brilliant, self-taught English philologist who murdered a friend, Daniel Clark, in 1745, believing that Clark had committed adultery with his wife. Afterwards Aram lived a virtuous and valuable life studying, teaching, and compiling an etymological dictionary until the crime was detected in 1759. He confessed and was executed. Bulwer Lytton's novel *Eugene Aram* (1832) is based on the story.

(2) *William Andrew Horne*: Horne's sins as a young man were many. He debauched maid-servants, committed incest, and murdered a servant girl pregnant by him. In 1724 he murdered his natural child, and was executed for this in 1759. Unlike Aram, Horne did not lead a spotless life in the interim.

Page 252. *the cross*: 'Market crosses were usually polygonal buildings with an open archway on each of the sides, and vaulted within, large enough to afford shelter to a considerable number of persons' (*OED*).

Page 258. *Aristarchus*: a critic, philologist, and Homeric scholar of ancient Greece (died *c.* 145 B.C.).

Page 263. *Duke's Place*: a street in the eastern part of London, north of the Tower. The main Jewish place of worship, the Great Synagogue, was in Duke's Place.

Page 270. *Bow-Street*: location of the London police court.

Page 273. *Hunks*: Gines's nickname for Mr. Spurrel. A hunks is a miser.

Page 314. *Janissaries*: the Turkish sultan's guard, from the fourteenth to the nineteenth century, often powerful enough to control the destiny of the government.